RICH

Benson Security 5

JANET ELIZABETH HENDERSON

ISBN 978-0-473-51644-4

Also by Janet Elizabeth Henderson

Lingerie Wars

Goody Two Shoes

Magenta Mine

Calamity Jena

Bad Boy

Here Comes The Rainne Again

Caught

Reckless

Relentless

Rage

Ransom

Rich

Can't Tie Me Down

Can't Stop The Feeling

Can't Buy Me Love

Red Zone

Red Awakening

Laura's Big Break

Mad Love

The Davina Code

A Little Something Extra

Acknowledgments

A huge THANK YOU to my copy editor Liz Dempsey who was incredibly patient with me over this book. You rock! And another massive thank you to my beta readers Mary Willard, Kylie Couvelha and Iona Jones. You spotted things I would have never guessed were missing and this book wouldn't be the same without you. So, big hugs from me!

Prologue

"**A**re you sure you don't want me to call your family?" the nurse said. "Or maybe a friend?"

The woman's voice was an echo inside Rachel Ford-Talbot's head, making the dizziness she felt so much worse. Picking a point high on the wall above the window, she concentrated on it until the room stopped spinning. How long it took, she didn't know. Time was distorted, and a strange sense of disorientation clung to everything she did.

She tried to speak, but her mouth was too dry. The nurse murmured something before she felt a plastic beaker being gently held to her parched lips. Water. Lukewarm and tasting slightly chemical.

A sharp, stabbing pain shot down her throat with each sip before she sagged deeper into the bed. "Don't call anyone." Her voice was a croak. "I don't want anyone."

"You need someone." The woman's voice overflowed with compassion. "If you were my daughter, I'd hate to think you were going through this alone."

"Please." Rachel couldn't bear to look at her and see pity. Not again. Never again. It was all she'd seen since arriving at the hospital. Instead, she focused on that same spot high on the wall. Was it a scuff mark? A cobweb? A shadow that was nothing at all? "Please, don't call anyone."

As soon as she'd woken up on the floor of a hotel room she didn't recognize, with several Polaroid photos beside her, she'd known she couldn't tell anyone what happened. She'd understood the warning in the photos without even reading the threats scrawled across them.

"The police are here," the doctor said as she came into the room.

"I don't want to talk to them."

All Rachel wanted to do was sleep. Possibly forever. Her limbs were leaden, sinking into the stiff mattress on the hospital bed. Her head throbbed—an aftereffect of the drug that had been slipped into her drink in the nightclub. Her throat ached from the finger marks around her neck. There were bruises and scrapes all over her body. Some in places she couldn't bear thinking about. Not yet anyway.

Maybe never.

She felt a touch on her hand and jerked it away, hugging her arms tight to her body as she concentrated on the mark on the wall. Was it getting bigger? Was the blackness growing?

"It's okay, honey," the nurse said softly. "You're safe here."

"Rachel"—the doctor walked around the bed and stood between her and the smudge that kept her grounded—"the police are here to help. They can find the people who did this to you."

Rachel winced. *People*. Not *person*.

"I can't tell them anything. I have no memory of what happened, and no evidence." She'd ripped the photos into tiny pieces and flushed them down the hotel toilet, along with the contents of her stomach. Not that there had been anything in the images that would help identify her attackers. The only face that could be seen was hers.

"Let us do a forensic examination," the doctor said gently. "Let us collect evidence. It may help the police find who did this."

She shook her head, and nausea assaulted her. The bile surged up into her mouth before she could even attempt to stop it. Hands helped her to sit up. A basin appeared under her nose, and the two women waited while she tried to empty a stomach that had nothing left in it.

They eased her back down onto the bed, and the nurse wiped her face with a cold cloth before letting her sip some more water. This time, it tasted of vomit.

"I don't want to file a report," Rachel said when she'd had enough to drink. "Tell the police to go away."

She stared at the spot. It was definitely getting bigger. Darker. Blacker.

"Okay," the doctor said slowly. "We'll let you rest, and we'll talk about this again in a little while. You might change your mind."

The nurse and doctor spoke to each other, but Rachel wasn't listening. There would be no changing her mind. The note on one of the photos had made sure of that, as it told her that the drug used to spike her drink had come from her family's pharmaceutical company. Her family business had played an unwitting part in her attack.

It was just the kind of scandal the newspapers loved. The company name, her family's name, would be dragged through the mud. People would question what kind of security was in place at TayFor that allowed drugs to be stolen from the research labs and used in this way. It would never end. Not until all the good her family had achieved was trampled into the dirt, and her parents' life work was gone. No, she couldn't tell anyone about the attack.

Even if it meant giving up everything she'd ever wanted.

"If you need anything, just buzz," the nurse told her. "I'll be right here. But please, honey, think about talking to the police. Nobody should get away with what happened to you."

Rachel didn't reply. She just stared up at the mark on the wall as the lights dimmed and the door closed softly. All that was left to keep her company was the beeping machines, that sterile hospital smell, and the dark, spreading smudge.

And while Rachel stared at it, she fought through the haze clouding her brain, attempting to figure out what she was going to do with her life now. She was due back in Glasgow soon, to begin her final year at university. She'd always planned to return to her family business once she graduated. Her mind had been set on becoming CEO from the moment she'd realized what those letters meant.

That wouldn't happen now.

But there was something she could do. Her friend, Harry Boyle, was a programming genius, poised to start his own company and clueless about how to go about it. She would help him. And she'd tell her parents that being away from home had changed her goals. She no longer felt her future lay with TayFor Pharmaceuticals.

And that was the truth.

Because the message spread across the photos of her rape had stated that if she were to return to the company as planned, details of the worst night of her life would be made public. The press would receive copies of the photos, along with proof that the drug used to spike her drink came from her family's very own labs.

It would ruin them.

It would ruin her.

The inky darkness that had started as a minuscule spot high on the wall grew large enough to fill the room. It engulfed Rachel. Seeping into her pores. Settling in her

DNA. Changing her forever as it made itself at home deep within her.

And as she fell asleep, she thought it only right. The darkness could live in the place that once held hope. The place that was now empty.

Chapter One

Rachel Ford-Talbot should never have allowed her father to hire her company. There were plenty of other security experts in London who could have worked with him just as easily. But no, she'd let sentimentality get the better of her, just because he'd had one teeny, tiny heart attack, and now she was the one suffering. If that wasn't a lesson in why you shouldn't help people, she didn't know what was.

"I don't see why I have to get involved in the investigation," she told Callum McKay, one of her business partners.

As usual, the Scotsman was in a bad mood. One that'd started the day he was retired from the SAS after losing both legs to a bomb in Afghanistan. Even though he had state-of-the-art prosthetics now, he was still permanently grumpy—unless you were his wife or his children. For them, he tried to act human.

"Because," he said through a jaw clenched so hard it was a wonder he could talk at all, "you're familiar with your family's pharmaceutical company, and you're the one who can get us close to the family members on the board." He folded his arms over one of his many gray Henleys and glared at her.

Like that would have any impact. Honestly. Didn't he know her?

"You have a professional spy leading the investigation." Rachel waved a hand in the general direction of Michael Carter, whom everyone called Harvard. She had no idea why, since he'd studied at MIT. Sometimes it was as though everyone she worked with was still in middle school. Shouldn't nicknames be banned as soon as you hit your twenties? Wasn't there a law making it so? "Surely a former CIA agent can take care of this investigation on his own. After all, it isn't like he has to infiltrate Al-Qaeda; we're talking about a pharmaceutical company in Surrey. Compared to investigating ISIS, getting to the bottom of some industrial espionage should be a walk in the park."

On the other side of the conference table, Harvard sat back in his chair, relaxed and smiling. Those dark eyes sparkling at her in challenge. Something he'd been doing ever since joining Benson Security months earlier. It was as though he knew a secret, a sexy secret, that he was willing to share with her if she'd just take a step toward him. Which was not going to happen. She didn't do relationships. And she definitely had no intention of entering into a casual arrangement with a colleague. No matter how much he tempted her.

"Rachel," her father said with long suffering, "you know as well as anyone that Harvard can't get close to the family without help."

"Then you help him. You know the company and the family members on the board even better than I do."

The vein throbbing at his temple brought back many childhood memories. Apparently, that particular vein hadn't even been there before Rachel was born, and she was the only one out of her siblings to cause it to throb.

"How exactly can I help him?" His tone was clipped. "Should I tell everyone he's my long-lost son?"

Rachel cocked her head as she considered the idea.

"Don't even think about it," Callum snapped. "Nobody would buy it."

"Because Harvard's African-American?" Rachel prodded her partner, as making him snap was too much fun to resist. "How very narrow-minded of you. Father could just as easily have had an illicit affair with a black woman as a white woman."

"I haven't had any affairs," her father barked.

She gave him what she hoped was a sweet smile. "As you keep telling me, this situation isn't real. We're pretending, and it's only for the duration of the investigation. If I can pretend I'm engaged to my bodyguard, surely you can pretend you have an illegitimate son."

"And have my reputation ruined in the meantime? Do you seriously want your mother to have to deal with that kind of gossip? Stop being so difficult. We both know you wouldn't let her suffer like that any more than I would."

Roger Ford-Talbot pushed back his chair and started pacing the length of Benson Security's conference room. Pacing was something else he seemed to do more often around her than her brothers.

"Rachel," Callum rumbled, "just suck it up and do the bloody job. You're best suited to it, and you know it. How hard can it be to pretend you're engaged to Harvard? You hardly take your eyes off each other anyway."

Harvard cocked an eyebrow at her in challenge. Daring her to deny Callum's claim. Like she cared one way or another what any of them thought.

She absently tapped her red nails against her iPhone screen. "My strengths lie in business management, not in espionage. Or even in any type of fieldwork. And goodness knows I've been in enough field situations to know I'm not suited to it. I don't see why we can't just give the job you want to give me to Harvard. As director of special projects, he'd have no problem getting close to the family members employed at TayFor."

"Because," her father said as he paced, "the company would never appoint someone to a role like that without them going through the interview process, and that involves the whole board. There would be no way to guarantee he got the job, and even if he did get it, it would take months to put him in place within the company. Months where this thief is free to steal whatever they like from us. Whereas you're a family member and a shareholder, so you could take up the position without delay or any argument from the board."

Which reminded her—she was still angry about that little deception too. "When I turned thirty, I told you I didn't want my shares in the company. I told you to get rid of them."

"And I assumed you were making an emotional and irra-tional decision that you would regret later, so I kept them for you."

Callum snorted. "Aye, the first thing anybody thinks when they meet Rachel is that she's emotional and irrational. Listening to you talk, I wonder if we know the same person."

Her father ran a hand through his pristinely coiffured silver hair. "Regardless of everyone's perception of my daugh-ter, it's a good job I kept hold of her shares in TayFor. Other-wise there wouldn't be any way to get your team in place to investigate the family." His head fell forward and he shook it. "I can't believe it's come to this. I can't believe that someone I trust is stealing from us."

Rachel rolled her eyes. "Really? You can't believe it? Uncle Theo's on marriage number five, while the payments for his first four marriages are crippling him financially. Not to mention, we have no idea what connections the new wife brought into the family. I believe he picked this one up in a strip club. Cousin Rupert has a well-known gambling problem —the problem being he never wins. Aunt Clarissa has been in rehab three times. And when she relapses, she'd sell a kidney to get a fix, so it isn't a stretch to believe she'd sell company secrets instead. And that's only scraping the surface. Who knows what everyone else is doing behind closed doors? Although I'm sure that information will be fascinating once our tech team digs it up. You may as well face facts; we're a family of criminals. We just do it wearing Prada."

To emphasize her point, she brushed some imaginary lint from her black Prada pantsuit.

"Do you really have to be so facetious, Rachel?" Her father dropped back into his seat, looking frustrated. "This is serious. Someone almost stole the details of our flagship drug. We've invested ten years in research and development for that drug, and if there hadn't been a glitch in the system, the information would have made it into the hands of our competitors. If anyone had put it into production before us, it would have meant millions of pounds down the drain. Who knows what our spy has already sold or is planning to sell now? All I know is that if we don't stop them fast, it will be the end of the company. Is it too much to ask that you sacrifice a few weeks of your life to help prevent that?"

"Is it necessary to be so dramatic?" she asked him.

"Apparently it is, because you aren't taking this seriously."

"Oh, I'm taking it very seriously. I just don't think I'm the best person for the job."

"You're the *only* person for the job." Callum thumped a fist on the table. "Stop being such a whiny wee wean."

Rachel gave him an icy stare. "If you're going to insult me, could you at least do it in English?"

He made a growling sound that was neither Scottish nor English.

Harvard shifted in his seat, drawing all eyes to him. The seams of his blazer strained against his shoulder muscles as he sat up straight. She couldn't help but appreciate the cut of his jacket and matching black shirt. They'd obviously been tailored to fit his larger-than-average frame to perfection.

When she eventually looked at his face, he had that secretive little smile again. She frowned, and he smiled wider.

"Gentlemen," he said, his focus still on her, "could you give us the room for a second? I think Rachel and I have to discuss this alone."

"I disagree," Rachel said as her father and Callum practically ran out the door.

"Don't forget we're having a family dinner tomorrow night," her father called over his shoulder. "We're expecting you at seven. No excuses." He caught Harvard's eye. "I'm hoping you'll be able to bring your fiancé along too."

"Father—"

Callum cut her off. "Family later. Work now." And then he slammed the door shut behind them, leaving her alone with the man who drove her crazy—even in her dreams.

She narrowed her eyes at the tall American with his rich brown skin and dark, dark eyes. "There's nothing to discuss. I'm not a security operative. I'm a managing partner."

"I disagree." He clasped his hands on the table in front of him. "I think what you are is a coward."

Rachel gave him a cold smile as she drummed her blood-red nails on the tabletop. "I don't much care what you think. As I pointed out earlier, I'm your boss. I gave up worrying what employees thought about me before I turned ten."

"I'm not one of the maids at the family mansion. And you've been involved in the security world long enough to know that the team leader has authority over every member of their team. Even if that member is a partner."

"You might be team leader, but I'm not a member of your

team." She stood, slinging her favorite Hermes handbag over her elbow. "This discussion is over. I'm sure you'll find a way to run the investigation without me." She walked around the table, heading for the door. There was a bottle of Merlot at home calling her name.

"What's the problem exactly?" Harvard turned in his seat to face her. "Are you worried your high-class friends and family will think less of you for bringing home a black man? A working-class American black man at that. They'll know I'm your employee—especially seeing as I'll also be playing the part of your bodyguard. They'll think you're screwing the help. Tut-tut. That's even worse than good old Uncle Theo."

If he thought his poor attempt at riling her would get results, then he was seriously deluded. "I don't have to explain myself to you, and as I've said before, I don't much care what you or anyone else thinks either."

He got out of his seat and positioned himself between her and the door. "Or maybe it's the thought of returning to the company you'd once planned on running. The company you suddenly turned your back on ten years ago. Is that what's freaking you out? One day you're talking about becoming CEO of TayFor, the next you're gone, and telling the family to give away the shares you'd inherit. Why did you walk away, Rachel? I've done some digging, and no one seems to know."

Which was exactly how she planned to keep it. "Not everyone follows through on their childhood ambitions. I simply outgrew the family business. And unsurprisingly, I've outgrown this conversation too. Prove you're the ace spy we were led to believe you were when we hired you and do the job without me."

Instead of backing off, as most reasonable people would have done, he took a step closer. For a second, it seemed as though the air was rushing from the room, and she felt quite light-headed. Harvard always smelled like the ocean. Like freedom. Or recklessness...

"Tell me what's going on and I'll help you," he said softly.

Jumping beans started bouncing in her stomach. "Nothing's going on. I just don't want to revisit the past. Or deal with my family on a daily basis. There's nothing you can say that would make me go undercover with you, so you may as well give up."

"How about this?" He lowered his head to whisper against her ear, making her shiver as his breath swept over the sensitive shell. "The word around the office is that you're scared to play the part of my fiancée. People are saying you won't be able to separate fact from fiction." He touched her hair, running the straight length through his fingers, and she swore she could feel it right to her toes. "There's a betting pool. Ryan's bet a thousand pounds that you won't be able to resist me. In fact, most of the bets are on the side of you giving in to the attraction between us."

"There's no attraction between us." Had that sounded breathier than usual? No. No, it hadn't. She sounded the same way she always did—cold and distant. Precisely how she liked it.

His eyes warmed. "Oh, Rachel, I know you're gonna lie to me, but you should at least be honest with yourself."

She forced a snort of amusement. "Arrogance isn't an attractive trait in a man."

"Arrogance, or confidence?" His lips skimmed the flesh beneath her ear, and every inch of her skin was electrified. There were only a few millimeters between their bodies, and the heat from his much larger frame engulfed her. She was warm when she usually felt cold. He was lulling her into a false sense of security. Teasing her with his presence. Daring her to reach out and close the distance between them.

She took a step back instead.

His smile was pure male amusement. "You should know I've placed a five thousand pound bet you'll be in my bed before the mission ends. What do you think my chances are?"

"About the same as getting me to fall for this juvenile attempt at reverse psychology. Did you really think I'd jump at the chance to prove you and the other idiots placing bets wrong?"

"No, but I thought you might like to prove the women on the team right. They all bet against me." He gave a self-deprecating smile. "Elle said there wasn't a guy on the planet who could tempt you if you'd already decided against him. Megan placed a side bet that you'd shoot me before the investigation was over."

Now *that* was interesting.

Damn it, the man was playing her, and she was beginning to fall for it. Although, it would be good to prove him and the other annoying men she worked with wrong...maybe...

She seriously considered whether being close to Harvard would be a problem for her. Sure, he was big and sexy and had muscles that made her mouth water. But that didn't mean she had to give in to the urge to touch. She was famous for her stubborn streak. It'd helped her resist princes and Hollywood stars. She could definitely resist the advances of one overly confident ex-spy.

All amusement disappeared from his face. "We really do need you on this, Rachel. If there was another way, we'd have found it by now. Without you, there's no way we'll have the access we need."

And, unfortunately, he was right. They all were—even Callum. But she didn't have to like it. "Fine," she said with a good measure of bad grace. "I'll play my part, but that's all I'm doing. Don't expect anything else." She brushed past him to open the door. "And tell the idiots who bet against me to get their money ready. I don't lose."

"Oh, you wouldn't lose, Rachel. Even if you did give in, you'd still come out a winner. I'd make sure of it." His voice was a purr of promise that made her thighs clench.

"You know what they say about a man and his ego," she said as she walked away. "The bigger the ego, the more he feels he has to prove."

His deep, echoing laugh followed her as she strode past reception and out into the London sun. Hailing a cab, she took a steadying breath and straightened her shoulders. There was no place for emotion in this. The decision was made. She was going back to TayFor.

And to the past she'd fought to leave behind.

Chapter Two

Rachel hadn't said more than ten words during the hour-long drive from central London to the heart of Surrey. You didn't have to be a genius to know what was bothering her. They were on their way to dinner with her family, where he'd pose as her fiancé. To say Rachel wasn't thrilled would be an understatement.

"You realize you've got a real-life spy in your James Bond car," Harvard said into a silence that was so thick it made it hard to breathe.

If looks could kill, the glance she shot in his direction would have incinerated him. "*You* are no James Bond."

Rachel's hands tightened on the steering wheel of her Aston Martin, making the emerald cut diamond in her engagement ring catch the light and gleam. He'd spent days hunting down the perfect ring for her and had finally settled on a solitaire diamond in a platinum setting. Icy and elegant, just like Rachel, it was worth every cent he'd spent. Although well aware this was purely an undercover op, he hadn't been able to resist the urge to see *his* ring on her finger. Of course, being Rachel, when he'd given it to her, she'd slipped it on without a word. But that alone had told him she liked it. If she hadn't, she wouldn't have worn it.

"I know, I'm no James Bond." He relaxed back into the gray leather of the passenger seat and smiled at her. "He makes stupid decisions that would get him killed in real life. Plus, he's a chauvinist asshole."

She did that dramatic eye-roll thing that made his dick stand to attention. Damn, she was sexy as hell. All class and ice and keen intelligence. From her sleek mahogany hair falling against pale porcelain skin to her professionally mani-cured blood-red fingernails, she was perfection. Ever since he'd set eyes on her, he'd wanted to touch. But Rachel was resisting. He just wasn't sure why—yet.

He'd seen the way she watched him when she thought he wasn't looking. The woman practically drooled. And it wasn't like she was a nun either. She'd dated in the time he'd been at Benson Security. One date per man. Which was the only reason Harvard had let them live—their lack of repeat access to Rachel.

"Why don't you keep the flowers I send you?" The ques-tion popped out, even though an idiot could guess the answer.

"Maybe because I don't want them." She arched a perfectly groomed brow at him. "Or you."

Oh, it was on the tip of his tongue to call her on her lies. On more than one occasion, he'd caught her touching the petals of the flowers he had delivered to her office every Monday. There had been a wistful softening in her face before she'd lifted the vase they'd come in and dumped it in the trash.

He hadn't imagined it either. Elle Roberts, their resident computer genius, had alerted him to her behavior when she'd asked why Rachel didn't keep the flowers she so obviously wanted. Like everything else about the woman who fascinated him, the answer was a mystery.

Unfortunately for Rachel, Harvard loved mysteries. He'd always been a sucker for a puzzle other people couldn't solve. And for women who could kick his ass. Yeah, Rachel was his dream woman.

There was no denying he had issues.

"This is a complete waste of time." She didn't bother to signal before cutting someone off. "The only person at this dinner who doesn't know our engagement is fake is my sister-in-law. Why do we have to pretend for Amelia? It isn't like she's involved in the family company. All she thinks about outside of Jonathan is her precious cello. She's hardly likely to notice there's anyone else in the room, let alone that you're supposed to be my fiancé."

"Your father seems to think this dinner will be good practice for convincing the rest of your family."

"I honestly don't see how."

"Just go with it. There's no point in letting it upset you."

"Upset me?" She cast him a glance full of outrage. "This isn't upsetting me. This is nothing but an irritation. I'm more annoyed that my weekend plans were ruined by your pathetic need for my assistance."

Oh yeah, she could flay the skin off his balls with one sentence. And why the hell did that make him want her more? Harvard was beginning to think his closest friends were right: his taste in women was going to get him killed one day.

But what a way to go.

"Why are you smiling like a lunatic?" Rachel demanded as she raced through the motorway traffic at a speed that would likely get her pulled over by the cops. Then, of course, he'd have to step in to make sure she didn't make things worse by opening her mouth. It was one of Benson Security's standard operating procedures for anyone who had the misfortune of being a passenger in her car.

You had to love a business that had company guidelines for dealing with a boss who enjoyed breaking traffic rules.

"Stop smiling like that," Rachel snapped. "It's disturbing."

He did his best to appear somber. "We need to get our story straight before we reach your parents' house."

"What's there to get straight? Even I know that spies do a better job when they stay as close to the truth as possible. So, we tell Amelia we met at work, and"—she grimaced—"we fell in love."

"Yeah, say it exactly like that. I'm sure you'll convince everybody present that your feelings are genuine."

"I don't need to convince everyone. Just Amelia. Surely we can work out the details of this farce before we meet everyone else."

She slid between two cars, barely missing one, and it promptly blared its horn at her. From the look on her face, Harvard would bet she was wishing her Aston Martin was as tricked out as Bond's so she could fire a rocket at the offender.

"It doesn't matter that this dinner's only close family. It doesn't even matter that most of the people present are in on the lie. This is a chance to establish our story for when other people ask questions. Which we should have been doing today." Instead, she'd disappeared off the face of the planet and refused to take his calls. "Did you read over the cover information I sent you? We need to be on the same page here."

She shot him an irritated glance. "Of course, I read it, and our cover story isn't exactly a stretch to memorize. We met at work. We clicked. We're getting married. What else is there to say? It's going to be harder to convince everyone I need a bodyguard. Couldn't you just turn up at TayFor to visit me?

Do you really need to act as my bodyguard to get access to the offices?"

"Rachel, would you ever, under any circumstances, let a lover hang out at the office with you?"

He didn't need to hear the answer to know what she'd say because, along with every single person on the planet who'd ever spent ten minutes in her company, they both knew the answer was no.

"Perhaps I've softened now that I'm betrothed?" She looked a little nauseous.

"Yeah, I can't see us selling that either. But we can sell the fact that you pissed off some dangerous people during your time at Benson Security, and until the threat they represent disappears, you need a bodyguard. That's where I enter. Who better to protect you than the man who adores you?" If only that weren't true.

"I think I vomited a little in my mouth."

"And they say romance is dead."

"Are we hiding the fact that you used to work for the CIA?"

"See? That's the kind of thing we should have talked about today."

She glared at him.

"Nope," he said. "We aren't hiding my past career. It won't make any difference if they know about it anyway, but let's lay off the spy references and tell them I was an analyst instead."

"Does anyone ever believe that?"

"The CIA has hundreds of analysts. Offices full of them. It isn't a fake job."

"If you say so."

She shot across three lanes at full speed to take the exit she needed. Horns blasted and her car missed the barrier by an inch. Harvard was actually quite proud that her driving wasn't making him sob like a baby and cling to the panic handle.

"Fine," she said in a tone that mocked him. "We'll tell everyone you were a CIA desk jockey. I'll let you explain why you look like the black version of Thor."

"Thor has more hair." He ran a hand over his shaven head. "And I have more muscle."

"My point is, you don't look like you spent your life behind a desk," she said slowly, as though he was incredibly thick. Only Rachel would look at the master's degree he'd gotten from MIT and still think he was an idiot.

"Not pale enough?"

"You really aren't funny."

"Only you think that. But, seriously, don't worry about the details of my cover. Plenty of office guys work out. I'll tell everybody I spent years doing MMA training in my spare time."

"Did you?"

"Yeah. We all did. Joe, Grunt, Beast, Noah, and me. That's how we met. We started out as teens in a church-run boxing club and went into other martial arts disciplines from there. Beast was the only one who turned professional."

And now, all of his best friends worked for the same UK-based security company. After years of working alone in high-stress situations, it was good to know he had them at his back again. Although Beast wasn't often around. He was on permanent duty as head of security for his movie star wife.

"I would have said that you and Grunt were far too big and bulky for MMA." She lifted her nose in the air. "But if you think you can sell the story, then you may tell it to my family."

"Thank you, Rachel. As team leader, it's important to me that I have your permission to share *my* life story."

Her scowl made him want to laugh.

The car turned into a dark, tree-lined country road, at the end of which sat ornate ironwork gates. Rachel pulled her sun visor down, pressed a button, and the gates swung open.

In the distance, on a rise, sat Talbot House. One of Rachel's ancestors had built the eighteenth-century stately home and passed it down through the generations. With the house came the title of Earl of Ponterley. Or, in Rachel's mother's case, the Countess of Ponterley. As one of the few families in England that had an exemption for the firstborn to inherit the title regardless of gender, it had passed to the earl's only daughter. After Rachel's mother, it would return once again to the male line through Rachel's older brother, Jonathan.

Which made him wonder. "Do you ever wish you were the one who'd inherit the title?"

Rachel scoffed. "Hardly. Whoever has the title has to oversee the trust dealing with that monstrosity. I honestly don't need the hassle." She gestured to the house, with its many turrets, ornate chimneys, and carved detail.

Harvard had to agree. Even a cursory read through of their website had made him feel overwhelmed. With thirty bedrooms, countless social areas, and staff quarters, the vast limestone structure would definitely require a lot of upkeep. But he had to admit it was impressive. It glowed in the distance, lit by carefully placed lights and surrounded by two hundred acres of pristine gardens. Yeah, it was something out of a fairytale book.

"Did you grow up in there, or did you always live in the guesthouse?"

"We stayed in the manor until I was about eight, then we moved to the guesthouse, and the family seat became a full-time tourist destination."

"That's a shame," he muttered, trying to imagine what it

must have been like to live in a house so vast you could have your own wing and not see each other for days.

"Not really." She turned the car toward the private corner of the grounds where her parents' home sat. Something Harvard knew from spending a little too much time on Google Earth. "It was cold and dusty. So. Much. Dust. Even the staff couldn't keep on top of it, and Mother never wanted to hire on more people. She said there were enough strangers in her home as it was. Of course, when the trust took over the place, they upped the staff numbers and dealt with the dust. I hate dust."

"Yeah, I'm getting that."

"And we were forever shouting for each other. No matter who you needed, they were never in the same part of the building as you, and the intercom system wasn't always reliable. It would have been easier if we'd been allowed cell phones, but Mother refused to let us have them until we turned twelve—something about developing brains and radiation."

Harvard grinned at the thought of a house so big you had to phone your family to find them. "Was there anything good about living there?"

She thought hard for a second. "It was great for hide-and-seek. Although quite often, the games were unintentional."

As he burst out laughing, the guesthouse came into view. If he hadn't seen the other house first, he would have thought this one was the mansion. It was built out of the same pale limestone as the main house, but was less ornate in design. There were three rows of windows, the top row being much smaller—probably where they stashed their servants. Wide sweeping stairs led up to the double front doors—which currently stood open.

And standing in the doorway were Rachel's parents.

Her mother, Lady Francesca Ford-Talbot, the seventh

Countess of Ponterley, beamed at them as she practically bounced on the spot with clear excitement. Meanwhile, her father's body language screamed, "Oh shit."

Harvard couldn't help but grin. This was going to be even more fun than he'd anticipated. "Remember, you agreed to marry me. Which means we're in love. So, act like you adore me and can't keep your hands off me, and everything will be fine."

The look she gave him would have made a lesser man lose control of his bladder. "After this is over, I *will* make you suffer." Not waiting for a reply, she climbed out of the car.

Harvard took a second to admire the way she smoothed down her dress. The black knee-length sheath had an asymmetrical neckline that was too damn tempting for a man who was supposed to be on his best behavior. And those signature black heels of hers? They slayed him.

Shaking his head to clear the daze of lust Rachel induced, he climbed out of the car and went to meet the parents.

Chapter Three

❧

"Darling!" Her mother held out her arms to Rachel as soon as she stepped from the car. The countess was always impatient when she was excited. And in her mother's mind, Rachel bringing home a man was definitely cause for excitement. Even when that man was purely a work colleague, which her mother knew full well.

Rachel narrowed her eyes in suspicion as she strode up the steps to wrap the slender woman in a hug. Unlike her friends, Rachel's family didn't do air-kisses. No. They did proper hugs. It had been the source of much humiliation as a child. "There's no need to pretend when we're alone," she said.

"Nonsense," her mother whispered, as though there was someone to overhear. "Your lovely gentleman told Roger it would be best to stay in character at all times. It's thrilling. I haven't had this much fun since the sixties."

And that there was exactly the reason Rachel had suggested keeping her mother in the dark.

Breaking the embrace, she stepped back and felt a hand come to rest on the small of her back. She stiffened before remembering she was supposed to be familiar with Harvard's touch. Forcing a smile, she set about getting the introductions over.

"Mother, this is Michael Carter. People call him Harvard. I have no idea why. Michael, this is my mother, Lady Francesca Ford-Talbot."

"Michael, or should I call you Harvard?" her mother exclaimed. "I'm utterly delighted to welcome you to the family. It's about time Rachel settled down. I can't wait to get to know you better." And with that, she enfolded Harvard in a hug.

As her father groaned and looked skyward, Rachel glared at him. This whole thing was his fault. He, more than anyone, knew his wife had a wicked sense of humor that would get them all into trouble.

"Call me whatever you like," Harvard said when her mother released him. "I'm sorry we weren't able to meet before this."

Great. Apparently, they were *all* pretending, even when there was absolutely no need.

"Please, don't apologize." Her mother shot Rachel a chastising look. "It isn't as though Rachel lives in my pocket. If it weren't for these monthly dinners, I'm not sure when I'd see my daughter." She took Harvard's arm. "Do you know, you're the first man she's ever brought home? And I do mean ever. Although, there was her friend Harry, but he doesn't really count as it was never a romantic relationship. I very much hope you'll be a good influence on her and make sure you both visit more often once you're wed."

Okay. That was it. Rachel had known from the start that taking part in an undercover op with her family was a bad idea, but if her mother was going to use the situation to make digs all evening, she was going home.

She turned back toward her car, but her father caught her

arm. "We're suffering through this together," he muttered to her as he strode into the house, taking her with him.

"This is all your fault," she told him. "You're the one who came to Benson Security and demanded I take part in the investigation. And now look what's happening. Mother is taking advantage of the situation to drive me crazy."

Her mother smiled over her shoulder. "Come along, you two. Everybody's waiting."

Rachel tripped on the rug, and her father's hold tightened on her arm. "Everybody?"

"Oh, yes." Her mother sounded dangerously pleased with herself. "My only daughter is getting married. That calls for a celebration. I've invited the whole family."

Any second now, Rachel's head would explode. She felt the pressure build as she glared up at her father. "And you couldn't send me a text to let me know what she was up to?"

He looked pained.

"No, he couldn't," her mother said. "I swore him to secrecy. If you'd got even a whiff of there being a party, you would have made an excuse not to come."

"So, you decided to blindside me instead?"

"Yes." Her mother was clearly delighted. "I'm thrilled it worked. Now, come along. It isn't every day your daughter brings home a fiancé that her mother hasn't even met."

"She does know this isn't real, right?" Rachel whispered to her father.

"Yes, she does, but she's decided to use our unusual circumstances to make a point."

The point being that Rachel was too distanced from her family and not settling down fast enough for her mother's liking. "If she doesn't calm down, I won't visit for a year after this is over."

Her father clutched his chest as though in pain. "Don't even joke about it. The woman would hunt you to the ends of the earth if you did that, and she'd drag me along with her. And then we'd all suffer. Isn't one heart attack enough for me? Do you really want to give me another?"

"Whatever," Rachel grumbled, "but I'm definitely making Harvard pay."

"That I can live with," he said.

THE INTERIOR OF THE HOUSE WASN'T WHAT HARVARD HAD expected. He'd obviously seen one too many English historical dramas because he'd thought the place would be wall-to-wall burgundy flocked paper and ornate moldings. He'd imagined darkly painted portraits of previous generations and antique furniture with the kind of spindly legs that a man his size would worry about breaking.

Instead, the walls were cream and the floors a polished wood, strewn with tasteful throw rugs. There were a few pieces of contemporary art, most of which he recognized as being the work of well-known British artists. The furniture was sleek, solid and modern. The kind that would entice a person to sit awhile and relax. In fact, it was exactly the type of house Harvard would have liked for himself.

"The stuffed animal heads, suits of armor and bad Renaissance paintings are all in the main house," Francesca said with a twinkle in her eye.

"I was that obvious?" Usually he was good at hiding what he thought. His life had depended on the skill on more than one occasion.

"No, it's the reaction most people have if they haven't been inside Talbot House first. It was a good bet you were thinking the same. When Roger saw Talbot House, he told me it was magnificent, but he had no desire to live in it. As soon as we were married, he had plans to get us out of there.

And he was right. It was a terrible place to live, but a wonderful place to share. If buildings had feelings, I've always thought the house must be happier now that it's being fully used. And I do love it when we host a wedding there. It brightens the place up."

Harvard liked her reasoning. He also liked the woman. It was clear Rachel took after her mother in looks. They shared the same height and lithe figures, the same creamy skin and dark hair—although, given her age, he suspected Francesca's color had more to do with regular visits to a top-class hair salon than any genetic predisposition. Yeah, there were a lot of similarities. But it was the differences that intrigued Harvard most.

Where Francesca had a mischievous glint in her eye, Rachel's eyes were mostly filled with irritation. Where Rachel was distant, Francesca was friendly and welcoming. Where Rachel preferred her own company, Francesca was known for her social events. Having met Rachel's older brother and their dad, Harvard was beginning to wonder where exactly Rachel got her personality from. It was just another piece in the puzzle that was Rachel Ford-Talbot. And he loved it.

"Here we are," Francesca said when they stopped in front of the double doors at the end of the hallway. "Ready?"

"Absolutely." He returned her conspiratorial smile.

"In case anyone is interested, I'm not ready," Rachel snapped.

"No, darling." Her mother released her hold on Harvard. "No one's interested." With that, she threw open the doors and stepped inside. "Here they are," she called above the chatter of a roomful of people. "The guests of honor. Rachel and her fiancé, Mr. Michael Carter, from America."

The large entertaining room was decorated in complementary pastel shades, broken up with faded floral prints. Artfully arranged couches and tables provided plenty of opportunity for guests to make themselves comfortable. And there were a *lot* of guests in the room. It was filled with family members he recognized from the research Benson Security had done on everyone connected to TayFor. They cheered, applauded, and whistled at Francesca's announcement. Harvard wrapped an arm around Rachel's waist and pulled her to his side. She stood stiff as a board and scowled at everybody.

He leaned into her, as though nuzzling her neck, and whispered, "You're supposed to be happy you're with me. You look furious."

"I am," she said through gritted teeth. "This is *not* a small family dinner."

"No, it isn't. And you need to stop freaking out and roll with it." He pressed a kiss to her cheek, inhaling her hothouse scent before smiling at her family.

"I. Do. Not. Freak. Out." She forced the words out.

"Excellent." He smiled at her. "Then we're good to go."

Rachel scowled at him, took a deep breath, and addressed the room. "Please, don't get up. I know you're all deliriously happy for me, but there's no need to interrupt your evening to congratulate us straight away. I'm sure we'll have a chance to chat with all of you over the next few hours." The woman was lying through her lush red lips.

There was laughter and one murmur of, "Typical Rachel, taking charge as usual."

"Right," she said to Harvard, "that should stop us drowning in well-wishers for the time being, but it won't last long." She let out a heavy sigh. "We're going to have to mingle. You should know, I'm keeping tally, and you will be held accountable for every single little thing that irritates me during this nightmare."

"Do I get to keep a tally of all the things that irritate me, so I can even the score once this is done?"

She barked a laugh. "You can try."

"DON'T TELL ME YOU TWO ARE HAVING RELATIONSHIP problems already?" Rachel's older brother, Jonathan, sidled up to them. The look of pure delight on his face screamed that he was more than enjoying her predicament, and like her mother, he planned to milk it for all it was worth.

"Go away, Jonathan," she told him. "I can only deal with one idiot at a time." She pointed at Harvard. "I already have my quota for the day."

Of course, he didn't go away; instead, he grinned at Harvard. "Insults are how Rachel shows her love. Welcome to the family." He held out a hand, pretending it was the first time they'd met and that he wasn't fully aware of their fake romance and the investigation. "If you could pop out a couple of kids as soon as possible, that would keep the heat off me for a few more years."

"We'll do our best." Harvard looked highly amused.

Rachel just glared at both of them.

Jonathan wasn't intimidated. She'd long been aware that her ability to intimidate didn't work on immediate family, and she hated it. What was the point of having a superpower if it only worked with *some* people?

"Has Mother told you all the childhood stories about our Rachel?" Jonathan asked with a wide grin.

"Be careful what you say, Johnathan," she warned. "Pay-back's a bitch—called Rachel. I know where all your skele-tons are hidden. Don't forget it."

"You don't scare me," the idiot said. "I was there when Mother brought you home from the hospital, and all you did was poop and wail. And I was also there when you used to take a stuffed rabbit everywhere because you were scared of

Talbot House. Don't even get me started on the times you lost it. I swear you woke ghosts with your screaming." He looked at Harvard. "I was always the one who had to hunt the damn thing down, and do I get any appreciation? No." He beamed at her, clearly enjoying himself. "She still has it, you know. The bunny."

Harvard chuckled, and Rachel elbowed him. It was like elbowing a tree.

"I wish Sebastian were here," Jonathan said of their younger brother, who was off researching in Borneo. "He could tell you about the time he was dragged along when she bought her first bra. It traumatized him for years. A preteen boy shouldn't have to suffer the lingerie department at Self-ridges. Especially seeing as Rachel only wanted a bra so she could beat Cousin Samantha in the race to get one first. Oh!" His face lit up. "I must tell you about the time she made Seb and I spray tan her. We all ended up looking like Oompa-Loompas. Mother wasn't happy at all. Father found it quite funny though. Took forever for that stuff to fade."

"That's it," Rachel snapped at them. "I need a drink." She shrugged out of Harvard's hold, ready to head straight across the room to the bar her mother had set up.

"Rachel," Harvard called after her, "can you get me my usual?"

His sparkling eyes told her he found it funny that she had no idea what his usual was, and she couldn't exactly shout back across the room to ask him.

Instead, she inclined her head and smiled sweetly. "Of course." She turned toward the bar, hoping they had pink umbrellas for the drinks, because Harvard was getting all of them.

~

HARVARD WATCHED HER WALK AWAY, GRACIOUSLY accepting congratulations from family members as she weaved through the crowded room. Her dress clung to the curves of her ass as her hips swayed. Man, she made his mouth water. Even when she was plotting to poison him.

"You're keeping her safe, right?" Jonathan said, his eyes on Rachel too. "I mean, I know this isn't exactly a dangerous assignment, but some of the jobs Benson Security have taken over the years have gone downhill fast. I worry about her."

"I won't let anything happen to her," Harvard assured her brother. "Now, is there any chance you could introduce me to some people? There's no way in hell Rachel's going to do it." He glanced over to where she was talking with another one of her cousins. "I figure I have about half an hour before she sneaks off and leaves me stranded in Surrey."

Jonathan gestured around the room. "Who do you want to meet first?"

"Everyone who's on the board *and* works for TayFor."

"We call those people the partial board." He nodded. "Of course, I work there, as do Mother and Sebastian—when he's in the country. Sebastian isn't a member of the board yet, as he's under thirty. That's the age we inherit our company shares, which gives us a place at the table. But, of course, you know all this. And your investigation has already cleared us, or we wouldn't be having this conversation in the first place."

Harvard kept his eye on the room as they spoke, ensuring no one was close enough to overhear them. "With Rachel going undercover, we had to clear her immediate family. It would have been too complicated otherwise."

"Find anything interesting while you were digging around in our lives?"

"You sing Barry Manilow in the shower."

Jonathan's face turned beetroot. "How on earth do you know that?"

Harvard chuckled. "Rachel told us."

"My sister will be the death of me," he said, before muttering, "If I don't get her first."

"There are seven members on the partial board, aren't there? And fifteen on the general board of directors, which includes all family members with shares. Is that right?"

"Not quite." His lips quirked. "There are eight on the partial, and sixteen on the general. You're forgetting Rachel. As of Monday, she'll be working at TayFor, and she still has her shares, which gives her a say in the company. Father was on both boards, but he retired after his heart attack last year. Now he's only the chairman of the general board."

"And the largest shareholder." Something Harvard had flagged as a possible motivation for the theft of industrial secrets. Perhaps the thief wasn't driven by greed, but rather by feeling slighted at the power Roger Ford-Talbot wielded. That was why he'd asked his team to keep an eye out for family members who held a particular grudge against Rachel's father. So far, nothing had come up. But they were still digging.

"Yes," Jonathan said. "Father is the largest shareholder by far. Uncle Theo would have been second, but he kept losing wads of his shares in his divorces—until he wised-up and had them written into a prenup. Now his first wife, Aunt Anne, has more shares than he does and more power within the board."

"How does Theo feel about that?" Harvard glanced over at the man.

Theo kept himself in shape and took pride in how he dressed. From his gray hair to his polished Italian shoes, he was every inch the sexy silver fox the tabloids liked to call him. And apparently, he was just as shallow as they reported too.

Jonathan snorted. "I'd say he misses the money, but he

doesn't particularly care about his first two wives having more of a say in the company than he does. Theo doesn't exactly relish the responsibility that comes with privilege."

"How much access does he have to the research and development department at TayFor?"

"You don't suspect Uncle Theo, do you?" Jonathan looked more bewildered than affronted. "I don't think he has the patience to pull off something like this."

Harvard shrugged. "Just doing my job."

"Everyone in this room is related to me. I grew up with them. It's hard to think that someone here might hate us enough to try to destroy us."

"I don't think it's about destroying the company," Harvard said. "This kind of crime is usually about the money."

"And that's another thing." Jonathan gestured to the room. "Do any of us look like we're hurting for cash? We make a good living from TayFor. Some of us also have inheritances behind us. What would be the point in risking it all to get more?"

"Greed doesn't need to be logical," Harvard said. "It's nasty and dirty, and it doesn't care who suffers because of it. Greed is always hungry, and no amount of feeding satisfies it."

"I don't understand." Jonathan thrust a hand through his hair, and Harvard suspected that the man really didn't.

A streak of honor ran straight through him. One that had prompted him to set up the charities the company ran on the side and kept him fighting to make drugs cheaper for those who needed them. There was a lot to like about Rachel's brother.

Harvard slapped a hand on his shoulder. "Come on, let's get these introductions over with."

Jonathan nodded and headed off in the direction of the fireplace, where two of Rachel's male cousins stood glaring at their father as he pawed his new, young bride.

Chapter Four

"So, you're the chap who nabbed our Rachel," Preston Talbot said once they'd been introduced. "You're a brave man."

The eldest of the two brothers was in his late thirties and had inherited his playboy father's good looks. His blond hair was thick and wavy, his chin strong, and his physique that of a man who played lots of sport. If Harvard remembered his research right, Preston was a tennis player. In fact, he could have turned pro if he'd wanted. Instead, he'd gone into the family business as the company lawyer. Unlike his father, Preston had been happily married for fifteen years.

"You know what they say," Harvard drawled. "Fortune favors the bold."

"Good one." Preston lifted his glass in salute.

"Life with Rachel certainly won't be boring," his brother, Marcus, said.

Unlike Preston, Marcus had not only inherited his father's looks, but also quite a bit of his natural charm. As manager of the research and development department at TayFor, he often used that charm to negotiate government grants and private funding. It was a position that put him close to the information being stolen and high on Benson Security's list of suspects.

"No," Harvard agreed. "Life definitely isn't boring with Rachel."

There was only a year between the brothers, and they were very close. Partly because of the slight age difference, and partly due to having to deal with their father together.

They had three younger half-siblings: two sisters from their father's second wife and a brother from his third. Wives four and five hadn't produced any offspring. But it was still early days for wife five.

Unlike Preston, Marcus was already on marriage number two. And if the Benson Security research was correct, his eye had started to roam yet again.

"I see you're working your way through the cousins." A feminine voice had them turning to see a tall, svelte blonde sashaying toward them, champagne flute in hand. "So I thought I'd come introduce myself too. The three Talbot brothers—our grandfathers—started the company. Which really makes us second cousins, not first. But it would be tedious to say that all the time, don't you think?" She held out a perfectly manicured hand. "Samantha Talbot, delighted to meet you," said TayFor's marketing director. Unlike her cousins, Samantha was very happily single and seemed to have a thing for younger men.

Harvard recognized interest in a woman's eye when he saw it, and as soon as he'd finished shaking her hand, he put some distance between them.

"Where's Rupert?" Preston waved his empty glass at one of the waiters discreetly doing the rounds of the room. "He was supposed to be here—and at work yesterday." Preston didn't even glance at the young man who took his glass. "Gin and tonic," was all he said.

"Rupert's my younger brother," Samantha told Harvard before addressing Preston. "He's gone to Paris for the weekend with his latest fling. Didn't he tell you?"

"No." Preston was clearly irritated at the news. "And it isn't a matter of telling me; he's supposed to request time off, not just take it whenever he feels like it."

"I don't think Rupert understands how employment works." Samantha sipped her champagne. "You know this is the first proper job he's ever had. He'll eventually get the hang of it. To be fair, he does seem quite serious about getting to know the company now that he's come into his shares."

Marcus caught Harvard's eye. "I suppose Rachel's told you that every direct descendant of the original three brothers inherits shares in the company on their thirtieth birthday. Of course, I don't think the grandfathers thought there would be quite so many children when they came up with their plan. In a few years, the board will be overrun with Father's ex-wives and kids."

"You're exaggerating," Preston said. "There are only two of his ex-wives on the board. He discovered prenups after he divorced for the second time. Mainly because I shoved one under his nose and demanded he sign it. It's a miracle Father has any income to live off at all."

"I'm just grateful that wife number four didn't get any shares from their divorce." Samantha shuddered. "Can you imagine having to take someone called Honey seriously in a meeting? Honey? I mean, honestly. And that wasn't even an assumed name; her parents actually chose it."

"Not as bad as Sasha Darling." Marcus grimaced. "Stepmother number five picked her own stage name and kept it when she married Dad."

"Stepmother number five is the same age as your younger sister," Samantha said with barely hidden glee as she smoothed a hand down her pink satin sheath of a dress. "At lunch last month, Sasha Darling asked me where I'd gone to school. I said Oxford, and she said, 'Is that a comprehensive in Slough?'"

"It's best all round if you just don't talk to her," Marcus said. "I smile and nod. Then run at the first opportunity. It's mortifying that our father married a stripper who's barely out of her teens. The only upside is that he did it in Vegas and didn't make us attend."

"You must think we're terrible snobs," Preston said to Harvard, appearing a little shamefaced at the conversation. "The truth is, we have nothing against the girl. It's just the cliché of it all. Our sixty-year-old father married a twenty-year-old stripper. It's straight out of a bad Hollywood movie, and we're related to it."

"I disagree," Samantha said. "I *am* a terrible snob and I own it. It takes a lot of effort to be this elitist, and I feel I should get the credit for the time I've put in."

Harvard couldn't help his chuckle. "Then well done. That was the perfect level of snobbish disdain."

Samantha pretended to take a bow. "At last, some recognition," she said before sipping her champagne.

A WALKING STICK JERKED OUT AND NEARLY TRIPPED Rachel on the way to the bar.

"Gran, are you trying to kill me?" She frowned at the slender octogenarian, who was seated on the ornate high-backed chair she always claimed when she visited. As usual, her clothes would have given Grace Kelly a run for her money, her snow-white hair was fashioned into a tasteful chignon, and her lips were painted the faintest shade of sparkling pink.

"Darling girl, if I were going to kill you, I wouldn't do it with this cane. It's my favorite." She poked at an upholstered stool. "Sit down and tell me all about this man you're marrying."

Rachel knew an order when she heard one, and seeing as her grandmother was the only person on the planet she took them from, she sat. "What's there to tell? He's American, he's a former spy, he's beyond smart, and he looks like that." She pointed over at him as she did her best to avoid lying to her gran. "Who wouldn't marry him?"

Mary Prudence Talbot was clearly suspicious. She gave her granddaughter the considering glare that only a dowager countess could pull off. Rachel tried to appear innocent. Unfortunately, it wasn't a look she'd ever been able to do well.

"I suspect there's more to this than meets the eye," her grandmother said. "I'll get the information out of you eventually." Her eyes strayed back to Harvard. "Are you going to rescue him? The barracudas are circling."

Rachel glanced over to where her cousins had congregated around her fake fiancé. "He can take care of himself."

"Samantha's trying to seduce him."

"No, she isn't. She's just being Sam." Which meant flirting with anything that had a penis.

"You're very certain of your fiancé's devotion."

"Trust me, Harvard has no interest in anyone but me." But definitely not for the reasons her grandmother envisioned.

"Are you going to bring him over here so I can meet him?"

"No. I have no idea what will come out of your mouth, and I think I'll spare him the experience."

Her gran put her hand to her chest. "I can feel some pain in the general vicinity of my heart. Might be an attack. Best not to exacerbate it by making me anxious."

Rachel rolled her eyes. "Remind me again. When was the last time you had a heart attack? Oh, never. That's when."

"There's a first time for everything. I do believe I'm feeling faint. You'd better call your mother over."

"Oh, for the love of Prada, don't involve Mother. She's already causing enough trouble as it is."

"Perhaps I'd feel better if I was distracted, say by a handsome American man…"

Rachel let out a sigh as she stood. "When are you going to grow out of this manipulative streak of yours? You don't even do it very well."

"And yet, it's still effective." She smiled serenely. "Do bring me a sherry when you return with your man."

"Honestly." Rachel let out a huff as she stalked to the bar. She asked them to deliver a sherry to her smug grandmother, then took the drinks she'd ordered for herself and Harvard and made her way back across the room.

"I hear you're Rachel's bodyguard," Preston said, in a clear attempt to change the subject away from his father's many wives.

"Yep. Have been for a few months now." He went with the story his team had come up with when they'd first taken the job of investigating the thefts at TayFor.

"Why on earth does she need a bodyguard?" Marcus seemed genuinely bewildered as he knocked back his scotch. By Harvard's count, that was his third since they'd started talking.

"Benson Security deals with some shady people. Rachel was in the wrong place at the wrong time and ended up on the radar of someone we'd rather didn't know about her. I'm sticking close until the situation's resolved."

"In other words, Rachel managed to irritate the wrong person," Marcus said with a guffaw. "No surprise there."

"Don't blame her," Samantha reprimanded. "She can't help how she is."

"There's nothing wrong with my sister," Jonathan told her.

Samantha shrugged. "That's what I meant."

Marcus held up his hands. "We all know that Rachel delights in offending everyone she meets, why pretend otherwise?"

"She doesn't delight in it," Samantha said. "As I already told you, she simply can't help it."

"Oh, but I can." Rachel stepped up beside Harvard. She handed him a drink, making him grin. "I got you your usual, darling. Sorry it took so long, but I got waylaid by Grandmother."

Preston and Marcus gaped at him as Samantha started to giggle.

"Your usual is a strawberry daiquiri?" Jonathan asked.

Harvard took a large gulp and managed to quash the resulting shudder. "Can't get enough of the stuff." He draped an arm around Rachel's shoulders. "Thanks, honeybunny."

Her cousins and brother all worked hard to stifle their laughter as they looked anywhere but at Rachel, who stared at him with the promise of death in her eyes. Harvard made a mental note to Google more annoying pet names for her as soon as he got home.

"Let me see the ring," Samantha gushed, taking Rachel's hand.

To Harvard's surprise, she didn't tug it free. Instead, she sighed as Samantha admired her engagement ring.

"Platinum and diamond." Samantha arched an eyebrow at him. "Very chic setting too. Your man has good taste. And deep pockets for a bodyguard it would seem."

Rachel extracted her hand. "I do hope you aren't being so

crass as to question how he could afford it." Her eyes narrowed at all of them. "Because that would be beneath you."

Damn, she was glorious. Harvard tugged her to him, earning himself a frown of disapproval. "Rachel's worth every penny I spent." And wasn't that the truth?

"Rachel," Preston said, obviously over discussing her ring. "Who did you insult to earn a bodyguard?"

Rachel didn't miss a beat. "The South American drug cartel that blew up Father's private plane."

Jaws dropped.

"Are you crazy?" Marcus said at last.

"No." Rachel calmly sipped her red wine. "Just very angry. I promised Father I'd return it in one piece, not thousands."

"And now you can't go anywhere alone because your life is in danger." Preston shook his head at her. "You've become reckless. I'm not sure being involved with a security company is good for you." He glanced at Harvard. "No offense intended."

Harvard inclined his head at him. "None taken."

"I don't think it's all bad," Samantha said, her eyes on Harvard. "After all, it did get her a bodyguard *and* a fiancé. I'm actually quite jealous. I think I need to get a bodyguard too." Her eyes widened. "It just occurred to me that you're paying your fiancé to *take care* of you. How very liberated."

If anyone else picked up on the double meaning of her words, it didn't show. From the look on her face, you would assume she was innocent enough and that any subtext had been a mistake. But her eyes told a different story. Her eyes stayed on Harvard. And they were tinged with desire.

"Have you two set a date yet?" Preston asked.

"No," Rachel said at the same time as Harvard said, "Preferably soon."

Jonathan laughed, while Harvard waggled his eyebrows at his supposed fiancée. She wasn't amused.

"Oh, do let me pick the bridesmaid dresses," Samantha pleaded. "I'd just die if I didn't get the right color for my complexion."

"We wouldn't want that," Rachel said dryly. "Who said you're a bridesmaid anyway? Last I checked, the bride got to choose."

"Of course, I'm going to be one of your bridesmaids. Possibly your only one." She arched an eyebrow at Rachel. "We all know how good you are at making friends."

"Point taken," Rachel said. "I'll allow you to act as a bridesmaid."

"And the dresses—assuming you manage to find more than one bridesmaid? We both know I have better fashion sense than you. Otherwise you would have ducked out of our seasonal shopping sprees years ago."

"Fine, but the dresses better not upstage the bride."

"Would I do that?" Samantha feigned horror.

"In a second," Rachel said.

"I hate to be the voice of doom," Preston said, "but you do have a prenup, don't you? If you don't, I have experience in drawing them up, even though it isn't my area of expertise." He cast a wary glance at Harvard. "You really should have one. You never know what the future might hold."

"In other words," Harvard drawled, "he's worried your lowly American bodyguard is after your money." If only they knew how much he was worth on his own. While at MIT, he'd discovered that not only did he have a knack for analytical methodologies, but he was also damn good at playing the stock market too.

Preston turned red and blustered. "I don't mean to be insulting, but Rachel is a very wealthy woman, and she should protect herself."

It was clear her cousin meant well, so Harvard let him off the hook. "I wouldn't marry her without one. I don't want Rachel's money—I want her body." He winked at her. "And her heart." And wasn't that the truth. "I'll sign whatever you draw up."

"My goodness." Samantha fanned herself. "An honorable man in this day and age. Where did you find him?"

"I thought we'd already established that I rent him by the hour," Rachel said, making Harvard laugh. At least she'd picked up on her cousin's earlier dig. "And let me tell you, services the likes of which Harvard provides don't come cheap." Solemnly, she looked up at him. "It's no wonder you don't need my money. You make enough of your own."

"You know." Samantha considered her cousin. "I think you've also become more sarcastic since you went to work for this security company."

"I don't work for them," Rachel said. "They work for me. I'm a partner."

"Well, you *were*," Jonathan said, reminding them of the other half of their cover.

"You were?" Marcus leaned forward, yet another full glass of whiskey in his hand and a glazed look in his eye. The man was at least three sheets to the wind. "Did you sell your stake? What are you doing now? I thought you'd found your niche at Benson Security."

"I did find my niche, but now it's time to move on. After I came into my TayFor shares last year, my interest in the company returned, and I found that I wanted to be more involved. As of Monday, I'll be working at the main office with the rest of you. Meet the new director of special projects." She gave a little bow.

After a few seconds of stunned silence, her cousins erupted.

"I'm so glad you're coming back." Samantha pulled her

into a hug. "I hate being the only female in our generation who's there. Now I'll have backup."

"I never understood why you left in the first place," Marcus said. "I always expected you'd become CEO after your father retired. Not that Jonathan isn't great." He winced in Jonathan's direction before holding up his drink in a tipsy salute. "Sorry, old chap."

Jonathan's laugh was good-natured. "I thought the same thing. In fact, if Rachel is back for good, I might try to talk her into taking over."

"As the official company lawyer," Preston said, "I'd like to point out that you can't exactly hand the CEO role over to your sister. Which, given that you also studied law, is something you should know. It's got nothing to do with her ability. We all know she could boss us around blindfolded. It's more to do with perception. To the rest of the pharmaceutical industry, Rachel is an unknown. You'd be wiser to offer it to the family members who already work at TayFor first, then if they—we—decline, it's all Rachel's."

"Don't worry," Rachel said. "I don't want to become CEO. Jonathan is stuck with the role, but it will be interesting to be back in the fold."

"We need to celebrate," Marcus said then looked around. "Oh, wait. We already are." He cheerfully swayed in place, sloshing his drink over the front of his shirt. He didn't seem to notice he was now wearing his whiskey. "Listen up, every-one," he shouted.

The noise gradually died down as he gained their attention.

"Is this necessary?" Rachel sounded bored as she toyed with the locket she always wore.

"Yes, it's necessary," Marcus said before raising his voice. "It turns out that it's a double celebration tonight."

There was a gasp, and every eye shot to Rachel's mother.

She had her hands on her cheeks, her eyes wide, just like the poster image for *Home Alone*. "You're pregnant?"

"What? No!" Rachel snapped. "Honestly, Mother. That's the first place your mind goes?"

"A woman can hope." She shrugged.

"Anyway," Marcus slurred loudly. "The news is that Rachel is coming back to work at TayFor. From Monday morning, we'll have another Talbot in the building. Where she belongs."

There was a cheer.

"About time," her Uncle Theo called.

"Welcome home, Rachel," her father shouted.

She shook her head at them in disgust before turning to Harvard. "Well, that was unnecessary. Come on, Grandmother insists on meeting you. Once she's done embarrassing me, I'm going home. I've had enough for one night."

He was kind of impressed she'd told him her plans rather than skipping out on him. "Lead the way," he said as he nodded his goodbyes to her cousins.

Chapter Five

"I like your family," Harvard said during their drive back to London. For some reason, his voice sounded deeper and more sensual in the dark intimacy of the car. "Your immediate family, that is."

"You seem surprised. Is it because they're nothing like me?"

Rachel was very much aware that she was the black sheep of the family. She always had been, even before she'd decided on a career outside of TayFor. She'd been born with a cold edge and a knack for biting sarcasm that her parents and brothers didn't have. Although she suspected her grandmother's nature was quite similar to her own. The main difference between them was that Gran knew how to play nice in public, and Rachel couldn't be bothered.

"Rachel," he purred her name, making her insides melt. "There's *no one* like you."

"True."

"They care about you deeply."

Was he bewildered? That was just insulting. "Of course they do."

"No, I don't mean because they're your family and they have no choice. I mean, they genuinely adore you for being you."

"And you can't understand that." She wasn't offended; most people couldn't.

"No," he said softly. "I understand it all too well."

She wasn't going to touch that statement with a ten-foot pole. Or wonder why his words caused a strange warmth to surge through her.

Driving onto Albert Bridge, they passed Battersea Park, its vast expanse a dark void in an otherwise glimmering city. Beneath them, the city lights bounced off the choppy waters of the Thames, and she caught a glimpse of a party on the deck of a houseboat.

"Did your super-spy senses tell you who's stealing from TayFor?" Rachel asked as they waited for the lights to turn green on the Chelsea side of the bridge.

"It doesn't quite work like that, but I did pick up a few interesting things. Your cousin Marcus likes his booze, which makes me wonder what kind of control he has in other areas of his life. Meanwhile, Preston's chomping at the bit to helm TayFor. And I suspect Samantha would have tried to get me into bed if she'd had the opportunity."

"Sounds about right."

They drove through Chelsea, past the townhouse her parents used when they were in the city, and into Westminster, where Rachel turned into the street that housed Benson Security. The converted Victorian terrace house had a couple of apartments above the offices that staff used when needed. Harvard was currently housed in one of them, as he hadn't found his own place yet. It seemed to Rachel that he hadn't made much effort to either.

"You aren't bothered that your cousin tried to seduce your fiancé?"

"I would be if you really were my fiancé."

"Rachel." The way he said her name was like a caress, even when it was tinged with long suffering. "You have to act like I *am* your fiancé, and if your cousin comes on to me, you need to tell her to back off. People are already suspicious about our relationship because you act like you'd rather be anywhere than by my side. You need to get into the role. If I was your fiancé, what would you have done to Samantha?"

"I would have calmly explained that you're already taken."

"Rachel..."

"Fine, and then I would have signed her up for a week at a clinic for sex addicts but told her I was sending her to a spa— my treat."

His laughter felt like bubbles on her skin.

"That's my girl," he said as she parked in front of the office.

"I'm not your girl. I'm not a girl at all. I'm a full-grown woman who's playing pretend with her work colleague." She held his gaze. "Don't get confused about what's happening here."

"I wouldn't dare." He threw the door open, climbed out and said, "Back in a minute," before he rounded the car.

She opened her window. "Wait," she called after him. "Why are you coming back?"

He seemed confused by the question. "I'm picking up my bag, and then I'm moving in with you for the duration."

A cold resolve took root at his words. "Oh, I don't think so."

"I'm your fiancé. We need to get to know each other. We need to get comfortable being around each other. The only way to do that is to spend time together. What if someone in your family drops by? They're gonna think it's pretty damn weird that I live here. We already gave the impression I have to be with you twenty-four seven. I can't do that from here." He pointed to the building behind him.

Rachel didn't bother arguing with him. It wasn't happening, and that was that. Instead, she closed the window, put the car in gear, and drove away. In her rearview mirror, she saw him pull his phone out of his pocket. A few seconds later, her iPhone buzzed from its spot attached to the dash.

While stopped at a red light, she read his message: *You get a reprieve until Monday morning. I'll pick you up at seven.*

Rachel narrowed her eyes as she zoomed toward Kensington and her home. He'd learn. It might be the hard way, but he'd definitely learn that Rachel did *not* take instruction well.

COME MONDAY MORNING, RACHEL WASN'T WAITING AT her apartment for a pickup as she was supposed to. Harvard wasn't even sure why he'd expected to find her there. Stupidity maybe.

Teeth clenched, he drove the forty minutes to TayFor Pharmaceuticals' complex alone. It was the last time he'd do it. Because one way or another, this little power struggle over his position at Rachel's side would be sorted that morning.

The admin section of the TayFor complex was housed in a gray stone Victorian mansion that had been renovated into offices when Rachel's grandfather first started the company. Since her father took over, the land around the original building had been developed as TayFor's research complex and contained several newer buildings. All of which sat in manicured grounds. To Harvard's eye, the setup was typically English. *Upper-class* English. Everything about it said genteel, sophisticated, understated, and very wealthy. It was a complex designed to put even the most nervous of business partners at ease.

He let himself in through the main doors of the TayFor office and headed straight for the smiling woman behind the reception desk. "I'm Michael Carter, Rachel Ford-Talbot's fiancé and bodyguard."

"Of course, Mr. Carter." The woman, who appeared to be in her fifties and very efficient, pointed to an iPad propped on the desk. "I'm Sandra Caird. If you'd follow the instructions on the screen, I'll fetch your ID. Ms. Ford-Talbot informed me you would be in around now."

Harvard was sure she had, probably smiling like a shark while she did it. "Has Rachel been here long?" Instead of waiting at her apartment for him like they'd agreed she would during their call the day before.

"About an hour. Do you have your passport with you?"

He reached into the inside pocket of his suit jacket and handed it over. Sandra was very careful to match the image inside to his face and then scan the document for their records. Meanwhile, Harvard logged in to the iPad and pressed his fingers to the scanner beneath it so that it would record his prints. As security setups went, it wasn't half bad.

"Here you go," Sandra said. "Your passport and your ID. Please wear it at all times. You'll need it to access the areas you've been cleared for."

He took the lanyard with the card—the photo he'd submitted the week before already on it—and hung it around his neck. "Thanks. Can you point me toward Rachel's office?"

"Certainly." She gestured to the security door at the end of the spacious reception area, where a guard sat beside a scanner. "If you pass the guard and go through the door, you'll find a lift on your left. Take it to the third floor. Ms. Ford-Talbot's office is to your right when you exit."

"Thanks." He flashed her a smile before heading to the security guard.

A familiar face grinned at him. "I see you've already lost the body you're supposed to be guarding." Ryan Granger kept his voice low as he spoke. The ex-soldier, who was only slightly younger than Harvard, had been with Benson Security since the first office opened in Scotland. He was a good man to have at your back, although his sense of humor and constant eating took a bit of getting used to.

"Don't worry," Harvard muttered. "I know exactly where to find it again."

"If you'll just walk through the scanner," Ryan said, using a louder tone that would carry to the receptionist, "that would be great. Please empty any metal objects from your pockets before you do so."

Harvard took out his keys, phone, and wallet and placed them on the table for the bag scanner to check before walking through the metal detector. He knew his teammate had turned it off so the gun in his shoulder holster wouldn't set off an alarm.

Ryan had already been in place with security for two weeks. Only the head of his department knew who he was and why he was there. To everyone else, he was merely a new employee.

"Do me a favor." Harvard put his belongings back in his pockets. "Disable Rachel's car. She's going home with me at the end of the day."

Ryan struggled to hide his amusement. "Unless she calls a taxi and sneaks out when you're looking the other way."

"Just sort the car. I'll deal with Rachel."

"Aye aye, boss." Ryan was clearly unconvinced.

"Did you do your rounds?" Harvard asked quietly.

"I scanned Rachel's office for surveillance devices as soon as I got in this morning. It was clear. I didn't get a chance to do the other offices on the exec floor because my shift partner was too damn nosey."

"At least Rachel's office is clear; that's something. Anything else I need to know?"

"Nothing that can't wait until the team meeting. You're bringing pizza, right?"

Harvard stared at him.

"Guess I'll bring the pizza," Ryan said at last.

"I'll talk to you later," Harvard said. "I have a runaway fiancée to deal with first."

"Now you know why no one else on the team volunteered to partner with the Queen of Darkness." Ryan sounded amused. "We totally warned you, dude."

Since he wasn't supposed to know the security guard, Harvard didn't think it appropriate to flip him off. Instead, he headed for the elevator.

And made it five steps past the door before he was waylaid by yet another of Rachel's relatives.

"We haven't met," the man said. "I'm Charles Talbot, financial director and Rachel's uncle." He didn't hold out his hand.

"People call me Harvard." His trained eyes took in every detail of the man before him.

In his early sixties, with steel gray hair and a bit of a paunch under his tailored pinstripe suit, he looked like the stereotypical English gent. All ruddy complexion and permanent air of disapproval. After reading the file on the man, Harvard had pitied Rupert and Samantha for having him as a father. And their research had revealed that his wife wasn't much better. Clarissa was the definition of simpering English flower—when she wasn't stoned or drunk, that is.

"Congratulations on your engagement," Charles said, in the same tone others would use to give their condolences.

"Thanks." Harvard thrust his hands into his pockets and

waited. He'd had many conversations like this over the years and knew how to read the signs of what was to come.

"I never imagined Rachel would...*couple* with an American." He sneered the word, as though American was synonymous with dirt. "And an African-American at that. I hear you're also her bodyguard. How very...modern of you both."

Yeah, Rachel's uncle was a racist asshole.

"According to the tabloids," Harvard drawled, "if the peerage doesn't modernize, they'll die out. Probably a good thing Rachel's bringing in some new blood."

Charles puffed out his chest. "As her uncle and an elder to you both, I feel I should point out that the gossip rags will have a field day with your relationship. I say this only to spare Rachel the upset of going through the pain of such an experience, you understand. You must have noticed the way they raked Prince Harry's wife over the coals, and she wasn't nearly as...dark...as, well, you are."

Oh, he wanted to punch the unctuous little prick right on his glowing red nose. "I didn't realize the UK had a sliding scale for racism. Guess that wasn't covered in my *Welcome to England* package."

"I don't believe you're taking this seriously. It isn't only the color of your skin that will cause issue, it's also your *class*." He lowered his voice. "For Pete's sake, you're *working class*. And American. It's as though Rachel deliberately went looking for a man who ticked the most controversial boxes and dragged him home to her parents. Can't you see what this is going to do to the family? To Rachel? We'll be the laughing-stock of the town. Do you really want to put her through that?"

Harvard's hands curled into fists inside his pockets as he visualized the damage one good right hook would do to the man. "Just going from this conversation, I'd say people are already laughing at you."

Charles' face turned a strange shade of purple. "I don't understand what Rachel could possibly see in you. You're obviously only out to get your hands on her money, and I intend to make her aware of that at the very first opportunity."

"You do that." Harvard pushed the button for the elevator. "But you might want to invest in a bulletproof vest first; she carries a gun in her purse, and she's quite the shot. She'll shoot your balls off at twenty paces. She's that good. Even a target that small won't faze her."

"Well, I never," Charles blustered.

The elevator doors opened, and Harvard stepped inside. He turned to face good old Uncle Charles. "And another thing. While I was in the CIA, I learned a thing or two about torture and body disposal. You might want to keep that in mind the next time you spew racist shit in my direction."

The doors closed before Charles had a chance to reply.

Chapter Six

The first thought Rachel had when she opened her desk drawer and saw the photo sitting in it was that she should have waited at her apartment for Harvard. Not because she needed a man to protect her, but because she would have been too busy dealing with him to get her office ready. But no, she'd just had to mess with him and come in early. Which meant boredom had led her to organizing. And organizing had led her to open the drawer.

She should have come to work with Harvard.

But then, who knew how long that photo would have sat there, waiting for anyone to find it...

Rachel was aware her thoughts were muddled and somewhat inane, but that couldn't be helped. Her inner voice rambled as her mind struggled to comprehend what she was looking at. Which was stupid in itself, because she'd been expecting this.

As soon as she'd known she was returning to TayFor, she'd been waiting for something to happen. She just hadn't been as prepared for it as she'd thought she was. But then, how did you prepare for suddenly coming across the photographic evidence of an attack you only remembered in fragments of broken dreams? Was that even possible?

And now that she thought about it, was she supposed to feel shame when she saw the image? Was she supposed to run and hide? It had been ten years since it was taken. She wasn't the same person anymore. She'd learned a lot since then. Grown up. Become stronger. Now she knew the photo didn't show *her* shame. It showed the indignity of her attackers.

The victims didn't own the shame.

It wasn't theirs to carry.

Ever.

"Victim," she whispered, trying the word. Trying to imagine it as describing her. It tasted alien on her tongue.

Stretching a surprisingly steady hand toward the Polaroid, she hesitated to touch it. As though, somehow, confirming that the photo was real would make what happened more concrete too. But then, when the memory of your assault was a blank, a photo of it was the only reality left.

As Rachel's fingertips touched the edge of the Polaroid, her office suddenly disappeared. She no longer stood beside her ugly desk. Instead, she was back *there*. On the floor of that hotel room. Naked. Alone. Hurting. And desperately wishing...

A flash of memory slammed into her, ripping her open.

Hands around her throat. A body heavy on top of her. Moving inside of her. The thick, sickening scent of incense. And laughter. So. Much. Laughter.

None of it hers.

As past and present merged, the walls pressed in on her. Was she in her office? Was she back at the hotel? The floor beneath her feet wobbled and roiled until she felt dizzy. The air became thick with the cloying fragrance of incense, making it hard to breathe. Or maybe it was the pressure on her chest that cut her oxygen. The weight crushing her as the body moved over her...

"No," she moaned.

She had to get out of there, had to escape. But even without the hands holding her down, her legs were too weak to carry her. She needed a plan. She needed to think. But the world wouldn't stop spinning long enough to allow her to have one single coherent thought. Just one. All she needed was one.

"Rachel?" a voice snapped. "Rachel? You with me?"

She blinked rapidly, the hotel room beginning to fade. Dragging air into her lungs, she forced herself to stay still. Very still. Until she knew she was safe. The light became brighter, and the floor stopped moving beneath her feet. Slowly, her office came back into focus, and the thick, pungent aroma filling her senses dispersed from the air. But her heart felt like it was trying to break out through her rib cage, and her legs were weak.

"Rachel, you okay?" As a deep voice rumbled, she tore her gaze from the photo to focus on the person talking to her.

Harvard. It was Harvard.

His massive frame filled the doorway, dressed from top to toe in black and looking every inch the deadly assassin he'd trained to be. She reached for her water bottle and took a sip, her heart still hammering inside her, making her feel nauseous. But she kept her gaze on the man watching her so intently.

"Rachel," he said again, "is everything okay?"

As casually as she was able, she slid the drawer closed. "Why wouldn't it be?" Slowly, she lowered herself to the seat behind her desk.

Okay, that was weird. She hadn't lost herself like that before. The brief flashes of memory she did have usually turned up in her sleep. Taking a slow breath so that Harvard wouldn't notice her fighting the urge to hyperventilate, she let it out carefully. Once. Twice. On the third breath, her sense of control returned.

"Is there something you wanted?" she asked, relieved to hear her voice sound as cool and even as usual. She took stock of her body. Her legs had stopped shivering, her heart was beating steadily, and her mind was clear. Everything was back to normal, meaning the moment had passed.

Harvard closed the door behind him and leaned back against it, folding his arms casually as he blocked her only exit. "What just happened?"

"Nothing." She waved a hand at him. "If you have nothing to discuss, you may leave. I'm rather busy."

He narrowed his eyes at her, making it clear that he was only dropping the topic of her mini-meltdown because he chose to. "Yeah, I have something to discuss. How about you dodging me this morning? That's twice you've dumped me and run. It won't happen again."

Rachel frowned at him, feeling more herself with each passing second. "That's a bit presumptuous, given that I don't answer to you."

"For the duration of this undercover assignment, you do."

Now that was just irritating. "I said I'd do this job for you; I didn't say I'd do everything you told me to."

Harvard wasn't like the other men at Benson Security. They tended to get loud and over-emotional when she confronted them. Not Harvard. He was just as calm as usual. There was no throbbing vein on his forehead, no clenched jaw, no dark frown. There were only those piercing brown eyes of his, boring straight through her. It was disconcerting, and she wasn't quite sure how to handle him yet. All she knew was that she never felt threatened by him, and he definitely didn't feel threatened by her. Which was such a shame.

"A lot of people are depending on you to do your part in

this investigation. And to do it professionally. You're part of a team, whether you like it or not, and we can't function properly unless we can rely on each other." He arched an eyebrow at her. "Can I rely on you, Rachel?"

For some reason, those words said in that gentle tone of his felt like more of a reprimand than anything he could have shouted at her. A strange sensation stole over her, and it took her a second to realize she felt shame at disappointing him. It wasn't a feeling she was used to nor one she enjoyed.

"I'm playing my part in this team," she objected.

She was in the damn office, wasn't she? She'd stood at his side while being ambushed by her mother's attempt at telling the world they were a couple. What else did he want from her?

"Are you playing your part? Can you honestly say that? A security operation is about trust. As team leader, I need to know you're where I tell you to be, doing what I tell you to do. Lives could depend on it."

She rolled her eyes. "We're here to find a thief; we aren't taking on the Taliban."

"It doesn't matter what the assignment is, Rachel. It's about team trust. We don't know where this job will lead. Hopefully, it'll be a safe, easy walk in the park for all of us. But if it goes south, if the shit really hits the fan, your team needs to know you have their backs." He held her eye. "Right now, the only person whose back you're covering is your own."

His words shouldn't have mattered to her, but they did. They felt like a slap. And she couldn't understand why. "Is this because I wouldn't take you home with me on Saturday night? Or because I came to the office on my own this morning? Don't you think you're overreacting?"

"No. I don't. This isn't a game for me. It isn't something I'm doing reluctantly, putting in the minimum effort. This is my profession, and I take pride in doing it to the best of my ability. I need a functioning team that also behaves professionally at my back. You're a partner in the business you're representing. How you behave, what you do as part of this team, reflects on Benson Security and on me. And, your family is relying on you to get the job done for them. So, no. I don't think I'm overreacting. I think I'm dealing with a woman who's acting out because she didn't get her own way."

She would *not* let him see the blow his words had been. "I care very much about resolving this for my family *and* ensuring Benson Security performs as a company at the top of its field should. I resent your comments."

"Then change your behavior, so I won't have to make them. Work *with* your team instead of against us. Treat your undercover role with the same dedication you treat every other aspect of your business life. I've seen how you work. You push yourself to attain the highest standard in everything you do and expect us to do the same. Why is this assignment any different?"

Because she didn't want to be there.

Which meant he was right.

It was a knife to her stomach.

If there'd been any challenge in his demeanor, any anger in his voice, she would have fought him on the issue—even though she knew she was wrong. But he hadn't given her even a sliver of a reason to keep on arguing. Her only saving grace was that there was no one around to watch her concede. But holy Yves Saint Laurent, it was hard to get the words out of her mouth.

Studying him carefully, watching for any sign of amusement or gloating, she postponed the inevitable. But there was no avoiding it. She had to say the words he needed to hear and hope he didn't hold them over her forever.

Rachel cleared her throat and said, "I apologize. I will

make every effort to perform as part of this team from now on."

She was going to be sick. Bile actually raced to her mouth. This was hell.

The air in her office felt electrically charged as she waited for Harvard's reaction. Would he rub her face in her apology? Would he continue to lecture her and explain things endlessly as men were wont to do? Would he laugh at her?

"Thanks," he said as he pushed away from the door. "You want a coffee? I need one."

That was it? That was all he had to say?

She shook her head. "No, thank you."

He nodded and left, closing the door quietly behind him.

Hesitantly, Rachel opened the drawer and took out the photo. Calmer now that she knew she wasn't alone. That Harvard was there if she needed him. Not that she would, but the knowledge helped.

She stared at the photo as though looking at an image of someone else. It showed a woman being held down by one man while being raped by another. The only face in the photo was her own. And there were tears on her cheeks.

Fury burned white hot at the sight of the tears.

The bastards had made her cry.

And Rachel *never* cried.

It was tempting to shred the photo and flush it, but she'd done that once before. And she wouldn't do it again. She wasn't that scared girl anymore. So, instead, she dropped it into the side pocket of her handbag and zipped it tight. She'd figure out what to do about it later. Because there was no doubt in her mind that she'd have to deal with it eventually. There was no ignoring the photo this time, nor the message scrawled across the bottom.

The one that said, *You shouldn't be here.*

As soon as he'd closed the door behind him, Harvard pulled out his phone and stepped into the outer office. He dialed Ryan, who answered immediately. "I need cameras inside Rachel's office. Today." He kept his voice low, so Rachel couldn't overhear.

"What happened?" As usual, when it came to work, Ryan was completely professional. No hint of amusement in his voice at all.

Harvard flicked on the coffee machine that sat on the counter against the far wall. While it did its thing, he turned and leaned back against the counter, facing Rachel's office. "If I had to guess, I'd say some sort of flashback."

"Who had a flashback?" Ryan sounded confused.

"Rachel." He shook his head. It didn't make any sense. Her history was clear of trauma—unless it was from something that'd happened since she joined Benson Security. The team hadn't exactly lived nice, safe lives these past few years. "Has she had any counseling? Treatment for PTSD? Any help with processing the stuff that happened in Peru?"

"What stuff? You mean when her dad's plane was blown up and we got into a gunfight with the cartel?"

"Yeah, that stuff." He kept his eye on the door to Rachel's office. It was silent inside.

"We all had counseling. We were all cleared. Are you sure you saw what you did? Rachel doesn't suffer trauma; she causes it."

"I know a flashback when I see one." Hell, he'd had enough himself to recognize them. "Has she ever spaced out at the office? Started sweating, closed down, looked like she might pass out?"

"Not that I know of, and if she had done something like

that, the word would spread fast. The general consensus is that nothing affects Rachel."

"Then it has to have been triggered by coming back here." Which put a whole different slant on her argument not to be involved in the investigation.

"Harvard, my man, are you sure you aren't just overreacting because you've got the hots for her? Maybe she hasn't woken up properly yet. Or maybe she was just thinking about something else. There doesn't have to be a sinister reason for her checking out for a minute."

"She said the word no." He closed his eyes tight at the memory. "Never gonna forget how she said it. Like she was pleading. Like she'd given up and it was hopeless."

"Well, hell."

That about summed it up. "I'll get Elle to dig deeper into her background. In the meantime, you get surveillance up and running in her office."

"I'm happy to do that, but I need to ask—is investigating Rachel's past the best use of Elle's time right now? We're in the middle of an investigation. You sure you want to derail it by making this a priority? It's only happened one time. Maybe you should try talking to Rachel before you go crazy."

Harvard barked out a laugh as he pinched the bridge of his nose. "Have you ever tried talking to Rachel about anything? If she doesn't want to tell you, it ain't getting told."

"Then we need to hope she tells you sooner rather than later, because we're up to our ears in this investigation, and we can't stretch our resources too thin."

He let out a sigh. Ryan was right. "Okay, just install cameras for now. I'll bring in Elle if it happens again. But I have a bad feeling about this whole thing, and I'm beginning to regret making Rachel come back here."

"She isn't alone," Ryan said. "We've got her back. She

might use us for target practice if she finds out we're looking out for her, but she's still one of ours."

"Yeah. You're right."

"Wait," Ryan said. "Can you say that again? I need to hit record first."

Harvard hung up and turned to fix his coffee. There was no denying something was going on with Rachel. Something that might affect the job they were on. And Harvard didn't want his team to be blindsided by whatever she was hiding, which meant he had to talk to her about it.

It would be easier to squeeze blood from a stone.

Chapter Seven

Just before lunch, when Rachel had given up on her PA ever turning up for work, she bounced through the door to her office.

"Should I have knocked?" Elle Roberts, Benson Security's resident hacker, said. "Do PAs knock when it's their own boss's office? I've never been a secretary before. Guess I'll have to make it up as I go. How do I look?" She held her arms out and twirled. "I'm calling this outfit *Office Minnie.*"

She was dressed in a full red skirt, à la nineteen fifty. It was covered in white polka dots and teamed with a short-sleeved black cardigan that fit her like a glove. She'd buttoned it right up and wore it as a top, with a silver Minnie Mouse brooch pinned to it. There was a black and white polka dot bow in her bright red hair, which, if Rachel wasn't mistaken, was a wig. To finish the outfit off, Elle wore reading glasses with cat-eye-shaped frames.

"I thought the glasses made me look more secretarial." Elle was obviously proud of herself.

"I would never in a million years hire a PA who came to work dressed like that," Rachel said.

"I know." Elle looked particularly pleased. "It will help our cover. We aren't supposed to get on. People will take one look at you in your boring black Gucci dress and me in this awesome outfit and instantly know that there's no way we're best buds." She grinned at Harvard, who'd gotten out of the seat he'd been parked in all morning to offer it to Elle. "I rock," she told him as she plopped into the vacated chair.

"I'm getting more coffee," Harvard said with an amused shake of his head. "Want some?"

"Totally." Elle bounced in place.

"It looks like you've already had too much caffeine. And this dress is Chanel, not Gucci," Rachel felt the need to point out.

"My mistake." Elle didn't sound contrite. "Anyway, I'm going to ignore the fact you've sent me about a million texts —some of which were pretty damn insulting—asking why I wasn't here catering to your every whim. For your information, I got in at five this morning and spent the hours before the IT department turned up checking their protocols. After that, I was given a tour of the facility as part of my orientation. I didn't complain as it was a good way to scope out the place. And now I'm here. *Not* playing video games, as you so rudely suggested."

Rachel sat down in her desk chair again. It was like sitting on rocks. Slippery, jagged rocks. The shiny leather meant her backside kept shifting forward, while hard little lumps under the cushion made it painful to move. Or stay still. The chair had to go. She could put up with everything else—the furniture that looked like it had been used in the production set for the movie *Wall Street,* walls painted a delicate shade of vomit green, and overhead lighting that wouldn't have looked out of place in a government building. But she could *not* sit on that damn chair a second longer.

She grabbed her phone and stood while she opened the website of a reputable office supply company. "One second," she said, as she ordered a top-of-the-line desk chair—in red. "Okay, carry on. What were you saying?"

"It's good to know I have your full attention. I was saying that TayFor's head of security has a bug up his butt the size of a VW Beetle."

"Terrance? He seems capable enough. What's the problem with him?"

"You mean apart from the fact it's Terrance and never Terry?" Elle was saying as Harvard came into the room and handed her a coffee.

"Terrance King knows what he's doing," Harvard said. "He's just an asshole about it. He thinks he could have handled this situation in-house and sees bringing in Benson Security as a slight to his ego. Big-fish-little-pond syndrome." He looked around for another chair, but there wasn't one.

"Have mine," Rachel told him and watched carefully as he sat. He didn't appear uncomfortable. "Don't you feel like you're sitting on rocks?"

"Nope." He sipped his coffee.

"Well, you can keep the chair. I've ordered another one that should arrive later today. Sitting on that is agony."

"Don't know what you're talking about; this feels fine."

"Either Rachel has a really boney backside—" Elle piped up.

"Rachel's ass is perfect," Harvard interrupted.

"Or," Elle carried on, "this is a case of *The Princess and the Pea*. Which I could totally see, because if ever there was a princess..." She trailed off and glared at Harvard. "Stop looking at her backside. There's no place for flirting on this job."

His grin was wicked. "If I don't flirt, how will I tease her into giving in? There's a bet to be won."

"Could we please focus on the reason we're here?" Rachel snapped.

Harvard's wide smile seemed far more intimate than it should have. "Tell us what you found on the servers, Elle," he said.

Elle looked up from her laptop and reached for her drink on the small glass and steel box that served as a coffee table. "To cut a long story short, there's been no tampering with the main backup server in the basement. It's locked up like Fort Knox. Someone would need access from security and one of the tech team at their side to get in there. Any hacking of research files must have been done in the labs."

"And we're sure we can strike the IT department techs off our suspect list?" Rachel asked.

Ever since accepting the job from her father, Benson Security had been hard at work investigating the staff and eliminating them from the suspect pool. Unfortunately, all the clues they'd uncovered so far had led the team to believe that a senior staff member of TayFor must be selling secrets. And most of the senior members were family.

"The IT department isn't involved." Elle took another gulp of her coffee and followed it with a blissful sigh. "The way things are set up, they wouldn't recognize the pertinent information in order to sell it. All research files are encrypted before storage. The only way you'd know what they were would be if you knew the research and went in looking for particular information."

"In other words," Harvard said, "the IT team has the ability to steal from the system but can't read the files, so they wouldn't know what was worth stealing."

Elle nodded. "The only thing they could do is copy everything and sell it in bulk, hoping whoever bought it could crack the encryption and find something useful."

"It would narrow down the search for the thief if we knew whether they were selling encrypted files or ones they'd already decoded," Harvard mused.

Elle's attention snapped to him. "If they were unencrypted before they were sold, that would mean someone had to have read them here. The encryption key is localized to this complex. But all TayFor files are automatically encrypted when they're saved or copied..."

Elle stared at Harvard, but it was clear her mind was elsewhere. It was fascinating. You could almost see her brain working.

"We need to run a search for anyone who might have acquired a copy of the encryption key. That would be damn hard to get. It's coded into the system. I doubt even the IT guys know what it is. But...if someone has one, there would be a ghost trail on their computer. With the right program, we can find it."

"All I'm hearing is blah, blah, blah computers," Rachel complained. "Which makes me think we could have run this investigation from Benson Security, so I didn't need to come here in the first place. Surely you could have hacked the system from there?"

"Rachel!" Elle sounded shocked. "Please tell me you know that most of the computers at TayFor aren't connected to the internet."

"I haven't been here in ten years; how would I know that?" Now she was definitely losing patience. She paced her office, feeling the walls close in on her with every step she took.

"Each building is a standalone network with its own server that backs up everything in an encrypted format. And that's backed up by the server in the basement. Even the connection between that server and the others is a closed system. In other words, no way to get into it from the outside."

"How on earth do the research scientists communicate with the outside world if they don't have internet access in their labs?" Rachel asked.

"The office building has internet access."

"So, all the thief needs to do is download the research onto a thumb drive, take it to the office building, and email it out," Rachel said. "Shouldn't we check those computers and get this over with?"

"No." Elle shook her head, making the bright red waves bounce. "Apart from the fact most computers have all unnecessary USB ports disabled, every machine in the building's fitted with a program that records downloads. If one occurs, both security and the section boss are sent an automatic notification. Even if they did somehow manage to download the files without being noticed and email them from their office, there are firewalls upon firewalls to stop anything like that getting out. It just isn't possible."

"Could they have transferred it to their phone and sent it that way?" Rachel said.

Harvard answered, "Phones, smartwatches, any personal devices are left at the security station in each building. Staff then go through metal detectors and scanners. No form of electronic storage is allowed into the labs—including thumb drives."

"Okay, but they must have laptops they take home to work on." Rachel's parents had often brought work home, some of it sensitive.

"Any data that's taken outside the building has to be approved by department bosses, and it's only allowed out on TayFor's own encryption-enabled laptops," Elle said. "Each of which is examined by the IT division when it's returned, to check there's been no unusual activity. No personal laptops are allowed within the facility."

"This is impossible." Rachel threw up her hands in disgust.

"No, but it's going to be hard. The thief is hacking the system from inside, somehow. We just need to figure out how." Elle's voice had lowered as though she wasn't even aware they were in the room with her anymore. "I need Harry's help. He literally writes the code to catch ghost programming. I'll shoot him an email and see what time zone he's in, maybe set up a meeting."

"He's in Scotland," Rachel said. "They're busy setting up home in Invertary. I'm not entirely sure he'll be available to help. He has other priorities now he's sold his share of Benson Security."

Elle blinked at her. "Harry will make time. This is your family's company we're talking about."

"I don't see what that's got to do with it."

Elle and Harvard shared a look that Rachel couldn't quite interpret.

"You really don't, do you?" Elle said. "Harry cares about you; you've been friends since uni. You're the reason he was able to set up his programming company in the first place. Before you guys bought into Benson Security. This will be important to him because it's important to you. That's how friendship works, Rach."

Rachel arched an eyebrow at her. "It astonishes me just how naïve you are. The world doesn't work like that. Harry's moved on. He's busy with his own life, and he has no interest in mine."

"Wow," Elle said. "What happened to make you this cynical?"

"What happened to turn you into such a Pollyanna?"

"Honey," Elle said, "I was born this way."

"Hello," a voice called. "Anyone in there?"

"Remember your covers," Harvard ordered as the door opened, and he moved to stand slightly in front of Rachel.

"Oh my, you do take your responsibilities seriously, don't you?" Cousin Samantha purred as she eyed Harvard's protective stance. "I swear I don't intend Rachel any harm. There are no weapons on my person, but you're welcome to frisk me if you'd like."

Harvard just gave her a polite smile. Sam smiled back before turning to Elle, and that's when her jaw dropped. The sight almost made Rachel laugh.

Putting on her best *boss* voice, she stepped around Harvard. "That will be all, Elle. We'll go over my schedule later. Samantha, this is my new PA, Elle Roberts. HR sent her up. Elle, this is Samantha Talbot, director of marketing."

Elle gathered her things and stood, beaming at Samantha. "It's lovely to meet you. I'm so excited to be working at TayFor. My last job was behind the reception desk at a local cat rescue place; this is going to be so much more fun." With that, she left the room, closing the door behind her.

"I don't know what to say." Samantha seemed genuinely stunned.

"Are you here for a reason?" Rachel asked, letting her impatience show.

Not that it bothered Samantha. "Yes, I came to get you for the board meeting. I wasn't sure if you'd remember where the conference room was located."

"Unless it's moved in the past ten years, then I remember fine."

"Has it really been ten years since you were here last?" Samantha hooked her arm through Rachel's and led her out of her office. "Do grab her bag," she called over her shoulder to Harvard. "Oh, I remember. That was the summer you interned for your father and I worked on the

PR for the new drug launch. We had fun then, didn't we? I miss those days. Even now that you're back in London, I don't see you nearly as much as I did when we were still students, and that says a lot given that we studied in different cities."

"People get busy," Rachel said as they walked down the corridor to the corner of the building where the conference room sat.

"Well, get unbusy because I've found the most delightful little boutique full of bridesmaid dresses that are to die for. And, of course, wedding dresses," She added, almost as an afterthought. "We are going to visit it. No excuses."

"You found the perfect bridal shop between Saturday night and this morning?"

"I *might* have started looking last week as soon as I heard the news of your engagement." Samantha pouted. "Don't be mad at me. We both know you need me for this."

What she needed was some serious counseling to help her assess her life choices.

Harvard stepped in front of them to open the conference room door, handing Rachel her handbag as he did so. "I'm going to familiarize myself with the building while you're in the meeting. Text me when you're done, and I'll escort you back to your office."

"I hardly think that's necessary," she said. "I can practically see the door from here."

"Just humor me until I'm confident you're protected while inside TayFor."

Even though she knew it was all pretend, Rachel couldn't help the little flip her heart did at his words. Especially seeing as she was very much aware of the photo tucked inside her bag, and the fact that she hadn't felt truly safe since the night it was taken.

It seemed the all too observant man read something in

her demeanor that bothered him, because he leaned in to whisper, "I can stay if you need me."

She stepped back with a jerk, holding her head high. "I'm fine. Thank you."

"Oh, oh," Samantha said. "I suspected you two had had a falling out. It's all in the body language."

"We haven't had a falling out," Rachel snapped.

"Well, you don't look like a couple in love." Sam cocked her head and studied them. "There's something that isn't quite right, and I can't put my finger on it. But as soon as I do, I'm going to sort the two of you out." She patted Rachel's arm. "Don't worry, I've had *many* relationships. You can trust me to help."

"You haven't had *any* relationships," Rachel told her. "You've had affairs. There's a difference."

"Rachel!" Her cousin Rupert elbowed his way past his sister. "It's fabulous to see you back in the fold and congrats on the engagement." He wrapped her in a quick, hard hug before pumping Harvard's hand. "Welcome to the family." He turned back to Rachel. "Can you believe I'm on the board now? And I work here."

"Sometimes," someone barked from inside the room.

Rupert looked sheepish. "Preston's mad because I went to Paris on Friday instead of coming to work. Apparently, I have to be here every day. Who knew?"

Rachel shook her head at her cousin. Even though there was only a year between them, she often felt decades older than him.

"Look at us." Rupert wrapped an arm around her shoulder and his sister's. "The gang back together again. We should go clubbing. For old times' sake. We haven't done it since you two were in uni. Let's do it. What do you say?"

"I say," his father, Charles, shouted from inside the room, "let's get on with this blasted meeting, shall we?"

"I'm in trouble again," Rupert whispered, before giving her one last squeeze.

After running his fingers through the blond hair that matched his sister's, he tugged at his tie as though he wasn't used to wearing one and entered the room.

"Come on," Samantha said as she took Rachel's arm. "Let's go save Rupert from the wolves."

And then the door closed behind them, leaving Harvard on the other side. And Rachel feeling strangely alone.

Chapter Eight

Rachel took one look at her disabled car before turning to Harvard. "You got Ryan to do this, didn't you?"

Harvard scratched his chin and made a mental note to have a quiet word with his teammate. "I thought he'd be more subtle."

"That fool doesn't know the meaning of the word." She glared back at her car. "The wheels better be back in place by morning. This is a travesty. That car is a classic and he's propped it up on common garden bricks."

Okay, now she'd lost him. "Should he have used gold bars?"

She ignored him. "Do you know what this means?"

"That Ryan had too much time to think about this?"

"No, that his infantile sense of humor has returned. Months of brooding, and now he's back in puppy mode." She narrowed her eyes at him. "Make it stop."

"How?" Ryan had lost his sense of humor after being conned and abandoned by a woman in South America. And if he was coming out the other side and joking around once more, Harvard didn't plan on making him miserable again. He wasn't that kind of guy.

"You honestly don't know?" Rachel tapped on the iPhone that never seemed far from her hand, then held it to her ear. "Ryan, my car will be in one piece by first thing tomorrow, or there will be consequences. This is exactly the sort of juvenile thing you did before that woman in Peru used and abused you. What was her name again? Oh, yes, you called her Essie, didn't you? It was terrible the way she walked all over you like that. A lesser man would never have forgiven and forgotten as easily as you have. But still, I'd prefer it if you didn't use your newfound lightness to mess with my car. Sort it please." She hung up. "That should have him brooding again by the morning."

Harvard folded his arms. "That was a crappy thing to do."

"And necessary. I can't cope with him bouncing all around me right now."

Yeah, other people might let her get away with that sort of shit, but he wasn't one of them. "Rachel, behaving like this is beneath you."

"No, this is who I am. Which makes me wonder if you even know the woman you've been trying to woo for months. And I use the word *trying* in every sense of the word, as your efforts have been seriously *trying* my patience."

"Oh, I know exactly who I've been *wooing*. It's you who's confused. I know you've got a bitch streak a mile wide, and it needs some serious boundaries to contain it. I also know that you hide behind that streak when it suits you."

Rachel's chin went up as she tossed her long sleek hair over her shoulder and gave him a look that was pure disinterest. "I have no idea what you're talking about, and I have no interest in it either."

"You show the world the bitch, so they won't notice when

you go out of your way to do something nice for the people you care about."

"Do you actually need me here for this conversation? Or are you happy to carry on alone?"

"I know all about the ways you've smoothed the paths of the people around you. Take Isobel's kids," he said evenly. "She was having trouble getting them into a decent school. You stepped in, and suddenly they were getting offers from the best schools in London. Only, they didn't know it was you because the schools told them they were picked up through the entrance exams they did for other schools."

"That wasn't me being *nice*." She waved a dismissive hand. "I was sick of listening to Isobel whine about it, that was all."

"Then there's Harry's literacy charity. Does he realize how many strings you pulled through your connections in government to get him access to the countries he wanted to work in?"

"Again, a purely selfish move on my part. I can't stand his wife, Magenta, and he was talking about moving to London with her." She shuddered. "I couldn't allow that to happen."

"Callum's prosthetic legs," he carried on. "There's a waiting list a mile long at the clinic that produces them. Not only that, but he got the state-of-the-art prototypes that are barely out of testing, and I know for a fact he didn't pay what they're worth. Didn't your brother go to school with the CEO of the company that developed those prosthetics? And I do believe you and Jonathan had dinner with him a couple of weeks before Callum got the call that he was on the short-list. Right after you made a huge donation to their research fund."

"Coincidence." She looked bored. "As much as I enjoy our little chats—which is about as much as I enjoy having gyneco-logical exams—I have an appointment with my wine cellar." She lifted her phone, ready to call for a car.

Harvard swiped it from her. "I have a car, and I'm going back to your place with you."

"Over my dead body." She didn't bother reaching for the phone, but he knew she was itching to retrieve it. There was the promise of payback in her eyes.

"Rachel, I won't kill you, but I will tase your sexy ass and throw you in the back of my vehicle. And no one here would object. In fact, I'm betting I'd get a standing ovation."

She glanced around at the employees lingering to watch them and to snigger over her car. No doubt they were waiting for her to lose her mind and eviscerate someone. He sighed. What was with everyone and their fear of Rachel's reputation? Couldn't they see she deliberately cultivated it just so she didn't have to deal with them?

"Get in the car." He pointed at his SUV.

Cold hazel eyes stared at him while she considered her options. "Fine. Have it your way." And then she swept past him and into the car. The *back* of the car. As though he was her damned chauffeur instead of her supposed fiancé.

He glared at their amused audience before climbing behind the wheel. In the back seat, Rachel sat with her hands clasped on her lap and her feet crossed at the ankles as she gazed out of the window. It wouldn't have surprised him in the least if she'd affected a royal wave for the TayFor staff.

"Couple more things," he said as he pointed the car out of the parking lot. "Stop being a bitch to the people who care about you and apologize to Ryan."

"Of course," she said politely. "I'll have my new PA schedule it for me. I do believe I have an hour free around about the twelfth of never. Now, would you be a dear and return my phone? I really must text everyone I've ever dealt with and tell them to keep their mouths shut about my business. Especially if an irritating ex-spy comes asking questions about whom I help, and why I do it."

All Harvard could do was toss the phone back to her. If there were two things he'd learned in the CIA, they were to pick your battles and to exercise patience. The exact same skills he needed in dealing with Rachel.

The drive into London from Surrey took a little longer than expected, thanks to the rush hour traffic, and Rachel spent the time tapping away on her phone. Harvard dreaded to think what she was doing. If Rachel wanted to, she could start World War Three armed purely with an iPhone.

"I need your keycard," he said, rolling down his window as they approached the garage under her apartment building.

Grudgingly, she handed it over and let out a little strangled sound filled with irritation when he pocketed it instead of handing it back. Ten minutes later—after Rachel had reluctantly added him to her list of approved visitors at the reception desk in the foyer—they were in her apartment. And it was just as spectacular as he'd envisioned.

Set in a part of Knightsbridge that overlooked Hyde Park, it allowed her to call Kensington Palace her neighbors. Rachel owned one of two split-level penthouses with uninterrupted views of the city, the park, and royalty.

The vast open-plan living area, with its polished dark wooden floors and thick white rugs, paled in comparison to the views framed by the floor to ceiling windows. And, even better, good sound insulation meant they couldn't hear the endless London traffic far beneath them. It was an oasis of decadence right in the center of one of the world's busiest cities.

She'd furnished the large living space with overstuffed sofas in shades of white and cream. But the different textures that made up the upholstery meant they didn't seem spartan. The cream walls were decked with contemporary art; she seemed to have a thing for huge, bright abstract paintings.

By the window was a baby grand piano and an oversized

armchair. A handknitted blanket in cream, of course, was thrown over it. A book lay on the seat. Rachel's reading nook, maybe. Apart from that, no personal mementos or photos cluttered up the place. Rachel obviously liked clean lines and plenty of space.

"Have you finished psychoanalyzing me based on my home?" she asked as she strode into the room.

"Not quite. Got to see the rest of the place first before I come to any conclusions." Harvard dropped his bag on the thick rug by the sofa and turned. He stopped dead. "A red kitchen?" Not just red. The cabinets were a lacquered red: the shade of blood. "Inviting," he muttered, wondering if she cooked in it or just dissected things.

"You don't need to stay here if you don't like it." Rachel strolled past him and into the kitchen from hell. "Wine?" She reached into the wine rack against the far wall and took out a bottle of red, then grabbed two glasses from the cabinet behind her.

"Red wine?" He looked around. "In this apartment? You like to live dangerously, don't you?"

"No. I like to live alone."

He stifled a chuckle as he peeked into the dining area off the kitchen. It held a large wooden table, stained black, and red upholstered chairs. "Do you eat in there, or just drink blood?"

"Vampire jokes? How very ordinary." She sashayed toward him, handed him a glass of wine, then kept on walking. "Since there appears to be no getting rid of you, I'll show you to your room." She flashed a dark look over her shoulder. "We aren't sharing."

Yeah, he hadn't thought they would be. Sipping the wine, which wasn't half bad, but still wasn't beer, he followed her along the hallway from the living room.

Rachel pointed at doors as they passed. "Study, lavatory,

cloakroom, laundry room." They turned a corner. "The pool is up those stairs." She pointed to a short staircase in the corner. "You'll find extra bathing suits in the closet."

"Pool?" In London? Was it an ice rink six months of the year?

"It's indoors, heated, and on the small side. But it suffices." She strode up the steps and opened the door, so he could look inside. And sure enough, there was a decent-sized pool with a small bar in one corner and several seats and loungers dotted around.

"I can only imagine how hard it is to have to make do."

Her lips twitched, but instead of smiling, she sipped her wine.

"Is that a gnome?" He stepped into the room, grinning at the giant concrete gnome perched on the edge of the pool as though fishing in it. "Doesn't exactly go with the rest of your décor."

"My brother, Sebastian, gave it to me for my birthday. It was his idea of a joke. As soon as I get around to it, I'll have it deposited at the bottom of the Thames, where it belongs."

Harvard suspected she'd take years to get around to it and wondered how long it had been there already. He didn't plan to ask though; there was no way Rachel would admit to being sentimental over a gift.

They left the pool room and Rachel led him to a set of stairs that headed downward, winding around until they stopped in a short hallway. There were four doors.

She pointed to the one farthest away. "That leads out to the fire escape stairway and service elevator. There's a small entryway beyond that door that I never use. Both the interior door and the one leading into the rest of the building are locked and alarmed." She cocked a thumb over her shoulder to the door behind her. "That's my bedroom." She stepped past him and threw open the door nearest Harvard. "This will be your room."

Harvard entered to find that it was decorated in yet more shades of cream. There was a king-sized bed, which, thankfully, meant he wouldn't be sleeping with his feet hanging off the end, a desk and chair, a dresser, and two armchairs positioned by the window but angled for a view of the TV facing the bed.

"Bathroom is through there." She indicated one of the doors. "The other door is to the closet."

"Thanks," he said. "What's on the other side of the last door on this floor?"

"Just another guest room that looks much like this one. I keep some exercise equipment in there, but I rarely use it. I prefer the pool."

"Mind if I check it out?" He headed back into the hallway.

"Be my guest. Oh wait, I'd have to have invited you for that to apply."

He grinned as he stuck his head inside the other bedroom. It was almost identical to his, but with a treadmill and elliptical trainer instead of armchairs. "You okay if I set up this room as command center? Whiteboards and computers, that sort of thing."

"Do whatever you like. Just be invisible while you do it." She turned toward her bedroom, clearly done with him for the day.

"Are you going to show me your room?" he couldn't resist asking.

"Yes." She opened her door. "I've penciled that in for right after I apologize to Ryan. I'll see you in the morning, which thrills me no end." And then she closed the door in his face.

Chapter Nine

T hree days later, the team congregated around Rachel's dining table to discuss their progress— which, to Harvard's dismay, wasn't a whole lot.

"Are any of you listening to me?" Ryan said, showing the irritation everyone else felt. "Or am I wasting my time giving my report?"

"I'm listening." Harvard reached for his beer, which sat in front of him on the dining room table.

As had been the case for the past three days, Rachel sat as far away from Harvard as possible and pretended he was invisible. Oh, she was polite enough when they met in the hallway or drove to work together. And she was polite in front of her colleagues and workmates at TayFor. Yeah, she was *very* polite. What she wasn't being was what everybody expected a fiancée to be, and that worried him.

"And?" Ryan demanded as he reached for the bag of chips and proceeded to demolish them. "What do you think?"

"About what?" Rachel asked as she studied her manicure. "Your update hasn't exactly added anything to the investigation. It's fabulous you've managed to bug all of the executive offices, but it hasn't produced anything of use yet. And discovering that Cousin Marcus is having an affair with one of the sales reps isn't exactly a shock. Everyone in the family knows his second marriage is already on the rocks."

"Divorce costs money," Ryan said around a mouthful of food.

"Yeah, but Marcus isn't his father," Rachel said, sounding bored. "He has a prenup. The divorce won't affect his finances too much; Preston saw to that."

"For a dude who's supposed to be an expert in company law, that Preston guy seems to write a whole lot of prenups," Ryan said. "As for Marcus, I still don't like the guy; he drinks way too much. Who knows what stupid shit he's done while drunk? My granddad always says a drunk man is an easy mark." He tossed the empty bag onto the table and looked around for more food. There wasn't any, because the pizza hadn't arrived yet. "But then again, Granddad also spends his retirement hanging around my work and playing at war in the basement training room, so not sure how much stock we can put in his wisdom."

Harvard grinned. Ryan's granddad and granduncle treated the carpentry work they did for Benson Security as a hobby. Mainly they were there for the entertainment and gossip.

He turned his attention to Elle. "You got anything for us?"

"A whole lot of nothing." She folded her arms over her pale blue T-shirt emblazoned with the words *Trekkies do it on the starboard bow*. Her hair, minus the red wig, was back to its usual pale blue. "The program Harry wrote to search for ghost activity on the TayFor computers has come up blank."

"Have you managed to get it onto every machine?" Harvard took a sip of his beer as he glanced at Rachel. She was paying more attention to her iPhone than to the meeting.

"Pretty much," Elle said. "There are a few laptops I still need to get my hands on, as they're out on assignment, and our friendly head of security is slowing me down. Basically, he reckons he could find the thief faster if we just got out of his way. He's even mentioned a few times that he could go to Jonathan and get us fired."

"In his small-minded dreams," Rachel said, her eyes still on that damn phone. She was like a teenager with it, and Harvard was getting to the stage where he was about to snap and confiscate the thing.

"The guy's a dickhead." Ryan wandered over to Rachel's kitchen, looking for some more snacks to tide him over until the pizza got there.

"Don't. Touch. Anything," Rachel ordered, still not looking up. "You get so much as a fingerprint on my cabinets, and I will hurt you."

"But there's food in here now that Harvard's moved in," Ryan whined. "Real food. Not just yogurt, designer water, and wine. Harvard, my man, you bought the food, you should get a say in whether I can eat it or not."

"Sit down," Harvard said. "Pizza will be here soon. You can survive that long without chewing on something."

"He can't," Rachel said. "He's like a puppy. Always has to chew on something. Would you like one of Elle's shoes?"

"Hey! Give him one of your own," Elle snapped.

"These are Louboutins. You bought yours at the supermarket. Where no shoes should ever be sold." She shuddered at the thought.

"Keep your shoes on," Ryan said. "I'm not chewing on any of them." But he didn't sound too convinced.

"Focus, people," Harvard said. "Terrance is only trying to do his job, and he sees our involvement as a threat to it."

"It's not that I don't understand where he's coming from," Ryan said. "There's always the suspicion that if he'd been more on the ball, the thefts wouldn't have gone on this long. He feels he has to prove he didn't screw up and let the thief slip past him. That doesn't mean I don't think he's a dickhead though. He almost blew my cover today. I caught it in time, but it's affected how the rest of security are dealing with me. They know he hates me, and they don't see the point in getting to know me because they figure I'll be gone soon. Makes it hard talking to them."

"I'll deal with him tomorrow," Harvard promised. No one messed with his missions. Ever.

"Meanwhile," Elle said, tapping at her keyboard and making Harvard want to grab a basket, put it in the middle of the table, and force everyone to put their devices in it for the duration. This job was turning him into his mom. "Word came back on young Rupert's trip to Paris. The upshot is, he wasn't in France at all. He was playing the German casinos, and he lost a wad of cash. Far as I can tell, he hit his mum up for a loan when he got back, but she's broke right now too because she fell off the wagon and snorted her money. Uncle Racist, or Charles as he likes to be known, doesn't know about any of this."

"What about Samantha?" Harvard asked. "Has anyone in her family asked her to finance their habits?"

"No idea." Elle shrugged. "Samantha's a hard nut to crack. Her finances are wrapped up tight, and her social media is full of fashion advice, hashtag blessed life photos, and hashtag hunk content. There's a ton of banal stuff on there, and it's taking me forever to wade through."

"You think there's any chance she's the one stealing secrets?" Harvard asked. "Maybe to help out her brother and mom?"

"I honestly don't think so," Elle said. "But I wouldn't put anything past her. As far as I can gather, if Samantha wants something, she'll do anything to get it—including sending one of her boy toys to fetch it for her. I get the impression Samantha doesn't like to get her hands dirty."

"With the amount of money Samantha spends on her wardrobe, I doubt she has any left to help out her family anyway," Rachel said to her phone.

That was it. Harvard stood and calmly walked around the table. He removed the phone from Rachel and the laptop from Elle before heading back to his seat.

"Hey!" they both shouted.

"No devices at the table," Harvard said firmly.

"Are you going to ground them?" Ryan asked as he laughed.

The concierge chose that moment to buzz up to tell them their pizza was there. Before Harvard could ask someone to get it, Ryan was out of his seat and running.

"There won't be any left by the time he gets back," Elle complained, her attention on her laptop. Harvard could have sworn there were tears in her eyes.

"So," he said, placing his contraband on the seat beside him, "if there has been internal hacking in the system, the ghost program would have found it, right?"

"Right." Elle nodded.

"Then how are they stealing the files?" Rachel said, looking pretty pissed off.

Pissed off he could cope with; it was miles better than politely distant.

"I don't know." Elle's head dropped to the table and stayed there.

Okay, so that's what happened when you took away her favorite toy.

Rachel got up and brought back plates, napkins, and silverware, which she put on the table. "There's no need to be barbarians," she said when he cocked an eyebrow at her.

It was the first time they'd sat down together at the table to eat. Normally, on the way home from work, Rachel called for delivery from one of the hotel restaurants she liked.

When it arrived, they dished it up, and Rachel took hers to her bedroom, leaving him alone. Harvard hated to admit defeat, but he was beginning to wonder if he'd been mistaken in thinking the attraction between them went both ways.

When Ryan came in with the pizzas, he was already eating a slice.

"Told you," Elle said, her head still on the table, but angled to watch Ryan.

"There's still plenty left." He put the boxes down on the table, opened the lids, and started piling up slices on his plate.

"Not for long," Elle muttered, sitting up to get some before Ryan demolished it all.

Rachel just stared at the boxes. "What is this? Where did we get it? This isn't the pizza I usually get."

Ryan shook his head at her, but there was a twitch of a smile around his lips. "That's because your pizza usually comes from a Michelin star chef and is dusted with gold."

"As it should be," she answered with a completely straight face.

"Just try it," Harvard said. "You might like it."

When she made no move to get any, he took a slice from the meat lover's pizza and put it on her plate. She stared at it as though it'd dropped from Mars.

"You can do it, Rachel," he said with a grin. "I have faith in you."

Shooting him a glare, she picked up her knife and fork and cut off a piece, which she delicately put into her mouth.

"That's not how you eat pizza!" Ryan was outraged. He was also covered in pizza sauce.

Rachel ignored him and inclined her head in thought as she chewed. "This is tolerable," she said at last, making Harvard chuckle.

Harvard went to the wine rack and grabbed a bottle of red wine for Rachel. He put it and a glass beside her. Then he sat back down, picked up his beer, and ate pizza the way normal people did it—with his fingers.

"Okay," he said once he'd finished a slice, "I have an idea. What we need to do is give the thief a window of opportunity they can't resist and hope they take it. If they do, and we don't manage to catch them, we'll still be able to narrow down the ways they might be using to steal from TayFor."

"You want to set a trap," Ryan said.

Harvard nodded. "We tell everyone the network's compromised, but only for a very limited time. Then we monitor the cameras and run when the system says there's been a download."

"That would mean we'd need to access the program they use for flagging downloads," Ryan said, showing that food improved his mental ability. "And if we start looking at that, we'll scare people off. I mean, none of us have official access. People are going to talk if we suddenly start checking who's downloading what."

"But," Elle said, her eyes wide, "we're the only ones with access to the ghost program, and that's on all computers. I can reconfigure it to send us an alarm when something's downloading."

Harvard reached for more pizza and put another slice on Rachel's plate for her too. "How long will that take?"

"An hour, maybe." Elle narrowed her eyes at him. "It depends when I get my laptop back."

"Will this work?" Rachel asked them. "Will it help us catch the thief?"

"It will help us get a damn sight closer, that's for sure," Harvard said.

And he got the first smile he'd had from her in days. Of course, she was probably smiling about the end of their mission being in sight, which meant she could get rid of him.

But hell, he'd take whatever he could get. A smile was still a smile.

"COMING BACK HERE MUST FEEL LIKE PUTTING ON A favorite pair of shoes," Jonathan said as he stood at Rachel's side the next morning, looking out over the TayFor complex. "I never understood why you walked away from this. You were born to run the family business." He gave her a self-effacing smile. "I wanted that for you. Even though I'm the eldest, I always felt as though I was born to support you."

Rachel kept her eyes on the manicured grounds. Her brother was right; it did feel a lot like coming home. It was all she'd ever dreamed of—an office in this building, a place in the heritage her family had built. She turned her back on the view to glance around her office. Dreams changed, and she didn't regret her choices.

"You don't need me here, Jonathan." She strode across the thick gray carpet and took a seat behind the sleek glass and steel monstrosity that made up her desk. If this had been her permanent office, the desk would have been gone. At least her gorgeous red office chair sat behind it, and she didn't have to suffer the torture of the previous chair. "You've done a fine job running the company. I know Father's proud and has no regrets putting you in charge."

"Oh, I can do the job." He turned to rest against the windowsill, his hands in the pockets of his blue pinstripe suit. "But you were the one with a passion for it."

"And what exactly would you have done if I were at the helm? Wandered the world surfing?" Her lips twitched into a smile. It was a standing joke. Jonathan was terrible at watersports.

"I rather thought I'd help with the legal side of the business. After all, I do have a law degree that's woefully underused."

"Not sure how Preston would feel about sharing. He does enjoy being in charge of his little kingdom."

"There is that. But dealing with Preston's still preferable to being CEO. My job is endless meetings and issuing orders." He grinned at her, suddenly looking much younger than his thirty-six years. "See what I mean? That's more up your street than mine. The first words you ever spoke were an order. I remember distinctly. You looked me in the eye and said, *Joh, gimme*, then pointed at that damn stuffed rabbit."

"You totally made up that story. I still can't believe the parents believed it."

"I didn't make it up," Jonathan said. "You're a born leader and you belong here."

"Jonathan," she cautioned.

"Just think about it." He straightened his suit. "Use this time with us as sort of a trial run—to see if you still have an interest in the place and think you might fit here. That's all I'm asking."

"It won't make any difference."

Jonathan shrugged before walking to the door. "Then there's no harm in trying, is there? If you need anything, shout out. I'm in meetings most of the day, but my PA can interrupt if it's urgent." He hesitated. "Do you think this trap will work?"

"I have no idea," Rachel said honestly. "But right now, we don't have a clue how the information is being stolen. This could give us that, at least."

"Then I'll try to act suitably surprised when the email circulates saying we have a problem."

"You do that." Although his acting sucked, so Rachel wasn't sure he could pull it off.

"Hi, Jonathan," Elle said as she passed him on her way into Rachel's office. "Looking dapper today."

Jonathan blushed and mumbled something before disappearing into the corridor.

"You do that on purpose," Rachel accused once the door closed behind her brother.

"He's so cute when he blushes. I can't resist."

"His wife thinks his blushes are cute too."

"I'm not flirting, Rachel. I'm teasing. There's a difference. Anyway, my heart belongs to mystery man. Even though I still can't find him. He's disappeared off the information grid entirely, and the last thing he did was warn me not to look for him." She smiled evilly. "Of course, I totally listened to his warning, which means it's just a matter of time before I pinpoint his location."

"You don't even know which security agency he works for," Rachel pointed out. "It could be the Chinese or the Russians. If you keep looking for him, you'll end up waking one day to find yourself in a Russian cell, being interrogated about a man you've barely even kissed. Ask yourself, is he worth it?"

"It was a spectacular kiss, Rachel. Spectacular."

It was clear that there was no saving the woman from herself.

Elle took a small signal jammer out of the pocket of her circular skirt, which today was a shocking blue with applique images of white poodles. "Okeydokey," she said once she'd activated it. "Ryan swept our offices this morning as usual, but I say better paranoid than sorry."

"What's happening with the trap? Is it set?" Rachel tapped the end of a pen on the glass top of her desk, hating the sound it made.

"We're activating it now. Basically, we're setting it up to look like IT is having issues. An email will go out to everyone shortly, telling them not to transfer any sensitive data between buildings or to the main backup server until the issue's fixed. We're letting them think the transfer system's been compromised and isn't as secure as it should be. We'll tell them that we're adjusting the download protocols to make them more secure, but over the next hour, downloading of information from any server is forbidden. It's the perfect scenario for a thief. Anything that goes missing within the next hour would be chalked up to a security breach from outside the building."

"And if they do, your ghost program will find them."

Elle tapped at her keyboard and didn't look up. "Fingers crossed. We really need a new name for the program; it sounds like we're carrying out a paranormal investigation." She looked at Rachel. "Do you think ghosts are real?"

"I think that if you don't get to the point quickly, I may kill you, and we'll find out when you haunt me."

Elle beamed at her. "And the bitch is back."

"She never left. Now tell me what's happening."

"She might not have left, but she's been pretty distant for the past few days. Anyway, Ryan's in security, monitoring the camera feeds from around the building. Harvard is stationed outside, so he can run for whatever building trips our alarm. And we're in here, setting it all in motion." She cracked her knuckles. "Ready?"

Rachel lifted her phone, her thumb poised over the 'go' message she'd already typed, ready to send it to Harvard and Ryan. "Ready."

Elle hit the keys. "Then we are Go. The email has been sent."

Rachel sent the text to tell the boys. And then...

Nothing.

"Well, that was a bit anticlimactic," she said to Elle.

"People need time to read the email, Rach," Elle said with a sigh.

"Still, this isn't the most exciting of missions, is it?"

Elle's eyebrows shot up. "Better this than people shooting at us."

Rachel wasn't so sure. She liked her enemies where she could see them.

Chapter Ten

One hour and forty-three minutes after the email went out, Harvard's phone buzzed an alarm.

"West Building, second floor," he snapped into the comm unit attached to his lapel.

"Bringing up all the cameras now," Ryan said through Harvard's earpiece as he ran for the building.

They were lucky. It was the closest one to the main office, where he'd been waiting.

Ryan cursed. "One of the cameras is out in that building."

"Where?" Harvard snapped as he raced through the door.

"The connecting office to the second-floor research lab."

What the hell? "On my way."

"That's my mother's office," Rachel's voice bit out in his ear. "You can't possibly think she has anything to do with this. Wait for me; I'm coming over."

"No," Harvard ordered. "Stay in position. Let me deal with this."

There was no reply from Rachel.

He scanned his security pass, pushed through the doors, and sprinted up the stairs two at a time.

"Rachel and Elle are heading your way," Ryan said. "Damn, Rachel can move in those heels."

Harvard didn't say anything. There was no point. He'd just have to deal with the women when they arrived, and then later, he'd go over why a member of a team *never* broke position. In the meantime, he tamped down his anger and focused on getting to that office.

Two more stops to scan his card and he was in the corridor outside the second-floor labs. Each door had a biometric lock that Harvard didn't have access to, but he didn't need it because Francesca's office door stood wide open.

Daily training meant Harvard wasn't even out of breath by the time he reached the doorway. He scanned the room, taking in everything within seconds—the most important part being Francesca sitting at her desk, talking to Samantha, who sat on the opposite side.

When Rachel's mother noticed him, she beamed. "Harvard, we were just talking about you. Come in, come in." She angled her head to look around him. "Rachel isn't with you?"

"She's on her way," he said as he stepped into the room.

"Shouldn't a bodyguard stay with his charge? Had enough of her already?" Samantha said with a wink.

"Samantha," Francesca reprimanded, but it was filled with affection. "Not everyone knows when you're joking, darling. You need to remember that."

Yeah, Rachel's mom being one of them, because Samantha had been deadly serious. He glanced around the room, but nothing jumped out at him as being out of place.

"What are you doing over here?" Francesca said, motioning for him to take a seat.

Harvard shook his head, indicating he was happy to stand. "We thought we'd take you out for lunch. I came ahead to make sure we caught you, as Rachel's tied up in a meeting."

"Well, you must think it's safe at TayFor if you're letting her wander around alone." Samantha tossed her wavy blonde hair over her shoulder and crossed her legs, making sure Harvard got the best angle. "That's good news for our security. I guess they're doing their job."

The sound of heels on vinyl flooring came from the corridor outside the office, along with panicked whispers. Rachel had arrived. Harvard was watching the doorway when she strode through it. Her eyes went straight to her mother, then to him, where they narrowed, and lastly came to rest on Samantha with interest.

"Darling," Francesca said, "Harvard just told me you want to do lunch. Let me get my jacket, and we can go."

"Am I invited to this lunch too?" Samantha purred, her eyes on Harvard.

"No," Rachel said coldly.

Samantha looked amused while her mother tutted. "Sometimes, I despair of your manners. I often wonder where I went wrong with you."

Elle hovered in the door behind Rachel, looking a little panicked. Quickly taking in the situation, she approached Samantha.

"Samantha," she said, "Jonathan's been trying to get hold of you. He asked me to pass on the message if I saw you. He'd like to see you in his office as soon as possible, something about a problem with the marketing for the new Alzheimer's relief drug."

"Copy that," Ryan said in Harvard's ear. "Calling Jonathan right now to tell him to manufacture a crisis and expect his cousin."

Samantha stood with a sigh. "It's so inconvenient that we aren't allowed cell phones outside of the office building." She smoothed down her tight lemon-colored shift dress and smiled at them. "It seems I won't be available for lunch after all. Even if I was welcome."

Rachel folded her arms over her black suit jacket and drummed her red nails on the sleeve. The look on her face shouted that she'd run out of patience with her cousin.

"I'll walk you back to the main building," Elle said. "I've been meaning to ask you about that wonderful advertising campaign you did last year. It must have taken ages to put that together."

Samantha's whole face lit up as she sashayed to the door. As she drew level with her cousin, Rachel's hand snapped out to take hold of her arm.

"Please remember that Harvard is my fiancé and is therefore off-limits for any kind of flirting, loosely veiled suggestion or outright seduction." Her tone was a whip that could flay the skin from the recipient.

"Rachel, darling, I would never *try* to seduce your fiancé; surely you know that."

Harvard was betting he wasn't the only one who heard the emphasis on try.

Rachel released her cousin, and Elle could be heard chatting a mile a minute as they made their way down the corridor. As soon as they were out of sight, Rachel closed the door.

"What the hell do you think you're doing?" she snapped at him.

Her mother's eyes widened as she looked between them. "Aren't we going to lunch?"

"No," Rachel said, her body vibrating with fury. "We're going to talk about why Harvard thinks you're stealing from TayFor."

How could he think her mother was involved? Rachel was so mad she could have taken off her shoe and bludgeoned him with the heel.

"I never, for one minute, suspected your mom had anything to do with the thefts. If you'd given me a chance to deal with the situation before you came charging over here, you might have known that." He folded his arms and gave her a stony-faced stare. All the while, his tone never rose or changed, which made her sound like the one being unreasonable.

"You rushed up here even when you knew whose office it was."

"Because there could have been someone else in here." He pointed to the corner of the ceiling. "The camera's been covered. There was no way of knowing who was in the room."

Rachel looked up, and sure enough, there was a very familiar hat covering the lens. "Mother…"

Her mother's hand fluttered to her face, her cheeks turning pink. "I don't like being watched while I work."

"Oh, for the love of Dior, do you realize how bad that looks?"

"You can't think I covered the camera for nefarious purposes." Looking stunned, her mother sat down with a thump.

As Rachel looked at Harvard, her anger seeped away, leaving her a little deflated. "I—" she started, but he held up a hand to stop her.

"I'm going to need a minute with your daughter," he said to her mother, striding toward Rachel. Harvard grabbed her hand and took her out into the corridor.

She had to hurry to keep up with him as he led her to the female bathroom. After checking inside, he locked the door and turned to face her, hands on hips and eyes blazing with fury.

"This is the last time this happens," he said evenly. "You're either on this team or you aren't. What's it gonna be? Because right now, you're causing more damage than good, which makes me think the team would be better off coping without you. Choose now, Rachel."

"On the team," she said through gritted teeth.

"Then this stops now. No more leaving your position when you're ordered to stay put. No more undermining my leadership. And no more acting like a lone wolf. You got me?"

Rachel let out a heavy breath. "Yes," was all she could say.

He stared at her for a moment before nodding once. "Okay," he said. "Let's get back to your mom's office and see if we can get to the bottom of this." His face expressionless, he turned toward the door.

Three days she'd avoided and ignored him. Being close to him felt like too much of a temptation, one she wasn't sure she could resist. Instinctively, she knew that this man, and only this man, could change her life forever. Could change *her* if she let him.

Deep down, she must have expected that he'd keep on chasing her—even though she'd given him no encouragement. He was right. They all were. She was a first-class bitch, and she had no idea how to be any other way. But the cold, blank look on his face made courage rise up inside of her, in such a wave that it overwhelmed her fear of being vulnerable, just for a second.

And without thought, Rachel reached out and placed her hand on his arm to stop him from leaving. She couldn't give voice to the turmoil inside, but she could tell him why this particular situation had made her react the way she had.

With that same blank face, he looked back at her.

Rachel swallowed hard. "She's my mum. I've always done whatever I could to protect her and the rest of my family. My close family. The ones who love me regardless. I've *always* protected them, and I didn't think about what that meant to the investigation, or to how people saw our cover story, or even how it would affect the team." She willed him to understand the things she couldn't say. That after spending ten years making choices to protect her family, the behavior was hard-wired into her now.

His expression softened to the one she'd grown to expect when he looked at her. The one she hadn't known she'd miss until it was gone, and the relief on seeing it again almost made her crumble.

"You are so much trouble," he said. "Billions of women on the planet, and you're the one who keeps me awake at night." He shook his head as if he couldn't quite believe his own behavior. "You've got secrets piled on top of more secrets. You have layers of barbed wire wrapped around you that rip anyone to shreds if they try to get close. And you insist on hiding the best parts of you behind a wall of disdain and disinterest. Why is that, Rachel?"

"I don't know." And she didn't. Part of it was nature, and the rest was just what she did to survive.

He let out a scoffing laugh. "Come on, your mom will be wondering what we're doing in here."

Dropping her hand from his arm, she squared her shoulders. "I can't apologize twice in a decade, but I will make more of an effort to be part of the team."

He took her hand and led her out of the bathroom. "Well, here's hoping your effort doesn't get us all killed."

Really, there was nothing she could say to that.

IT TOOK ELLE OVER AN HOUR TO FIND WHAT THEY WERE looking for in Francesca's office. Through it all, Rachel and her mother sat at the desk she used for paperwork, eating lunch and watching Elle like she was daytime reality TV.

Harvard would have been amused by their behavior if he hadn't been busy hunting down his own clues. He'd scanned the room for anomalies but had found no surveillance devices. He had, however, discovered that someone had tampered with the biolock, basically rendering it ineffective. Anyone who pressed their hand to the scanner could unlock the door. How long it had been like that, he didn't know. It wasn't something you'd notice unless you tried to get unauthorized access in the first place.

"Hot diggity dog!" Elle shouted from under the computer desk in the corner of the room. "I've got it. I can't believe how stupid I am. All this time, I've been looking for hi-tech answers, like hacking and server tapping, when it was a low-tech heist." She wriggled out from under the desk with a tiny black box in her glove-clad hand. It was about the same size and shape as a chewing gum packet. They all leaned forward to examine it.

"What is it?" Francesca asked.

Elle let out a disgusted laugh. "A Wi-Fi memory card reader. It sets up a Wi-Fi hotspot, a private network essentially, between a couple of computers or phones. Its transmission range is only about twenty meters, and it's mainly used for transferring files between devices without using a USB port or Bluetooth." She popped open one of the little slots. "The information's saved to a micro memory card." When she held up the card, it was barely the size of a fingernail.

"Like the cards from our phones or cameras," Francesca said.

"Exactly like those. Easy to hide and won't set off a metal detector." She glared at the box, as though it'd personally offended her. "This is seriously low-tech. I can't believe I didn't think of it."

"How does the box thing work?" Rachel stared at it intently.

Harvard answered, drawing her gaze, and finding a softer aspect to it than he'd seen before. "Someone would have to set it up on the computer to use it. But basically, all that means is getting the computer to recognize it, then typing in the Wi-Fi password."

Elle nodded. "It'd take five minutes at most. Especially if they were lucky enough to catch the computer while it was still running, but before the security screen kicked in. That thirty seconds to a minute or so wait time would be enough to get in there and keep the computer awake long enough to set this up."

"And then," Harvard said, "the box would lie dormant until someone gave it the command to save files from the computer. Triggering the Wi-Fi on the box would knock out the Wi-Fi the machine normally connects to, but it would only be for a matter of seconds. Hiccups that you'd barely notice, Francesca."

"Oh, I noticed." She frowned. "I also complained about the Wi-Fi in here several times over the years. I told them it glitches sometimes. The last time it happened, the head of security and IT, Terrance, came over himself to tell me it was all in my mind. I've never liked that man."

"Yeah, well," Harvard said. "It definitely wasn't your imagination. Elle? Is that thing battery powered?"

She turned it over to look. "Yep. Rechargeable. Judging by its size, I'd say they'd be lucky to get two or three hours out of it before it needed charging again."

"But they'd only use those hours in intermittent bursts of just a few seconds, right?" Rachel said.

"Right." Elle looked at the box in disgust. "Depending on how often they used it, it could go for months without needing a recharge. Even then, all they'd need to do is plug it into any micro USB port to do it. It's probably never left this room. If it were me, I'd have charged it here."

"How much memory does it hold?" Harvard asked.

"Total capacity's five hundred and twelve gigabytes." She looked up at him. "That's more than enough space to download the files our thief needs. Hell, you could save all of the *Lord of the Rings* movies onto these—twice."

Harvard turned his attention to Francesca. "During the time Samantha was in here, was she out of your sight at any point?"

"No, not at all. She'd only been here a few minutes before you arrived, and we spent it chatting about the wedding."

"Did she touch your desk or computer?"

Francesca shook her head. "Definitely not."

Rachel looked up at him with an openness he hadn't seen from her before. "What do we do with it?"

Elle's head almost shot off her shoulders as she swiftly looked from one of them to the other, appearing shocked that Rachel had deferred to him.

"We dust for prints and swab it for DNA, and then we have Elle replace all of the files with copies she's edited to make them useless, just in case we lose control of the data." He looked at Elle. "Make sure you check anything you find against Samantha's prints first."

"And what about after all that's done?" Rachel pressed.

"After that, we set up cameras and wait for the thief to return."

Francesca almost fell out of her chair with excitement. "I'm going to be part of a sting."

"You need to carry on as usual," Harvard warned. "You can't do anything that will draw attention to yourself."

"I can absolutely do that. My acting is superb. Isn't it, Rachel?"

Rachel groaned, and Harvard decided it would be wise to

keep his amusement to himself. He was about to wind up their time in Francesca's office, when Ryan's voice came over his comm unit. "Harvard? You read me?"

"Go ahead," Harvard said, drawing the attention of the women in the room.

"We've got another problem," Ryan said.

Chapter Eleven

❧

"This is ludicrous," Rachel complained for the twentieth time since Harvard had explained to her that *she* was the new problem the team faced. "We announced we're getting married. So what if people are gossiping about us and saying our relationship is fake?"

"Because," Harvard said in that same patient tone he'd used since Ryan stuck his oar in, "if people don't believe we're in a real relationship, they'll watch us more carefully, and the chances of our cover being blown become a whole lot higher."

Rachel glared out of the window of the taxi, into the night, as they sped through London's streets. Going who knows where, because Harvard had said it was a surprise. An activity that would help them. If it was couples counseling for their fake relationship, she would smack him silly.

"We're here," he said as the taxi pulled over.

Rachel let out a groan. He'd brought her to Brixton, of all places. At night. In the dark. And it wasn't even a good part of Brixton—if there was such a thing—it was a backstreet behind the train station.

"Come on," he said, climbing out of the taxi and holding the door for her.

"I'd rather not." Rachel stayed put.

From what she could see, graffiti covered every wall around her, and it wasn't Banksy. No, this wasn't art of any kind. It looked like a three-year-old had just learned to spell their name and decided to scrawl it everywhere.

"You're being pathetic," he said with a grin.

"Are you getting out or not?" the driver demanded.

With a huff, she climbed out of the car and watched it drive away.

"If I'd wanted to visit a third-world country," she said, "I'd have gone back to Scotland. Why did I agree to come here with you?"

"I'm still trying to figure that out." Harvard smiled at her. He wore a white shirt with the sleeves rolled up, which he'd left untucked over faded jeans. If there had been a style called sexy casual, then he'd be the walking embodiment of it.

She, on the other hand, wore a black cocktail dress with a cute flared skirt and her usual heels. Harvard had told her to dress casual and flirty, suggesting she wear jeans. Seeing as she didn't own any, the dress was the best she could do.

"So, tell me then," he said. "Why did you agree to come with me tonight? I expected you to put up more of a fight."

"You were there for our conversation this afternoon, weren't you? I promised to make more of an effort. I didn't promise I wouldn't complain while I did it."

"And I appreciate it. The effort part, that is."

Placing a hand on the small of her back, Harvard guided her toward a gate between two rundown tenement buildings. Goodness only knew what she was stepping in as they approached it; there was a distinct lavatory smell to the place.

"I've changed my mind," she said as he opened the gate. "Whatever we're doing here, there has to be another way we can work on being more physically comfortable with each other. I know, why don't we go back to my apartment and have sex? It would be more sanitary."

"As attractive as that proposition is, this will be fun too." He took Rachel's hand in his, engulfing hers, the warmth of his touch shooting up her arm. "Besides, you aren't ready to sleep with me. *Yet*." He waggled his eyebrows before stepping in front and leading her down the alley between the buildings.

"Your ego knows no bounds, does it?" she said.

Harvard shrugged. "I'm a big man. I have a big ego."

She wasn't going to touch that comment. Instead, she concentrated on following him down the narrow alley without brushing against the walls. Who knew what she'd pick up if she did?

"Is this really necessary?" she asked. "I'm touching you now, and look, no wincing."

"Yeah, because you're too worried about catching something from just being in Brixton to worry about anything else." He glanced over his shoulder at her. "Rachel, you have issues."

She honestly couldn't argue with that, so she said nothing. Without warning, he stopped and turned into a nondescript doorway with something written on it in Spanish. He pushed it open and stepped inside.

"Careful," he said. "We're going downstairs."

"We're going underground? In Brixton? Are you crazy? There are probably rats."

"Don't worry, I'll protect you." He was laughing at her.

"I am perfectly capable of protecting myself."

"Then, you can protect me."

Irritating man. "And who'll protect you *from* me?"

"Rachel, I don't *want* to be protected from you. So do your worst; I welcome it."

Before she could cut his oversized ego down to a more

manageable size, he pushed through the door at the bottom of the stairs, and they entered a small cloakroom area.

"Harvard!" A young woman ran around the counter to throw herself at him.

Harvard dropped Rachel's hand to catch the stranger, annoying her more than was reasonable, but she put it down to being out of her element. Which extended about a two-mile radius from her Kensington home.

"Where have you been?" the woman demanded. "We've missed you." Honestly, if she pouted any harder, Rachel was going to smack her.

"Been doing spy stuff, Jenny. But I'm back now," Harvard said.

Rachel couldn't help but roll her eyes. "Do you tell everyone you were a spy? Didn't your government swear you to secrecy?"

He extricated himself from Jenny and wrapped an arm around Rachel's waist to tug her into his side. "I'm retired. I can tell whoever I like."

Hmm, now that she thought about it, he never gave any details, and he always joked around about his previous career. No doubt, everyone thought he was making it up. Sneaky man.

"Who's this?" Jenny asked loudly, and somewhat snarkily, making it clear she had a baby crush on Harvard.

"This is my fiancée," Harvard said. "Rachel, meet Jenny. Her parents own this club."

"Fiancée?" Jenny's voice went into dog-whistle territory.

"Yes," Rachel gushed. "Isn't it wonderful?" She'd had enough of the teen. Looking up at Harvard, she patted his stiff, muscled stomach—and he said she never touched him. Honestly, all this drama over nothing. "Come along, darling. You promised me a fun night out."

His eyes sparkled at her, as though he was getting a kick

out of everything she said and did. "Gotta go," he told Jenny. "A promise is a promise."

Once they were out of earshot, Rachel smacked those same muscles. "Why are you introducing me as your fiancée?"

"Rachel," he purred, "a good spy knows you never break cover once you're established. Now, stop asking questions and try to relax."

He threw open the double doors and led her into a large, dimly lit room. Dotted around the area nearest her was an odd assortment of wooden tables and chairs. Faded posters covered the walls, advertising everything from soap to tequila in Spanish. In the corner stood a well-stocked bar, with orange and pink neon signs above it that read *Dance, Love, Live*. And on the far side of the room was a packed dance floor.

Rachel gaped at it. "We're salsa dancing?" *Did he not know her at all?*

"No, Rachel, we're Bachata dancing. It's like salsa, only a whole lot slower, and a whole lot sexier. You ready to have some fun?"

She looked at the people rubbing up against each other on the dance floor. They all seemed to know what they were doing and moved like professional dancers. The club was for people in the know. And that definitely didn't describe her.

She frowned at the man who was deliberately elbowing his way into her life. "No," she said. "No, I'm not ready."

"Don't worry." He took her hand and dragged her toward the dancers. "I promise you; this won't hurt at all." When they reached the edge of the dance floor, he asked, "Do you want a drink first, or do you want to dance?"

"I don't want to do anything here. What I do want is to go home. I can't believe you thought this would help us with our cover. It's a stupid idea."

"No, it's a great idea. By the end of the night, we'll be so comfortable with each other it will be obvious to anyone who sees us. Gotta stop that gossip, Rachel."

She wasn't buying that 'we' rubbish. He meant her. She was the one who jerked away every time he moved to touch her. It wasn't deliberate. She just wasn't comfortable with public displays of affection, especially ones coming from colleagues. And as much as he might want things to be different between them, she couldn't get past seeing him as purely a colleague.

No, that wasn't true.

She definitely noticed Harvard as a man. But she didn't want to. Because every instinct told her that if she were to give the man an inch, he'd take everything. And Rachel couldn't allow herself to be that vulnerable with anyone. She'd been vulnerable once, and it had been devastating.

"What will it be?" he said. "Drink or dance?"

Oh, she wanted the drink. But if she asked for one, it would only extend their time in the club. How bad could this be, really? She'd survived formal dancing in high school; she could get through this. Right?

"Dance," she said determinedly. "Let's get this over with."

"That's the spirit," he said as he nodded to a few faces he recognized and dragged her onto the floor.

THE MUSIC THRUMMED THROUGH HARVARD'S VEINS, THE vibrations and rhythm making him sway. He loved to dance. He loved the darkness of the clubs, the beat of the music, the mass of bodies on the dance floor. It was his happy place, and he'd relaxed as soon as they'd walked through the door. Rachel, on the other hand, looked like a rock at the edge of the ocean with waves crashing over it.

"This isn't going to work." She raised her voice to be

heard over the music. "I studied ballet as a child, and I can waltz. But I don't know how to do this. I don't even know what they're doing." She pointed to a couple in the middle of the dance floor. "I think they might be having sex."

Trying not to laugh, he held out his hands for her to take. "Don't panic; I'll teach you."

"I never panic." Her eyebrow arched. "Do you actually know how to dance like this?"

He reached forward and took her hands in his. "Why would I bring you here if I didn't?"

She looked genuinely perplexed. "I did wonder."

"I think this evening will go much better if you don't talk. Now watch my feet. We're gonna go left to right in a straight line. Two small steps, keeping your legs under your body, don't stretch them out, then tap and repeat it in the other direction. Got me?"

"I think I can manage to move side to side." She could also manage a quick stamp on his toes for pissing her off.

"Okay, let's go then." They moved together flawlessly. "That's great. Now loosen your hips. Look around you. See the sinuous way the other women are moving?"

Her hands tightened in his as she glanced around. "I'm not sure that's physically possible. Are you sure these people are English? Because the English weren't born to move like that. We have different joints. They're stiffer. Like our upper lips."

Man, she was funny. "I've seen the way those hips of yours sway when you're walking away from me. You were totally born to move like that. Give it a try; see how it feels."

They stepped side to side some more while Rachel focused on loosening her hips. And it was focus. She looked like she was sitting an exam—in a subject she hated.

A woman twirled close to them and beamed at Rachel.

"*Lo estás haciendo genial, cariño*," she said, and then she was gone again, dancing into the crowd.

"She said you're doing great," Harvard told her.

"You speak Spanish?" Again, she looked surprised that he wasn't all brawn and no brain. It was just as well Harvard wasn't an insecure man because Rachel would rip one of those to shreds.

"Yeah. Now, we're gonna try moving back and forth together. You ready?"

"It's walking, Harvard. I've been doing it for thirty years."

"Okay, three steps forward, then back, tap behind your foot with your other toe when you stop. I'll lead with my left, so it's right foot forward for you. Here we go. And don't forget those hips."

Rachel frowned in concentration as they moved together.

"Not bad," he encouraged. "Now let's try some turns." He took his time, talking her through some more basic moves. "I'm gonna spin you and bring you back against me, and then we'll move together. Your back to my front. Okay?"

She hesitated, then nodded. Harvard spun her out and drew her back quickly. With her back pressed to his front, their hips moved in rhythm together. He flattened his right hand on her stomach while his left still held her left hand against his chest.

Her long sleek hair brushed against his arm as she gazed up at him. "What do I do with my free hand?"

"Whatever you want." He lifted his chin toward a couple close to them, who were dancing the same way. The woman's hand covered her partner's on her stomach, as her face turned into his throat. They moved in perfect sensual movement, lost in each other and the beat of the music.

Slowly, tentatively, Rachel rested her hand on his. He resisted the urge to tighten his hold, to pull her even closer.

Instead, he quietly talked her through some other moves, feeling the loss when they separated.

But it wasn't for long. Harvard pulled her into his arms, in the classic hold used for a waltz, only closer, and rested one hand on her hip while the other held hers against his chest. Their bodies touched as they moved, repeating the footwork they'd already learned, but this time, fully together.

It was perfect. Rachel's ballet lessons came back to her, and she moved easily with the music, gradually relaxing in his hold. Harvard gently tugged her closer, resting his cheek against her hair as the music engulfed them. The tension eased from her body as she sank into the beat, her movements gradually becoming more sensual and lyrical.

Feeling her soften, watching her let go, was one of the best experiences of his life so far. For the first time since they'd met, he felt like she was allowing him to see a part of her that people rarely—if ever—saw. The honor of her trust made his chest swell with pride.

Harvard was realistic. He knew that the sarcastic, cutting, painfully smart woman who tormented everyone around was who Rachel truly was. He didn't have some misguided savior complex. There was no believing that with the right man to love her, she'd transform into someone lighter and more forgiving. No, he liked Rachel exactly as she was, bitchy tendencies and all. But he suspected there was more to her than met the eye. A soft little underbelly that she never exposed to anyone.

And he wanted to be the man she trusted enough to let him see it.

Which meant baby steps. Because you didn't win the trust of an alpha female overnight. That took time, patience, and an ego made of Teflon.

THIS WASN'T LIKE THE NIGHTCLUB EXPERIENCES RACHEL remembered from her youth. Those dark, crowded dance floors where you either moved around beside someone but never touched or fought off some guy who wanted to rub himself against you. This was different. More intimate. And...safer.

While she couldn't explain it, she could feel the difference. It was as though Harvard created a little box with his arms, defining how far she could move from him. It was a box that no one else was allowed to enter, one meant for them alone. A place where she could relax and let herself go. Where she was protected. Where she was secure.

She shook her head at the thoughts as her body moved to the rhythm of the music. No one looked at her; they were all lost in their own little worlds. No one knew who she was or expected anything from her. It was freeing.

And with each step she took, her muscles remembered what it meant to dance, to move in synchronicity with someone else. It wasn't like ballet, nothing like it, although the movements were familiar. But where ballet was all about distance, comportment, grace, this was about closeness, sensuality, and expression. It was a strange new world. One Rachel found she enjoyed exploring.

As she followed Harvard's lead on the dance floor, the rest of the world faded to insignificance. There was only the darkness, the music, and the feeling of their bodies as they touched and moved together. For the first time in years, there was peace in her busy mind.

Harvard didn't push her boundaries, didn't try to make the experience more intimate than it naturally was. His hands didn't stray; his touch didn't linger. And yet, each gentle brush of his skin against hers was a caress that sank straight into the depth of her being.

He did that thing again, where he cradled her against him,

her back to his front as they moved. Her hips swayed of their own accord, feeling his strength, his solidity against her, and her eyes drifted closed. In that moment, there was only the man guiding their dance and her own desire to move.

The music changed, and Harvard turned her. "Put your arms around my neck," he whispered against her ear.

Her arms obeyed before she made the conscious decision to follow his instruction. His hands on her hips, they moved to the new beat, and Harvard's low voice sang softly to her. Rachel didn't understand the language, but she understood the feeling behind the words. He was serenading her.

Her breasts flattened against his chest as her hips swayed under his hands. Eyes closed, she pressed her face into his throat, breathing in his ocean scent. He smelled of adventure. Of freedom. Of beautiful, clean waves.

"What does it mean?" she whispered, her voice so low and intimate she barely recognized it.

"It's a love song," he murmured. "The singer is desperately in love with his woman, and no one can understand how deep it is. It's beyond anything ever seen before. It's eternal. Immortal. That's what the song's called: *Inmortal*," he finished in Spanish.

"I...like it."

"I do too." One of his arms wrapped around her, holding her close.

She didn't feel vulnerable or exposed; she felt strong and courageous. Because he made it possible for her to feel that way. There was no judgment in anything he did or said, no expectation. Only delight...and promise. As though he knew he was giving her a safe space, somewhere just to be.

"Are you thirsty?" he asked. "Do you want a drink?"

For once, the experience of someone taking care of her didn't grate. "Let's keep dancing," she said as she turned in his arms. She liked having him at her back, resting her head against his shoulder, feeling his arms around her.

"Whatever you want." He nuzzled her temple.

As the music flowed over and through her, Rachel let herself be transported into an alternate dimension where she didn't always have to be in control. A place where there was no need to be on her guard or constantly proving herself to people who should have already figured out how capable she was. Here, in this moment, with the music and the man, she could just be Rachel.

And she found she liked it very much.

They danced until close to midnight, stopping to sip water, but not saying very much to each other. Rachel was grateful. She didn't see the need to dissect the evening. They'd come to dance and get used to each other, and that's what they were doing. The last thing she wanted was any comment about her enjoying herself. Mainly, she was just hoping Harvard hadn't noticed.

When he walked her to their taxi, Rachel found herself leaning into his touch instead of away from it. And they sat close beside each other all the way back to Kensington. Neither of them commented on their thighs touching.

They made their way downstairs to their bedrooms in silence but paused before opening their doors.

"Successful night," Harvard said, his hands stuffed deep into the pockets of his jeans, making her wonder if it was an attempt to keep from touching her. He'd reached for her so frequently throughout the evening that it almost felt strange to have any distance between them now.

"I'm glad," Rachel said. "Hopefully, people won't have any suspicions about our fake relationship now."

"Hopefully." His smile made her stomach flip flop. "Good night, Rachel."

She put her hand on her door and hesitated. "You know, it

might be a good idea to go dancing again—once or twice. Just to make sure we do everything we can to maintain our cover."

He didn't turn back to her, but she could have sworn he was smiling. "Say the word, and I'll take you anytime you want. Anything for the mission, you know that."

"Exactly." Rachel walked into her room and quietly closed the door behind her.

Chapter Twelve

O ver the next week, Rachel found she'd settled into a kind of routine with Harvard. They went dancing whenever she asked him to take her—purely to help them maintain their cover, of course. She let him drive her to work and home again, and during the day, he wandered in and out of her office at random times, doing who knows what the rest of the time. He'd soon made friends at TayFor, showing his skill for obtaining information from people without them even knowing it was happening.

He usually updated her on what he'd uncovered over a shared dinner. Sometimes they ordered in. Sometimes he cooked. And he was a surprisingly good cook. Rachel had begun to wonder if there was anything Harvard couldn't do well, because the list of his skills seemed infinite.

Which irritated her no end.

"What's up with you?" he asked as they entered her apartment.

That was another thing. She was never alone. Either Harvard was in her space, just *being* there, using the air. Or everyone assigned to the TayFor investigation was hanging out around her dining table, talking over their progress. Why, she didn't know. Because they weren't making any progress. One week after finding the memory card reader, and they still had no clue who'd put it there.

She threw her suit jacket over the back of one of her sofas. At this rate, the investigation would never end, and Harvard would have moved in with her permanently. And how was she supposed to resist him then? He was upending her whole life—a life she'd managed to arrange perfectly to suit herself. And he smiled while he did it. That damn sexy smile of his was a continual temptation.

He was driving her mad.

"Rachel," he said in that way of his that made her name sound intimate. "You want to tell me what's wrong? You've been in a foul mood since you woke up this morning, and I can't understand it because you were fine after we came home last night."

She rounded on him. "This is not your home. It's my home."

"I know that." Harvard stared at her as though he could see right through her. "And I appreciate you allowing me to stay here for the duration."

"That's the thing; I didn't allow it." She threw up her hands in disgust. "You just moved in and took over. You're everywhere." She gestured around her living room.

"Not sure I understand what you mean," he said. "I keep my belongings to the guest room. Everywhere else looks exactly as it did before I moved in."

"It's not. It's all different." Rachel stormed over to the fridge on the heels she hadn't bothered to kick off, wishing the pencil skirt she wore wasn't quite so tight so she could take bigger steps. Throwing open the fridge, she pointed inside. "There's food in here," she accused.

"Okay, I don't see—"

She cut him off. "There was never any food in there before you moved in. It's like I don't even know my own fridge anymore. And then there's your smell."

"I smell?"

"No. Yes. You don't smell bad. You smell like the blasted ocean. And it's everywhere. What do you do? Douse yourself in aftershave, then rub up against the furniture like a cat? Are you marking your territory? Because this is *my* territory."

"I know it's your territory, and I don't rub myself against anything." Harvard shot her a look that was equal parts confusion and amusement, which just irritated her more. "I'm trying to be a sensitive and considerate guest and keep out of your way."

"Well stop it. It's driving me crazy." She glared at the kitchen counter. "You make coffee in the mornings. You stock the fridge with pastries. You cook dinner, and it tastes like something I'd order from the Savoy. Which I don't understand. When did you have time to learn to cook when you were off being a spy? It isn't normal. None of this is normal." She pointed at him. "You aren't normal."

"Okaaaaay, should I stop cooking?"

"Yes! And while you're at it, stop being so damned perfect at everything else." Rachel started pacing the length of the living room. "You cook, you dance, you sing in Spanish, you smell like the beach in summer, you make friends easily, you clean up after yourself." She came to a halt in front of him and poked at his chest. "You look like that! Muscles everywhere. Which I don't understand because I never see you work out. And then there's the way you dress...it's too sophisticated. I mean, look at you. A stylist at Selfridges couldn't have done a better job of putting you together."

She waved a hand down his body, indicating the bespoke suit in the perfect shade of pale gray that he'd teamed with a crisp white shirt and a classic Rolex. A Rolex!

"How can you even afford a Rolex? You worked for the CIA." She stopped talking as a thought occurred to her. "Please tell me that this perfect version of you isn't real and that you made your money being a double agent." She held her breath, waiting for the answer. Hoping her guess was right.

"You *want* me to be a traitor?" The look in Harvard's eye made it clear he was worried about her.

"Yes," she snapped. "I want a sign. Just one sign. That you aren't so perfect that you practically come wrapped in the original packaging."

She watched his muscles flex while he hung his suit jacket over the back of one of the stools at the breakfast bar.

"So, let me get this straight." He unbuttoned the cuff of his shirt. "You think I'm too perfect, and it's driving you nuts. Is that right?"

He rolled up the sleeve to just below his elbow, and it was mesmerizing. And sensual. Why was it sensual?

Watching him do the same to his other sleeve, she licked her lips. "Yes. Being around you is frustrating." Watching a man roll up his shirt sleeves shouldn't be sexy. "And stop doing that too." She pointed at him.

Harvard froze mid-roll. "Fixing my sleeves?"

"Yes. You're deliberately flirting with me when there's no need. We're alone. We don't need to protect our cover. Stop being so sexy."

They'd unintentionally worn matching gray outfits for the day, although Rachel had teamed her gray skirt with a pink blouse. Along with everything else, the matching aspect annoyed her. They weren't the bloody Beckhams. They were nothing to each other except colleagues. Annoying, irritating, always-together colleagues.

"We need some new rules," she said. "No more dancing. We've danced enough. No more cooking for me. I can order food in. And get rid of that aftershave, or deodorant, or whatever it is. In fact, I'll buy you a new one. One that smells terrible. Yes. That's what I'll do. Harrods is still open; I can get one there."

As she strode past him to fetch her handbag, Harvard's hand shot out, and he grasped her arm. He twirled her into his hold, the same way he'd done a thousand times while they danced. Suddenly, Rachel found herself pressed back against his body. His hand on her stomach as his scent and warmth enfolded her.

"What are you doing?" She sounded breathless. Her heart raced out of control, and she felt as though she were frozen in amber, waiting to be freed.

"I'm fixing the problem," he said as he nuzzled her hair with his jaw. "I'm gonna address each of your issues for you. First"—he held her left hand in his as he swayed to music only he could hear—"I'm far from perfect. I can be arrogant and manipulative when I want something bad enough, or when it comes to my job. I don't like anyone messing with me professionally. If they do, there are always repercussions."

Rachel sank back against him, her body already trained to relax against his from the few evenings they'd spent dancing.

"Second, I can only cook about half a dozen meals real well," Harvard's deep voice rumbled. "After that, it's hit or miss. And the coffee you drink every morning? That's delivered. My coffee sucks."

She angled her head to look up at him. "How do I know you aren't lying?"

"I'll wake you tomorrow before it arrives. And that's the third point on my list. While you're still sleeping, I'm working out in the gym in the basement or running around Hyde Park. These muscles require an effort to maintain, and staying in shape for my job is important to me. Having you pay attention to them doesn't do my ego any harm either."

"It wasn't like I was studying you," she huffed. "The muscles are big, and you're often in my line of sight. It would be impossible not to notice."

He brushed a kiss against her hair. "And lastly, the deodorant that offends you? That's gonna have to stay, because I don't think it's offense you feel, Rachel. I think you like that scent a little too much."

She started to shake her head, but he spun her out and back into him. This time, their bodies were pressed front to front, his palm flat against the small of her back.

"As for my imperfections, they're too many to list," he said softly, holding her gaze with his.

"Try," Rachel ordered, but there wasn't the same demand behind it as usual. She was more interested in the sensation of his shirt under her fingers as she stroked his chest.

"Okay then, gotta tell you that I'm a bed hog," he said, gently moving them to a silent rhythm. "I also poke my nose into everything that interests me. I'm stubborn. It's well known that I don't have much of a temper, but there have been occasions where I've punched first and asked questions later. And, although it may look like I'm the master of self-control, I think I've reached the limit where you're concerned. As for me being too sexy, whatever I'm doing, I intend to keep on doing because I want to tempt you. I want you to touch me."

Harvard lowered his head until his lips were against her ear. A shiver went through her at the feeling of his breath against her skin, and she felt like she was melting inside. "We're never gonna stop dancing, Rachel, not if I have my way. So you can forget about that rule. As for your other frustrations, I'm pretty sure I have the solution for those too."

Damn, he was far too cocky for *her* own good. "You're very sure of yourself, aren't you?"

His cheek brushed against hers, and then their mouths

were touching. Just a whisper of a touch. Yet it was enough to make all of her concerns disappear. She waited, aching to know what he'd do next. Hoping it would be everything she needed to calm the raging unrest within. To still the hunger inside of her that had been there since Joe's and Julia's wedding in Peru, when she'd first told Harvard to go to hell.

"No, Rachel. I haven't been sure of anything since I met you." His words were butterfly kisses against her lips. "All I know is that I've been waiting forever to kiss you."

As her knees weakened, she was glad his hold on her was firm and strong. "You've only known me a few months."

"And yet, I've been waiting a lifetime." And with that, his lips gently brushed over hers. "Put your arms around my neck."

It was the same order he'd given on the dancefloor, and again, she found herself complying without a second thought. "What now?" she whispered.

"Whatever you want," was the reply.

"Then show me if you kiss as perfectly as you do everything else."

"When you put it that way, it makes me feel as though I have to screw this up to get you to like me."

"Poor you. Such a dilemma. Now stop talking and kiss me."

Her eyes drifted closed as she felt his smiling lips against hers. And then, while they swayed in place in the middle of her living room, his mouth moved over hers. Sweet, gentle, teasing kisses. Small playful nips with his teeth. The sensual slide of his tongue against hers before the kiss turned languorous, and the world disappeared entirely.

Rachel's hands stroked up the back of his neck, caressing the bare skin at the base of his skull where hair would normally be. Even that was sexy. She felt his muscles flex as he deepened the kiss. Heard herself whimper with delight as their bodies moved together in a sensual dance. Those strong, capable hands of his traced over her back. And that scent. The one that haunted her in every single room of her house. That scent made her heady with desire.

Slowly, reluctantly, he eased them apart, and Rachel rested her forehead on his chest. His hands flexed on her hips as they stood motionless together.

"You even kiss perfectly," she accused. "Which means we can never do that again."

"You wanna tell me why?" Harvard said softly, sounding as distracted as she was.

And because her brain was scrambled and her focus still on the hum of pure ecstasy vibrating through her body, she gave him the truth. "Because you make me feel out of control and exposed."

He didn't reply; they just stood there quietly in each other's arms for a few precious moments.

"Go get changed," he said, breaking the spell he'd woven around her. "The team will be here soon for our meeting."

Feeling both reluctance and relief, Rachel stepped away from him to retrieve her handbag. "I'm going to chalk up what just happened to the stress of this investigation," she said as she headed for the staircase. "Let's never talk about this again."

"No, *talking* definitely isn't what we need to do," he said with heavy meaning.

Rachel didn't answer. All her focus was on walking away without letting him see just how unsteady she was on her feet.

She managed to project an air of cool indifference until her bedroom door closed with Harvard on the other side. Sagging against it, she brushed her fingertips over sensitive lips. Dumb. It had been so dumb to kiss him. And yet, all she wanted was to do it again. But how could she? When each step that took them closer to each other also made her feel more vulnerable. Flattening a hand over her stomach, she fought the anxiety-induced nausea that spiked. One kiss would have to be enough. She couldn't risk more.

It was time to put that kiss behind her and get on with the rest of her life. Which meant another damn meeting about their elusive thief. But first, she planned to shower, change, and empty her handbag, so it was ready for the morning. She took the bag to her bed and emptied the contents.

And that's when she found it.

A second photo.

It was in the open-topped pocket on the rear of her bag. Anyone could have slipped it in there at any point during her day.

The photo fell to the silk-covered bedspread. And the shock of seeing it on her bed made her gag. She snatched it up and hastily backed across the room. The photo shaking in her hand, a strange feeling of detachment overtook her as she stared at the image.

It was a younger version of herself with two men she didn't know, their faces hidden while they did unspeakable things to her body.

Closing her eyes for a moment, she concentrated on steadily breathing in and out until the nausea passed. And then, she turned her attention to the message written in blue ink across the white border at the bottom of the photo.

You have until Friday to get out, or you'll regret it.

As cold resolve steadied her, Rachel shook her head in denial. No, she wouldn't be the one to regret her choices. Not this time. No matter what it cost her. No matter what it took. This time, things would be different. Because she wasn't the same person she'd been when that photo was taken. Now, she was stronger, scarier, and had the resources of Benson Security at her back.

She wasn't a naïve university student who trusted too readily. She was a formidable woman who didn't scare easily. In other words, she was the bitch who was going to take them all down with her.

Chapter Thirteen

Harvard laughed at Ryan and Elle as they bickered over which Chinese dish was best. He wasn't sure why they were arguing. Or whether Ryan ever ate anything slow enough to register how it tasted in the first place. Hearing a sound behind him, he turned to include Rachel in their conversation.

And stopped dead; everything within him instantly on high alert. Because this wasn't the same woman who'd gone to her bedroom not half an hour earlier.

Instead of changing into lounge pants and one of the camisole tops that she liked to wear at home, she was still dressed in the gray skirt and pink top she'd worn to work. More telling, her feet weren't bare; they were clad in the mile-high silver pumps she'd donned for the office.

She was wearing her business armor.

With her shoulders back, chin held high, and absolutely no emotion showing on her face, she made her way to the end of the table farthest away from them all, holding an envelope in her hand. Suddenly, the table was as much of a barrier between Harvard and Rachel as the distant expression on her face.

Slowly, Ryan and Elle realized that the atmosphere in the dining room had changed. Become tense and expectant. They lowered their chopsticks and gave their attention to Rachel.

She didn't even glance at them. Instead, she focused on Harvard. "I'm being blackmailed."

As Ryan froze and Elle gasped, a jolt of shock shot through Harvard's body, ensuring that every inch of him was focused fully on Rachel. "Go on," he said without any sign of the inner turmoil he felt.

"Before I tell you all this, I must insist that none of you get emotional. It really isn't worth it. And I would appreciate it if you'd wait with questions until I'm finished talking. Am I clear?"

Ryan and Elle murmured their agreement, sounding worried. The tension in the room shot up by about a million degrees. Nothing good could follow a warning like that. Nothing. Fighting the urge to walk around the table and hold her while she talked, Harvard said instead, "We'll be professional."

It must have been enough of a reassurance for her, because she nodded and took a visible breath. "Ten years ago, I spent my summer break from university living at home and interning at TayFor. While out one evening at a nightclub, I was drugged and raped by several men."

What the fuck?

Ryan shot to his feet and started pacing. Elle covered her mouth with her hands.

As for Harvard, the world as he knew it exploded around him. Years of training in tamping down his emotions kept him from reacting to the flying shrapnel and out-of-control blazes that only he could see.

When he didn't move a muscle, but instead kept his eyes

glued to hers, Rachel let out a long, very controlled breath that he wouldn't have noticed if he hadn't been studying her so intently. "I don't actually know how many men were involved." Her voice was flat, as though she were reciting London's underground schedule. "Thanks to the drug they used, I have no memory of the actual assault. Sometimes, I have the faintest of flashbacks. Usually when I dream, more recently, when I'm awake."

For a split second, the tip of her tongue peeked out to wet her lips. "After the incident, I woke up in a strange hotel with photos of the assault lying beside me, and a message demanding I never return to TayFor, or the images would be made public."

Ryan cursed under his breath, and a muffled sob came from Elle. But Harvard remained outwardly calm and strong —for Rachel. He didn't dare break eye contact with her, as he suspected that focusing on him was giving her the strength she needed to tell her story.

"I destroyed the photos and took myself to the hospital. I didn't file charges, as there was no one to file them against. Even in the photos, the only recognizable face was mine." Her throat bobbed as she swallowed, and he could only imagine how dry it must be.

"Ryan," Harvard said in a calm, steady voice, "get Rachel a bottle of water."

Rachel kept her eyes fixed on Harvard as Ryan stalked to the kitchen, grabbed a bottle of water, opened it and gently handed it to her—all without saying a word.

After she drank, she continued, "The drug used on me that night was from TayFor. I know this because it was in the note my attackers left behind. Clearly, if that information came out, along with the photos, the resulting media atten-tion would destroy the company. And my parents." She took another drink without taking her eyes off him. "I didn't tell anyone in my family what happened. When I got out of the hospital, I went straight back to university in Glasgow. I asked Harry to hack the hospital and the police to remove any records concerning me or the attack. And then I made him promise never to tell a soul."

Elle made a little moaning sound, filled with agony, while Ryan continued to pace, fury emanating from his every step.

Harvard buried his emotions deep. The rage and pain he felt weren't what Rachel needed from him. She needed his usual steady, even approach to life. She needed an anchor. And even if every muscle in his body snapped from being held so damn tight, he would give her what she needed.

She cleared her throat. "I had intended to work for TayFor once I graduated, but as that was no longer possible, I went to work for Harry's tech start-up instead, and I heard nothing more about the attack." The water bottle shook slightly as she took another drink. "Until last Monday, when I found this in my desk drawer."

She reached into the envelope she'd placed in front of her and took out an old Polaroid photo, which she slid across the table to Harvard. He didn't look at it but focused instead on the woman who was ripping him up inside. The photo could wait until she was done telling her story.

His teammates did look. Elle let out a gasping sob, and Ryan slapped a hand down hard onto the table, the sound echoing through the room.

Rachel didn't even seem to notice their reactions. "Tonight," she said, "I found a second photo tucked into the pocket of my handbag." Another photo joined the first.

Now Elle was sobbing hard and had given up trying to hide it.

"For fuck's sake, Rachel," Ryan exploded, agony lacing his voice far more than rage. "Why didn't you let us go after these bastards years ago?"

She didn't answer him, but Harvard suspected Ryan hadn't expected her to.

"I had intended to ignore all of this," Rachel said to Harvard. "Mainly because it occurred to me that the person doing this must work at TayFor. And one would assume they wouldn't want to ruin the company that employs them. Also, we're in the middle of an investigation, and if this and the thefts were to be made public, it would be the end of TayFor. A pharmaceutical company is only as good as the trust their customers have in them."

It sounded like the measured, responsible response a politician would give after a crisis, and Harvard couldn't keep quiet any longer. Gentling his voice, he asked, "Why tell us about it, then?"

"Because this latest warning gives me three days before something else happens. I don't know what that will be."

"No." Harvard leaned forward, closing the distance between them. "Why tell us about it *now*?"

She blinked several times, her bottom lip trembling for a split second before she got it under control. "I emptied my handbag onto my bed," was all she said.

And having the photos of her assault in the place where she felt most secure, the place where she'd been able to let down her guard, had been the last straw. Damn it to hell, he couldn't take any more of this distance she'd put between them.

"Ryan," he said, in a tone that couldn't be mistaken for anything other than an order, "take Elle for a walk."

As a former soldier, Ryan recognized a commander's instruction when he heard one, and he didn't hesitate. He wrapped an arm around Elle's shoulders and helped the sobbing woman from the room. "Come on, Ellie, let's get you some air," he said softly.

As soon as the door closed behind them, Harvard was on his feet and heading for Rachel.

She held up a hand to ward him off. "I don't need comforting."

It was the biggest load of bull he'd heard in years. "Rachel, I just sat and listened to the woman I care about tell me that she suffered a horrific assault. You might not need comforting, but I sure as hell do."

For a second, she seemed stunned by his words, then she walked straight into his open arms and held him tight. Giving him some of her endless strength. Humbling him in the process.

"It's going to be okay," she said into his chest, comforting *him*.

And his heart was shredded.

WHEN THE MEETING PICKED BACK UP, IT WAS A SOMBER affair. With her reddened eyes and tear-stained cheeks, Elle appeared wrung out. Ryan looked like he wanted to punch something. And Rachel? From what Harvard could see, she was pretending it was business as usual.

"The mission objective has changed," Ryan stated harshly. For once, he wasn't eating, even though there was a plate full of Chinese food in front of him. "I don't give a damn about the stolen information; I want the people who did this." He pointed at the photos, which were lying facedown on the table beside Harvard.

"As much as I appreciate the sentiment"—Rachel poked at the egg fried rice on her plate as though it had come from another planet, and she wasn't quite sure what to make of it —"we've been hired to do a job. And, I have no idea who my attackers are. All I have are those two photos, and there's nothing in them that even hints at my attackers' identities."

Pushing away her plate, she leaned into Harvard's side and rested her head on his shoulder. "Be a darling and make me something to eat that's actually edible."

Harvard could practically hear Ryan's and Elle's jaws drop, but he didn't care. All he cared about was that Rachel had turned to him. And sure, she was manipulating him, but considering what she'd revealed, he'd give her a pass for the evening.

"There's still some pasta left over from yesterday. You want me to heat it?"

"Yes, please." She moved away again and gazed at him expectantly.

Obviously, he wasn't moving fast enough for her.

With a smile, he got up out of his chair and headed for the kitchen.

"No, no, no, no," Elle said. "This can't be happening. You two are far too comfortable with each other." She pointed a finger at Rachel. "You touched him. You never touch anyone."

"She touches me all the time," Ryan complained.

Elle shot him a look of disgust. "She *smacks* you; she doesn't touch you. But she's touching Harvard, and I don't like what I'm seeing. You'd better not have lost the bet for me, Rachel Ford-Talbot. I will hack your life and give you online herpes if you have."

"The bet?" Ryan almost choked. "You're worried about the bet after everything we found out tonight? The bet's off. We can't bloody wager on whether they sleep together after this. After finding out that Rachel was... No." He shook his head. "I'm dissolving the betting pool and taking back my money. I don't want a payout based on Rachel having sex with Harvard. No. Just no."

"What?" Rachel lifted an imperious eyebrow at Ryan.

"You think Harvard won't desire me now that he's seen those photos?"

"What? No!" Ryan's head turned a vicious shade of red. "It's just wrong. I feel like my bet is pressurizing you into sleeping with him. I don't want to do that. I don't want to be like them."

Elle paled. "He's got a point. I'm sorry, Rachel. I meant to lighten the mood a little. If that's even possible."

"It isn't possible," Ryan said darkly. "There's no getting away from the fact she was—" He slammed his mouth shut and shook his head.

"Raped?" Rachel asked with a casual air. "Assaulted? Abused? Victimized? Brutalized?"

"Stop, please." Ryan sounded like he was the one in agony.

"Why?" Rachel pinned him with her dark eyes. "Why should I hide from the words? Why should I be ashamed of saying them aloud? Would a person who'd been stabbed or robbed or shot have the same problem? No. It's only the victims of sexual assault who're expected to carry the shame for their attackers." She reached for her wine glass, noticed it was empty, and got up from the table to fetch the bottle off the counter.

"But he's right," Elle said. "This changes everything. Before, it was a bit of fun to bet about the sexual tension between you two. Now it feels like we're turning sex into something disposable, just like those guys did."

"That wasn't sex." Harvard took the pasta out of the microwave. "Rape isn't sex. Don't ever confuse the two."

"Honestly," Rachel said. "I don't care if the silly bet stands or not. I plan on doing whatever the hell I please, regardless. It didn't offend or traumatize me if that's what you're thinking."

"How couldn't it have?" Ryan asked, looking pained. "The

memories it must bring back. The way it must have affected how you see sex..." He shook his head.

"Ryan," Rachel said as she returned to her seat, "there is absolutely no way I'm ever going to discuss my sex life with you. I have a therapist. She's infinitely more qualified than you are to deal with anything I have to tell her, and much more pleasant to talk to. If you want her number, I'd be overjoyed to pass it on. Goodness knows you could use some counseling."

To his credit, Ryan huffed out a laugh. "Great. I'm glad you're coping, but I still don't want any part of the bet. I don't care what everybody else does, but I'm withdrawing from it and butting out of your sex life. Sleep with Harvard, don't sleep with him; it's up to you."

"Did you hear that?" Harvard said as he placed the plate in front of Rachel. "We have Ryan's permission to sleep together. It's just what we were waiting for. You want to skip dinner and head downstairs?"

"How can you joke about this?" Ryan asked.

Harvard held the man's gaze. "Because I'm not going to tell Rachel how she should deal with an assault that happened to her, not to me. I'm going to trust her when she tells me she's fine."

"I'm not ashamed of what happened to me, Ryan," Rachel said. "The reason I hesitated in sharing those photos is I'm a private person. It's not like I've been ignoring this for years. Believe me, Harry and I tried to find out who raped me, but there was no trail. The room was rented under an assumed name, check in was done remotely, and no one remembers who collected the keycard. If there had been an online trail, Harry would have found it."

Ryan looked pained. "Why didn't you let the police investigate? There might have been forensic evidence that led to those shitheads."

"Yes," she agreed as she sipped her wine. "I'll admit, I regret refusing the investigation at the time."

"What the hell?" Elle snapped at him. "Are you saying this is Rachel's fault that these guys weren't caught?"

"No!" Ryan clasped the back of his neck with both hands and let out a frustrated sigh. "I just hate the thought of these bastards getting away with this. I hate that Rachel went through it. I hate that somebody's using it against her right now. I hate feeling..."

"Helpless?" Rachel raised her glass to him. "Welcome to my world. I hate it too. Which is why I refuse to feel that way. One day, I'll find out who they are, and I will eviscerate them. Then they'll discover that I'm not the same girl they toyed with years ago. Until then, I have to do what's best for Benson Security and for my father's company, which means doing my job. Elle can take the photos and see if she can find any clues in them, but until we have something concrete to go on, we're better off focusing on finding TayFor's thief."

"So, we're just going to ignore this?" Ryan said.

"No," Rachel said. "We're going to do what I've been doing for the past ten years. We're going to live our lives."

Harvard took his seat beside her, resisting the urge to wrap his arm around her while she ate. He had the good sense to realize that the boundaries he could push in private weren't ones she'd tolerate being pushed in public. "We'll expand our investigation to include finding out who sent the photos. We know they have a vested interest in TayFor, and we know this situation with Rachel is personal for them. What we don't know is whether the person who's blackmailing her was involved in the attack, or if they came across the photos some other way."

"Do we bring the rest of Benson Security in on this?" Elle tugged her laptop closer.

"That's up to Rachel," Harvard said.

As all eyes turned to her, she dabbed her lips with a napkin. "The warning gave me three days to leave TayFor. Let's hold off telling everyone else for now. Until we have something more to go on."

Ryan's jaw clenched tight, and it was easy to guess he wanted to rush the building with every man he could find, interrogating every staff member until he found the culprit.

Looking Rachel in the eye, Elle cleared her throat and said, "You are amazing, and we'll investigate your attack any way you choose. Whatever your plan, I have your back."

For a second, it looked like Rachel didn't quite know what to do about Elle's declaration, but then she caught Harvard's eye and said, "Is there any more pasta?"

"Yeah." He stroked a hand down her back. "I'll get you some."

Chapter Fourteen

Elle took the photos away to have them tested for prints and DNA and to see if she could get anything off them digitally. Ryan lingered to talk to Harvard, no doubt to argue for more drastic measures to find her attackers. And Rachel said goodnight to both of them before retreating to her bedroom.

Where she currently stood, staring at her bed. Staring, but unable to actually get into it.

She'd showered and changed into a silk camisole and boy shorts set she liked to sleep in. She'd moisturized, tidied away her things, set the alarm for the morning, and checked the temperature of the bedroom. In other words, she'd done everything she could to avoid climbing into the bed she usually loved.

But no matter how determined she was to get past what had happened, when she looked at the blue and black Japanese silk of the bedspread, all she saw was that photo. No, not the photo, the images it contained. On. Her. Bed.

Thinking that changing out the cover might help, she

replaced it with one that had the most gorgeous silver embroidery over black silk.

It made no difference.

She just couldn't bring herself to get into bed.

And that made her furious. Ten years earlier, her attackers had stolen so much from her. They weren't taking this. All she needed was a little help to get past this latest setback and return to normal, nothing more. And she knew just where to find it.

Rachel shrugged into her short black robe, tying the belt tight as she stalked across the hallway to the guest room. Her knock was firm. A few seconds later, Harvard opened the door, wearing black pajama pants that sat low on his hips and nothing else. At the sight of his muscular chest, she momentarily forgot why she was there.

"You okay?" he asked in that calming voice of his. Nothing ever seemed to rile the man. And goodness knows she'd tried often enough.

She raised her chin. "I need you to sleep with me tonight." She narrowed her eyes. "Just sleep."

That penetrating gaze of his seemed to bore straight through her. With Harvard, there was always the feeling that he was seeing far more than she'd like him to see. It was disconcerting.

He flicked off the light switch and stepped toward her. "Lead the way," was all he said.

Turning on her heel, Rachel wondered at his lack of curiosity over her sudden invitation but was thankful for it. To explain would make her more vulnerable than she already felt. And she didn't want that.

When they stepped into her bedroom, she tried to imagine how Harvard would see it. Unlike the rest of her apartment, her bedroom was decorated in shades of blue against warm white walls.

"Blue," he said, looking around the room.

"The red clashed with that." She pointed at the ceiling, which was the glass bottom of her pool. The gentle blue lights in the water wouldn't do anything good for a red color scheme.

"You could have used red lights in the pool, but I'm thinking that might have given you nightmares."

With the things going on in her head these days, he wasn't wrong. "I sleep on the right."

Harvard looked at the bed, then at the door. "The right is closest to the door."

"And that's a problem why?"

"Because if I'm going to sleep beside you, I'd rather be between you and anything that might come through that door."

A link in the chains around her heart gave way. "This apartment is locked up tight and alarmed, which you know, as you check it every night. I'm safe here."

"Rachel," was all he said, in that deep rumbling tone he used solely for her name.

"Whatever." She threw up her hands in surrender. "Sleep on the right if that makes you happy."

After flipping the door's lock, which she never used, Harvard threw back the bedspread and climbed in. The sight of him reclining on the black sheets, the perfect embodiment of raw male power, made her heart race and her breathing grow short. But it wasn't from fear. Harvard would never threaten her. It was from awe.

He was beautiful. It was the only word to describe him. All glorious muscle and endless strength married with a smart brain and too perceptive gaze. He was everything she tried to avoid in a man, because she wasn't sure she'd ever be able to resist him.

And he was in her bed.

Swallowing nervously, Rachel toyed with the necklace she only took off for sleeping. The locket that had been passed down through the female line of the Talbots for generations. The one her grandmother had given to her mother, who'd given it to Rachel when she turned eighteen.

The locket was empty. Her mother had told her, "When you find your future, this is where you'll keep it. Over your heart."

Why she'd thought about that while staring at Harvard, in her bed, where no man had ever been, she didn't know. It had to be nerves. Or anxiety. Or fear. All things she never allowed herself to feel.

Never again.

With pure determination, she cast Harvard a look filled with challenge as she slipped off her robe and unfastened her necklace, which she gently placed on her dresser—beside the ring he'd given her.

"Pretty," he rumbled, his eyes on her body. "Do you wear stuff like that every night?"

"Yes. But don't expect to see this again. Tonight is a onetime deal." Without hesitation, she rounded the bed and climbed in beside him, making sure to keep some space between them. It felt strange, lying in bed with someone. It wasn't something she'd ever done, well not since she'd had pajama parties with her cousin Samantha when they were children. And Harvard was nothing like Samantha.

Rachel lifted the remote from her bedside table and switched off the lamps dotted around the room. Now, there was only the soft blue glow rippling from the pool above them.

"Do you need me to draw the shutters over the pool?" Automatic panels built into the edges of her ceiling slid out to hide the pool if needed.

"Do you usually close the shutters?"

"No."

"Then I'm fine."

She put back the remote and lay there, staring at the water above her and feeling tense. It was then that she realized she hadn't once thought about that damn photo since Harvard had stepped into her room, nor had she felt anxious about getting into bed.

A relieved breath escaped her. All she'd needed was a distraction. And they didn't come much bigger than Harvard. Part of her considered sending him back to his room now that she was in bed and didn't need him, but a niggling fear at the back of her mind told her not to. What if she ended up lying there alone, thinking about the photo, or worse, thinking about the attack? No, she was much better off with Harvard beside her. For tonight anyway.

"Are we just gonna sleep side by side like this?" His deep voice broke into her thoughts. "Or can we snuggle?"

That made her look at him. "Snuggle?"

Harvard lay on his back, one arm behind his head, making the bicep bulge, the other resting on his stomach. His eyes were on the pool above them.

"I told you I wasn't perfect and that I had issues, same as everybody else. One of those issues is that I'm a snuggler." He turned his head to grin at her, all wicked playfulness and tempting sensuality. "I also told you that I'm a bed hog, which means even if we aren't gonna snuggle, you'll wake up during the night with me wrapped around you anyway. I snuggle in my sleep."

"Oh, for the love of Prada. Fine. We can snuggle." Honestly, he was completely exasperating. "How do you do it?"

His eyes went wide. "You don't know how to snuggle?"

Rachel frowned at him. "Do you have an opinion on that?" Because she'd bloody well send him back to his own bed if he did. She'd rather sleep in the other guest room than deal with any mockery. But only if she were desperate, because the last thing she wanted was to let *them* win by giving up her bed.

"I have absolutely no opinion on your lack of snuggling experience," he said with mock solemnity and a mischievous sparkle in his eyes. "I'm real glad that I'm the one who gets to show you how to do it. Now turn on your side with your back to me. We'll start with a basic snuggle position—spooning."

"You couldn't just say you wanted to spoon?" she complained as she turned. "I know how to spoon." She'd just never done it.

She felt his warm body move up behind her, curving around her. "Lift your head," he said gently. And she did so. Making her wonder if she followed so many of his demands purely because he used that gentle tone. If anyone else told her what to do, she gave them hell, she definitely didn't comply.

He slid an arm under her head for her to rest on, and then wrapped his other arm tight around her waist. "This is beginner snuggling. I'll teach you the more advanced versions another time."

"What makes you think there will be another time?"

"A man can hope."

They lay there in silence as Rachel relaxed into his hold. It was familiar to her from dancing together. As her weight sank deeper into the bed, she wondered if she'd ever get his ocean scent out of her sheets. Or her room. It had been the only place in her home that didn't remind her of Harvard. Now that had changed too.

Inch by inch, the man was slowly inserting himself into her life, and she wasn't sure what she thought or felt about it. Because he did it so sweetly, in such an unthreatening manner, that she'd barely noticed it happening.

The heat of his body along her back made her muscles turn limp in a way that no massage had ever achieved. With his arm around her and his bulk protecting her, she felt as though she were cradled inside a cocoon.

She felt safe.

And as her mind drifted, she found thoughts escaping from her lips that she normally wouldn't allow free. "Years back," she said quietly, "before you joined Benson Security, we had a case that involved a sex trafficker."

He said nothing, but his thumb stroked lazily against her stomach.

"I used my connections with TayFor to acquire a drug to disable the man so that one of our team could get the information we needed to shut his operation down." She paused, remembering that time and the complete lack of remorse she'd felt at her actions. "It was the same drug they used on me."

They remained silent for a long time before Harvard spoke. "And you think that makes you the same as the guys who attacked you?"

"Not the same, but it did allow Megan to assault the man in a way that meant he wouldn't rape anyone else. It's a fine line, isn't it? Between what I did and what was done to me."

She liked that he took his time to consider his answer before giving it.

"What I think," he said at last, "is that it sounds like poetic justice. There are people in this world who don't play by the rules, but they expect everyone else to, and they use that against them. There has to be someone willing to cross the line and deal with those people." He nuzzled her temple.

"I don't feel bad about what I did," she whispered, confessing the part that made her worry about herself the most.

"I've done a lot of things that I don't feel bad about. Things other people would say I should regret."

"None of which you can talk about, or you'd have to kill me."

"Exactly." She heard the grin in his reply. "But sometimes, the things I had to do come back to haunt me in my dreams. I feel like I deserve that."

Rachel placed her hand over his and wriggled closer. "Thank you," she whispered before falling asleep.

DEEP IN THE NIGHT, ONCE RACHEL WAS SOUND ASLEEP, Harvard slipped out of bed and crept to the guest room to place a call.

"Who the hell is this?" the sleep-roughened voice demanded.

"This is Harvard," he said, keeping his voice low so that it didn't carry back to Rachel and wake her. "From the London office. You just wrote a program for my operation. We need to talk, but not about the TayFor case, about Rachel."

"Crap," Harry Boyle said in his deep highland brogue. "Gimme a minute to get out of the bedroom."

There was the sound of muffled conversation and a drowsy female voice asking what was going on, and then Harvard heard a door shut.

A minute later, Harry came back on the line. "What about Rachel?" he said, sounding wary.

"She told me about the rape."

A long stream of cursing battered Harvard's ear before Harry let out a heavy sigh. "Does she know you're talking to me?"

"It's three in the morning, what do you think?" For a genius, Harry wasn't impressing Harvard too much. But then, to give him his due, it was the middle of the night, and not everyone woke up battle-ready like a former spy.

"Okay, okay," Harry said. "Let me start some coffee while we talk. What do you know? Bring me up to speed on what she's said."

"I know the basics of the attack ten years ago, that you covered up the aftermath for her, and then tried to hunt down her attackers. She says you hit some dead ends and gave up. My guess is that you only led her to believe you gave up, but you kept on hunting. Probably still are."

"Smart man," Harry muttered. "She wanted to move on, so I stopped telling her what I was doing. To be fair, I never came across enough information to go on anyway."

Harvard's sixth sense tingled. "But you did find something."

"Aye."

Chapter Fifteen

Keeping one ear open for any sign that Rachel might wake, Harvard asked, "What'd you find out?"

"About a year before the attack, Rachel was doing some work at TayFor during a break from university." Harry clunked around doing who knows what while he talked. "You have to understand that back then, Rachel was always thinking about TayFor and spent every free minute working in their offices. She had huge plans for the company and was interested in every tiny detail. It fascinated her."

Which made Harvard wonder why her family hadn't pushed harder to find out why she suddenly changed her career path.

"Anyway," Harry continued, "during that particular visit, Rachel came across evidence that two guys were stealing from the company. It was just petty crap, but they'd been getting away with it for a while. They fired the guys but didn't lay charges because the company didn't want the public to think they had security issues." He snorted with clear derision. "That seems to be standard practice at TayFor—cover up or avoid the problems instead of coming clean and explaining things properly to your clients."

The hair on Harvard's arms stood on end. "You think those two guys were the ones who attacked her?"

"I don't know. What I do know for certain is that they spent the year before the attack bad-mouthing TayFor, Rachel in particular. But I only know what they did before the attack because they disappeared straight after. As in, completely gone. No online trail. No record of them anywhere. Nothing."

"How soon after the attack did they disappear?"

"Following day."

Harvard remained silent for a moment while processing this new information. "That's a helluva big coincidence," he said at last.

"I know. Every few months, I run a search on them, but they still haven't popped up."

"Can you send me all the information you have on these guys?"

"Sure. I'll do it as soon as we're done with this call."

"When you were looking for them, did you contain your search to the UK?"

"They were minimum wagers. I figured they didn't have the resources or skills to move abroad."

Harvard had that sinking feeling in his stomach that he always got when random patterns in a mission started to make sense. "They would if someone paid them."

Harry cursed. "Why the hell didn't I think of that? I'll extend my search."

"I'll help," Harvard said. "I have connections you might not have the ability to tap into."

"One more thing." Harry sounded like he was sipping coffee between words. "Not long after the attack, it occurred to me that if the drug they used on Rachel came from TayFor, there might be a record of who took it, or of its theft, on the backup server." He let out a sigh. "I never brought this up with Rachel because she was determined to keep the whole thing a secret from her family, and there was no way I could get access to the server without them knowing. But you could get access now."

"If you tell Elle what to look for, she can do it." Harvard took a deep breath. "You gotta know, Rachel's been receiving old Polaroids of the attack since she returned to TayFor. Second photo arrived with a warning written on it telling her to leave the company."

It took so long for Harry to reply that Harvard began to wonder if the call had disconnected. "Elle isn't searching those servers," he eventually said in a tone that was pure steel. "I am. I'll be on the first flight down tomorrow. But I'll need a cover story if we're still flying her assault under the radar."

"Elle can—"

"No," Harry interrupted. "Rachel's my best friend. She might not see it like that, but there are days when I wonder if the reason that we're friends in the first place is because we're both crap at picking up on social cues. She's been there for me since we were in uni. I'm coming down to help her with this—whether she wants me there or not."

"Okay." Harvard pinched the bridge of his nose. "I was kinda hoping to keep our conversation quiet. You turning up is gonna blow that right out of the water."

"She'd find out anyway. Trust me. In all the years we worked together, I couldn't get anything past her."

"Great. You need to know that she was very specific about keeping the attack quiet right now. She's waiting to see what information Elle manages to get from the photos."

"Aye, that sounds like Rachel. She's all about controlling everything around her."

There was no arguing with that. "I'll see you tomorrow. Contact Elle if you have any questions about the server setup at TayFor or what she's doing with the photos."

"Will do. And good luck explaining this call to Rachel."

"Thanks." Harvard hung up. He needed all the luck he could get.

As he sneaked back into bed beside a gently snoring Rachel, he decided the conversation could keep until the morning. Lying on his back, he pulled Rachel closer until she was almost on top of him. With her arm around his waist and her leg over his thigh, he held her tightly.

"This is snuggle position number two," he whispered. "Sleep well, Rachel. I'll watch over you."

And then he stared up at the bottom of the pool while planning exactly what he'd do to the men who'd attacked her once he found them. And he would find them. If it was the last thing he did.

THANKFULLY, HARVARD HAD THE GOOD SENSE TO GET OUT of bed before Rachel woke up. She wasn't sure what she'd have done if she'd woken to find them all over each other. This way, she could pretend the previous night had never happened. Which might make it easier to convince herself that she didn't want a repeat of it.

She ran her hand over his side of the bed and found it was cold. Obviously, he'd been gone a while. A glance at the clock told her it wasn't yet seven a.m., which was her usual time to get out of bed. Crazy man was probably off running laps of the park or working out in the building's gym.

Her imagination provided her with an image of Harvard, muscles flexing and a light sheen of sweat on his skin as he worked on his fitness. Her cheeks heated with the memory of his body wrapped around her the night before. And then the heat deepened as she remembered his strong hands holding her as they'd kissed. He'd tasted of hot, sensual temptation. A taste she could easily become addicted to.

But the kiss had come before everything had gone to hell. And Rachel couldn't help but wonder if he'd treat her differently now that he knew her history. Part of her thought it would be for the best if he withdrew. Another, worryingly larger part, knew she'd think less of him if he did.

The bottom line was, she was becoming far too familiar with Harvard's touch.

Covering her face with her hands, she groaned. "What are you doing, Rachel?" she admonished aloud.

Playing with fire. That's what she was doing. And it had to stop. She liked her life the way it was, liked the distance between herself and everyone else. When people got too close, it made her feel exposed.

And yet...Harvard had a way of shielding her from that exposure without making her feel like he was smothering her...

"No!" she snapped at herself. "Stop being so weak. You can resist."

As her arms dropped to her sides on the bed, she opened her eyes and looked straight at the bottom of the pool. She should have kept them closed. Because the man who drove her crazy was right above her, cutting through the water with the grace and ease of a dolphin. But Rachel wasn't fooled. Harvard was no friendly sea creature; he was as much of a predator as she was. He just hid it better.

All thoughts of getting out of bed fled now that she had Harvard to watch. No sane woman on the planet would give up the opportunity to ogle that. And if that made her a pervert, she didn't care. It wasn't like she could help it. He was only fourteen feet above her, with just the glass between them.

Fourteen feet. *About four meters.*

A surge of adrenaline shot through her, propelling her from the bed. She rushed to the bathroom to use the facilities and quickly brushed her teeth and hair—because even in a hurry, there were still standards one must adhere to. She didn't bother getting dressed though; Harvard had already seen her nightwear. Instead, she raced up the stairs and slammed through the door to the pool room.

Rachel picked up a float she used when she worked out in the pool and lobbed it at his head. Of course, she missed and hit that ugly gnome instead. Her aim seriously sucked. But it was enough of a disturbance to get his attention. He came up out of the water like Neptune, muscles flexing as the droplets ran down his skin. For the love of all things haute couture, it was distracting.

"Hey, gorgeous, you're awake." His smile was wide and intimate and had her second-guessing her decision to talk to him before getting dressed for the day. "You coming in?" As he dragged his hands through the water, her eyes followed the movement. It was mesmerizing.

She shook her head. "No. Something's just occurred to me. We need to check the cameras outside West Building." The block that housed her mother's lab. "Elle said there was a script running on the computer that enabled an automatic download to the Wi-Fi card reader periodically. Her theory was that the only time someone handled the reader was when they swapped out a full memory card for a fresh one." She took a deep breath.

"Go on," Harvard said, moving closer.

"What if the files stolen during the time we set the trap weren't taken on schedule? What if someone was outside the building, using their phone to tell the card reader to copy files? To take advantage of the security issue. The reader has a range of twenty meters. It's possible someone could have been close enough to the building to communicate with it."

He nodded slowly. "And phones aren't banned from the grounds, just the buildings."

"Exactly." She smiled at him. "We need to look at the security footage. Should I call Ryan and tell him to pull it?"

Harvard angled his head and smacked his ear, as though clearing water out of the opposite one. "Say that again," he said. "I'm a bit clogged."

"I said"—she leaned closer—"should I call Ryan or wait until we get to the office to talk to him?"

He shook his head and frowned. "Nope, still only getting bits. I'll come closer." He swam to the edge, until he was directly under her. "Sorry, tell me again."

"I said—"

But nothing else came out, because he reached up, grabbed her, and tugged her into the pool. Rachel screamed until water filled her mouth. She kicked to the surface, wiping her face as she glared at him. "I am going to kill you for that."

The lunatic laughed. "Aw, come on, Rachel, the situation was begging for it."

"No. It wasn't." She started swimming toward the steps.

The pool was about seven feet deep, except for a wide ledge around the edges, where the glass ended. That ledge varied in height, making it possible to sit in some parts of the pool. But right now, she was in the middle, and she couldn't touch the bottom.

As she passed Harvard, a strong arm wrapped around her waist from behind. "You're cute when you're all wet." He nuzzled the spot where her neck met her shoulder. "What will it take to make you forgive me?"

"There is nothing you could do that would make me

forgive you." She wriggled against his hold, their legs moving gently in the water, keeping them afloat.

"Nothing?" he whispered against her ear, and her body melted a little.

"No. That was uncalled for and juvenile."

"Maybe a little," he conceded. "But I'm trying to teach you how to play."

"What you're doing is driving me crazy."

"Again?" His teeth nipped at her earlobe, making her clutch his arm. "I know how to fix your crazy. Didn't I help with it yesterday? When we got home from work and you told me that I was too perfect?"

"I don't recall that conversation." She remembered the kiss though, all too well. "It couldn't have been very memorable."

"Then, let me remind you." Before she could even decide if she wanted to object, he turned her and pinned her against the side of the pool, where she was able to stand on the ledge. The water lapped at her body, sliding over it in a sinuous tease.

"I told you that I didn't want to kiss you again," she said, sounding a little breathless.

He cupped her cheek, turning somber. "I won't ever take anything you don't want to give." Suddenly, she found their positions reversed, with Harvard leaning back against the side of the pool and her standing between his legs. The width of the ledge made it impossible not to be within touching distance. "If you want me," he said in that dark, deep voice that made her shiver, "you can have me. I'm all yours. I promise not to touch until you ask me to."

Chapter Sixteen

Come on, Rachel. While Harvard outwardly appeared relaxed, inside he was a knot of desperation. *You know you want to; come on. Take the step. Come to me. You know I'll take good care of you. Come on...*

Her usually guarded expression had disappeared, and the war of indecision waging inside her was written all over her face. Harvard said nothing; he just waited. Willing her to take the step toward him. Wanting her with every molecule of his being.

Dark hair fell in thick, tangled strands, clinging to her cheeks and throat before falling around her shoulders. The black silk of her tiny pajamas was plastered to her like a second skin, revealing everything. He wanted to look his fill at her lush curves, the swell of her breasts, the hard nubs of her nipples. But he couldn't. Not yet. Maybe never if Rachel chose this moment to decide he definitely wasn't worth risking her heart over.

Choose me, Rachel. Want me. Need me the way that I need you...

Eyelashes fluttered as her gaze met his. "This doesn't

mean anything," she said, her upper-class English accent sounding a little rough around the edges.

Harvard didn't reply. She was lying to herself. They both knew that if she touched him, it meant everything.

She watched her palms flatten on his chest as if in slow motion. Her pale pink skin stood in decadent juxtaposition to his own rich brown. They were a study in contrasts. She was slender and delicate; he was bulky and strong. She was classy and sensual; he was rough and raw in his sexuality. She could be volatile and cutting, while he was calm and measured. There was darkness within her, and he was more than willing to be her light.

If she let him.

"If you're doing this to help me get over what happened to me, then I can tell you, it's pointless," she said absently, her fingers tracing the ridges of his abdomen. "I dealt with that a long time ago."

"Rachel," he said, his voice a rumble filled with need, "trust me when I say sexual healing isn't foremost in my mind. You're forgetting that I've been chasing your touch since the first moment I set eyes on you."

"Oh, no, I remember." Her smile was pure devilment. Most likely, she was replaying their first encounter, during which she'd slapped him.

"For the record, I thought that slap was an overreaction."

She stopped touching him and gave him a cold stare. "And I thought you were just another rude American."

Ouch. Well, that's what happened when your pickup line got lost in translation. "Let's not talk about that," he said.

"Wise choice." Rachel's hands started moving again.

It was agony and ecstasy all in one. Each touch sent shock waves through him, making him desperate to return the favor.

"You're still using that scent," she half accused, half purred.

Harvard didn't answer. If his deodorant had this effect on her, he planned to use it until he died. He made a mental note to stock up, just in case it was discontinued.

Slipping her arms around his shoulders, she stepped into him. Her breasts pressed flat against his chest, making his mouth water. Damn, he wished she was naked. That they both were. He wished he could feel the slide of her cool skin against his warmer one, feel the water swirl between them, caressing them as they caressed each other.

Go slow. Don't rush it. Let her come to you. It was the hardest thing he'd ever had to do.

Rachel's face nuzzled into the crook of his neck, breathing him deep. Her body moved against him in a sensuous wave. His hands clasped tight on her hips. She was killing him.

A groan escaped when he felt her tongue on his skin. Tiny kisses trailed up to his ear before she tugged the earlobe between her teeth.

"Let me off the leash, Rachel." If he sounded desperate, then it was only the truth.

She shook her head, her hair rubbing against his skin. The tip of her tongue teased his ear. Her breath was loud, echoing through his whole body. He heard the desperate rhythm to it, the hitch when she rubbed her sensitive breasts against him.

"I need to touch you." Hell, he'd beg if he had to. He was that desperate.

"Not yet." Her voice was a dark, needy purr as she moved her legs until she'd captured his thigh between them.

His arm wrapped around her as his other hand clenched at his side. She nibbled along the edge of his jaw, her hips undulating, pressing her hot, needy sex against him. His head fell back. His eyes closed. Nothing existed but the woman writing against him, using him for her pleasure, torturing him with her desire. For a man who was constantly aware of his environment and the threats within it, he wasn't sure he'd notice an army if they launched an assault on the room.

"Rachel, let me loose. Let me touch you. I'll make it good for you, I promise."

Her answer was a kiss to his throat as she moved against him. Holding her tight, he forced himself not to take over her movements, but to keep his promise and let her have her way.

"So good," she groaned as she rubbed against him, using the firm muscle of his thigh as though it were her own personal sex toy.

"You're killing me," he complained.

He felt her smile against his throat. The wicked woman enjoyed torturing him. He should have known she would.

"Kiss me," she said.

He wasn't sure if it was an order or a plea.

Her slender hand clasped his jaw, turning his face toward her. He went willingly, and what he saw in her eyes made him want to roar with primal possession. But desire didn't mean she was his. Not yet. Maybe never.

Please, please, he prayed, *don't let me screw this up.*

Holding his gaze, she leaned in to sip at his lips. Harvard couldn't even describe the noise that escaped him. It was a feral explosion of pure need. Those long lashes of hers drifted down as she changed the angle of her kiss.

Harvard fought to give her the control she needed when all he wanted to do was clasp the nape of her neck and take the kiss deeper. Her teasing tongue toyed with the seam of his lips.

"Let me in," Rachel whispered, her mouth brushing against his when he refused her entry.

"Say please." This was a war, and she was a strong fighter; he couldn't let her win every battle.

She rumbled her approval. "Please?"

That was enough. He opened his mouth, tasting the playful longing in her kiss as she retreated each time he followed, always staying just out of reach. Never taking it as deep or hard as he wanted.

When they broke apart, he groaned in frustration. "Rachel, stop messing around and let me off the leash. Let me please you. Let me drive you wild. I want to. Can't you feel how much I want to?"

She nuzzled his throat. "Mmm, I don't believe I have felt how much you want me," the temptress said as her hand slid down his stomach.

"You're putting a lot of faith in my self-control if you touch me there. You sure about this?" Damn it, he wasn't sure he could keep his hands to himself if she kept moving lower.

Her head went back, and her eyes captured his. She stared into them for an eternity, her hand poised at the waistband of his shorts. "Yes," she said at last. "I'm sure. You'll keep your promise."

As her quiet belief in him disarmed him, his head fell forward and his eyes squeezed shut. Silently, Harvard cursed out his need to be honorable while his heart swelled at her faith in him. Her trust. There was only one thing he wanted more—her heart.

"Do your worst." He braced for her touch, knowing it would be sweet agony.

~

HE WAS SO BEAUTIFUL IN HIS RUGGED MALENESS, STANDING there, straining his control for her. Had anyone ever given her that much of themselves? She couldn't remember if they had.

As her hand drifted under his shorts, moving south, feeling her way, Rachel studied his face. Eyes scrunched shut, jaw clenched. He was a leashed lion. And in that moment, he was hers.

Her fingers brushed against the coarse hair of his groin until they reached the base of his firm length. She hesitated to go further. She hadn't lied to him about getting over the assault and having no anxiety about sex. What she'd neglected to mention was that she hadn't slept with anyone since it'd happened. Because to have sex meant to be vulnerable, and she hadn't trusted any man enough to allow herself to feel desire.

Until now.

Until Harvard.

Her heart raced, and her breathing grew shallow. As a glorious lightness invaded her mind, she felt like she was floating in a vat of champagne bubbles. Her skin was almost oversensitive, making her aware of every single place her body touched Harvard.

No, not Harvard. That didn't feel right. Not now.

"Can I call you Michael?" she whispered, feeling a little foolish at the request.

His eyes snapped open, and she feared he read far more in her gaze than she'd intended to share. Slowly, he nodded. "I'd like that."

It was suddenly impossible to breathe. Keeping her eyes locked on his, she wrapped her hand around his thickness. His hold on her waist tightened for a second, his eyes turning black with unspoken need.

"Rachel." His voice was a hoarse whisper.

Taking her time, she slid her hand along his length, feeling the softness and solidity of him. Learning him, she listened to his breathing speed up and watched a vein at the base of his throat throb along to the tempo of his heart.

Having all that strength at her mercy was a heady experience. And she needed more. She wanted *all* of him. Not just the part he'd tethered for her enjoyment.

"Michael," she whispered.

His eyes opened gradually, as though the eyelids were too heavy.

"I'm letting you loose," she said, feeling a wave of anticipation at the words.

And, of course, he didn't think about himself. Instead of rushing at her, he said, "Are you sure?"

Rachel's fist squeezed his hard length, making him groan. "Yes."

He moved so fast that her breath caught in her throat. One second, she was in the water, and the next, she was sitting on the edge of the pool with Harvard standing between her legs on the ledge.

A desperate hunger emanated from him. "If you want to stop, we stop. Just say the word."

It was clear that he didn't intend to do anything else until she gave her answer. "Okay," she said, her stomach doing somersaults. She felt as if she were suspended on the edge of a precipice, waiting to see what happened next.

She didn't have to wait long. His hand clasped her nape as his mouth descended on hers. The kiss robbed her of what little reason she had left. All that remained was the ability to feel, to revel in the sensation. She swam in it, her skin electrified by his touch as he stole the air from her lungs with his lips. Their kiss was endless, sending her spiraling into a free fall of pure sensual delight.

When he leaned away from her, she swayed after him. A large hand pressed gently against her breastbone.

"Lean back," he said softly. "Prop yourself up on your hands."

She did so without hesitation, feeling the cool tiles surrounding the pool beneath her palms. Harvard leaned into her, his hands at the small of her back, supporting her as he trailed kisses down her throat.

"Yes," she panted. "Do more of that."

She felt the smile against her before he resumed kissing, down her throat, over her collarbone, to the curve of her breasts.

"I'm sorry," he muttered before clasping two handfuls of her camisole and ripping it down the middle. The silk was no match for his strength. "I'll replace it."

"You'd better," she said breathlessly as she watched his head lower to her exposed breast.

His eyelashes lifted, and his eyes captured hers just before his mouth covered her nipple. With a gasp, Rachel's head fell back. The pull against her breast as he sucked the sensitive little bud was a fiery torture.

"More," she demanded.

His tongue played with the firm nub, eliciting a groan. The sound echoed through the pool room, bouncing off tiles and water, and returning to stroke over her skin. Yet another sensation to drive her wild.

One large hand kneaded her other breast while his sinful mouth drove her to distraction. Rachel locked her elbows. It was the only way she could stay upright. The hand in the small of her back tugged her nearer, and she willingly arched her body closer to him.

The room spun. She was delirious. And wanting.

"Michael," she pleaded, unsure whether she'd said the words aloud, or if they were just in her head. "I need you."

His tongue swiped over her nipple. "I don't have any protection here. Didn't think I'd need it for a swim."

She noted the humor in his voice, and it made her smile. Okay, he was probably more than a little funny. But she was too needy to appreciate it. "I'm protected."

He let out a long moan, his forehead falling to her breastbone, where it was cradled by her breasts. "I'm clean. I promise."

"I believe you. Now, can we get on with it?" And yes, she sounded a little snippy. But she was losing the buzz from his touch, and reality was creeping back in. Rachel didn't want reality. She wanted to soar.

"This is a matching set, right?" he said, before his hands fisted in her boy shorts and ripped them in two. "Better keep them matching," he muttered as he tore them from her body.

There was something deliciously caveman about his actions. "Michael, hurry up."

A hand at the back of her head straightened her until she was staring into his exasperated eyes. "It's a good thing I like bossy women." And then he was kissing her again.

Rachel wrapped her arms and legs around him, feeling his hot length against her sensitive core and wondering when he'd gotten rid of his shorts. Hands grasped her behind and scooted her even closer to the edge of the pool, and she'd never been more grateful for that raised ledge because it allowed him to achieve the perfect position. A hand slid between them, trailing through her own particular wetness, making her gasp. Then he was guiding himself inside her.

Bliss.

Perfection.

His width stretched and filled her. But the feeling wasn't just physical. She was sure he'd also seeped into her soul. Warming the cold places. Soothing the anger that always seemed present.

His lips took hers in a rapturous assault. The room was spinning, and he was her anchor. She tightened her legs around him and again felt his hand between her breasts.

"Lean back," came the rasped order.

Her arms refused to hold her, and she fell to her elbows, vaguely aware Harvard was holding her weight so that she didn't hurt herself. Her head fell back and her eyes closed, her focus on the feeling of him moving inside her.

She felt his mouth on her breast, nipping, licking, sucking. It was all too much.

"You can handle it," he said before resuming his glorious possession.

A hand splayed low on her body, his thumb angled over her clit. A long moan escaped as he gently strummed that bundle of nerves while moving inside her and teasing her breasts.

It was like nothing she'd ever felt. This was no fumble in the dark as she'd experienced as a teen. And far removed from the empty encounters she'd attempted as an adult but had been unable go through with. This was something else. Something much more. Playing her body like a virtuoso, he was taking her over. Speaking to her with his touch.

Making love.

And she felt the chains around her heart loosen. Then one by one, they broke and fell away until all but a few were gone. She'd never survive this. He was changing her, inside and out. And she wasn't sure if she was desperate for it or terrified.

The tension in her body grew, building to a crescendo, taking her higher and higher until she rode atop a wave of such vast proportions that it almost overwhelmed her. Secure in his arms. In his touch. In his care.

"Give it to me, Rachel," he growled the words.

His thumb pressed on her clit. His length surged inside of her. And the wave broke with her cry, "Michael."

Strong arms enfolded her as she floated away.

In the back of her mind, a breath of a voice whispered, *So this is love*. And then it was gone, as though it'd never been there to begin with.

Chapter Seventeen

By the time they reached the TayFor offices, Rachel was back to acting like she hardly knew Harvard. Which wasn't a surprise. Retreating behind a wall of ice was how she coped with change. All he could do was wait her out. Just as well he had an abundance of patience.

"I'll be in the security room looking at footage with Ryan if you need me," he told her once he was sure her office was secure and there were no more nasty photos waiting for her.

"I won't need you." She turned her attention to the open laptop in front of her, dismissing him.

With an amused shake of his head, Harvard closed the door on her. "Got anything for me?" he asked Elle, who was busy at her desk.

"You mean apart from being glad the bet's off?" She pointed at his throat. "That hickey would have cost me fifty pounds."

He wasn't embarrassed. "A hickey isn't evidence of sex."

"It is with Rachel. That wouldn't be there unless she'd decided to let you have access. Trust me, I know the woman. It's all or nothing with her."

He hoped so, because he wanted everything. "What've you got from the photos so far?"

Blue hair bobbed as she let out an exasperated sigh. "Nothing. No prints, no DNA that's of any use. I'm running them through a digital analysis program. The computer might find something in the images that we can't see. But I have to be honest; I'm not holding out a helluva lot of hope. Which pisses me off no end. These guys shouldn't be able to get away with this."

"They won't." He had to believe that as long as the blackmailer was communicating with them, they'd leave some clue as to who they were dealing with. Everybody slipped up at some point. It was just a matter of patience.

For years, his friends had joked about his endless patience. Between Rachel and these investigations, they were about to find out just how much he had to go around.

"Harry called me at the crack of dawn, so I stopped off at the shop on my way to work and got you this." Elle handed him a bag with a sportswear logo. "It's a protective cup—I had to guess your size." She grinned. "If you wear it all the time, it should offer some defense against Rachel when she finds out you involved Harry. Of course, it won't save you from her putting your balls in a vise while you sleep."

"Thanks for the nightmares."

"Just calling it how I see it."

Harvard handed back the bag. "As much as I appreciate you thinking of me, I don't want to go walking through the building with it."

She patted the bag before stuffing it in her desk drawer. "It's here when you need it. Which should be very soon. Because Harry's on his way."

"When's he due to arrive?"

"Around lunchtime. I've set up his cover as working with the company that installed the server. He's coming in under the pretense of doing some routine maintenance." She frowned. "I haven't clued in the head of security about his arrival. Terrance thinks this is a legitimate job."

Harvard focused in on her, reading the non-verbal clues, just as he'd been trained. Weighing them with her words to get the whole story. "Is there a reason you're keeping him in the dark?"

A gentle pink stain covered her cheeks. "I don't like him."

And from the looks of things, it was way more than simple dislike. Elle was suspicious of the man; she just didn't know why, and that meant she couldn't put it into words. It was instinct. One she obviously wasn't used to listening to. But Harvard had learned never to underestimate his own instincts or those of the people around him.

"He doesn't need to know," he assured her. "The investigation into Rachel's past has nothing to do with the job he's been briefed on. It's a good idea to keep it that way."

Her shoulders slumped a fraction, signaling relief. "Do you want me to come down to security with you to look over the footage from outside West Building?"

"Not right now. Ryan and I can narrow it down. We'll call you in when we find something." He grinned at her. "Then you can do your magic and clean up the images enough to, hopefully, get us something to go on. Sooner we close this investigation, sooner we can focus on more important stuff."

"Like wooing Rachel?" She waggled her eyebrows at Harvard.

"Yeah, and eliminating the threat to her."

Elle nodded solemnly. "That too."

Glancing back at Rachel's door, he lowered his voice. "Keep an eye on her. Don't let her out of your sight. I don't like that someone was able to get close enough to slip a photo into her handbag. If she goes to the restroom, you follow. If she bitches—and she will—tell her it's the team leader's orders."

"If I tell her that, you can *definitely* kiss goodbye to a repeat of whatever you did to get that hickey. Just saying."

"Don't worry about me. I can handle Rachel."

Elle snorted. "Famous last words, huh?" she said to his back as he let himself out of her office.

After taking the elevator down to the basement, he walked along a plain gray corridor and let himself into the security hub, using his pass. One that Ryan had helpfully coded for full access to all areas of TayFor.

The security hub sat opposite the IT department, and both were overseen by the head of security, Terrance King, a man who'd been with TayFor since leaving the police force over a decade earlier. Security and IT were definitely King's domain, and he never let anyone forget it. Which was one of the reasons Harvard had come looking for the man.

He was easy to find, standing right in the middle of the surveillance room, watching the wall of screens over the shoulders of his staff who were tasked with monitoring them. And neither staff member looked relaxed about having their boss at their backs.

Although the former police officer was in his fifties, Terrance kept himself in shape through daily workouts. His hair was graying at the temples, which Harvard suspected he liked, as it gave him an air of respectability that only came with age. He was a generically handsome man, kind of like a grandfather version of Ken Doll.

Glancing over his shoulder at Harvard, he frowned. "You could have given me a heads-up about raiding the security's footage."

The two security guards instantly perked up as they blatantly eavesdropped. Something they couldn't help but do when Terrance stood right behind them. It was sloppy professionalism on his part, which made Harvard think Ryan was right—the man's ego was getting in the way of his better judgment *and* their operation.

"How about we take this into your office," Harvard said coldly. It was an order, and everyone in the room knew it.

The two guards instantly became very focused on their task in an obvious attempt to fly under their boss's radar. Interesting. Looked like Terrance was the kind of manager who took out his frustrations on his people.

"Get back to work," Terrance snapped at them, even though it was clear they were working.

It was on the tip of Harvard's tongue to tell the man to stop being an asshole. But he wasn't there to educate Terrance on how to lead a team. He was there to get his own job done. And if that meant stepping all over Terrance's ego to achieve what he needed, then he could live with that.

Terrance straightened his back and gestured toward his office. "If you'll follow me. I've been meaning to talk to you about several issues that have arisen around Ms. Ford-Talbot's protection."

Harvard didn't bother to pull him up for pretending the meeting was his idea. He'd let the guy give the impression he was about to chew Harvard out over something that had put his nose out of joint—this time. But he could have told him that you didn't earn the respect of your team by puffing out your chest and pissing in corners to mark your territory.

"What the hell?" Terrance snapped as he closed the door behind them.

He stalked around his vast mahogany desk, which wouldn't have looked out of place in the CEO's office, and sat in his leather office chair. It was an interesting setup for head of security and fit in perfectly with his tailored suit and polished shoes. The man had ambition, a taste for the good things in life, and an overly developed sense of his own worth.

Terrance pointed at Harvard. "You are only here with my cooperation, which means you don't get to come into the office before work to download security footage without *my* permission. The CEO will hear about this. Benson Security has overstepped the line, and it's time for you to go."

If Terrance had hoped to intimidate with his threats, he'd picked the wrong guy. "Funny thing, I came in here to talk to *you* about lines." Standing on the other side of the desk, Harvard casually picked up a glass paperweight and studied it. "This is your only warning. Don't risk my team by exposing their covers. Don't interfere with our investigation. Keep your opinions to yourself and bend over backward to be helpful, or…"

"Or what?" His lip curled into a sneer.

The glass paperweight seemed a strange choice for a man like Terrance, because tucked inside the heavy orb was the three-dimensional rendering of a flower. Harvard cocked his head. It looked like purple heather, but not quite. Patchouli, that's what it was. He turned it over and read the inscription on the base: *Welcome to TayFor.* He returned it to the desk.

Harvard unbuttoned his suit jacket and thrust his hands into his pants' pockets as he sauntered over to look at the photos on the wall. It was a gallery dedicated to Terrance's ego. Photo after photo showed him standing beside somebody famous. It was clear that working for TayFor afforded the man many perks that other jobs couldn't. Access to the elite definitely being one of them.

"You spent a few years in the army before you joined the police force," Harvard said conversationally, his attention on the photos.

"What the hell has that got to do with anything?" Terrance snapped.

"Just making conversation. I was never in the armed forces." He turned to look at Terrance. "Not officially anyway.

Did a couple of operations when I was with the CIA that blurred the lines though." He sauntered to the door. "Did you serve in a hot zone? No? Shame. It forces teammates to bond in a way that's stronger than family. You come out of it knowing you have brothers at your back. It's a good feeling."

"Unless you have a point to make, get the hell out of my office."

Harvard inclined his head. "Officially, having already served your country, you're eligible for recall if your government deems it necessary. Now, it just so happens that one of the men I consider a brother is pretty high up in your military. Not so long ago, he was saying he needed men with experience for tours in Afghanistan. Men with some life under their belts, who wouldn't go off half-cocked and get their fellow soldiers killed. Men like you."

Terrance leaned back in his seat, trying to appear relaxed, which he might have pulled off if his jaw hadn't been clenched so tight. "You think you can have me recalled and sent to Afghanistan?" he mocked.

"No." Harvard flashed a friendly smile as he opened the door. "I know I can." With that, he walked out, closing it quietly behind him.

The two guards manning the desk shot him curious but wary looks. Harvard nodded to them. "Doing a good job there," he said. "Staring at screens all day long isn't easy. Has your chief got you swapping out every few hours?"

They shared a look before the man nearest to him spoke. "Uh, no. We work on a weekly rotation. Night shift for a week. Patrol, front desk, security checkpoints. That sort of thing. Each one lasts a week, sometimes more. Depending on who's on."

"Or who doesn't turn up," the other guy said.

"Well," Harvard said pleasantly, wondering how Terrance had managed to get this job when it was clear he had no idea how to do it, "that's another option." Not one he'd use, but this wasn't his circus, and they weren't his monkeys. "You know where Ryan is?"

"Sure," the first guy said. "Conference room. Down the corridor, third door on the left."

"Thanks." He squashed the urge to give them tips on staying vigilant and keeping track of details while they were on desk duty. If Rachel were there, she'd have smacked him upside the head and asked what the hell was he thinking taking on more work when he had enough of his own.

Thoughts of Rachel filled his chest with warmth and his head with images that were pure distraction. He took out his phone and dialed her number.

"What?" she barked when she picked up.

"You okay?" he asked as he thumped on the locked door to the conference room.

Ryan threw it open and motioned him inside.

"Of course I'm okay," Rachel snapped. "What do you want?"

His eyes took in the multiple stills from different cameras that Ryan had up on the projection board. "Nothing. I just missed you."

She hung up, making him grin before he focused on the screen. "Looks like our Samantha was texting on her way into the building."

"Yep. Not only that, but we also have Charles shouting at someone on his phone just under Rachel's mum's window." The screen changed, and sure enough, there was Mr. Racism himself, cheeks ruddy and spittle flying as he screeched into his phone.

"What's that?" Harvard pointed to the blank space opposite Charles. "Are those shoes?"

Ryan zoomed in on the bottom left-hand corner, and sure enough, there were the toes of a pair of men's dress shoes peeking out from one of the side doorways. The doorway was locked, but it would be a good place to shelter for a moment, out of sight of the cameras.

"We got a visual on that door?"

Ryan tapped at his keyboard. "No camera." He frowned at Harvard. "Why would they leave a gaping security hole like that? Far as I can see, the door's locked and alarmed, but there's no camera on it."

"Why indeed," Harvard mused as the hairs on his arms became electrified. "Do you recognize those shoes?"

Ryan looked at him like he was nuts. "Do I come across as somebody who notices other men's shoes?"

No, he didn't. But Harvard would bet if the man had a sandwich in his hand, Ryan could describe the filling. "Go back ten minutes, see if we can get a shot of whoever that is before they hid in the doorway."

As they spooled through the footage, Harvard felt that familiar knot in his stomach that told him he was missing something. And he hated to miss details. Suddenly, one of the camera feeds from outside West Building turned to static before coming back on, then going off again. It cut in and out for about fifteen minutes.

"Signal jammer?" Ryan said. "Pointed at the camera covering the door?"

"While Charles was walking and waving his arms around? That would be hard to maintain and obvious to anyone watching. Can you go check the camera?"

Ryan was out of his seat and heading for the door as Harvard dialed Rachel again.

"Stop. Calling. Me," she said. "It's clingy and annoying."

That was his girl, always making him feel wanted. "I need you and Elle down in the security department conference room."

"Well, why didn't you say so?" was her irritated reply before she cut the call.

With a smile and a shake of his head, Harvard turned his attention to the image showing the man's shoes. Where had he seen them before?

Chapter Eighteen

"Seriously?" Rachel said to Harvard as he pointed at the screen in the utility closet that security called a conference room. "You brought me all the way down here to identify shoes?"

The infuriating man just folded his arms and stood there, staring at her.

"Fine," she huffed. "They're Gucci Horsebit loafers. I can't tell the color because..." She waved a hand at the black and white images. "I can tell you that they're regular calf leather and not crocodile skin."

His smile was slow and far too sexy for the workplace. Rachel glanced at Elle to see if she'd noticed, but her attention was on her laptop—as usual.

"You have a family member who's partial to those shoes?" Harvard asked.

Rachel couldn't help but roll her eyes. "Um, all of them? Those Gucci shoes are a wardrobe staple. I can't think of one man in my family who doesn't own a pair. They've sold like hotcakes ever since John F. Kennedy wore them, and they've been one of Gucci's flagship designs since they first released them in the fifties. And, of course, the horsebit name is a nod to their history of making saddles."

"Of course." Elle snorted. "How do you know this stuff?"

"Doesn't everyone know about Gucci?"

"No, Rachel." Elle gave her a look that said she clearly despaired of her. "Not everyone has Gucci's history memorized."

Rachel shrugged. "Whatever. Now, is someone going to tell me what you found?" She glanced around. "Where is Ryan?"

"Right here." He walked into the room holding a ziplock plastic bag with a tiny black box inside. He flashed Rachel a grin. "Did you miss me?"

"Why is everybody asking me that today? I don't miss any of you when you're gone. Usually, I'm just thankful."

"You wound me." Ryan handed the bag to Harvard. "Found that attached to the camera. It's a basic jammer with a receiver. Set it up with your mobile phone, and you can use an app to switch it on and off. You can buy them every-where." He sneered at the box. "It's like our thief went into Currys and loaded up on over-the-counter tech. This is bargain-basement stuff. I can't believe they got away with stealing for this long."

"I know, right?" Elle said with equal disgust. "That's exactly how I felt when I found that low-tech piece of rubbish glued under Francesca's desk. It's insulting. Couldn't they have put a bit of effort into their illegal activities?"

Rachel caught the confused expression on Harvard's face. "What is it?" she asked.

"Currys?" he said.

"Britain's Radio Shack."

"Gotcha."

"Did you see that?" Ryan said to Elle. "They're totally sleeping together."

"And the bet is off. Remember that. I don't owe anybody any money because the bet is off."

Ryan hung his head. "I could have been rich."

"Dear, sweet, man-child," Rachel said. "A few thousand pounds isn't rich."

"No," Ryan said. "But then, it's all relative isn't it? Not everybody has your millions. What does it feel like? Being rich. Just for a second, let me live vicariously through you. Describe it to me."

"Being rich means never having to put up with idiots, unless you choose to," Rachel said. "You can either pay them to go away or remove yourself to an island."

Ryan nodded in all seriousness. "I need to get rich."

"Okay," Elle said. "I can't clean up the images any more than we have. You need to talk to the head of security, Rachel. TayFor needs better quality cameras with a higher resolution if they want to do the job properly."

"I'm sorry." Rachel flattened a hand to her chest as though shocked. "Did you forget I don't actually work here?"

"Wow." The blue-haired wonder narrowed her eyes. "Sex makes you meaner."

"Maybe Harvard isn't doing it right." Ryan turned to him. "If you want any pointers, shout out. I've got your back."

"As much as I appreciate the offer, I think I'm okay." Harvard grinned.

"Hear that?" Ryan mumbled to Elle. "He's *okay*."

"Children," Rachel snapped. "Focus. What do we have?"

"Three suspects." Harvard turned deadly serious. "Samantha, Charles, and whoever's wearing the Gucci shoes."

"So, we have nothing." Rachel folded her arms over the blood-red pantsuit she'd donned for the day. She'd styled it with her standard black pumps and a killer black leather belt to cinch in the waist. It was her "don't piss me off" outfit, and it matched her manicure perfectly.

"No, we've got a lot more than that." Harvard ran a hand over his smooth bald head, making her wonder what he'd look like if he didn't shave. She shook off the thought, reminding herself that she didn't care. He'd be out of her life soon. And that's exactly what she wanted. Mostly...

"We know," he continued, "that someone's phone is connected to the memory card reader in your mom's office, and also to the signal jammer on the camera. All we need is to check everybody's phone and see which one it is."

Rachel pulled out a chair and plopped into it. She folded her legs and swung her foot. "You might as well ask people for their firstborn. No one is going to hand over their phone for inspection."

"They don't need to," Ryan said. "They just need to leave them at security in a building that doesn't allow them inside. Then I can check them."

"And how do we do that?" Rachel said. "If I have a meeting in another building, I lock my phone in my desk drawer. I don't take it to the building because I know it will end up sitting in security, being stroked by someone's grubby fingers." Three sets of identically incredulous eyes stared back at her. "Don't try to tell me it doesn't happen," she said.

Ryan started to say something but shook his head. "To hell with it. I give up; she's your problem now, Harvard. Good luck."

"I'm not anyone's problem," Rachel told the man-child.

"So," Elle said, "is there no way we can get everyone to bring their phones to one of the secure buildings?"

"What if we told them that all phones need to be handed in and scanned as a security measure?" Ryan mused.

"Won't work," Elle replied. "If I got a heads-up, I'd wipe my phone before I came to work. Or bring in a backup to hand in instead."

"Then how the hell do we get hold of their phones?" Ryan was beginning to lose patience.

Harvard and Rachel shared a look and, for a second, it felt like they were tuned in to the same wavelength. It was almost as though she could hear his thoughts.

Breaking eye contact, he said, "There's a board meeting on Monday." And it felt strangely right that he should speak for both of them, because it almost felt like they'd had the discussion and come to an agreement.

Honestly, her life was becoming stranger by the day.

Rachel continued where he left off, "We can stop everyone on the way into the building. We'll tell them there's been a security breach, and phones have to be left at the desk until we get on top of it."

Harvard nodded. "We keep it under wraps and spring it on them when they come in. That way, nobody has time to swap out or wipe their phones. In the meantime, I'll call headquarters and see if they have some free bodies we can use to watch Samantha, Charles, and our Gucci-loafer-wearing suspects—Preston, Marcus, and Rupert."

"You want them *all* watched?" Ryan looked at Rachel. "Will TayFor pay for another five team members?"

"Yes." If they argued about it, she'd personally make her father and brother suffer for the rest of their natural lives. She needed this investigation over. She needed to get back to her life. And woe betide anyone who was a stumbling block to that plan.

"Okay." Harvard turned to her. "Want to get some lunch?"

Before she could answer, Elle shouted, "No!"

When Rachel looked at her, Elle flushed as her eyes went suspiciously wide. "I mean, it's too early for lunch. We need to go over this footage a little more anyway. See if there's anything we missed." She was making bug eyes at Harvard now, as though trying to get him to read her mind.

Rachel considered them both and spotted the second Harvard realized what Elle was trying to tell him. "Yeah, you're right. Lunch can wait. Bring up that footage of the shoes again."

Honestly, they must think she'd been born yesterday. "Have fun." She stood and headed for the door. "I'm finished here."

"No." Elle shot to her feet. "We need you."

Rachel sighed. "Please, for the love of Yves Saint Laurent, never ever try to bluff anyone for money." With that, she threw open the door, took two steps into the corridor, and ran straight into Harry Boyle.

"Hey, Rach," he said with a sheepish smile. "How've you been?"

And at that point, her head spun and her eyes shot bolts of lightning as she shouted, "Harvard."

"I tried to warn you," Elle hissed as Harvard strode across the conference room. "Didn't I tell you he was arriving now? The IT department's right across the hall. All you had to do was keep her in here for five more minutes." She folded her arms and glared at him. "You can deal with the fallout on your own."

Ryan sat back in his chair and put his feet up on the conference table. "I propose a new bet. Five hundred pounds says Harvard's back in his own bed tonight and Rachel announces the engagement is off."

"Twenty-five on him sporting a black eye when we see him next," Elle said.

"There's nothing quite like your team having your back," Harvard muttered as he passed them and strode out into the hall. He hooked a hand each through Rachel's and Harry's arms and dragged them back inside the conference room. Once he'd locked the door behind them, he asked, "What part of *undercover* do you people not get?"

Rachel narrowed her eyes at him. "The part where you're partnered with a backstabbing, interfering Neanderthal of a man who should have minded his own business."

Harry, who turned out to be about six foot of lean muscle and overgrown sandy brown hair, held up his hands in an effort to appease her. "Don't be mad with the Yank. This was my idea. I didn't give him a choice."

"Ha!" She threw up her hands in disgust. "*You* forced *him?*"

Harry looked Harvard up and down, taking in his size and bulk. "It happened over the phone. It was more of a mental challenge than a physical one." He stuck out a hand at Harvard. "Good to meet you in person. You look like Grunt. Only black. And you talk way more."

It was like meeting a puppy. A genius puppy who could hold a conversation, albeit a bizarre one. "Grunt and I aren't related." He kept his tone deadly serious so that Harry wouldn't know if he was joking or not.

"Are you sure?" Harry said. "I read an article once about a set of twins who were born with different skin tones. One black, one white. It was fascinating."

Ryan groaned as Elle smothered a giggle.

"I'm sure," Harvard said.

Rachel stepped forward and poked a finger into Harry's chest. "Will you pretend to be normal for five seconds? What are you doing here?"

Harry blinked a couple of times, as though it took great effort to stop hypothesizing what a reality would look like where Harvard and his taciturn behemoth of a friend were twins. "I came to find your rapists."

The air became so thick that Ryan choked a little.

"And how do you plan to do that?" Rachel's voice was pure ice.

"Um." Harry split a nervous look between Rachel and Harvard. "I thought I'd hack the server they use to store historical data to see if it gave me any clues as to who stole the drug they used on you. Then I thought Harvard could, I don't know"—he shrugged—"torture the person to find out who else was involved. To be honest, I didn't really think past the hacking part."

With a look of pure naivety, he asked Harvard, "You learned torture and interrogation techniques in the CIA, right? Or do we need to call in Grunt? He scares the crap out of people just by being in the same room." He snapped his fingers. "That's what's different about you! You're way friendlier than Grunt."

"Yeah," Ryan drawled. "*That's* the difference."

"I am surrounded by imbeciles," Rachel said of an MIT graduate, a tech billionaire and sought-after hacker—and whatever the hell Ryan was. "Go back to Scotland, Harry." She sounded suddenly weary. "We can handle this, and you can't leave your wife alone for long, or she might bite someone. And rabies is a death sentence."

Harry grinned. "Magenta says hi too." He turned somber. "I can't let you do this alone, Rach. You didn't abandon me when I was a scared kid in uni. If you hadn't taken me under your wing, I would have dropped out and moved into my parents' basement forever."

"I didn't take you under my wing," she snapped. "Do I look like a mother hen? I simply organized you. Goodness knows you needed it." She glared at his hair. "You still do. Doesn't Magenta care that you're going around looking like that?"

"What? I'm growing it long so I can wear a leather queue."

"A queue?" Ryan said.

"It's what guys call a hair tie, so it sounds manly," Elle said.

And yet again, Harvard felt like he was Arnie in *Kindergarten Cop*. "We about done here? Because, in case you guys forgot, we have two cases we need to get sorted. And time's a-wastin'."

"You don't have two cases," Rachel said. "You have one." If looks could melt your face off, his would be gone.

"Rachel," Harry said, "if you let me do this for you, I'll make Magenta name our first child after you."

"I need popcorn for this," Ryan muttered.

For a long time, Rachel stood fuming at him, and then she pointed at Harry's chest. "I don't want a baby named after me. But I do want Magenta to swear that she'll be nothing but sweet and delightful every time we meet." Her eyes narrowed. "No matter what I say or do."

Harry ran a hand through his hair, making it look even worse. "I don't know if I can pull that off. She kind of hates you."

That revelation was stated in such a matter-of-fact voice that it took a minute for it to register with Harvard, who then barked out a laugh. Which earned him a smack to his chest from Rachel.

"Give me your word that you'll make this happen, or you can go home right now," she told Harry.

"Fine." He sighed. "But this sucks."

"Whatever." She waved a hand toward the door. "You may hack to your heart's content."

"Thanks!" Harry wrapped Rachel in a hug, and she patted his back like she didn't quite understand how touching worked.

"Okay," Harry said when he was done. "I'd better get going. It'll take a while to go through all this stuff, so I'll call when I'm done." And with a cheery wave, he disappeared through the door.

"Do you think he realizes that he just promised a debt in order to do *you* a favor?" Elle asked, sounding bewildered.

"I don't think Harry knows what day it is, let alone what just happened," Ryan said.

"I'm going to my office." Rachel swept past them. "Please don't follow. I've had enough of you all." And then she was gone too.

Ryan let out a long sigh. "I am the only normal one here," he said.

Chapter Nineteen

After a long, annoying day, full of people that irritated her, all Rachel wanted to do was go home. But Harvard had other ideas.

"We've got to eat," he said as he drove them toward Soho instead of Kensington.

"That's what ordering in is for."

"This place doesn't do takeout."

"Well, order from somewhere that does."

He ignored her. "Can you walk in those shoes?"

"Do these look like walking shoes to you?" They were four-inch pumps, and yes, she could wear them all day, but not if she had to walk a marathon through London's streets.

"I'll try to park as close as I can then."

"Good luck with that," she scoffed. Even on a Thursday night, Soho would be packed.

Of course, he found a spot not two doors down from the restaurant he insisted on eating at. Typical.

He jumped out, rounded the car and opened the door for her. "Let's go," he said. "I'm starving."

With a sigh, she climbed out of the car. Honestly, there

wasn't a whole lot she could do other than comply. Her usual tactics for getting people to keep their distance didn't seem to work with Harvard. She'd yet to figure out what did.

As they walked to the restaurant, he took her hand.

Rachel tried to tug free of his hold, but it was useless. "There's no one around," she told him. "We don't have to pretend we're in a relationship."

"Rachel," he drawled, "I've told you a good spy never breaks cover."

It was completely maddening that he had an answer for everything.

The tapas bar had barely any frontage and a sign that needed a good repaint. It wasn't reassuring.

"There's more space in back," Harvard said as though that would ease her mind.

He placed a hand on the small of her back and led her through the open door. The décor was "explosion of color", with a variety of bright tablecloths on different-sized and - shaped tables, small vases of flowers sitting on each one, and mix 'n' match paintings depicting all things Spanish crowding the walls. The chairs, floor, and table legs were all the same dark wood. Which just made Rachel think how easy it would be to hide stains.

She shuddered. If she touched anything sticky, she was going straight home. "Do you deliberately hunt down all the places in London that decorate by throwing everything they have at the room?"

"No, but now that I think about it, maybe I should."

A cheery blonde waitress with a Polish accent led them to a table right at the back of the room, where the space widened out to three times the size of the frontage. Their table had a bright blue cloth, yellow flowers and, thankfully, no sticky residue anywhere.

"How about we do one of everything?" Harvard asked her as the waitress offered them the laminated menus.

If it meant she didn't have to touch those, she'd agree to anything. "That's fine with me. And wine. Dear Gucci, I need wine. A bottle. Sealed." She didn't trust anything that came in a glass. Who knows what they were serving and calling a decent vintage. Actually...

She glanced at the drinks menu, which sat propped up against the flowers. It was worse than she thought. The wine only came in *red* or *white*.

"Forget the wine," she said. "I'll take a bottle of beer. Something light. And please open it at the table." To her credit, the waitress didn't so much as blink an eye at Rachel's instructions.

After the waitress disappeared, Rachel watched Harvard shrug out of his jacket and hang it over the back of the chair beside him. With a sigh, Rachel placed her handbag on the seat next to her and did the same with her jacket.

"Just once," she said, "could we eat somewhere that's regularly inspected by the health department?"

He threw back his head, laughing deep and long. Rachel glanced at some of the nearby diners, who were smiling at him. Noticing one or two of the women had speculation in their eyes, she glared at them. It had nothing to do with her pretending to be his fiancée; it was just plain rude to size up another woman's dinner date.

Of course, Harvard caught her actions. "Getting a bit possessive?"

"Don't be ridiculous. Why would I be possessive? Because we had sex?" She made a little scoffing sound. "I don't know you well enough to want to keep you."

"You could. Know me, that is." He spread his arms wide, making his shirt tighten at his shoulders. "I'm an open book. Ask me anything. I dare you."

She couldn't help but roll her eyes. "I'd have to be interested to ask."

He leaned forward and clasped his hands on the table, his eyes pinning hers. "Aren't you even a little bit curious?"

"No."

"Liar."

He was bloody well amused again. "Fine. Tell me about being a spy—if that's what you really did. Tell me something you've never told anyone. And make me believe it."

"You think I'd lie to you." His eyebrows shot up.

Rachel let out an exasperated breath. "Actually, I don't think you'd lie to me. I'm fairly certain you'd just skirt any topic you didn't want to discuss."

Her answer seemed to please him. "For your information, I was definitely a spy. Not a desk-jockey analyst. Although I started out doing quite a bit of that." His smile was self-deprecating. "It came with my area of expertise—data mining, pattern analysis, statistics, that sort of thing. But I also have other skills." He winked at her, and she felt heat travel through her body.

Damn cocky man.

"What other skills?"

"Languages, the ability to make friends and win confidences, staying calm when other people are stressed, and hand-to-hand combat training." He shrugged as though it was all nothing. "I was kinda born to be a spy."

Against her better judgment, Rachel found herself intrigued. "Did you enjoy it?"

"Sure, there were parts I enjoyed. Mainly I got a kick out of the challenge. The puzzle, the game, the adrenaline rush of trying not to get caught."

She folded her arms and rested them on the table. "Were you ever caught?"

Dark, somber eyes met hers. "Yeah."

Rachel knew other women would back off at his tone. They'd demur and tell him he didn't have to answer if he didn't want to. She wasn't other women. The man knew practically everything there was to know about her life. As far as she was concerned, that meant share and share alike.

"What happened?" she asked, wondering if he'd tell her. Wondering what it meant if he did.

"I spent three days being interrogated by Al-Qaeda extremists in northern Africa."

He seemed perfectly relaxed, calm, no tension at all. But somehow, Rachel knew he didn't mean a few questions in a back-country jail.

"Did they hurt you?" She couldn't bring herself to say torture, but that's precisely what she meant.

"Yeah." His smile was rueful. "And now you know something that no one outside of the US government knows about me."

Rachel pretended she didn't notice that her arms had unfolded and her hand had sneaked across the table to cover his. "And I bet you were far too stubborn to tell them what they wanted to know so they'd let you go. Honestly, that stubborn streak of yours is a danger to you *and* everyone around you. I should know."

The corners of his mouth quirked as his hand turned over to clasp hers and, again, she pretended it wasn't happening. Because Rachel Ford-Talbot did *not* hold hands in public. Especially with a *fake* fiancé.

"Next time, I'll seriously consider just giving in and spilling the goods," he said. "Although Al-Qaeda isn't known for setting prisoners free if they cooperate. Just sayin'."

"Well, how would you know if you didn't even try?" Her hand flexed in his, squeezing tightly for a second. "We'll never know the answer to that anyway, will we? Because you aren't a spy anymore?" Had that last part come out as a question? No.

It was just her mind playing tricks. She didn't care if he still worked for the US government.

"No." His voice softened as though reassuring her, which was just silly. "No, I'm retired from all that."

Rachel knew she should leave it there. Harvard's business was none of hers, but she couldn't help asking, "Why did you retire? Do spies age out of the CIA?"

"I got fed up being alone," he said, staring into her eyes. "It's hard to have a family when you're traveling the world, putting yourself in danger, and being forced to lie about it. Some try, but I wasn't one of them. I want honesty in my relationship. And I want to be home with the woman I love."

The room around them disappeared as Rachel fell into his gaze. Her heart raced; her mouth went dry. She wasn't sure if she wanted to run or surrender. And she wasn't sure why she felt she needed to do either.

"This is so romantic," a female voice gushed, snapping Rachel's attention back to their waitress.

She pulled her hand from Harvard's and folded her arms as she sat back in her seat. What on earth was she doing, pretending there was a relationship between them when they were purely colleagues who'd had a physical *slipup*? The man was infuriating, and she couldn't help but think he was using some tricks he'd picked up in the CIA to lull her closer to him.

Well, she was onto him. And it was stopping now.

"Sorry to interrupt," the waitress lied as she clearly showed no remorse. "I have your order."

Once the woman was gone, Rachel helped herself to some food from the assortment of tiny dishes that held everything from olives and roasted mushrooms to lamb strips and prawns.

"I'd like to be clear," she said as she dished calamari onto her plate. "As soon as we're finished here, I'm going home, and I'll be sleeping alone tonight, as usual." She took a bite of the calamari, her eyes going wide.

"Good?" Harvard asked.

It was delicious. "I'd rather have had takeaway."

Harvard just smiled.

RACHEL LASTED UNTIL ONE A.M. BEFORE SHE COULDN'T stand being alone in bed any longer. No matter how hard she tried, the images from the photos entered her mind unbidden and refused to leave. It made her furious to feel so helpless—as though her own brain was working against her.

With a growl of pure irritation, she got out of bed, donned her robe, and stalked across the hall to the guest bedroom.

When Harvard opened the door a few seconds after she'd thumped the hell out of it, she glared up at him. "Don't. Say. A. Word," she threatened before turning on her heel and stomping back to her room.

It never once occurred to her that he wouldn't follow, which was good because she didn't have a backup plan if he decided to go back to his own bed and ignore her.

She tossed her robe onto the armchair and climbed into the side of the bed farthest from the door. Harvard was already in the room, closing and locking the door behind him.

He put his phone on the bedside table and got in beside her. Lying on his back, he curled an arm around her and drew her into his side. Rachel wrapped her arm around him and threw a leg over his thick thigh as she settled her head on his shoulder.

Slowly, gently, and without saying a word, Harvard stroked the bare skin of her upper arm, and she felt herself relax. The images that had filled her mind were now gone, replaced by the all-consuming awareness of the man holding her.

This couldn't go on. She couldn't rely on him to chase away her demons forever. Could she? No. She was being stupid. It was tiredness that was making her think such foolish thoughts.

"I'm not weak." Even to her own ears, she sounded belligerent.

He kissed the top of her head. "No one would ever think that of you."

With the rippling blue light of the pool washing over them, they lapsed into a comfortable silence. Rachel's eyelids became heavier as she sank into his heat.

"I have nightmares," Harvard said softly, dragging Rachel back from the brink of sleep. "I can lash out, thinking I'm still there, in the hole they kept me in between beatings. Sometimes the dreams are about betrayal or things I've seen. There's a lot of shit in my head. Stuff people shouldn't see in several lifetimes."

Betrayed? Kept in a hole? Rachel's arm tightened around him. "You aren't weak either." It was all the comfort she knew how to give.

"No." His hand smoothed down her back and came to rest on her hip. It was a proprietary touch, but she found she didn't have it in her to object. "Still, if I start shouting or thrashing around, just wake me up, okay?"

She nodded, her cheek rubbing against his skin. "I'll look out for you."

"Thanks."

With that one word, he assured her they were in this together. Partners in dealing with the residue of their respective trauma. And Rachel didn't feel so weak anymore.

"Go to sleep," Harvard said. "We've got another long day ahead of us tomorrow."

"Please promise me one thing," Rachel murmured as her eyes closed.

"What?" His bristle-roughened jaw nuzzled her hair.

"Let me pick the restaurant tomorrow. I have a headache from the décor of that tapas place."

Listening to the deep sound of his chuckle rumble through her, she fell asleep, feeling safe and comfortable in Harvard's arms. But knowing it wouldn't last. Friday was coming. Her blackmailer's deadline loomed. And there was no way of knowing what it would bring.

Chapter Twenty

Thursday came and went with no word from Harry about what he'd found on the server, which Harvard took to mean he'd found nothing. There were no further incidents at TayFor, so it seemed the thief was either laying low or blithely carrying on with their set schedule. The Benson Security staffers they'd brought in to follow Samantha, Charles, and the Gucci loafer brigade had reported nothing out of the ordinary. They were in a holding pattern, waiting for the board meeting on Monday, when they could get their hands on everyone's phones and check for the apps used to steal from TayFor.

In the meantime, they had to get through the rest of Friday.

Harvard checked his wristwatch—half an hour until they could go home. It was thirty minutes too long. All day, the tension had built as they waited for something to happen. Waiting to see how the blackmailer would make good on their threat, as Rachel had no intention of quitting TayFor before the day ended. It had them all on edge. There was only so much time a person could spend in the brace position before they lost their minds.

As Harvard waited in Rachel's outer office for her meeting with the research division to finish up, he looked out over the grounds, studying every corner for something out of place. Anything that would give him a clue as to what was coming. But there was nothing.

He turned his back on the rain-soaked scene and leaned against the windowsill. Elle had gone home early to do some more work on the photos the blackmailer had left for Rachel. But she didn't hold out much hope of finding anything.

There were one or two leads Harvard could have chased, but he didn't want to leave Rachel's side. She was far too exposed at TayFor, and he wasn't letting her out of his sight until he knew what they were dealing with.

Her office door jerked open, and a half dozen shell-shocked and pale-faced scientists scurried out. Clearly Rachel was in full 'charm' mode.

"I've had enough." Rachel sailed out after them, handbag hanging from the crook of her arm. "I'm going home."

Harvard pushed away from the window, glancing toward the door to make sure no one was listening. "Check your bag first." He crossed the room and closed the door.

She let out a huff of air. "It hasn't been out of my sight all day." She narrowed her eyes at him. "Nor yours. Must you follow me so closely all the time?"

"Yeah. Now check the bag."

"Whatever." She smacked the bag onto Elle's desk before emptying each pocket.

Harvard watched her intently. "Wouldn't it be faster just to turn it upside down?"

"This bag is a limited-edition Hermes. It deserves to be treated with respect."

"Rachel, when you say things like that, people think you're a snob."

"I know," she said absently while placing the contents on the table. There wasn't much: a small notebook and pen, her ever-present iPhone, AirPods, tissues, lipstick, her wallet, and the small handgun Callum had given her, which she carried everywhere. Despite it being well known that she was a crap shot with it.

"I thought women were famous for filling their bags with everything they could stuff in there."

"Really, Michael? That's such a cliché. I expected better from you."

His heart skipped a beat at her calling him by his given name for the first time since they were together in the pool. "I'll try harder."

She gave him a cool look. "You do that."

"What about your pockets?"

"Nothing. I've already checked."

"Your desk drawer?"

"Only contains a stapler."

It didn't make sense, unless... "Maybe they're playing with us. Getting us stressed, then doing nothing."

"I'm not stressed," said the woman who'd practically slept on top of him for the past two nights while mumbling about photos in her sleep.

"You know you don't have to be tough around me," he said softly.

He expected her to tell him off or make some cutting remark, shutting him down. Instead, she suddenly looked lost. "I don't know how else to be."

"Damn, Rachel, you drive me crazy." He cupped her nape and pulled her into him, pressing a hand to the small of her back as he held her tight.

"This is the office," she snapped into his chest, but her arms slid around his waist.

"We're getting married; no one would be shocked to find us showing affection."

Again, she surprised him. Instead of reminding him that their relationship was fake, she said, "My family would be."

She was off her game, which meant she was far more worried about her blackmailer than she'd let on. Understanding Rachel required a masterclass in reading body language and a superhuman ability to understand subtext because, on the surface, nothing was what it seemed with her.

"Whatever's coming, we'll handle it together." He stroked her back, breathing that heady hothouse scent deep into his lungs.

She looked up at him. "But we aren't together."

Did she honestly think that? Or was this just her ability to live in denial, reformatting the world around her to suit herself?

"Rachel," was all he said, feeling her name straight to his soul. There was no point in arguing with her; she had to reach the conclusion on her own. Instead, he could show her what they were to each other through every action. Every touch. Every word. He could show her that they were meant to be together. Call it destiny, call it fate, call it chemistry. It didn't matter. All that mattered was that they belonged.

Before she could object, he leaned in to brush his lips against hers. For a woman who insisted there was nothing between them, there was no hesitation in her returning kiss. Her arms snaked around his shoulders as she melted against him. Tasting of pure sensuality and utter temptation. She was a tiger caged, a flame contained; she was a tempest in a beautiful china cup.

She was Rachel.

And Harvard loved every facet of her to distraction. Even

the ice-queen side that the world knew. She'd burrowed under his skin, like a tick that couldn't be removed. Not the most romantic of descriptions, but he was sure she'd appreciate the humor in it. If he ever managed to tell her without making her run for the hills.

Slowly, he broke their kiss. He watched as her heavy eyelids gradually lifted, and she looked up at him through thick black lashes. "Feel better now?" she asked in a husky voice that made his blood run south.

Man, she was funny. "Much better, thanks."

She straightened and tugged down the jacket of her black pantsuit. "Good. Can we go home then?"

"Come on." With a shake of his head, he headed for the door, opening it and checking the corridor to make sure it was safe before motioning for her to follow him out.

"You do realize the bodyguard thing is only a cover too, don't you?" she muttered to him as he locked her office behind them.

"Your safety is more than a job to me." *She* was much more than a job to him.

"I honestly don't understand you," she said as they headed for the elevator. "It's as though you come from another planet. And I don't just mean America."

"It's okay." He pressed the button for the ground floor. "I don't plan on going anywhere, so you have plenty of time to figure me out."

"Don't get your hopes up," she said in that snippy voice she used to intimidate her minions.

"Too late, they're already up," he drawled, making her roll her eyes before pointedly staring at the doors.

Honestly, there was no arguing with the man. He

seemed to have an unnatural knack for getting the last word in and a strange logic that only he understood.

But, he could definitely kiss.

Rachel took a deep breath and forced her mind away from such treacherous ground. It would be far too easy to become addicted to those kisses. And it was getting harder and harder to lie beside him every night without stripping him naked and climbing all over him.

It had gotten to the stage where she was taking care of business by herself in the shower rather than give in to temptation. But that wouldn't last. Because she didn't just want relief—she wanted Harvard.

As the doors opened, her cell phone sounded with her mother's ringtone—which was just a classical music intro. Rachel didn't do humorous ringtones. She took her phone from the pocket in her bag and put it to her ear as they exited the lift.

"Hello, Mother," she said as Harvard used his security pass to open the doorway into the main reception. "This had better not be about my avoiding Samantha and her ridiculous idea that we go wedding dress shopping together."

A teary gasp on the other end of the line stopped Rachel in her tracks. Her hand shot out and curled around Harvard's arm, clinging to him with a death grip that would probably leave bruises. He instantly went into full-alert mode, aware of everything and everyone around him, while still managing to focus on her.

"It's your father," her mother said. "He's had another heart attack."

Rachel's gaze fixed on Harvard's. "Where are you?"

"We're at the Royal London Hospital."

"Is anyone with you?"

"No." The word was shaky. "Rachel, darling, your father is going to be fine. But the reason for the attack...oh, my darling, I'm so, so sorry." Her mother sobbed. "I should have known. I should have been there for you. I should..." It was impossible to make out anything else she said.

But Rachel knew exactly what she was talking about. Her mother *knew*. This was what she'd been waiting for all day long. This was how her blackmailer planned on getting to her. Through her family. As the floor dropped away beneath her, Harvard's strong arm wrapped around her waist.

"Breathe," Harvard ordered as the line went dead.

Had she hung up? She didn't know.

A security guard called out to Harvard, but Rachel couldn't hear over the roar of blood rushing through her veins.

"No," Harvard barked. "I've got this." He backed Rachel against the wall, shielding her from prying eyes. "Breathe in and out with me. Put your hand on my chest. Feel it rise and fall." He matched action to words, moving her hand and gently placing it inside his jacket, over his heart. "In, out. In, out." He kept his gaze locked with hers, holding her in place with his will. "That's it. You've got it. That's better."

Once the rushing noise in her ears began to fade and strength returned to her legs, she wet her lips with her tongue. "I'm okay now."

"Yes. You are." He took a step back, still holding her hand to his chest as he shielded her from the world. "What did your mom say?"

Rachel swallowed hard, but with each passing second, she felt the walls inside her rebuilding, brick by brick. "Father's had another heart attack. They're in central London, in hospital. She said he was going to be fine, but..."

He leaned in to murmur against her ear. "Give me the ice queen, Rachel. That's who you need right now. Let me see her. I've got your back, and you can handle anything. I know it. You know it. Let's show the world."

She nodded, and he backed up again. Rachel straightened her shoulders and took her hand from his chest. "I suspect my blackmailer may have shared some photos with my father," she said, pleased that her voice sounded even and strong.

"Okay." His eyes turned deadly. "Has she called your brothers?"

"She didn't say." Rachel smoothed her suit and brushed her hair over her shoulder.

"We can call them from the car."

She was grateful he didn't suggest going upstairs and telling Jonathan in person. She wasn't ready for that yet. "Let's go. I'm alright now. It was just a shock."

"Come on." He took her hand, and for once, she didn't complain.

As they passed the curious guard and receptionist, Harvard called out, "That's what happens when you skip lunch. She's fine; we're going to get something to eat. Have a good weekend."

They smiled politely, but awkwardly, clearly unsure whether to believe him. Rachel didn't care. She just didn't want anyone calling Jonathan before she could talk to him.

Once in the car, Harvard handed her a bottle of icy water from the cooler built into the center armrest. She took it gratefully and sipped until her throat felt like it was working properly again.

"You okay to call?" he asked as he took them out into the traffic.

"Yes." She lifted her phone and brought up her brother's contact details. "Jonathan? There's been some bad news; Father's in hospital again with a mild heart attack." As she listened to his shocked response, they joined the motorway, and Harvard's hand reached out to clasp hers.

She held it tight.

"No, Mother said he'll be fine, and you know she wouldn't downplay it. I'm on my way there now." She gave him the details. "I'll meet you there. Will you tell Sebastian?"

Once he'd agreed, she hung up and reached for the water again.

Harvard squeezed her hand. "You okay?"

"It was just a wobble." She took another sip.

"We all have them. How do you want to handle this?"

And just like that, the last remaining links in the chain around her heart gave way. Any other man at Benson Security would have taken charge and tried to tell her what to do, but not Harvard. With one short question, he'd let her know that he had her back, and this was her show to run.

"I need to calm my parents," she said. "There will be questions about the attack. Emotions." And she wasn't great at dealing with those. It was tempting to leave them to get over the shock and then talk to them about it later. Maybe in a year or two. But she couldn't. They were her family, and she loved them fiercely.

"Just tap my arm if you need a reprieve," he said, sounding his usual calm self. "I can either take over the explanations or get you out of there for a few minutes."

"Tag team," she muttered.

"Yeah."

She stared out of the window as they zoomed past the landscape. Green hills turned gray in the pounding rain. "I really want to kill someone right now," she said.

"I'll help you bury the body," Harvard said darkly, leading her to think he had some very real experience in that area.

With her hand tucked in his, she kept her eyes on the road in front of them and tried not to think about where their journey would end. Or what she'd have to face when she got there.

Chapter Twenty-One

As they approached the door to her father's hospital room, Harvard asked, "Do you want me to come in with you or wait out here?"

His question came across as purely pragmatic, without even a hint of pity. Thank Gucci. "I honestly don't care," she said. "Do what you want."

He put a hand on her arm, his touch gentle but firm. "Rachel," was all he said, but his tone made it clear he expected a different answer.

"Fine," she huffed. "I want you to come in with me." She squeezed the words through a throat that was rapidly closing to keep them inside.

"Was that so hard?" He let go of her arm.

"You have no idea," she muttered.

"Would it make it easier if I promised to tell everyone I forced myself into the room with you?"

She gave that some serious consideration. "Yes. It would."

"Okay then," he said, while smothering a smile.

"I don't want anyone to think I've gone soft or become needy." She glared at him. "Because I haven't."

"Understood." Harvard reached out to brush her hair behind her shoulder. "I'm your backup in case you need it. I'm not a crutch."

"Exactly."

His eyes sparkled. "You want to pat me on the head and tell me well done, don't you?"

Honestly. "You are far more trouble than you're worth."

"We both know that isn't true. You ready?"

"As ready as anyone can be when they'd rather be anywhere else." Rachel hesitated, her hand on the doorknob. "I'm concerned about my father, but I'd rather the focus was on him—where it should be—than on my ancient history." She frowned up at him. "I have no idea why I'm explaining myself to you."

"Delayed shock?" he offered.

"Must be," she said as she opened the door and stepped inside.

As with hospital rooms the world over, this one was decorated in insipid pastel colors and gray machinery. The room was private, which meant there were flowers on the bedside table, a painting on the wall, some floral curtains that she assumed were supposed to be cheerful, and an upholstered armchair for her mother to sit in. The only thing about the room that was in any way delightful was the view out over London. Everything else would just make a patient feel even more ill.

"Rachel," her mother cried, jumping out of her seat and running straight at her.

The force of her hug almost swept Rachel off her feet. Instead, she felt the steadying hold of Harvard's strong hands before he took her handbag, freeing her up to return her mother's embrace.

"My baby," her mother said through tears, squeezing her tight. "My poor, poor baby."

"I'm fine." Rachel patted her back. "Really, let's concentrate on Father."

Over her mother's shoulder, she caught her father's eye, and it felt like the wind had been knocked right out of her. He stared back at her, his face devoid of color and his eyes filled with tears. Propped up on pillows, with wires coming from his chest and tubes in his arm, he suddenly looked much older than his years. It was a stark and awful reminder that she wouldn't have them forever. Something she couldn't even bear thinking about.

"It's okay," Rachel reassured him. "Honestly. It's fine."

"How can it be fine?" His voice was a rasp. "My daughter was...you were..." He shook his head as though nothing made any sense. "And we weren't there for you. Why, Rachel, why didn't you tell us?"

Her stomach formed a solid lump inside of her. "You received some photos then." It wasn't a question; it was merely confirmation of what she'd expected.

He visibly swallowed, his hands curling into fists. "Why didn't you tell us?"

"Were you ashamed?" Her mother stopped hugging her long enough to cup her cheeks. "Please tell me it wasn't shame that stopped you from calling us after the attack. You have nothing to be ashamed of. Nothing." Tears streamed down her cheeks. "I can't stand the thought of you going through that alone. Why didn't the hospital call us? Or the police?"

"I wouldn't let them. They wanted to, but it seemed like the best decision at the time." Rachel swallowed hard. "I'm okay, Mum. I promise. It was a very long time ago. And I wasn't ashamed. I was trying to..."

She looked at Harvard, hoping he had the right words because somehow she knew that explaining she'd been trying to protect them would only make things worse.

"Sometimes," Harvard said as she tagged him into the conversation, "the shock from a trauma can last for years. A person can withdraw and make decisions that they wouldn't usually make. Rachel was in shock. By the time she got past it, she didn't want to open old wounds. Which is what would have happened if she'd told you."

Her father's anger focused on Harvard. "But you knew. You knew my daughter was...attacked, and you didn't tell me. You knew when I didn't."

Harvard maintained that steadying calm of his. "Only because the photos started turning up when we arrived at TayFor."

With a curse, her father rested his head back against his pillows. "Blackmail." His eyes scrunched shut. "That explains the note with the photos."

"What note? You didn't mention a note. And blackmail? I don't understand." Her mother's wide-eyed gaze went to each of them, but she never let go of Rachel. Through it all, she continued to pet her and touch her, as though making sure she was real. Or trying to soothe away all the hurts that had happened so very long ago. "Why would someone blackmail Rachel?" Silent tears fell. "And with this? Who could do such a thing? Wasn't the assault enough? What sort of sick mind would save photos like that? Would use them again? I don't understand." She looked at Rachel for answers.

But there were none to give. All Rachel could do was pull her mother back into her arms. "I know you don't, Mum. I should have told you when it happened, but I was young, and I thought I had control of the situation."

"And you were protecting us," her father said gruffly.

Rachel's eyes caught his, and she saw complete understanding in them.

His jaw clenched tight for a second. "You knew they'd use those photos to bring down TayFor. They threatened you with a scandal, didn't they? And you chose to protect the company, and us." His face crumpled. "Don't you know that you're worth far more to us than that damn company could ever be?" A single silent tear ran down his aged cheek.

"I never, for one second, thought you cared more for the company than you did for me," Rachel whispered to him. To them.

"You were always too damn strong," her father said. "Determined that you knew better than everyone around you and so bloody smart that you were usually right. You spent your whole childhood protecting your brothers and cousins while pretending you weren't. As though none of us would notice. And nothing has changed. You're still taking all the weight on your own shoulders to spare the rest of us the burden. But, my baby girl, you never realized that the people who love you want to take the burden from you too. You should have let us carry this. You should have let us be there for you."

"I know." Rachel guided her mother over to the bed so she could enfold them both in a hug. "I know," she said softly, casting a panicked glance at Harvard. She had no idea what to do, how to comfort them, or how to make things right. She was completely lost in the situation, and all she wanted was for her parents to stop hurting. But she didn't know how to make that happen.

Harvard must have read the desperation in her face, because he cleared his throat. "How about we get some hot drinks and talk about how we're going to catch the bastards who did this?"

Her father came out of their hug to look at Harvard. "I want them to suffer. Nothing is more important than getting to the bottom of this. Not TayFor. Not the thief. Nothing."

"Yes, sir." Harvard nodded. "I understand, and we're on the same page. But"—he rubbed his chin and hesitated, as though unsure—"we need your help. Are you sure you're up to that?"

"Just you bloody well try and stop us," her father raged while her mother took a tissue from the side table and dabbed at her face.

"Let's crucify those animals," she said as Jonathan burst into the room.

Taking in the scene in front of him, he paled. "Dad, you okay?"

"He's going to be fine." Her mother rushed to comfort another child. "We've just had some bad news about Rachel."

"Rachel?" Jonathan looked prepared to hug her until she spilled the story.

Rachel caught Harvard's eye. "Tag, you're it. I'll get the drinks while you explain." There wasn't a chance in hell she was going through that again. "Maybe they have wine in the cafeteria."

"This is a hospital." Her mother sounded outraged.

"Well, if they don't have wine, maybe someone could sedate me until this is over." She opened the door and waved a hand at them. "I'm fine. Father was the one who had a heart attack. Harvard has a plan for getting to the bottom of this whole situation and the skill to torture everyone involved. Please, for the love of all things Prada, get the hugging and tears out of your system while I'm gone."

With that, she closed the door behind her.

Harvard grinned at the door before becoming aware that all eyes were now on him. Yeah, there was no hiding that he was far more than a work colleague to Rachel—even if she wasn't willing to admit it. Yet.

Running a hand over his bald head and absently noting it

needed a shave, he turned to Rachel's family and gave them the truth. "I'm in love with Rachel. I'm pretty sure she loves me too, although getting her to admit it is turning out to be a challenge. But you should know that if I have my way, this wedding you're planning will be the real deal."

There was a stunned silence before Rachel's mother burst into tears again and rushed at him. As she enfolded him in a hug, Harvard patted her back and gave the men a bewildered look.

"Welcome to the family," Jonathan said with a shrug. "We like to hug."

"I'm so glad she has you," Francesca said between sobs muffled against his chest. "She needs a strong man to love her. To see her for who she really is and appreciate all of her."

"That's a good point," Jonathan said. "You sure you know what you're getting into?"

"Yeah." Harvard smiled. "I'm sure."

"Okay then." Jonathan went over to place a hand on his father's arm. "They've said it was a mild attack. I thought you were taking your medication and laying off that fatty food you enjoy too much. You need to take your doctor's instructions seriously. I'm not sure if *my* heart can take another scare like this. Not to mention poor Sebastian. He's scrambling to find a ride out of the Borneo jungle, just to check for himself that you're still alive." His voice softened. "Seriously, Dad, let's make this the last time."

Roger patted his hand. "I couldn't agree more. I just had a terrible shock, that's all."

Jonathan frowned. "A shock involving Rachel? What has she done now? Was anyone injured?"

"Sit down," Roger said before giving Harvard a helpless look.

"I wouldn't mind taking it from here if that's okay with you, Roger," Harvard said as he led Francesca to her seat.

"That way, I can fill in some gaps while I bring Jonathan up to speed."

Roger sagged into the pillows with clear relief. "Please," he said, turning to Jonathan. "Son, prepare yourself. This isn't good at all."

Burying his emotions deep, Harvard tried to be as professional and caring as he could be while he explained everything to Rachel's family. Francesca kept a fierce grip on her husband's hand, her free hand dabbing at her cheeks with a tissue. Jonathan's head dropped forward, and he cursed softly with each revelation. Roger looked like he was clenching his teeth so hard they might crack.

When Harvard had finished, Jonathan looked up at him, his eyes red. "I hope she finds some whiskey in the cafeteria."

"If there's any to be found, Rachel will get it," Harvard said.

Jonathan took a visible breath. "She won't let us comfort her, bloody prickly woman."

"No," Harvard said. "She won't. But you have to remember, Rachel's had ten years to think about this; you've only just found out. She really is doing great."

Francesca's tear-filled eyes met his. "You can't always believe what you see with our daughter."

"I know," Harvard said softly, giving her a silent promise. "I'm watching over her. If she crumples, she won't be alone."

Her mother nodded as she turned to her husband, who wrapped his arm around her and comforted her.

Roger's steely gaze met Harvard's, reminding him that Rachel's dad had built a world-class company from the ground up, using grit, determination, and pure strength. Before he'd arrived on the scene, there'd been no TayFor. He *was* the For in the name—the man who'd single-handedly saved a failing company, making him both feared and revered within London's business community.

"What do you need from us?" Roger asked.

Harvard pulled up a chair. "I need the envelope, the photos, a detailed breakdown of where you were when you received them, and who was near you in the time preceding it."

Roger nodded. "You'll have it."

"What did the note say?" Harvard asked.

The man's eyes blazed. "It said *Rachel was told to leave TayFor. You get to deliver her last warning. Enjoy.*" He turned green. "It actually said that word. Enjoy. As though this was all just a game."

Francesca stroked a hand down his shoulder. "Whoever this is, they're very sick."

"Or evil," Jonathan said.

Harvard had to agree. "We've got someone searching the server for clues from ten years ago. Someone else examining the photos to see what they can tell us. And we have Rachel. She might not remember much, but she has flashes of detail that will help. On top of that, we believe the blackmailer works at TayFor, and we know they were involved in the attack. Otherwise, how did they get hold of the photos?"

"And we know that all they care about," Jonathan said, "is getting Rachel to leave the company."

Francesca shook her head. "Why Rachel? I don't understand how she's a threat to anyone—ten years ago or now. Why do they want to get rid of her?"

Harvard felt a chill run up his spine. "That's a very good question. One I've been asking myself, and I've yet to come up with an answer." But when he did, he knew it would point straight to the person behind the attack and the blackmail. The puppeteer. The one orchestrating Rachel's suffering for their own twisted ends.

All he had to do was figure out why and he'd have them.

"I'm very good at puzzles," he told Rachel's family. "It's why the CIA recruited me. I'll figure this out." It was a vow.

Before anyone could say anything else, the door swung open and Rachel walked in, a tray of takeout cups in her hand. "Oh good, we're finished with the hugging part of this visit. You'll be glad to know that there wasn't a spot of liquor to be found on the premises. The best I could do was coffee all round." She handed out the cups. "Except for you," she told her father. "You get orange juice and a lecture." She glared at him. "I had a word with your doctor, and apparently you've been a very naughty boy." She looked at her mother. "Did you know he's been sneaking bacon behind your back?"

Roger cringed as Francesca's face turned to thunder and Jonathan shot to his feet. Harvard sat back in his seat, sipping his coffee as he watched Rachel's family show their love for each other by shouting, threatening, and making demands. They seriously needed a calming influence in their ranks.

They should thank their lucky stars they had him.

Chapter Twenty-Two

"I'm having a bath and then going to bed," Rachel announced as soon as they were in her apartment.

They'd stopped for food on the way home, and Harvard had listened patiently to Rachel while she ranted about all the different ways she wanted her blackmailer to suffer. She was furious, and scared. He suspected the latter was mainly for her family rather than herself.

"I'm going to check in with Harry." Harvard shrugged off his jacket and tossed it over the back of one of her white sofas.

"Are you planning to leave that there?" she demanded.

"Are you trying to pick a fight?" He unbuttoned his cuffs and rolled up his sleeves. "Because I can think of other ways to work off your tension. Much more pleasurable ways."

"You"—she pointed a talon at him—"have a one-track mind."

"True. But it isn't just sex. It's all things Rachel."

She blinked at him, as though trying to figure him out. "I don't even want to know what that means," she said at last. "I'm taking a bath."

He watched her sashay away, moving like mist over rocks in those heels of hers as her long straight hair swayed across her back. Sexiest thing he'd ever seen.

As soon as she was out of sight, he pulled out his phone and called Harry. He wasn't used to dealing with someone like the tech genius. He was used to his teammates checking in and keeping him up to date with their progress. Harry, meanwhile, had dropped off the radar entirely.

"Harvard?" He sounded distracted when he answered.

"Yep. What's happening? You got anything for me yet?"

The answering silence stretched so long that Harvard wondered whether Harry had put down the phone and forgotten about it.

"I'll call you if I find anything," he said eventually.

"Do you think there might be something there, or are we chasing fog?"

"No, there's something here," he muttered, almost to himself. "There's some corruption in the memory systems. It's as if somebody tried to cover their tracks by deleting the information, but they did a cack-handed job of it. I just need a little more time to see what I can clean up. It doesn't help that I'm not dealing with the original data storage. The server was updated years ago and the information stored in it copied over to this one. But, maybe if I—"

The line went dead. Harry had lost interest in the call—if he even remembered it was happening.

But still, the programmer had given Harvard something to go on. The next person he contacted was Elle, and he did it as he made his way downstairs to the guest room.

"Before you ask," she said instead of hello, "I've already started going over the photos and envelope Rachel's dad couriered to me. It's too soon to report on whether I've found something or not, but when I do, you'll be the first to know." There was a silent but unmistakable *now stop bothering me* at the end of that sentence.

Elle had obviously gone to the same charm school as Harry. "That's not why I called. I just spoke to Harry, and he mentioned that there's corrupted data on the server, as though somebody had been trying to cover their tracks. Which means, someone from IT or security was definitely involved in Rachel's attack. I need you to dig out personnel information for that period."

"One of the guys Rachel had fired worked security back then."

"Yeah, but those two were fired long before the drug was stolen." Harvard kicked off his shoes beside his bed before bending over to tug off his socks. "We need to question anyone else working around the time Rachel was attacked."

"I'll get you the names." She took a deep breath. "Is Rachel okay?"

"She will be—once everyone involved in this is out of the picture."

"You mean behind bars, right?"

He meant *completely* out of the picture, and he'd be more than happy to make it happen. But the authorities tended to frown on that sort of thing. "I need to call Ryan. I'll talk to you tomorrow."

"Try not to kill anyone before then," she said drolly before hanging up.

With a smile, Harvard called his last team member. "Are you eating?" he asked as soon as Ryan said hello.

"I don't always eat, but yeah, I have pizza."

Harvard chuckled. "Did you check in with the surveillance team following our suspects?"

"Absolutely." There was the sound of a can opening and then Ryan taking a drink. "Samantha's out on a date this evening, with a young movie star who's barely out of nappies.

They've gone clubbing, and their tail thinks they called the paparazzi before they left her condo. Charles is in Kent, checking his wife into rehab yet again. Word is she was running around their garden naked trying to catch imaginary bubbles with a bucket."

"Okay," Harvard said. "Wasn't expecting that."

"I don't think her neighbors were either," Ryan said around a mouthful of food. "Then there's the shoe guys. What are they called again? Can't remember the name of the shoes. Doesn't matter. Anyway, Preston went home to his wife, had dinner, watched the news. Boring. Marcus spent the evening with his mistress, but his wife expects him home later—apparently, he's got a late emergency meeting. And Rupert's in the Hippodrome Casino, but he isn't gambling. Word is, he's wandering around stroking the tables and slot machines."

"Stroking?" Harvard arched his brows.

"I only report what I'm told, and his tail said there was definite stroking and he's resisted all attempts to get him involved in a game. The tail said he looks kinda sad."

Harvard pinched the bridge of his nose as the craziness of Rachel's relatives sank in. "Were any of them anywhere near Roger's house this afternoon when the envelope was delivered?"

"That's a negative. But then, they wouldn't have to be. I asked Elle to hack into the CCTV cameras on the road leading into the property and look for couriers."

"What about the cameras on the Talbot estate?"

"They're only on the main house and public grounds. Seems the family don't like cameras on their residence."

"I need to have a word with them about that." It was a dumb thing to do for people in their position. No matter how much you valued your privacy, safety came first. Harvard unbuttoned his shirt. "Keep surveillance on everyone over the weekend. In the meantime, prep what you need for Monday's board meeting. Hopefully, we can get some answers then."

"No kidding," Ryan said.

"Michael," Rachel's voice came from the doorway, "what are you doing in here?"

He turned to answer and froze. She stood there, hands on hips and completely nude, and not showing even the slightest sign of being self-conscious about it.

"You there?" Ryan said in his ear, but Harvard could barely hear him over the sound of all the blood in his body rushing south.

"Have we stopped sleeping together?" Rachel demanded. "I don't remember telling you to go back to the guest room."

"Harvard?" Ryan called.

Harvard ended the call and tossed his phone onto the bed. For a man who was known for being cool under fire and having an answer for everything, there were no words in his head.

"Are you coming?" Rachel glared at him before turning on her heel and stalking back across the hall.

For a second, all he could do was watch her go as his mouth watered and his pants grew uncomfortably tight.

"Michael?" she snapped as she disappeared from sight.

And with a grin, Harvard answered her summons.

~

HONESTLY, JUST WHEN YOU THOUGHT YOU HAD A MAN trained, they wandered off and did their own thing. Hadn't she made it clear they were sleeping together? What would be the point in him going back to his own room?

A thought occurred to her as she rounded the bed. "Are you trying to be sensitive because my father had a heart attack?" she asked him as he walked through the door. "Because it was only a mild one, and it was mainly due to the amount of bacon he's been scoffing in secret."

Harvard locked the door before staring at her. "You're naked."

Rachel rolled her eyes. That was the kind of astute observation she expected from an MIT graduate—*not*. "Yes. I am. I thought we might have sex. But you were in the other room."

He shook his head as if dazed. "Why do I get the feeling you're ordering sex the same way you'd order a pizza?"

Now he really was irritating her. "Have I misread the signs? Do you *not* want to have sex with me? Is the erection you've been sporting these past few days purely a medical issue? Do I need to take you to the emergency room? Because walking around like that surely can't be healthy."

His gaze flickered between her face and her breasts. "I know what you're doing, Rachel. You're picking a fight so we'll have angry sex and you can keep some distance between us. Well"—he shrugged out of his shirt and tossed it onto the chair, exposing an expanse of muscle that should be illegal —"I have news for you. I'm not going to help you. If you want to *make love*, you'll have to ask me nicely and make me feel like you want *me* and not just a body to use to ease your tension."

"Oh, for the love of Gucci." She threw up her hands. "When did men become all sensitive? It's only sex. If you don't want it, feel free to go back to the guest room." She tossed back the covers and climbed into bed, leaving him the side closest to the door.

"Yeah, you'd like that. Because you like distance. You don't like up-close and messy emotions. And you definitely don't like feeling vulnerable." He took off his trousers and underpants and stood, naked and proud, hands on hips, staring at her. A beautiful, thick, long erection pointed in her direction. Which was very distracting.

"Thank you for your analysis," she said, dragging her eyes from his hard length. "I could have saved thousands in therapy if I'd just met you sooner."

As usual, her comments didn't derail Harvard. He remained irritatingly calm. "Relationships are messy. They're emotional. And they don't work if one of you refuses to be vulnerable and trust that the other person will take care of you."

"This. Isn't. A. Relationship." She lay on her back and tugged the bedcovers up around her, then tightened them at her sides by slashing her arms down hard. "I don't understand why that doesn't sink in. I'm beginning to think it would be easier to train a cat."

"You don't train a lover, Rachel." He lay down on the bed and mirrored her pose, but without covering his body. Instead, he lay there like a cake buffet outside a Weight Watchers meeting.

"You aren't my lover." Damn, she sounded hoarse and achy. "Right now, all you are is a house guest who's in the wrong bed."

"That's not the way to get me to make love to you."

"Stop calling it that. It's just sex. A bodily function. Nothing more."

He turned onto his side and propped himself up on an elbow, and she practically salivated at the sight. "It is way more than *just sex* when two people have feelings for each other."

"The only feeling I have for you is irritation."

"Well, then. All of this"—he waved a hand down his body —"is off-limits until you admit we're in a real relationship. If you want to go further and admit you actually have feelings for me, then that would be great too. But I'd settle for you admitting we're in a relationship."

Never, in all the years she'd lived in her apartment, had Rachel entertained the idea that the glass bottom of her pool might crack and flood her bedroom. But in that instant, she almost hoped it would, and that the smug, stubborn, annoying man beside her would drown.

Keeping her eyes on the water, she said, "I'm going to sleep now." And then she grabbed the remote and turned off the lights, leaving only the glow from the pool above.

Forcing her eyes closed, Rachel tried to keep her mind from the naked man beside her and go to sleep. This was ridiculous. Why did he have to make such a big deal out of things? They were in the same bed. They touched. They spent time together. What difference would it make putting a label on whatever was happening between them? He was just trying to drive her crazy.

She took a few slow breaths, trying to calm her mind and relax. That's when she felt the bed move—rhythmically. Her eyes snapped open as she turned her head toward Harvard. And stopped breathing entirely.

He lay on his back, the soft light caressing his dark skin. One arm lay behind his head, the other...

She found it difficult to swallow as her mouth became suddenly dry.

"What are you doing?" she croaked, her eyes glued to his large hand wrapped around his stiff erection, sliding slowly, almost absently, up and down. Like a switch had been flipped, the tension that consumed her became a desperate desire to touch. To replace his hand with hers. To caress, taste, kiss.

"I'm trying to relax," he said.

At his low, rumbled words, her eyes shot to his. The sensuality in his heavy-lidded gaze had her clenching her thighs together.

"Well do it some other way," she told him. "I'm tense too, and you don't see me with my hand between my legs."

His eyes turned blacker. "I'd like to."

As a rush of pure adrenaline raced through her, she had to fight to stop from reaching for him. Her attention kept straying back to his slow, steady movements as he stroked himself. Why, oh why, was watching him do that such a turn on?

"Find another way to relax," she ordered, sounding breathless.

"I'd like to, but you're being difficult. All you have to do is say what I need to hear, and I can make all your tension fade away." His hand clenched the base of his erection, and he let out a low moan.

Rachel's fingers curled into the bedspread. "I don't know why I have to say anything."

"Rachel," he purred, "no more lies."

His thighs widened as he continued to stroke. This was torture. Pure, utter torture. "Fine," she snapped. "We're in a temporary relationship. Happy now?"

"No." Harvard's thumb slid across the crown of his penis. "There's nothing temporary about this. It's a relationship, period."

"Rubbish. No one knows how long something will last when they get into it."

"You can't use that as an out. I know you. You think you can admit there's something between us right now, then say it was good while it lasted come morning. No. We're in this together, and we aren't searching for an end date. It's a proper, normal relationship. And if you want my cock, you need to admit it."

"You're being completely unreasonable," she snapped.

"Then I guess I'll just carry on, all on my own, over here."

Was there ever a more annoying man? "Fine. You win. We're in a relationship." The words almost choked her.

His hand stilled. "For how long?"

"As long as it lasts," she gritted through clenched teeth, thinking it would most definitely only be until the morning.

"I want to hear you say that you don't plan to sabotage us and that you'll give us a chance." He stared at her. "Which means no dumping me in the morning to prove a point."

"Whatever." Could he read her mind now? "We're in a serious relationship, and we're going to see where it leads. Happy now?"

"Honestly? I'm a bit worried that you'll smother me in my sleep, but otherwise, well done."

She let out a feral growl. "Can we have sex now?"

"No." Harvard rolled to his side, propped himself up on an elbow and slung his other arm over her waist. "But we can make love."

And then, at last, he kissed her.

Chapter Twenty-Three

arvard woke up to a very naked Rachel draped across him and the sound of buzzing coming from the apartment intercom. Gently shifting her onto the mattress beside him, he reached over to answer the buzzing phone.

"Yup?" Rubbing a hand down his face, he glanced at the clock and noted it was seven a.m. It was a sleep-in for him. Usually he'd have been up, running and working out hours earlier. Yeah, he could get used to waking up late with Rachel.

"I'm sorry to disturb you, sir," the concierge said, "but I thought you'd like some warning that Mr. Harry Boyle is on his way up." He cleared his throat. "Mr. Boyle has a key, and we have standing instructions from Ms. Ford-Talbot that he may enter her apartment at will."

Obviously, the guy thought Rachel's other lover was about to walk in on them. "Thanks. Harry's welcome anytime. I appreciate the heads-up though."

"Of course," the man said before ending the call.

Harvard swiveled around to see Rachel lying on her front, her hair covering her face. The smooth, pale skin of her back proved too much of a temptation, and he stroked a caress down its length. Next time they made love, he was going to concentrate on her back, and the round, plump curves of her ass. His dick liked that idea a whole lot and decided it was time for it to wake up too.

With a sigh of regret, he gently shook her shoulder. "Rachel, time to wake up. Harry will be here in a couple of minutes."

"Go away," she mumbled into her pillow.

"Rachel, Harry's coming. You need to get up."

"Don't care if the Queen's coming. Need to sleep."

He ran a hand over the curve of her hip. "He wouldn't be here if he didn't have something important to tell us."

"Unless he's got coffee, I don't care." She brought her hands up to clutch her pillow, as though worried he'd take it from her.

It was tempting to do what his mom had done when he wouldn't get out of bed as a teen. A glass of cold water over your head once or twice was enough to sort that problem right out. But having just managed to get Rachel to admit they were an item, he didn't want to kill the buzz by enraging her. Looked like he'd have to deal with Harry on his own.

Harvard stepped into yesterday's pants, leaving the button undone, and reached for his phone—only to remember it was still in the guest room. Along with his gun. Some bodyguard he was turning out to be. Rachel had scrambled his brain.

He'd intended to run upstairs and get Harry settled, then return to the guest room to shower and change, but thumping on their bedroom door blew that plan to hell.

Throwing it open, he did a double take when he found not only Harry but also Elle and Ryan standing in the hallway. There was no way of hiding the sight of Rachel asleep and naked on the bed behind him. He could only be thankful that the sheet covered past her hips.

"You totally slept with each other," Ryan said. "That's not fair. We dissolved the bet, and I had a grand in it. I would have made a bomb." He glared at Harvard. "You owe me."

Meanwhile, Elle seemed particularly focused on his bare chest. Her hand came up and she reached for him. "Can I? Can I just touch?"

"No!" Ryan pushed her arm back down. "And stop drooling. You're embarrassing yourself."

"But, he's so pretty." She batted her lashes at Harvard. "You don't mind if I have a little touch, do you?"

"I do," came the muffled shout from the bed. "Now, everybody, get the hell out of my bedroom."

"Rachel?" Harry looked up from the iPad in his hand as though becoming aware of where he was standing. "Oh, good. I need to talk to you. I think I've found something." And the fool actually tried to walk past Harvard and into the room.

"Later." Harvard pushed him back out into the hallway. "First, you guys wait upstairs. Second, somebody make coffee. Third, I'll shower and wake the beast."

"Are you getting dressed too?" Elle asked, her eyes still on his chest.

"Yeah."

"Oh." She sounded so disappointed that he burst out laughing.

"Go. I'll be up in a minute. Don't forget the coffee." And then he jogged into the guest room.

Twenty minutes later, he was showered, shaved, and dressed for the day in jeans and a black tee. Ryan had made coffee, which was pretty damn good, and Harvard took a mug down to Rachel. She sniffed the air before sitting up, her eyes still closed and the sheet pooling at her hips.

"Gimme," she ordered.

He placed the drink in her hands and stroked her hair.

"You've got fifteen minutes to get upstairs, or I'm bringing the team down here, and we'll sit on your bed to debrief."

Her eyes opened a crack. "You wouldn't."

"Try me."

She cocked her head. "Now that we're in a *relationship*," she said, using the same tone that she'd use to describe inferior knock-off designer wear, "you'd think you would be nicer."

"Funny that," he said as he strode to the door. "Fifteen minutes."

She opened her mouth, no doubt to dump his sorry ass.

"Nuh-uh," Harvard said. "We talked about this. No backing out just because you woke up in a bad mood."

When her answer was a menacing growl, Harvard left her to it, wondering if he should have brought the whole coffee pot downstairs with him instead of just one mug.

It took Rachel close to forty-five minutes to get ready, and that was rushing it for her. She dressed for the day in white wide-legged trousers with a faint cream pinstripe, a white cashmere boatneck sweater, and four-inch pumps in cream. Her hair fell in a sleek waterfall over her shoulders, and she'd painted her lips a dark red. Around her throat, she wore her grandmother's locket, and on her wrist, a thick platinum bracelet and on her hand was the engagement ring Harvard had given her.

Every time she slipped on the ring, she felt a warming well inside her. It was exactly the type of ring she'd have chosen for herself, and strangely, wearing it made her feel like Harvard was standing right beside her, even when he wasn't. She shook off the strange bout of sentimentality; obviously circumstances were affecting her in ways she hadn't imagined. And she wasn't sure what to think or do about it.

With a toss of her hair, she swept out of her bedroom, ready to face whatever came her way.

"That's what you wear on the weekend?" Ryan said as she sailed into the kitchen.

The team, plus Harry—who looked even more disheveled than usual—were seated around her dining table. Although she kept her eyes from Harvard, the glance she stole told her that he was looking at her with open affection, laced with a heavy dose of amusement. The man obviously didn't know what circumspect meant. Which made her wonder what exactly they taught at the famous MIT.

"You look like you're auditioning for Christmas angel in the school play," Ryan said.

Rachel took in his rumpled T-shirt, with its faded print promoting something she'd never heard of, and his faded jeans. "Unlike you, I don't roll out of bed and put on the first thing I find." She pointed at his shirt. "And that isn't how you spell deaf or leopard."

"I can't even," Ryan said, shaking his head. "It's like you live on a different planet."

"Yes. One with clean clothes and decent manners. Now, for the love of Prada, use a napkin. You're getting crumbs everywhere."

Without taking his eyes from her, he lifted a large Danish pastry from his over-full plate and took a bite.

"And that there"—she pointed at him—"is exactly why you can't keep a girlfriend."

Harvard held up his hands. "Can we get on with this, or do I have to give you two a time-out?"

"She started it," Ryan said with a grin.

Rachel just filled a mug with coffee, helped herself to *one*

Danish pastry, and headed toward a seat far away from Harvard.

His eyes sparkling, he stood up and took the plate from her hand. "Let me help you." He put it on the table beside his seat and pulled out a chair for her.

Elle and Ryan seemed to hold their breaths as they waited for her to eviscerate Harvard. But she had no intention of doing the expected. Instead, she said thank you and took the seat. She'd deal with him later.

As he settled beside her, Harvard looked over at Harry. "We're ready when you are."

When he didn't respond, Elle leaned over and poked his arm. "We're waiting," she said.

"Oh, okay." Harry looked around the table, and you could tell the exact second when the people present came into focus for him. He gave that goofy grin of his before sobering. "I think I know who stole the drug they used on Rachel."

"So do I," Elle said.

Harry's head almost spun off his shoulders as he turned to her. "How?"

"Harvard told me you'd found corrupted data during a set time frame, so I pulled up staff for that period."

"So, you don't know the exact person, you just narrowed it down to a group of people?"

"Nope." Her blue curls bounced around her face as she shook her hair. "I've dug around in some backgrounds and came up with a motive. I'm fairly sure I've got the right person."

"Are you saying that I spent all night digging around in corrupted data, and it was pointless?" Harry frowned.

"How about"—Harvard leaned forward and clasped his hands on the table—"you both tell the rest of us who you think stole the drug."

Harry nodded. "Okay, it was—"

"Terrance King," Elle and Harry finished together.

Finding she'd lost her appetite, Rachel pushed the pastry away. "Are you sure? I didn't even know him back then. I barely know him now."

She sounded calm, and she felt weirdly calm too, as though disconnected from the conversation. But somewhere deep inside, questions kept bubbling up. Was he one of the men who'd attacked her? Had he taken the photos? Had he set all of this up?

"Why?" she said. "I don't understand the why."

Elle opened her laptop and tapped at the keyboard before turning it toward the rest of them. "This is why." She pointed to an image of a young woman, a teenager, walking with a younger version of Terrance King. He had his arm around her waist as they gazed into each other's eyes like lovers would. "That's Angelina Smith; she was seventeen when this was taken. Terrance was in his forties and still working with the police. He was also married."

"What's that got to do with me? I was a few years older than her when I was attacked, and I honestly don't recognize the girl."

"It's not who she is that's important," Elle said. "It's what she represents."

Harvard slid a hand over Rachel's shoulder to her nape, but instead of brushing him away, she found the gesture strangely settling. "Blackmail," he said to her. "Whoever's blackmailing you, probably used this affair to blackmail Terrance."

"Exactly." Elle hit some keys, and the screen changed, bringing up several photos and a written report. "I used our connections to private investigators in London and found a firm who was more than happy to help once they knew this was personal. I had to promise to keep their name out of it though. Nobody trusts a PI who shares information."

Harvard nodded, his hand still warm and solid on Rachel's neck. "Understood. What did they tell you?"

"That round the same time Terrance decided to quit the force and apply for the security position at TayFor, someone contacted them and asked them to investigate the man." She picked up her coffee and took a sip. "Nothing unusual, you might be thinking. It's routine for TayFor to check out their staff, especially security staff. But this didn't come through official channels. In fact, TayFor's name was nowhere near the job contract. The whole thing was done in secret. They didn't have a client name, just money up front, a contact number and a contract signed by a lawyer who was hired just for that purpose."

"So, someone used a private investigator to dig up dirt on Terrance." Rachel felt ill even saying his name. "And then used the fact he was having an affair with a schoolgirl to blackmail him into getting them the drug?"

"That about sums it up," Elle said.

"Which brings us back to our belief that someone inside TayFor is behind all this," Ryan said. "Otherwise, how would they know Terrance had applied for a position with them and that he'd be in a place where he could help the blackmailer?"

Harry nodded. "They must have approached him before he got the job at your family's company. Because the theft of the drug and the attempted cover-up on the server happened just a week or so after he started there."

Rachel looked up at Harvard. "Do you think the person who hired him is the same one who organized my attack?"

"Hard to tell." He caressed her neck with his thumb. "Could just be somebody who took advantage of the opportunity to use the new guy." He caught Ryan's eye. "We bring him in and talk to him. Give Joe a call; see if he's free to back you up. I want Terrance in the Benson Security holding room this morning."

"And if he doesn't agree to come along nicely?" Ryan's face said he already knew the answer.

"Convince him." Harvard's voice was steel. Looking somber, he turned to her. "We need to tell the rest of Benson Security before we turn up with this guy. It's time to bring everyone else up to speed. You okay with that?"

Rachel nodded. It wasn't anything she hadn't thought of herself. "You may tell whomever you choose."

"I'm happy to tell people if you don't want to." His gaze softened.

Which just annoyed her. She didn't need pity. Nor did she want it. "It's not like I'm ashamed to tell them, I just don't want to waste time repeating the story again and again."

"But it's okay to waste my time?" His eyes sparkled with amusement.

"It's one of the perks that come with being in a *relationship* with me. Aren't you glad you got what you so desperately wanted?" When she looked back at their team, they were staring at her openmouthed. She let out an irritated sigh. "Apparently we're in a *real relationship* instead of a fake one. Don't get all excited and start poking your noses in. It's unlikely to last."

With that, she got up from the table and went to fetch more coffee.

Chapter Twenty-Four

errance King sat at the table in Benson Security's interrogation room. Or, as they told anyone who asked, their basement interview room. Whatever they called it didn't change the fact that this room was sound-proofed, installed with cameras and a one-way mirror, and only opened from the outside. The table and chairs were bolted to the floors and the only way out was through one of the Benson Security staff.

Adjacent to this was a surveillance room. Which was currently overflowing with testosterone and badass attitude. On hearing about Rachel's past, it seemed the men of Benson Security had all decided to take over her life. Apparently, she wasn't even needed in the discussion on how best to approach Terrance King's interrogation.

The longer the men argued, the more Rachel eyed up the weapons storeroom and wondered how quickly she could tase them all and shut them up. Hell, she doubted they'd even notice she was missing until they were suddenly jolted with enough electricity to reboot their Neanderthal brains.

"I'll talk to him," Lake Benson said with absolute authority.

The former special forces officer, who'd started the company that bore his name, faced off against the rest of his team. He'd been in London, helping out on another Benson Security job, and for some reason, as soon as he'd heard about her past, he'd decided to postpone his return trip to Scotland and stick around to "help." Rachel had no idea why.

"To hell with that," Callum McKay, her other partner, snapped back. "The London office is mine. You put me in charge when you dragged me into this business. Now get out of my way and let me do my bloody job."

"I think," Harry piped up, taking his life into his hands by getting between two former SAS men, "that I should talk to him. I'm the one who found out he's involved."

"What the hell are you talking about?" Ryan demanded. "You aren't even part of Benson Security anymore. You sold your stake. I'm the one who should interrogate him. I know him best because I've been stuck working with his arrogant arse for weeks. He'll let down his guard with me."

Joe Barone and Noah Merchant, two of Harvard's childhood friends, started talking at the same time.

"I'm an ex-cop," Noah said. "I spent my career interrogating suspects. Trust me, you want me in there."

"I just want to punch him until he talks." Joe glared through the glass of the one-way mirror, to where Terrance sat relaxed in his chair.

Harvard, who'd been silently leaning against the far wall during the discussion, his arms folded and ankles crossed, flashed a smile at Joe before catching Rachel's eye. He cocked an eyebrow at her, and she jerked her head toward the door. When he nodded once, Rachel slipped outside. If anyone noticed her leaving, they said nothing.

A few seconds later, Harvard stepped out of the room,

closing the door quietly behind him. "What do you want to do?"

"I want to go in there and tell him what happened to the drug he stole. And I want you standing behind me looking scary while I do it."

He nodded. "Then lead the way."

Grateful that he hadn't asked her if she was up to the task, Rachel punched in the code to open the interrogation room door and stepped inside. She had to fight the urge to grin at the mirror, where no doubt all the men on the other side stood with their mouths hanging open. At least this would have shut them up.

"Terrance," Rachel said as she took a seat opposite him, "I'd like to tell you something."

He shot a wary glance at Harvard before glaring at her. "I hope you're going to tell me why the hell you've got me locked up in here. I thought I was coming in for a team meeting. To discuss the thefts. You'd better not be planning to pin this on me. I'm no thief." He practically spat out the last word.

"Well"—Rachel crossed her legs—"that isn't exactly true, is it? I mean, we suspect you have nothing to do with the current spate of thefts. But you're very much responsible for the ketamine and Rohypnol that went missing ten years ago, aren't you, Terrance?"

If she wasn't mistaken, he paled under his fake tan. Although, it was hard to tell. That tan was very orange.

"I have no idea what you're talking about," he protested. "Let me out of here at once. This setup is illegal. I'll have the Metropolitan Police down on you lot before you can snap your fingers."

"Good." She folded her arms and drummed her red fingernails against the white of her sweater. "While you're at it, you can explain to them why you stole date rape drugs from

TayFor and then tried to cover your tracks by deleting all record of your presence in the research facility on the day the drugs went missing."

"I see what this is." He pointed at each of them in turn. "You're trying to pin an old crime on me in the hopes that people will think I'm behind the new thefts too. This is nothing more than a pathetic attempt to protect your family. This is amateur hour; you don't have a clue what you're doing. Or who you're trying to do it to. I have connections. You won't get away with this. You know nothing. It's all lies."

"We'll see. In the meantime, let me tell you all the *nothing* that I know and see if we can't change your mind." She poured every bit of contempt she felt for him into her gaze and watched him shift in his seat.

He glanced over at Harvard, who leaned against the wall beside the door, looking to all the world as though he was perfectly relaxed. But Rachel knew that if Terrance tried anything physical, Harvard would be on him within seconds.

"Ten years ago, you had an affair with a teenager." When Terrance started to object, she held up a hand. "I have photos." He clamped his lips shut. "And so did the blackmailer. Because there was a blackmailer, wasn't there, Terrance? Someone with inside knowledge who knew you'd get the job at TayFor and asked you to do one small thing for them. All you had to do was sneak into the drug lockup and take a vial. They probably told you that no one would even notice it was missing."

She stopped drumming her fingers and focused on him. "But someone did, didn't they? And you knew they would; that's why you tried to wipe the evidence from the server."

"That's rubbish," he exploded. Harvard tensed and took a step away from the wall. Swallowing hard, Terrance sat back in his seat, clearly aware of just how much of a threat the American posed to him. "It's all rubbish," he said. "If this person worked at TayFor, they could have stolen their own damn drugs. Why use me?"

"To muddy the trail? To hide behind you? To ensure that, if someone did discover the theft, you'd take the blame? Again"— Rachel cocked her head at him—"I have evidence. Have you heard of Harry Boyle?" She could tell by the way his eyes shifted that he had. "Yes, the security programmer who literally wrote the code the government uses. Well, he went through our servers and uncovered the mess you'd left behind. He was able to untangle it, which means we have proof you were in the building, in the locked storeroom, and that you tampered with the server."

Terrance licked his lips as he looked from Rachel to Harvard. "I want a lawyer."

Rachel burst out laughing and shook her head. "You foolish little man. As you've already pointed out, there's nothing legal about this setup. We aren't the police. We haven't arrested you, and we don't owe you legal representation."

He tugged at the collar of his shirt. "My wife knows I'm here."

"No, she doesn't. You didn't tell her where you were going. You see, we've been watching you, Terrance, and we know that you rarely tell your wife what you're doing. Poor woman. She has no idea what a spineless little shit she's married to."

He exploded out of his seat, slamming his hands on the table. "You fucking bitch—" was all he managed before Harvard grabbed him and tossed him against the wall as if he were nothing more than a rag doll.

Terrance hit with a thud and crumpled to the floor.

Harvard picked him up and shoved him back into the chair. "Get out of that seat one more time, and I'll cuff you to it," Harvard said evenly. "And watch your mouth. I even get a hint you're insulting Rachel, I'll make sure you can't talk again without medical help. You get me?"

Terrance nodded as he rubbed the back of his head. For the first time since they'd stepped into the room, he seemed to realize that none of this was within his control.

"Let's get this over with quickly, shall we?" Rachel said. "Who told you to steal that drug?"

"*I don't know*," he hissed out. As Harvard moved fractionally closer to him, Terrance winced. "I honestly don't know. I got an envelope, with photos, and a note telling me what to do."

"And you just did it?" Rachel asked the weaselly excuse for a man.

"They were going to send the photos to TayFor, and I wouldn't get the job. Worse, they said they'd send them to my superior in the police force. And my wife. I would have been left without a marriage or a job. And for what? She was of legal age. All I was guilty of was—"

"Please," Rachel snapped, "don't say loving too much. We both know you're guilty of a whole lot more than that. The girl was *barely* legal, and you were a dirty old man who cheated on your wife."

"You're judging me?" He sneered at her. "If I'm guilty of anything, it's the exact same crime your family commits every single day—I was protecting my reputation."

"By stealing a date rape drug from a pharmaceutical company that trusted you with their security."

"It wasn't a date rape drug. It was a party drug."

"You were a police officer. You know exactly what people use that drug for."

"I was told they planned to party with it."

"And you believed your blackmailer?" She scoffed. "How very trusting of you."

"Nobody was hurt." He glanced at Harvard, suddenly looking very uncertain.

"Oh, Terrance, you unctuous little man. Somebody was most definitely hurt."

She cocked a thumb at herself. "Me. That drug was used on me. Without my permission. By the men who raped me."

For a second, he seemed completely shocked, then something like horror stole across his face. And before anyone could guess what he'd do, he turned, bent double, and vomited all over the floor.

"Open the door," Rachel called to the surveillance room. "And somebody get a bucket."

When Harvard and Rachel stepped outside the room, they were met with a wall of male outrage.

"Damn it, Rachel," Callum roared. "We hadn't finished deciding who'd talk to him."

"You were taking too long." She glanced back at the room. The smell coming out of it made her nauseous. "Feel free to take over. I'm sure he'll tell you whatever you want to know now. You might want to clean the floor first though."

"It's Saturday," Callum raged. "We don't have a cleaner. Just who do you think is going to go in there and wipe up the mess you caused?"

As one, every person present looked at Ryan.

"Oh, hell no," he said.

Two hours later, Benson Security's conference room was packed. Everyone who wasn't out on assignment had crammed inside to listen to Harvard update them on the theft investigation and the hunt for Rachel's attackers.

Rachel felt like the main attraction in a three-ring circus.

"So that's where we stand," Harvard said from the head of

the board table. "Terrance doesn't have a clue who blackmailed him, and he destroyed everything the blackmailer sent. He's a dead end."

Thankfully, he kept his eyes from Rachel while he spoke. Enough people were looking at her with varying degrees of pity as it was.

"Elle," Lake said, stepping up to the head of the table and looking very much in charge, because he was genetically incapable of doing otherwise, "where do we stand on the forensic tests you've been running on the photos?"

Elle, as usual, looked out of place in a room filled with ex-servicemen. She wore a blue and yellow polka dot dress and had a yellow headband in her blue hair. The look made Rachel long for her sunglasses.

"There's no trace evidence on the photos. Anything that might have been there years ago has degraded to the point of being useless, and the minute traces of latex tell me that our blackmailer wore gloves when they handled them recently."

"No visual clues from the images themselves?" Callum asked.

He and Lake stood side by side. Both had a military bearing that couldn't be hidden, but while Lake stayed stony-faced and icily calm, Callum looked like his head might explode.

"This isn't CSI," Elle said. "I can't enhance a ten-year-old Polaroid to the point where I see the reflection of a face in somebody's ring."

"A simple no would suffice," he snapped.

"No," Elle said tersely, obviously losing patience.

"Why don't we just break into everybody's houses and search for evidence?" Ryan was still in a huff after being made to clean up the vomit. The experience hadn't interfered with his appetite though, as he was currently snacking on popcorn.

"Like Rachel told the asshole downstairs, we aren't the cops. There's nothing stopping us."

"Uh"—Noah, the ex-cop, raised a hand—"how about the fact we could be arrested for breaking and entering? That should stop us."

Ryan shook his head in disgust. "You Americans are way too cautious."

"Law abiding. Not cautious," Noah corrected.

"We can up surveillance on everyone involved with the company's board," Lake said. "But we can't break into their homes." He ran a hand through his military-short blond hair. "What we're missing here is motive. Why does our blackmailer want Rachel out of TayFor?"

Everyone looked at her as though expecting to see the answer written on her face.

"I have no idea," she said.

"Maybe..." Harry piped up from where he sat beside Elle; their laptops open in front of both of them. "Maybe it's because you got those two guys fired. Maybe the blackmailer thought you'd poke your nose in where it didn't belong and get them fired too."

"It seems a bit drastic to drug and rape someone just to protect your job," Rachel pointed out.

At her words, everyone in the room shuffled in place, looking seriously uncomfortable. Everyone except Harvard.

"Uh, sorry, Rachel," Harry mumbled. "I didn't mean...hell, I don't know what I meant."

Oh, no. She wasn't putting up with this. Getting to her feet, she looked around at each person in the room. Most couldn't look her in the eye. Those who could manage were either close to tears, like Joe's wife—their office manager—Julia, or were full of pity, like Noah.

"Everybody look at me now," she ordered in the tone she only used when she was about to cause serious damage. All eyes met hers. "I want to be very clear. I am still the same rabid bitch you all knew last week. I haven't changed, and I don't intend to either. If you can't even look me in the eye, then you need to leave this room right now. I am *not* ashamed of what happened to me. And I won't accept having anyone around me who feels shame for me."

There were murmurs of apology before the person she'd least expected to talk spoke up. "Rachel," Julia said from the corner, where she hid behind a large office plant while being guarded by her husband. Julia didn't do well with crowds. Or people in general. "No one feels shame. We're all just shocked and hurting *for* you. This is how we show we care about you."

There were nods of agreement as Joe flashed an encouraging smile at the potted plant.

"Well, if you don't mind, I'd rather you showed how much you cared by expressing rage and a deep need to find the men who assaulted me and rip their testicles off before shoving them down their throats."

The room filled with pained groans as several men covered their privates.

Harvard shook his head and grinned at her.

Well, what did he expect? For her to put up with everyone walking on eggshells around her forever?

As she sat back down, Lake flashed her one of his rare smiles. "Whatever their reason, the blackmailer wants you gone from TayFor. If you walk into work Monday as if nothing's happened, there's no guessing what they'll do next. This could get violent."

"They haven't done so before now," Rachel said. "I suspect my blackmailer is a coward. Whoever it is likes to manipulate things while staying hidden."

"But," Lake persisted, "it only took one warning years ago to get rid of you. This time, you're still around after three.

They could be wondering what it will take to get you out of TayFor. That's a dangerous position for you to be in."

"I understand, but I'm not the same person I was ten years ago. I don't scare so easily. Anyway"—she waved a hand at Harvard—"I have a bodyguard."

"And a team at your back." Callum sounded defensive, as if expecting her to argue.

"You aren't alone this time, Rach," Harry said. "You've got all of us."

Everyone nodded, looking determined and deadly serious.

"Oh good," Rachel muttered. "How wonderful."

And Harvard burst out laughing.

Chapter Twenty-Five

❦

"Please put your phone in the tray," Ryan said to everyone as they entered TayFor's main building on Monday morning.

Harvard and Jonathan stood off to one side, keeping an eye out for anyone who objected. TayFor's CEO had lost his patience with anybody who didn't do exactly as they were told.

"Terrance?" Jonathan forced through gritted teeth for the umpteenth time, fury emanating from the man. "I trusted that bastard. Ten years I looked to him to keep this company secure, and all along, he was responsible for destroying my sister's life."

"Rachel's life wasn't destroyed." Hands in pockets, Harvard stood relaxed, taking in every detail around him.

"Derailed then," Jonathan bit out. "In the most horrific way possible."

That Harvard could agree with.

"This is killing Father." Jonathan cursed. "He hired Terrance. If he hadn't..."

"The person behind all this would just have found somebody else to do their dirty work."

Jonathan let out a heavy breath. "You're right. I...we... none of us can get our heads around this." His hands clenched to fists at his sides. "I want to hurt someone. Never saw myself as a violent man, but now all I can think about is ripping those bastards to shreds."

"Yeah, you're not the only one."

As they watched, Charles and Samantha came through the main doors. Samantha smiled and headed straight for them while Charles glared and strode toward security.

"Harvard," she simpered, standing a little too close. "You really must have a word with Rachel. She refuses to visit the bridal boutique I found for her. It was a terrible faff getting them to agree to see us. They're booked out months ahead, and I practically had to beg them to fit us in. Be a darling and make her come with me."

Pulling out his phone, Harvard casually increased the distance between them. "I'm making a note now, so I don't forget."

"You are a catch, aren't you? My cousin's a lucky woman." She stepped right up to him and patted his chest. "Are you sure I can't lure you away? Blondes do have more fun, or so they say."

To the casual observer, Samantha would appear to be playing, but Harvard knew better. He'd come across women like her a few times over the years. Their self-esteem depended on them believing that everyone in the room found them to be the most attractive woman available. The only way to get rid of them was to play to their ego.

He took her hand, patted it, and sighed with feigned reluctance as he released her. "If I wasn't completely in love with your cousin, you would be a serious temptation. But we both know that you don't need me; you could have your pick of any man around you."

Her eyes flashed with approval. "True." She took a step back. "Still, it's a pity. I shall always wonder what might have been."

"Now, that isn't true. I'm the kind of man who's easily forgotten, but a woman like you..." He left it hanging.

"I do believe you're a charmer." Samantha beamed at him, but all flirtatious behavior had vanished. "Now, don't forget to tell Rachel that we simply must visit this designer."

"You have my word." He placed a hand over his heart.

"Men," she cheerfully reprimanded before strolling away.

"You dealt with that pretty efficiently," Jonathan said. "I don't know whether I'm impressed or want to vomit."

"Yeah, let's keep that little exchange between the two of us. I don't want Rachel getting the wrong idea and ripping her cousin's eyes out."

"That would be inconvenient," Jonathan agreed. "Considering Sam's in charge of our marketing and needs her eyes to approve our visuals."

"Wouldn't want to get in the way of TayFor's success," Harvard said somberly.

"You know," Jonathan said, turning serious, "she's done that with every boyfriend Rachel's ever had; sometimes it worked. It's a miracle the two of them still get along."

"It's because Rachel never cared one way or another about those guys. And"—he kept his eye on the desk, where Charles was giving Ryan a hard time—"I'm not her boyfriend; I'm her fiancé."

"Does she know you aren't pretending?"

Harvard cocked an eyebrow. "Do I look like an idiot? Stealth is the only way to deal with your sister. You sneak in under her radar and slowly occupy her territory. Then one day, she looks around, and she's married and wondering how it happened."

"I almost feel sorry for you." Jonathan chuckled. "You have no idea what you're up against."

Harvard motioned to security. "Looks like Ryan needs rescuing."

"Typical. It's always bloody Uncle Charles. The sooner that man retires and gives us all peace, the better."

As they approached the desk, Preston and his brother, Marcus, arrived for the day. They nodded politely at Harvard before turning their attention to where Charles was arguing with Ryan.

"I will *not* hand over my phone," Charles snapped. "You're new here and obviously ignorant about our policy. Phones and personal devices are, and always have been, allowed within this building. Call your supervisor. I want to speak to Terrance immediately."

"Charles," Jonathan said as they reached the desk, "what's the problem?"

"The problem is that this *guard* here wants me to give him my phone. Where's Terrance? He needs to deal with this." He looked around as if expecting the man to manifest. Which was highly unlikely, given that he was still locked up in Benson Security's basement.

"I'm afraid Terrance has taken ill," Jonathan said, struggling to hide his distaste. "Since that left us rather in the lurch, I've asked Harvard to step in until we find a replacement."

"Harvard?" For a second, it looked like Charles' head was about to explode.

"Yes. Being former intelligence and currently employed by one of the most respected security companies in the world, he seemed the best man for the job. The fact that he's practically family is an added bonus."

Harvard smiled politely as Charles and Preston frowned at him. Marcus just looked confused.

"This is highly irregular," Preston said. "Important positions within TayFor are only filled after a lengthy interview process and approval by the board."

"I haven't given him a position," Jonathan said. "I've merely asked him to help out until Terrance feels better."

"This is outrageous," Charles snapped, spittle flying. "Do we even know anything about this man? In a very short time, he's not only managed to worm his way into our company but also Rachel's heart. I can't be the only one who's concerned about this. How do we know he isn't a conman?"

"Bloody hell, Charles," Preston said. "He's standing right there."

"I'm happy for you to check out my background and references," Harvard said with a relaxed smile. "But you can do it after you hand over your phone to Ryan. There's been a security breach. It will take a couple of hours to fix. In the meantime, the building's vulnerable to hackers using cellular devices to access our systems. You'll get your phone back as soon as we've secured the facility." He inclined his head. "As an owner of the company, I'm sure you're more than happy to ensure its continued security."

"Is that all this is?" Marcus reached into his pocket. "Here, take my phone. I'm going to grab a coffee before the board meeting starts." As he walked past Charles, he said, "Stop being a prick and hand over your phone." And then he pushed through the doors to the offices behind them.

"Well, I never," Charles snapped. "Has everyone around here lost all sense of decorum?"

Preston put his phone on the desk. "Just give the man your phone." He gave Harvard a sympathetic smile before following his brother.

Charles slammed his phone onto the table and glared at

them. "I will investigate you. Don't think for one second that I won't." Then he stormed into the building.

"Whoa," Ryan said. "That dude does *not* like you. What did you do to him?"

"I was born black," Harvard said. "You got everybody's phone now?"

"Yep." Ryan grinned and rubbed his palms together. "Let the games begin." He took the tray of cell phones and headed down to security, where Elle and Harry would hack each one.

"With any luck, we'll have your thief within the hour," Harvard said.

Jonathan's eyes turned dark. "Good. I could do with a target for venting my anger."

Couldn't they all?

THE BOARD ROOM WAS BURSTING WITH FAMILY MEMBERS. Every single one who had shares in the company had turned up—which wasn't usually the case. Even Rachel's grandmother and her Uncle Harold were there.

"I've come to see what trouble you cause," her grandmother had told Rachel after she sailed into the room, looking like Katharine Hepburn at a press junket for one of her movies, and took the chair beside her.

"Why on earth would you assume I'd cause trouble?"

"It's in your genes, darling." Her grandmother patted her hand. "Don't worry, you came by it honestly. I caused quite the stir in my day too. Be a dear and fetch me a cup of tea. I need to take my medicine." With a wicked gleam in her eyes, she held up an elaborately enameled flask.

"Really? You're going to spike your tea?"

"If you'd been to as many of these board meetings as I

have, you wouldn't need to ask that." Her eyebrows shot up. "What on earth? Does Theo think he's playing tennis?"

Rachel followed her gran's gaze, and sure enough, Uncle Theo had arrived, decked out in white tennis garb, complete with shorts and a jaunty ribbed jersey draped around his shoulders.

"Sorry about the getup," he said. "Got a match straight after this and no time to change."

"That explains the clothes, but what about the aftershave?" her grandmother muttered to her. "Please open a window while you fetch me my tea."

With a resigned sigh, Rachel went to do her grandmother's bidding.

They'd set up the refreshments table on the wall nearest the door, which meant Rachel was easy access for anyone arriving who wanted to chat. Yay for her.

"Rach!" Her cousin Rupert pulled her into an unwanted hug. "Did you know it's possible to 3D print small batches of drugs? If we were to make our own specialized 3D printers and rent them out to hospitals, they'd have a steady supply, and we'd cut the cost and risks associated with large-scale manufacture. Not to mention, if we cut down the need for hospitals to buy and stockpile our drugs, we could look into building our own smaller, more efficient manufacturing plant in the UK, instead of outsourcing to larger, established plants that will only commit to a minimum order."

Rachel was impressed. "I'm sorry, who are you? And what have you done with my cousin?"

He gave her an enthusiastic smile. "I never knew how interesting the family business was. The more I research, the more ideas I have. I didn't know it was possible to be this engaged and excited about something that wasn't a hand of poker. Look"—he pointed at himself—"I even bought a new suit so I'd look more professional and people might take my ideas seriously." He sobered. "I have a *lot* of ideas, Rach. I really think there are ways we could streamline production. Not only to save us money but also to make distribution more user friendly."

"Well, come talk to me about it later in the week. I am head of special projects and seeing as I have no idea what that means, I guess it can be anything I like. Revamping distribution seems as good a thing to look at as anything else."

"Thanks, Rach, you're the best." He pulled her into a bear-hug before bouncing off to find a seat.

"What was that about?" her grandmother asked when Rachel returned with her tea.

"Turns out Rupert likes working, who knew?"

"That boy." Her grandmother tutted as she added a liberal dose of liquor to her cup. "All he needs is a bit of encouragement, and he'll turn into a fine man. With Charles for a father, a mother who's high as a kite most days, and a sister who only cares about herself, he could use someone believing in him. Be nice to him, darling. I get the feeling he could be a good man one day."

"Is that the sound of you softening?" Rachel said. "Because years ago, you told me that at the first sign of you softening, I was to put you in a home and forget about you. I've been on the lookout ever since."

"Wicked child. I'm sure I said no such thing. Oh look, it's the wives Theo should have kept. His taste went straight downhill after those two."

Rachel turned to see Anne and Stephanie heading straight for them, smiling widely, their eyes warm with genuine affection.

"Rachel." Anne pulled her out of her seat and wrapped her in a hug. Which was exactly why she got on great with Rachel's mother. They were both huggers. "I'm so glad you're back. We need you here. And goodness, you look well, doesn't she, Steph?"

"Gorgeous as usual." Stephanie hugged her too.

Although roughly twenty years apart in age, the two women had formed a strange but strong friendship after Theo divorced them both. Anne's marriage had lasted eighteen years, Stephanie's only eight, but both of them had gained half of Theo's shares when they split. Which meant they both owned a hefty chunk of TayFor.

"Where's that hunky man of yours?" Stephanie looked around the room. In her early forties, with shoulder-length brown hair and a chic sense of style, she was the last time Theo had shown any taste in women.

Rachel waved a hand. "Off securing something."

"I see Theo's on the prowl again," Anne said, her eyes on their ex-husband. Having just turned sixty, Anne had decided to let her hair go gray. Twisted up into a sophisticated French knot, her silver hair complemented her beautiful pastel blue shift dress perfectly.

"How do you know?" Rachel asked, looking over at her tennis-garbed uncle, who was laughing raucously with Rupert.

The two women shared a look then said together, "The smell." Then they burst out laughing and went off to find seats.

One by one, the rest of the family arrived. Charles, looking annoyed as usual. Preston and Marcus, both businesslike and clearly eager to get the meeting over. Samantha, who insisted on talking to Rachel about wedding dresses. And her mother, who kissed her cheek and took the seat on the other side of Rachel.

"How's Father?"

"He's perfectly fine, but he has to take it easy for a few days." She gave Rachel a tight smile that emphasized the dark circles under her eyes. "I want to hire a keeper for him. Does

Benson Security do that sort of thing? I need someone who'll follow him around and ensure he keeps away from fried food."

Rachel swallowed her smile. "I'm sure we could find you someone." Ryan had been particularly annoying lately. It might do him good to go on bacon-watch for a few weeks. That evil thought made her grin.

Her mother rolled her eyes. "I forgot who I was talking to for a second. Forget I asked. I'll speak with Harvard; he seems the more sensible option."

Rachel leaned into her and lowered her voice. "Are you doing okay, Mum?"

"Yes, my darling, I'm fine." Her eyes turned glassy and she blinked back tears, straightening her shoulders as she did so. "I keep telling myself that the past is gone; that there's no point in wondering what we could have done differently. It's the future that matters now and the choices we make from here on in."

"Exactly." Rachel nodded. "Everything will be fine. I promise."

"My darling girl, you're far too capable for your own good. But I do love you."

"Why does everyone feel the need to clarify their love for me?" Rachel said dryly. "It's never just 'I love you,' it's always 'you're awful, but I love you anyway.'"

"Perhaps it's because they've met you," her grandmother said helpfully.

"Okay." Jonathan took a seat at the end of the table. "Let's get this show on the road."

Rachel's grandmother elbowed her and whispered, "I've run out of liquor."

"Too bloody bad," Rachel whispered back. "You can suffer like the rest of us."

Chapter Twenty-Six

✦

"Got it!" Elle's fists shot into the air as she grinned at everyone. "We've got our thief!"

The small gray-walled room they'd commandeered in the security department seemed to glow with her joy.

"Damn it." Harry shoved his laptop away from him in disgust. "I was about five seconds behind you on cracking that phone."

"Five seconds too late. Five seconds slower. Five seconds that get you second place. Who's the best?" Elle held up a hand for a high five. "I'm the best. Admit it. I totally rock."

Harry gave her a lame high five.

"Uh, Elle." Ryan, who'd helpfully paced the room while the tech geniuses hacked the phones in the search for their thief, had obviously run out of what little patience he possessed. "You want to tell the rest of us who it is?"

In reply, she beamed at them and flipped her laptop so they all could see her screen.

Harvard's jaw tightened. "Pack it up. We have a meeting to attend."

Ten minutes later, without knocking, Harvard led his team into the boardroom.

"What on earth?" Charles shouted. "Have you no manners?" He pointed a finger at Jonathan. "This is exactly why you should never have put this man in charge of security without consulting the rest of us first."

Jonathan ignored him. "Did you find something?"

"Yeah." Harvard glanced around the room and caught Rachel's eye. He winked at her, and she rolled her eyes at him, which almost made him grin and ruin his badass image. "How do you want this to go?"

Running his hand through his hair, Jonathan looked at his family. "You can give your report to all of us at the same time."

"Jonathan," Preston said, "what's going on? What report?"

It was Rachel who answered. "Harvard, Ryan, Elle, and myself—"

"I'm a late addition," Harry interrupted, giving everyone a wave and impressing no one with the printed image of bobblehead Einstein on his T-shirt.

Rachel frowned at him before continuing, "We all work for Benson Security."

"You mean *worked*," Marcus said, appearing confused.

"No. I mean, we're still currently there. I'm still a partner. These are still my minions." She waved a hand in their direction, making Harvard grin. "Jonathan and our father hired Benson Security to uncover who's been stealing research from TayFor for the past few years."

Charles shot to his feet. "This is out of order. Something of this magnitude should have gone through the board first."

"Not if it's a board member who's stealing from you," Harvard said.

"Do sit down and shut up, Charles," Francesca told him.

"We have more than enough to deal with without adding your tantrums to the mix."

"Well, I never." He sat down with a thud.

"I'm assuming you've uncovered the thief," Jonathan said.

"Elle?" Harvard indicated that she had the room. "Please do the honors."

Elle practically danced on the spot, making the blue bunches in her hair bounce along with her. "Okay, so we knew secrets were being siphoned off, so we set out to—"

Rachel held up a hand. "We don't need the *Columbo* version. We just need a name, and then the police can take over." She looked at Harvard. "You did call them?"

"No, I thought we'd just take the culprit down to the basement and put a bullet in their head." Of course, he'd called the police.

"I'm not staying here for this." Charles got to his feet again. "How do you expect us to believe a word you say when you can't even take yourselves seriously? I'll call in the police myself. If there's a thief, they can deal with it."

"Oh, there's a thief," Elle said. "And if I can't describe our process, then I'll just go for the big reveal. Ladies and gentlemen, I give you your thief"—she stretched out an arm, sweeping it left to right before stopping on one person —"Preston Talbot."

There was silence until Rachel's grandmother spoke up. "Well, that was a bit anticlimactic, don't you think?"

Harvard definitely had a soft spot for that woman.

Preston looked around the room. "You don't honestly believe them, do you?"

His mother, Anne, leaned forward, placing her hand on the table as though reaching for him. "Preston? Why would they think you stole from us?"

Pure fury flashed in his eyes before disappearing just as quickly. "This is clearly a mistake. I haven't stolen anything.

I'm sure my lawyer will deal with whatever information they have within minutes."

"We have your phone," Harvard said. "It has two apps on it. One connects to a signal jammer on the camera facing West Building. The app shows it was last accessed on the morning that the system went down, when everyone was told not to access the servers.

"And the other app connects wirelessly with the card reader that was hidden under Francesca's work desk and is linked to her computer. On top of that, now that we know who's behind this, we also know where to look for the money. Because money *always* leaves a trail."

Harry nodded from where he stood beside the door. "I'm running searches right now on your financials and any accounts set up in your name or your children's names."

"And I'm looking into your purchasing history," Ryan said. "If there's a record of you buying a Wi-Fi card reader and a signal jammer, I'll find it."

"And even though I did my bit by hacking your phone," Elle said, "I'm going through your contacts to see if I can find the people who bought your information. I'm sure I'll find them eventually. It's like finding a loose piece of wool in a sweater. Once you have it, all you need to do is tug to make the whole thing unravel."

"This is what we do," Rachel told her cousin. "And we're rather good at it."

"None of your so-called evidence would stand up in court." Preston loosened his tie and shifted in his seat. "A phone is a private device, and you certainly didn't have my permission to hack mine."

Anne gasped. "You aren't denying what they found on it? Just questioning their right to go looking for it?"

"And you're wrong anyway," Rachel said. "Everyone signed a disclosure agreement years ago that allows the company to search personal devices at their discretion. As long as they were in the building at the time and were used for work. We all know you make work calls on your phone; we've watched you. Which means TayFor was well within their rights to crack open your phone and peer inside."

"TayFor," Charles snapped. "Not Benson Security. Not *him*." He pointed at Harvard. "He has no right being here. None." He sneered at Rachel. "No one can stop you from making a foolish decision about whom you marry, but we can definitely stop management from putting him in a position of trust. I mean, what do we know about this man? How do we know he can be trusted? For all we know, he might be planting clues to dismantle the board and install himself. He's probably after Rachel's money and the company. Bloody gold digger."

"Charles!" Francesca shot to her feet. "I will not tolerate you speaking to Rachel like that."

"Of course you wouldn't." Charles gave her a look of disgust. "You made the same mistake with your choice of husbands. My father and his brothers started this company. It should have remained with them. It should still be called Talbot Pharmaceuticals, not TayFor. Roger Ford didn't start this business, he just wormed his way into it, exactly the same way this *boy* is doing."

Boy? Hell no. Harvard lost all sense of amusement. "You call me a boy one more time, and I'll escort you from the building. Through that window. This isn't some plantation, and you sure as hell aren't my white overlord. I'm sick of your racist shit, so do me a favor and keep talking, because I would seriously love to make you stop."

Charles' normally ruddy face paled as he shrank in on himself. His bluster disappeared as he obviously read correctly that Harvard wasn't joking.

"Everybody, calm down," Jonathan ordered. "The police will be here soon, and they'll get to the bottom of this."

"*This what?* This preposterous lie against Preston?" Theo snapped. "You've made a mistake. Go over it all again because my son wouldn't do something like this. Tell them, Preston. Tell them they're wrong." He appealed to Rachel, "Why on earth would my son steal from the company? This makes no sense."

Preston barked out a mirthless laugh that had all eyes focusing on him. "Do shut up, Father. You're making everything worse just by being here. Can't you tell when you aren't wanted? None of us..." He waved a hand to indicate his mother, stepmother, and brother. "None of us wants you. You're an embarrassment to us all and have been for years."

Theo's jaw dropped before he gathered himself. "You don't know what you're saying. It's shock from being so heinously accused. Don't worry, son, I'll look out for you."

"You'll look out for me?" Preston laughed hard.

It was cold and filled with bitter anger. Harvard had heard that laughter before and knew it only manifested in people who were broken. His eyes scanned the room, and he unobtrusively signaled to his team not to interrupt, but to stay quiet and watch.

"You'll look out for me?" Preston soared to his feet and leaned over the table toward his father. "The way you looked out for us when you walked out on our mother? The way you've walked out on every family you've had since then, so you could follow your dick all over London? Please, you can't even look out for yourself, let alone anyone else." He slammed his palms on the table, making several people jump.

Stephanie put her arm around Anne, who watched in horror as her son raged at his father.

"You're the reason this happened," Preston spat out. "You keep diluting the share base. Every child you have means more people on this board. Less profit for everyone involved. More stupid voices to listen to as they expound their inane opinions about a company that's nothing more than a meal ticket to them."

He slapped the table again. "You've diluted our heritage. Because of you splitting your shares with every divorce, our family's position on this board was weakened." He swung to Jonathan. "That seat is mine. I'm the eldest. I'm the one with the most experience. I should have been CEO. But no, you get to sit in the seat because your father managed to get his hands on the majority share of the company. A company that wasn't even his. It was ours, damn it."

He glared at his father. "So, yes, because you frittered away my heritage with your stupidity and inability to keep your dick in your pants, I took it back." He stood up straight and tugged down his suit jacket, fixing Jonathan with a suddenly calm and intelligent look. "You can't steal what you already own. As a shareholder in this company, the research belongs to me as well as everyone sitting at this table. It doesn't matter how much evidence you think you have. Because you cannot steal what you already own."

Anne sobbed quietly as the shock of Preston's confession sank in. Theo just sat there, pale and unmoving, as though disconnected from everything that was happening.

"You did it then?" Marcus asked his brother, sounding pained. "You stole from TayFor?"

Preston ignored his brother while he tugged at the cuffs of his shirt and fixed his tie. "I would like to call my lawyer now," he calmly told Harvard.

"The police are waiting in reception," Harvard said. "Ryan will escort you to them and accompany you to the station. You can meet with your lawyer there."

Preston nodded and strode toward the door, hesitating briefly when he opened it. "Think about who the real villain is here. Me for taking what I rightfully own? Or the Ford family for taking our heritage from the rest of us."

As the door closed behind them, silence fell over the room; all that could be heard was Anne's quiet sobbing. Until Charles cleared his throat. "He has a point. I mean, I don't agree with the stealing. He wasn't just taking what was his; he was taking from all of us. But he has a point about this company having been infiltrated by outsiders."

"Charles," Jonathan said evenly, "you're fired. Clear out your desk and hand in your security pass. I've already spent far too many years listening to your bigoted bullshit. I don't want to waste any more of my life on it."

"You can't fire me," he shouted. "I'm a shareholder."

"Actually," Rachel said, "being a shareholder doesn't automatically guarantee you a position with the company. Employment is at the discretion of the management. I should know; I helped Father draft the regulations."

"You always were an interfering little hussy," Charles told her as he got up and stormed toward the door. "I'll see you and your inbred family in court."

"Oh, to hell with it," Harvard said as the man approached him. He pulled back his fist and let rip.

Charles landed on the floor with a bloody nose and a spiteful glint in his eye. "I'll add assault to my litigation, shall I?"

"You'd need a witness for that to stand," Jonathan said. "I saw you run into Harvard's fist. I didn't see him punch you. Anyone else?" He looked around the table, his expression making it very clear that whatever answer the rest of them gave would determine what side they were on.

"Didn't see a thing," Marcus said, and others agreed.

Charles got to his feet. "Samantha? Rupert? Tell them what you saw." It was an order given by a man used to intimidating his family.

"I was looking at my phone," Samantha said. "Sorry, Daddy." She didn't look sorry. In fact, she didn't appear bothered at all.

Charles turned to Rupert.

"I saw you get what you deserved," Rupert said. "And don't worry. I'm okay with being disowned."

With pure fury, Charles strode from the room. Followed closely by Anne, who was still crying, and Stephanie, who was comforting her.

Theo blinked several times but couldn't look anyone in the eye. "I, uh, better go to the police station and see if there's anything I can do," he said before he left too.

"Marcus," Jonathan said, "if you want to go, I understand."

Marcus shook his head. "There's nothing I can do there. I'll see out the day, and then I'm going to find the biggest bottle of whiskey I can get my hands on and ask it what the hell happened with my brother."

Jonathan nodded. "Well," he said to the remaining board members, "it would seem we're a few short. With Charles and Preston gone, the management team will be stretched." He turned to Rachel, his face softening in apology. "Can you please stay on until we get this sorted?"

"Oh, come on," Rachel said. "That could take months."

"I know, but seriously, who else can I ask? Father's in no condition to come back to work. And no one knows the business like you. Even when you weren't here, you spent hours going over Father's reports with him, discussing tactics, formulating policy. No one else could step in and be up and running as quickly." He glanced over at Harvard. "And you'd be welcome as head of security. Until we sort that problem too."

Harvard shrugged. He didn't care where he went as long as it kept him with Rachel. "That's up to Rachel. Where she goes, I go."

"Oh, for the love of Gucci," Rachel snapped. "You don't need to stay by my side now that the job's over. Go play with the other boys. I'm sure Callum has someone he needs shooting."

Samantha stared between him and Rachel. "The wedding is still on though, isn't it?"

"Yes," Harvard said at the same time as Rachel said, "No."

"Thanks for clearing that up," Samantha mumbled before raising her voice. "Until you figure it out, I'll just carry on planning. Which means"—she pointed at Rachel—"you don't get out of visiting that bridal boutique."

"Rachel?" Jonathan said. "What will it be? I don't mean to pressure you, but I need you. Without Preston, I'll have to take on our legal work. I could do with another pair of hands to help run things. We could share the CEO role until we figure everything out."

"She'll do it," their grandmother said.

"Gran!" Rachel snapped.

"Oh, for goodness' sake, we both know you'll give in. You might act like a right little witch, but underneath, somewhere, you have a heart of gold. And you'd never leave your brother in the lurch."

Rachel just glared at her while Jonathan tried not to grin.

"Um." Rupert put up his hand, as though asking a question in school. "Are we carrying on with the meeting? Or are we too traumatized? Because I have some ideas about distribution that I'd like to run past everybody."

There was a moment where everyone just looked at Rupert, and then, as a group, they stood and made their way out of the room.

Harvard snagged Rachel in the hallway by wrapping an arm around her waist. "One down," he said. "One to go." Meaning they could now concentrate on her blackmailer.

"Don't talk to me," she said in that icy tone that made

him crazy to touch her. "Not unless it's to admit that this engagement is a farce."

"Don't say engagement," her mother snapped as she passed. "It's common."

"I truly hate my family," Rachel complained before heading to her office.

Chapter Twenty-Seven

When they got back to Rachel's apartment building, there was a package waiting for them at the concierge's desk.

"Did you order something?" Harvard asked as he reached around her and took the small brown padded envelope from the doorman, being careful to touch only its corners.

"Not that I remember," Rachel said coolly, but the look in her eye told him she was thinking the same as him—the blackmailer had sent it.

Harvard checked both sides of the envelope. "It only has your name on it. No address. No return information." He looked at the waiting doorman. "Who dropped it off?"

"A courier company." The man pulled a notepad toward him. "Atlantic Couriers." He ripped off the top sheet of paper and handed it to Harvard. "The phone number's on there. Ms. Ford-Talbot has never received a package without a return address, so I thought it best to note down all the details of the delivery. Just in case."

Harvard was impressed. "Good thinking."

The man merely nodded. "We have several wealthy, high-profile residents in this building. Security's good, thanks to your company, but it doesn't cover deliveries. That's why I never send anything up to the apartments unless I'm sure about it."

Harvard hoped to hell this guy was being paid well because, in that one sentence, he'd proved he was worth every cent.

"Thank you, Jeremiah," Rachel said. "As usual, I very much appreciate your vigilance."

They nodded to the concierge, then headed for the elevator.

As the doors closed behind them, Harvard said, "I hope he gets a hefty bonus come Christmas."

"Jeremiah's very well paid. And yes, he gets several bonuses a year. If one wants good staff, one must treat them well."

"Yes." He grinned. "One must."

She glanced down at the envelope. "You think it's from the blackmailer, don't you?" If she was worried, it didn't show.

"Yeah," Harvard said as they stepped out into her hallway. "Which means they know where you live."

"Anyone with access to TayFor's personnel files would know where I live."

In other words, it didn't mean the blackmailer was someone close to her.

Once securely inside her apartment, Harvard put the envelope on the dining table before sending texts to Ryan, Elle, and Harry. "I've asked the team to come straight over. We'll wait until they get here before we open this."

He looked up from his phone to find Rachel staring at the envelope. She'd taken off her jacket and had her arms folded over the severe, black form-fitting dress she'd chosen for work that day.

"I'd rather not wait." Her dark eyes captured his, communicating far more than the unemotional tone of her voice. Telling him just how wary she really was. "If there are more photos in there, I'd rather deal with seeing them without my colleagues watching me."

Harvard ran a hand over the dome of his head. "I don't know if that's a good idea. I've got a bad feeling about this."

She stared at him for a long minute before she said just one word, "Please."

He hung his head, knowing there was no way he'd refuse her this. "Okay. I need scissors or a knife and a pair of latex gloves."

"Why on earth would I have latex gloves lying around?"

Yeah, for a second, he'd forgotten who he was dealing with. "You've got kitchen scissors though, right?"

"How would I know?" She threw her hands in the air as if exasperated by his very normal questions. "You're the one who cooks. I can tell you where the bottle opener is, but I don't remember seeing scissors."

With a shake of his head, he strode to the knife block by the vast built-in cutting board. Sure enough, there were scissors. He held them up.

Rachel looked unimpressed. "My interior designer bought that block, along with everything else in the kitchen. I've never used it."

"When this is over, I'm teaching you to cook." Harvard grabbed two tissues from the box near the sink on his way back to the table.

The look of horror on Rachel's face was priceless. "Why on earth would I want to do that?"

"So you don't starve to death if the Savoy stops delivering?"

"But wouldn't you cook for me?"

Harvard almost tripped over his own feet. It was the first time she'd even hinted that they might have a future together, and apparently it was one where she expected him to cook.

"Yeah," he said, his voice softening. "I'll make sure you're well-fed."

She stuck her chin in the air. "See? No need for lessons. Now, let's get this over with before the hordes arrive."

Holding the envelope with a tissue, to preserve any prints that might still be on it, Harvard sliced across the top before turning it upside down and emptying its contents onto the table.

A thumb drive fell out.

"No photos," Rachel murmured. "Unless they've gone digital. Do you think that's what they've done? Scanned the photos so they can keep them, instead of giving them to me? I mean, they must have a limited supply. They are Polaroids after all."

"Don't know," Harvard said, but that bad feeling that had saved his life on several occasions was back and blaring at him to abort. "Maybe we should leave this until Elle gets here. She can plug it into something that won't be destroyed if it's infected."

"Michael." The way she said his name made his chest tighten. It was intimate. Personal. Just for the two of them. "I know you're trying to protect me, but I have to see what's on there when there's no one around to witness my reaction."

"Rachel, *I'm* here."

For a second, she seemed confused. "But you don't count."

The magnitude of that simple statement stole his ability to breathe. Because it meant she trusted him enough to let him see her vulnerable. To Rachel, he was an insider. Possibly the only one she had.

What a helluva time to discover she'd let him get that close.

With a curse, he rubbed a hand down his face and gave

her what she wanted. What she *needed.* "Okay, we'll do it your way. But we'll plug the drive into your TV first, that way it can't corrupt your computer. If there are photos on there, we'll be able to see them on the screen anyway, and if there are documents, we'll know if the files are malicious based on how the TV reacts. If it infects your TV, then I think it's safe to say, we shouldn't plug it into a computer without Elle being here to fix anything that goes wrong." It was the best he could do. The smallest measure of protection. That, and the fact he would be at her side.

"That sounds reasonable." Rachel turned toward the living room.

Harvard used a tissue to pick up the thumb drive before following her. "I'm not sure this is the wisest decision," he said as she picked up the remote and aimed it at the painting over the fireplace.

"Duly noted," she said, as the painting slid up into the ceiling to reveal a large screen TV.

Harvard went straight to the TV and positioned the USB at the port. "You sure?"

"Yes. Now hurry up, or the others will get here before I've had a chance to see what's on it."

There was nothing else he could do to stall or talk some sense into her, so he pushed the drive into the port. For a second, nothing happened, and then a message appeared on the screen. White text on a plain black background.

Resign Tomorrow.

He glanced at Rachel, who looked about as bewildered as he felt.

"They could have written that on a Post-it Note," she said.

"Here, gimme the remote." Harvard crossed the room to her, his back to the TV, and his gaze on her face.

And he saw the instant everything changed.

The color drained from Rachel's face as she whispered,

"No." She swayed as if about to topple, her eyes widening with shock. And then the sound kicked in, and a voice moaned, *"No, please, no."*

He spun to see a much younger Rachel on the screen. Two men stood over her, neither of their faces in shot. As a low groan sounded behind him, he spun back to *his* Rachel, who stood frozen in place, staring in horror at the TV while clutching the damn remote to her stomach.

"Turn it off," he ordered, reaching for her.

But she didn't hear him. For her, nothing else existed in that moment other than what was unfolding on the screen.

"Give me the remote." He tried to pry it from her hands without hurting her. "Come on, Rachel, we need to switch it off."

"This is what you want?" One of the men on the screen said to the person off camera. *"The necklace?"* He shrugged before removing the heirloom locket Rachel always wore. And then he wrapped it around his dick before—

With an agonized wail, Rachel crumpled to the floor, the remote tumbling from her hands. Harvard lunged for it and switched off the damn TV. Rachel wasn't looking at it anyway. She stared at nothing as she clawed at her throat, tears pouring down her cheeks.

"Get it off me." She scratched at her throat, trying to dig the necklace out from where it had become tucked inside her dress. "Get it off me. Get it off me. *Getitoffme!*"

Blood trailed down her throat as she scratched at the chain. Harvard fell to his knees beside her and grabbed her wrists to stop her. One of her hands slipped free, catching the chain at last and ripping the necklace from her throat. Sending it hurtling across the room as a long, keening wail escaped her.

"Look at me, Rachel. Look at me." He stroked her hair, trying to calm her. "Everything's going to be okay."

"It won't come off. I can't get it off." Her hands reached for her throat, her black eyes pleading. "Help me. Please help me."

Harvard caught her wrists before she could hurt herself again. "Rachel, damn it, listen to me. The necklace is gone. It's gone. You got it."

"No, no, no, no." She snatched her hands away, covering her mouth as her eyes went wide.

And then she doubled over, palms to the floor, sobbing and retching until her stomach was empty.

"Fuck, baby, please. You're killing me. Let me help. I need to help."

He rubbed her back and held her hair, feeling more help-less than he'd ever felt in his life.

At last, she stopped vomiting. As her head fell forward, Harvard gently tugged her away from the mess on the floor. "It was on me," she said hoarsely. "This whole time. On my skin." She gagged again. "They used it to—" She jerked away from him and fell to her hands and knees, retching. But there was nothing left to bring up.

Harvard pulled her back against him and held her care-fully. Knowing she was precious. Hoping she'd feel that knowledge in his touch. "It's gone, Rachel, I promise. It's okay. You're okay."

"I can still feel it on my skin, where it always sat. It's dirty. *I'm* dirty. Never, ever going to get clean. Never."

Cradling her to him, he got to his feet. "We'll make it clean. It's going to be okay." And then he strode down the stairs to the master bathroom.

"It's still on my skin," she whispered. "I wore it every day. Touched it all the time. And it was tainted." Her gaze met his, her dark eyes pooled with tears. "Like me."

"Never," he said vehemently. If only one thing got through

to her, he wanted it to be this. "You hear me. There's nothing tainted about you. Nothing."

"I can still feel the chain on my skin, the weight of the locket around my neck," she whispered, her hand drifting to her already torn throat. "It's like a noose."

Harvard settled her on the low stool in front of the bathroom vanity and started the shower before quickly shedding his clothes. With care, he undressed Rachel too. All the while, she sobbed silently, rocking back and forth, lost in herself.

He lifted her against him and stepped into the shower with her in his arms. The hot water beating down on them, Rachel lay limply against his chest.

"Can you stand?" he asked softly.

There was no answer, just those agonizing sobs. After carefully placing Rachel on her feet, he held her up with one arm while reaching for the shower gel and washcloth with the other.

"I'm going to make it all go away, Rachel. You hear me? We'll get rid of what's left of that necklace. It won't be there anymore. I promise I'll take care of it. Just hold on to me, let me do this for you. I've got you."

He lathered the cloth and tenderly wiped her throat, aware that the soap would make the raw scratches sting. "I'm so sorry," he whispered. "We'll get some cream on those soon."

"I wore it with everything." Her agony-filled eyes met his. "It touched all of my clothes."

He carefully ran the cloth over her breasts and stomach. "We'll get you new clothes."

"It was a family tradition." Her voice was an agonized breath. "I was supposed to put my future in that locket. When I met the man I planned to marry, when I had children, they were supposed to go inside." Silent tears fell from eyes that held such depths of pain. "They took my future."

He shook his head. "No, they didn't. Your future's standing right in front of you. They didn't take anything from you. Nothing. Because you're too strong. You hold it all tight inside of you, where they can't get any of it."

"I was part of a tradition..." Her eyes begged him to understand, to recognize all that had been stolen from her, and his heart broke all over again. "One that ended with me."

"We'll start a new tradition. One that we can pass down to our kids."

Her hand fluttered to her throat. "I can still feel it there."

"I swear, it's gone. You got it off, and you'll never see it again."

"Feel so dirty," she mumbled, mostly to herself.

"Don't you feel me washing it all away, Rachel?" He ran the cloth down her back and over her hip. "Concentrate on how it feels. Can you smell the shower gel? It's like flowers in the spring. Daffodils. Take a deep breath; let it fill you. It smells good, doesn't it? Fresh. New. Do you feel my touch, Rachel? My touch. Not theirs. Not anyone else's. It's just you and me here. Concentrate on that. On me washing all the memories away for you."

He added more soap to the cloth before making sure he wiped it over every inch of her. Head to toe. "When we get out of here, all the bad memories will be gone. Everything will be clean and fresh and new. But underneath it all, there will still be you. The you nobody can change or damage because you're strong and smart, and so courageous that you scare me half to death. All the rest of it, what they did, that's just on the surface, and we're washing it away. All that will be left is Rachel. The amazing, difficult, gorgeous woman I love so damn much."

She pressed her forehead to his chest, her fingers curling

into his hips as she cried herself raw. "Michael," was all she said.

"Yeah, I'm your Michael." He kissed her head before rinsing away the soapsuds and wrapping her in a thick white towel.

Once he'd dried her off, he carried her to the bed, where he climbed in and sat with his back against the headboard, Rachel cradled in his lap. He shut off the lights with the remote and held her close, protecting her in his arms as she cried herself to sleep.

A creak from the hallway had Harvard's head snapping to the open door. Elle appeared, giving him a sad little smile. It was clear she'd been crying, which meant Harry must have let the team into the apartment. They would have found the evidence and realized what had taken place.

Harvard held up a hand and signaled that Rachel was asleep.

"We've cleaned up," Elle whispered. "The rug's ruined, so we've taken it out of the apartment. Harry and I have the thumb drive, and we'll go through the video in detail. Hopefully, it will give us more to go on than the photos did." She looked on Rachel with love and pity, and Harvard was glad she wasn't awake to see it. "What do you want us to do with the necklace?"

He shook his head. "I honestly don't know."

"I'll bag it up and put it in the safe at Benson Security; that way, Rachel can deal with it when she's ready." She grimaced. "If ever."

Harvard nodded as he stroked the hair of the woman who'd become his life.

Elle watched him, her lips trembling. "We'll lock up. You'll call if you need us?"

"Yeah," he said. "Go find something for me, Elle. Some direction to point me in, so I can take these bastards out."

"You've got it," she promised before disappearing.

"It's going to be okay," Harvard whispered to a sleeping Rachel. "We'll get them."

If it was the last thing he did, he'd hunt down the people tormenting Rachel and wipe them off the face of the earth.

For her.

Chapter Twenty-Eight

When Rachel opened her eyes, the first thing she saw was Harvard sitting in the armchair facing her bed. He was decadence personified, wearing nothing but a pair of faded blue jeans that rode his hips, the top button undone. His knees spread, and his hands resting on the arms of the chair, he stared straight at her.

For a few minutes, they stayed like that, quietly watching one another. Her gaze caressed the planes and curves of his body, taking in the strength in his shoulders and the definition in his abs. The soft light from the pool made him seem as though he'd been staged for a fashion photoshoot. The kind where they bring in rugby players to give the clothes an edge.

"Is your father still handsome?" Rachel asked hesitantly, reluctant to break the peace of their silence.

His full lips quirked. "Don't think I'm the best judge of that."

"I bet he is. Genetics like yours don't just pop up out of nowhere, and you're definitely the type of man whose good looks will only get better with age."

"Guess you'll have to stick around to see if your theory proves true."

She licked her lips, detecting the faint aftertaste of mint but unable to recall when she'd brushed her teeth. "I'm considering it."

"Anything I can do to help sway the decision in my favor?"

"That depends; is it in your favor to spend the rest of your life with or without me?"

His eyes darkened. "Definitely in my favor to have forever with you. Is that what we're talking about, Rachel? Forever?"

While she'd never found the American accent particularly attractive, she couldn't imagine Harvard sounding any other way. That rumbling depth, rolling over those soft vowels, was something she'd never grow tired of listening to.

"Why don't you have a pet name for me?" she asked. "Callum calls Isobel his wee darling. Dimitri calls Megan Buffy. And Joe calls Julia baby."

His smile was so potently sexy that she was sure she could become pregnant just by looking at it. "You want me to call you baby?"

"Do I look like a child?"

"Yeah, that's what I thought." He turned serious. "You don't have a pet name because, as far as I'm concerned, your given name *is* a term of endearment. Can't you hear what I feel for you every time I say it? I'm telling you how much you mean to me every time your name passes my lips."

Her heart swelled at the words, and she stilled. For the first time in as long as she could remember, her heart didn't feel constrained. The chains had been removed by the man watching her so intently. He'd broken each and every link with his slow, systematic persistence.

Rachel no longer wanted the distance between them, but when she threw back the covers, she was mildly surprised. "I'm naked," she said as the air hit her skin.

"Mmm, so you are."

His eyes caressed her as she walked the short distance between them. Once there, she climbed onto his lap and straddled him, flattening her hands on his chest. His skin was soft and smooth, his muscle firm and warm, his scent familiar —the ocean on a summer's day.

"I don't want to talk about what happened earlier," she said.

"I figured." His right hand rested on the curve of her hip, his thumb caressing.

She took a deep breath and dismissed the ugliness of the memories. She was clean. Inside and out. And she only wanted to focus on the good—for now.

"Well, that's not entirely true. There's one thing I wouldn't mind discussing." She leaned into him, her nipples brushing over his chest as she whispered against his ear, "You told me you love me."

"Yeah, I did."

A warmth raced through her and settled in her newly freed heart. "Did you mean it?"

"Never been more serious about anything in my life."

Her throat tightened, and she knew she had to give him something back. Say something. But the words were stuck inside. As though what she felt was too big, too overwhelming to express. Or, she had just as much trouble admitting her feelings as she had apologizing.

Nuzzling the curve of his throat, she gave him what she could. "Make *love* to me."

"I think you should make *love* to *me*."

"Yes. That's a much better plan." She kissed along his jawline to his lips, teasing the fullness of them.

"Rachel," he whispered against her mouth.

And she heard it. The love overflowing from her name. Harvard's love for her.

"I'm not an easy person," she told him, leaning back to search his gaze for the honesty of his reaction. "I won't ever be any other way."

His hand cupped her nape, his fingers threading through her hair. "I like you fine exactly as you are."

"That's now." She felt she had to give him the brutal truth. "But after a while, people tend to find their patience wears thin with me." She wasn't apologizing for it. She was how she was meant to be, and she liked herself just fine too. But he deserved a warning. Just the one.

His smile was wicked. "Lucky for you, I'm famous for my patience."

"Mmm," she said, closing the distance to his lips. "Lucky for me indeed."

Their kiss, slow and sensual, was full of things Rachel might never be able to voice. But she could tell him with her lips, her body, her desire.

Slowly, thoroughly, she kissed her way from his lips, down his throat, and across his chest. She slid out of his lap and knelt on the floor between his knees. Keeping her eyes fixed on his, she took her time unbuttoning his jeans.

"You're beautiful," he told her, sounding awed.

He was the beautiful one. Inside and out. "Lift your hips."

It took seconds to remove his jeans and find he wore nothing underneath. She ran her hands up his solid thighs to the proud erection waiting for her. Tracing the thick vein that ran from the base to the head, she looked up at him.

"I was sure I didn't want this relationship," she confessed.

He sifted her hair through his fingers. "And now?"

"I never want it to end." She leaned forward and took him in her mouth, reveling in the gasp her touch elicited. Feeling deep satisfaction in the way his hand tightened in her hair and his thighs clenched around her shoulders.

As she loved him with her mouth, enjoying his musky

taste and scent, her eyes drifted up to his face, only to find him watching her intently.

"Come back up here, Rachel," he purred her name. "If you keep doing that, I won't last. And I want to be inside you. I want us to be connected."

She moaned around his thick width. Yes, she wanted to feel connected too. But she also wanted to keep him where he was—at her mercy.

"Rachel," he rumbled as he gently tugged at her hair. "I want to touch you. Come up here so I can make you feel good."

Shivering at the promise in his voice, she reluctantly released him. As soon as she freed him from her mouth, strong hands slid under her arms, and he lifted her back onto his lap. Her knees slipped into the space either side of him, between his hips and the chair, and she felt his hard length slide through her eager wetness.

With a gasp, she tried to get her hand between them, to guide him into her, but Harvard had other ideas. Using his strength, he kept her on her knees while lavishing attention on her breasts.

"Oh, yes," she moaned, clasping his head to her.

The room spun around her as his lips teased, nibbled, and sucked. Each delicious sensation shot through her body like a pinball in a machine, hitting all the best spots and ringing bells.

Panting, she tried to lower her hips and slide onto him, but he held her tight. A firm, steady hand moved down the length of her back and over her behind before cupping and kneading. She arched her body, pressing her rear into his hold.

"Yeah, push out some more, just like that," he said before engulfing a nipple in the heat of his mouth.

Rachel did as she was told and felt his hand slide down between her cheeks and lower to her aching wet core. Wicked fingers petted and teased, making her moan and beg and gasp in desperation. "Please, please, please…" she wailed, clutching him to her, straining against his tight grip as he kept her hovering above him. She'd never begged a man in her life. Not for something she wanted so desperately. She'd always seen it as weakness.

But Harvard was different. It wasn't a game he played with her. This was no battle of egos. He wasn't trying to prove anything by holding her on the edge of release. This was all about pleasure and trust and…love.

His merciless fingers teased her clit, dancing around it in ever-decreasing circles until he reached the very center and pressed. Her back bowed. Her muscles clenched. A long wail resounded through the room. Inside her head, lights flashed and danced in rhythmic explosions. And just as it began to ease, she felt him grip her hips and lower her onto his waiting length.

"So good," she cried out as he slowly filled her. He lowered her until she was sitting flush with him and they were completely joined.

"Connected," he said as he brushed kisses across her cheeks.

Rachel soared, flying high above them. Tethered only by the sensations rippling through her body. All she could feel, see, taste was him. His scent engulfed her, drugging her senses, leaving her desperate for more.

"Ride me, Rachel," came the gruff order as his hands moved her hips in a rhythm that pleased them both.

Once she started moving, she couldn't stop. Feeling the delicious stretch and rub as he filled her up, teasing nerves that only he could reach, giving pleasure only he could give.

Touching him was an addiction. One that made possessiveness rear its head and roar. "This body is mine," she declared, her fingers digging into his shoulders.

"And is this body mine?" His strong hands lifted her hips before slamming her down onto him again.

"Yes," she screamed. "Yes, it's yours."

He clasped her nape. "Then give me all of it." And covered his mouth with hers.

Their kiss was desperate, hungry, and lacking in finesse. But Rachel didn't care. All she could think about, all she wanted, was *all* of him. She moved faster, grinding her hips into his, gasping her pleasure into his mouth. Swallowing his sounds of need in return.

His arm tightened around her as she climbed again. Her limbs were weak, her movements uncoordinated, as thoughts fled and sensation took over. Giddy, she spun around inside her mind, trusting him to keep her safe.

His hips surged, pushing himself deeper. Once. Twice. Three times and they exploded together. His body tensed, his muscles clenched beneath her, around her, inside of her as they fell over the precipice, safe in each other's arms.

Gradually, as though emerging from a daze, Rachel blinked her eyes and the room came back into focus. She still straddled Harvard, a dead weight in his arms, their bodies slick with sweat and sticky with release. His heart thudded against her chest, their beats matching as they panted for air.

His hand caressing her back, he kissed her temple. "I heard you," he said, his voice full of emotion. "And I love you too."

Rachel's arms tightened around him. "I can't move."

His deep chuckle reverberated through her. "Then, we stay here."

It was as though they were secure inside their own cocoon, and neither of them wanted to do anything to jeopardize it. Rachel wasn't sure how long they sat like that as her mind wandered and her thoughts reordered themselves. But eventually, clarity and the world outside began to intrude.

"I'm not going back to Benson Security," she said at last. "I'm staying at TayFor. It's where I was always meant to be."

He squeezed her tight for a second. "They need a new head of security anyway."

"You don't have to take that job, Michael. I know it's not what you envisioned doing when you left the CIA. It's hardly the pinnacle of a security career."

She felt him shrug. "I'm not an ambitious man, Rachel. I wanted the challenge of working with the CIA, now I want the challenge of loving you and making our life together. I'll be fine. And if I get bored, I can always do some freelance work for Callum."

"You're sure you want to come with me?" Changing his whole life for her was a huge ask, and she feared he'd regret it.

"I'm sure, but there's a condition."

Her heart stuttered. "Of course, there is."

"No trust." He chuckled again. "I want us to get married for real. Those are my terms for sorting out TayFor's security and for watching your back for the rest of your life. You have to make an honest man of me."

"You are pathetically bad at negotiation." She felt a surge of pure happiness. "You should have held out for a higher salary and a better car."

"I don't need a higher salary. I'm marrying an heiress." When she sat up and glared at him, he laughed. "I'm worth millions, Rachel. I'm very good at playing the stock market. I don't need your money or the job at TayFor."

"Why didn't you tell me? Or my stupid cousins when they went on about prenups."

"Because it's not important. I was lucky with the stock market, that's all. Plus, I planned to keep you whether I had money or not."

She narrowed her eyes at him. "That arrogance of yours really isn't attractive."

"Yes, it is." He smiled, and it made her melt. "You haven't answered me. We're getting married, right?"

Letting out a heavy sigh, she rested her head back on his shoulder. "I suppose so. If we must."

"Your enthusiasm underwhelms me, but I heard a yes in there, and that's all I care about." His body flexed as something seemed to occur to him. "We're not going to triple barrel our names, are we? Rachel Ford-Talbot-Carter? That's just wrong."

"Don't be an idiot." She snuggled closer. "You'll just change your name, and that will be the end of it."

"Yeah, that ain't gonna happen."

"Men. You're always so difficult."

"You'd better believe it," he said as he stood with her wrapped around him. "Come on. This time, you can scrub my back." And he headed for the bathroom.

Chapter Twenty-Nine

R achel might have avoided the topic of the video during her night with Harvard, but the following morning, there was no getting away from it. Especially as her colleagues at Benson Security seemed so adamant about discussing it.

It was barely seven a.m., and the conference room was full. Everyone who was able had turned up for the meeting—and they'd brought breakfast along with them. There were donuts and Danish pastries, coffees and teas. And then there was Ryan, with a full English breakfast in front of him.

Rachel let out a sigh of disgust as she eyed the mountain of food in front of Ryan. "Do you have to turn every surface in front of you into a pig trough? You're heading for a heart attack." Not that she cared. She just felt the need to point it out.

"At least I have a heart." He grinned and held up his hand to Joe for a high five.

Joe just groaned. "Dude, that was lame."

"Yeah? Well, it's early."

"Aye," Callum snapped. "It is. Too damn early. Some of us

have been up most of the night. How about we get to the point of this meeting?"

"Isobel isn't sleeping too well during this stage of her pregnancy," Noah informed everyone. "So Callum isn't sleeping either."

"Did I ask you to update everybody on my life?" Callum barked.

Lake shook his head at his partner, his lip twitching in what approximated a smile for him. "Did Elle get something off the video?"

Well, that answered that question. Apparently, everyone was up to speed with the latest piece of her past that had slapped her in the face.

"No." Elle shook her head and yawned. "Harry's running every imaging analysis tool we can get our hands on. The pixel ratio isn't as good as we'd like, but then the video was shot on a ten-year-old phone. Cameras have improved a lot since then. After we run a comparative diagnostic, we'll take the video frame by frame and enhance the quality to isolate any details that may have been hidden. But that'll take time."

"What about the metadata?" Harvard asked.

"It was stripped." Elle looked annoyed. "But Harry thinks it was done recently by a newer app, so there might be a shadow of it left underneath."

"What's metadata?" Rachel asked. Must they speak in techie? And if they had to, couldn't they at least be polite enough to translate for the normal people?

"It's information about a file that's stored in a way that you can't see it unless you go looking for it." Harvard smiled at her. "Ten years ago, before people were fully aware of what extra data was saved with their files, and before guidelines and restrictions were put into place, there was a whole lot of sensitive info stored in the metadata. If the team can access it, they might get some personal info that you wouldn't get from a phone today."

Elle nodded. "Exactly. The video editing might offer up some clues too. If that's recent, then there might be some metadata transfer from the process that the blackmailer missed. It depends on how computer savvy they are."

Rachel waved a hand. "Blah, blah, blah, computer talk, more blah. Do we have something or not?"

Harvard rubbed the spot between her shoulders, making everyone freeze in place and stare at them.

"She gets cranky in the mornings," he said with amusement.

"I hope you know what you're doing." Ryan shook his head at Harvard. "Rachel's been known to eat her prey."

Callum glared at them. "Can we focus? What you're saying is, you don't have anything off the video yet, but you and Harry are working on it. Where *is* Harry?"

"Here." A hand appeared above the end of the table.

Rachel peeked underneath, and sure enough, Harry was sitting tailor style on the floor, surrounded by at least half a dozen laptops.

She straightened again and looked at Callum, whose head was red.

"Why the hell are you on the floor?" he shouted.

"Needed more space."

"Get your arse to the table for meetings. This isn't how we run a business."

"I swear," Rachel said. "If you start going on about how much better things were in the army again, I will tackle you to the floor, remove one of your prosthetic legs, and beat you to death with it."

There was silence before Harry said, "She's *always* been cranky in the mornings."

Lake leaned forward to clasp his hands on the table. "Let's

recap. We don't have anything from the video yet. We don't have any leads on the men who attacked Rachel. We don't know who's behind all of this, but for some reason, they want you gone from the family company. Did I miss anything?"

"No." Rachel folded her arms over her red and black color-block dress. "Except that I have no intention of giving in to a blackmailer's demands ever again. Once was enough, and I'm a whole lot older and less easy to intimidate than I was when I was twenty. They're going to be very disappointed when I don't resign today."

"You can't go back to TayFor," Lake said evenly, obviously under the misguided belief that he was the boss of her. "It's too dangerous. We don't know what your return might provoke."

"Plus"—Elle stole a sausage from Ryan's plate, earning herself a glare as he wrapped his arm around his food to guard it—"there's no need to go back to TayFor; we found the thief."

"That's not the only reason I have for returning," Rachel said, feeling strangely hesitant about sharing her plans. She glanced at Harvard, and his usual calm demeanor immediately eased her nerves. "Which is why I called you here this morning. I've decided to return to my family's company for the foreseeable future."

"Yes!" Ryan shot to his feet, fists in the air. "Best. News. Ever." He grinned as he pointed around the room. "Pay up because I won the bet. She's been lured back to the family company. I'm rich." He faced Rachel. "I could kiss you right now."

"And then I'd have to get a rabies shot, so please don't."

"What bet?" Harvard asked as Ryan sat back down and folded his arms over yet another T-shirt that Rachel didn't understand. This one said, *By the Power of Grayskull.*

"You know how we had to drop the sex bet?" Ryan said.

Everyone around him groaned. "What? We can't even mention the word now?"

"This is a business meeting," Callum snapped. "So, no, you can't mention sex."

Ryan pointed at Rachel. "It's not like it's a secret. They're obviously doing it, which means I would've won the first bet too."

"You shouldn't even be betting on your teammate's sex life." Callum glared at Ryan, as though that would somehow miraculously make his point sink through Ryan's thick skull.

"Exactly," Ryan said. "Once we realized that betting on Rachel's sex life might cause her to have a full-blown PTSD fit, we canceled the bet. But I started a new one on how long before she went back to TayFor for real. And I won. I am the master!"

"Please, for the love of Prada, stop talking," Rachel told him.

"I don't even care that everybody's in a bad mood. That's how happy I am," Ryan said before he got stuck back into his food.

"Rachel," Lake said, returning her attention to the man who'd started Benson Security, "explain your leaving." He was also a man of few words.

"It's really very simple; my family needs me right now. And I fit in there, in a way I never did here or with Harry's company. Programming is Harry's dream. Benson Security's yours. But TayFor has always been mine." She studied her nails for a moment, wondering if it was time to swap out the red. Perhaps for black. Or maybe an icy silver. "I don't plan on selling my share in this company. I'd like to remain a silent partner."

"Is that even possible?" Ryan asked, grinning at his own joke.

Rachel, along with everyone else, ignored him. "I intend

to start working for TayFor from today. There isn't much to hand over as far as Benson Security is concerned; the women's side of the business has only just started. Perhaps Julia could look after that in my absence."

"Me?" came a squeak from the houseplant.

"Yes. You. It takes a businessperson to organize it, and you are the most qualified." She pointed at Harvard. "Apart from that, I'm taking him with me."

"Bloody hell, Rachel," Callum exploded. "You can't just walk out on us and take our people with you."

"Of course, I can. I'm still a partner in this company, which means I own a stake in him."

There were groans throughout the room.

"Rachel," Elle said patiently, "we talked about this during our girls' night. You don't own the people who work for you. They...we aren't chattels."

"What Rachel means," Harvard said, "is that I'm *choosing* to go with her and take over as head of security at TayFor. You can consider this my resignation."

"Hell, no," Joe and Noah both snapped at the same time.

Noah glared at Harvard. "The whole point of the three of us joining the same security company as Joe and Grunt was to hang out together. Beast's already pissed off to follow his wife around the world. If you go too, that'll just leave me and Joe in London. Grunt might as well be on another planet instead of in Scotland; phone conversations with him are few and far between and consist mainly of me talking and him grunting. You talked me into moving my kids to London. And now you're backing out on us?"

"I'll still be in London, and I'll still get to hang out with you. It's not like we're moving to New Zealand; we'll see *all* of you."

"Speak for yourself," Rachel said.

There were a few people she'd be happy to see the back

of. Ryan being top of her list. She already had an annoying younger brother; she didn't need a second one. And Ryan had been trying to fill that role for years. Although without her around to keep an eye on him, he'd probably choke on a chicken bone. She sighed. She'd have to see the idiot after all. Responsibility sucked.

"Are you going to tell them our other news?" Harvard asked, loud enough for everyone to hear.

"No." She frowned at him.

His lips twitched. "Then how about I do it? We're getting married."

"Married?" Elle gaped at them. "For real?"

"Don't make such a big deal out of it," Rachel said. "I'm sure it won't last."

"That's what you said about your relationship to begin with," Elle accused, as though Rachel had deliberately lied to them. It wasn't her fault Harvard kept screwing up her plans.

"When we're done with this touchy-feely crap," Callum blared over all of them, "can we concentrate on Rachel's blackmailer and what we're going to do about that?"

"First, we need to talk about the guy locked up downstairs," Joe said. "We can't keep him there forever. The cops frown on unlawful imprisonment."

Lake and Callum shared a look of cold understanding.

"You can't kill him either," the potted plant said before Julia peeked out through the leaves. "That's just wrong."

Honestly, it was like working in a kindergarten. Which was one of the reasons Rachel was keen to get back to TayFor. At least that building was populated by adults. "Julia, why are you hiding? You know everyone in this room. I thought we got past this?"

"I'm not hiding," Julia said. "I just like sitting in the corner. And the plant smells nice."

"It's plastic," Rachel pointed out.

"I like the smell of plastic."

"Julia's right," Harvard told Lake and Callum. "You can't kill Terrance. But if need be, I could make him disappear."

"I didn't hear any of this." Noah put his fingers in his ears.

"One thing's for certain," Rachel said. "We can't keep him in the basement forever. His wife's been calling Jonathan daily to ask when her husband's top-secret work trip will end. At some point, she'll stop calling TayFor and start calling the police."

"Let him go," Harry said from the floor. "We have enough evidence to hand over to the police once we catch the blackmailer. Terrance isn't going anywhere in the meantime." His cheerful grin appeared over the edge of the table. "I canceled his passport and added his name to every no-travel list in the UK."

"Hackers rule." Elle patted Harry's head, and he beamed up at her.

"Plus," Ryan added as he pushed away his empty plate and reached for a donut, "we could microchip him, like they do with all dogs."

"I'm pretty sure that's illegal too," Julia informed them.

"Yes," Noah shouted, his fingers still in his ears even though that was obviously proving useless. "It is."

Her smile sad, Elle caught Rachel's eye. "You're going to miss this."

"Yes," Rachel agreed. "In much the same way I miss the bout of chickenpox that hospitalized me as a child."

"Right." Callum stood. "If nobody has anything to add, we're done here. Ryan, you're staying at TayFor until the blackmailer's found. Your priority is to keep your ears and eyes open, and to watch Rachel's back."

"Why me?" Ryan asked no one in particular.

"Elle, Harry, get us something to go on," Callum continued. "I'll set the bastard in the basement free once I've had another wee word with him. In the meantime, you can all get back to work." He looked at Rachel. "Except you."

As the room cleared, Harvard leaned in to whisper, "Do you want me to stay?"

"No." She shook her head. "I'll meet you downstairs in a few minutes."

With a nod, he headed for the door. He closed it quietly behind him, leaving only the three partners behind.

"Are you going to try to talk me out of this?" Rachel asked Lake and Callum.

"Hell no," Callum said. "Do I look like an idiot? I'm more than happy to find out what life will be like around here without you arguing about every bloody little thing."

Lake's lips twitched as his icy blue eyes met hers. "You sure this is what you want?"

"Yes." Did he expect her to break down in tears about leaving Benson Security? She'd felt more upset when she missed a hair appointment.

"Okay," he said. "But remember this. We're like the mob. Once you're accepted into our ranks, you can never leave."

"Unfortunately, he's right," Callum said. "We're family. Whether you like it or not. Expect to see a whole lot more of us until your blackmailer's behind bars. Or buried. Because you don't leave family hanging when they need you. Isn't that right, Rachel?"

If he was referring to the times she'd pulled his head out of his backside and forced him to stop feeling sorry for himself, then he was wrong. That wasn't about family. It was about having had enough of his endless self-pity. Honestly, the man had plenty going for him but was too damn stubborn to see it. Somebody had to shake him hard. Now that he had Isobel, there was no need to keep an eye on him. Isobel wouldn't suffer through his introspection any more than Rachel had.

"Are we finished here?" She stood and picked up her bag. Although she was just being polite, as she'd already decided it was past time to leave.

"Yeah," Lake said with a rare genuine smile that almost blinded her for a second.

"I'm going back to bed." Callum strode from the room.

When Rachel followed him out, she ran straight into Elle, Julia, and Isobel.

Elle held up her phone. "She's here," she said to whoever was on the line.

"I hear you're getting married." Megan Raast's voice burst from the speaker, making Rachel groan. Megan and her husband were on bodyguard duty in the Middle East, and she'd hoped to avoid the reckless Scot's opinion on her life, but Elle had blown that. "Do vampires get married? Isn't that illegal or something?"

"You're so brave when you're miles away," Rachel drawled.

"So, who's organizing your bachelorette party?" Megan carried on as though Rachel hadn't said a word. "It's me, isn't it?"

"Over my dead body."

"Perfect," Megan said blithely. "And as for bridesmaid dresses, if you choose pink, I will hurt you."

"It would clash with my hair," Elle said helpfully.

"I suit pink," Isobel said.

"I didn't ask any of you to act as bridesmaids," Rachel pointed out.

"Aw, it's okay," Megan said, sounding far too amused. "We wouldn't embarrass you by making you ask. Just consider it a given. We're more than happy to be part of your wedding. Aren't we, girls?"

The idiots nodded.

"And," Megan carried on, obviously enjoying herself, "Friday night get-togethers are still happening, as soon as I'm back in town and able to organize you lot. Which means you might want to warn Harvard. Because as long as you have the best apartment and a private pool, we're meeting at your place."

"I keep telling you," Rachel said. "I don't want to get together on Fridays. Or any other day. Why do you insist on harassing me like this?"

"It isn't harassing," Julia said softly, her eyes wide. "We're making sure you have fun."

"Friends don't let friends sit alone on a Friday night." Elle grinned at her.

"I'm not your friend," she reminded them.

"No," Megan said. "You're our project. We figure if we pool our resources, we can turn you into a real human being —in a decade or two."

"As delightful as this little chat is, it's time for me to go do just about anything else." Rachel gestured for them to move out of her way.

They didn't.

"We realize you're leaving Benson Security," Megan said through the phone. "But we want you to know we'll still be there for you. That's what a girl crew's all about. Ready, ladies?"

"Yes," the three women called before enveloping Rachel in a group hug.

It was a nightmare. And she couldn't even push them away because Isobel was pregnant and Julia bruised easily.

"I am going to kill you, Megan," she promised through gritted teeth as the other women held her tight. "I'm going to take my gun and fill you with holes."

"Not the way you shoot, you won't." With a laugh, the line went dead.

"Stop hugging me," Rachel demanded, but of course, no one listened.

It was then Rachel began to wonder if her superpower of repelling people was faulty. Because a few years earlier, one withering look would have stopped this hug in its tracks.

"Girl power forever," Isobel yelled.

"Dear Lord, save me from this hell," Rachel prayed aloud.

Chapter Thirty

The entire TayFor complex was abuzz with speculation over the missing management staff. And an email sent out by the CEO did little to quash the gossip. In fact, it probably added to it, as it stated that Rachel had taken on a larger role to compensate for the sudden vacancies and that Harvard had been appointed as head of security, effective immediately.

Whether Harvard liked it or not, Rachel had just announced to the world—and her blackmailer—that she had no intention of heeding their demands.

"Does she want the arsewipe to go to the press with the photos?" Ryan asked from his position in Rachel's outer office, where Harvard had told him to wait while he checked in with TayFor's security team. "Because that's exactly what's going to happen. Hell, she's practically daring them to do it. And how long do I have to play secretary to her highness?" He pointed at the pile of paperwork on the corner of the desk. "She's making me do filing."

Harvard checked his wristwatch. "Another hour and we're

done for the day. As your boss, I'm giving you permission to disappear early."

"Thank fu—"

"Oh," Samantha interrupted as she sailed into the room. "Does Rachel have two bodyguards now? Is she marrying you both?" She flashed a coy smile at Ryan. "She always did hoard all the goodies. Perhaps one of you could spend some time guarding this body instead?" She waved a hand down herself and, for a second, Harvard thought Ryan would start drooling.

"Is there something you wanted, Samantha?" Harvard asked.

"Yes." Her smile was bright and very determined. "I'm taking Rachel to her appointment at the bridal boutique."

"And that's my cue to run." Matching action to words, Ryan disappeared so fast you would have thought his ass was on fire.

Coward.

There was the sound of a collision and apologies in the corridor before Rachel's mother appeared in the doorway. "I'm fine," she said. "Almost got toppled by one of the guards, but I'm fine. Is she ready?"

"I haven't managed to get to her yet to find out," Samantha said.

"Hello, Harvard darling." Francesca reached up to peck him on the cheek. "Be prepared for fireworks." With that, she opened Rachel's office door and disappeared inside. "Pack up," she ordered. "We're going to look at wedding dresses."

"No, *we're* not," Rachel said from behind the desk she hated and was in the process of replacing.

"If you're getting married, you need a dress." There was no give in her mother's voice, which made Harvard think he was getting a glimpse into Rachel's youth. Only a strong woman would have been able to deal with a daughter like Rachel.

Rachel's eyes narrowed. "Then pick one for me. Any one you choose is fine. I'll only be wearing it for an hour."

"She's always been terribly romantic," Samantha said drolly.

"Rachel Mary Francesca Ford-Talbot, get up out of that chair this instant. I do *not* have the energy to deal with your tantrums today." Her mother pointed at the door. "Out. Now."

Harvard's eyebrows shot straight up his head as he watched Rachel glare at her mother while doing exactly as she was told.

"It's like watching an eclipse, isn't it?" Samantha said. "You understand the mechanics, but it's so bloody rare, you're still in awe. Only Aunt Fran could ever do this with Rachel."

"Don't say a word," Rachel ordered as she stalked past them. "Especially you." She pointed at Samantha, who made a show of zipping her lips.

Then Sam grinned at Harvard before following Rachel out the door.

Francesca linked her arm through Harvard's. "I assume you're coming too."

"Absolutely," he said. "You know, you could be a Southern Mother. My mom would welcome you into the club any day. I'm in my thirties, and I've yet to say anything to her except 'yes, ma'am'. She'd skin me alive if I disagreed with her."

"You are delightful," Francesca said as they made their way out of the building. "I'm glad she has you."

"Rachel feels exactly the same way," he told her, and she rewarded him with a grin.

❧

INSTEAD OF SETTLING BACK INTO THE FAMILY BUSINESS after a decade away, or chasing down her blackmailer with her team, Rachel was in a backstreet in Covent Garden, looking at wedding dresses. If ever there was a sign that the universe was against her, this was it.

"Isn't this fun?" her mother said as they sat on a replica Louis the Fifteenth sofa, complete with gold-leafed legs and embroidered satin cushions. "I needed a diversion from your father and his constant whining about bacon. Is it possible to have a bacon addiction? Maybe I should find a rehabilitation facility for him."

"Just buy him fake bacon and tell him it's real," Harvard called from behind the lush white velvet curtain that divided the fitting room from the waiting room. He sounded highly amused.

Her mother turned toward the curtain. "Didn't I hear you swear you'd act as though you were invisible?" she reprimanded, earning a deep chuckle from the peanut gallery. "It's bad enough we've brought the groom wedding dress shopping. The least you can do is pretend you aren't here."

"I'm not just her fiancé," Harvard said. "I'm her bodyguard. I go where she goes."

"Well, if she gets attacked by a bolt of lace, we'll call you in."

There was more deep chuckling from outside the dressing area.

"That's not true," Rachel drawled. "He's just being nosey. He doesn't need to be here."

"Oh, there's a need," Harvard said. "I'm here to make sure you actually buy a damn dress."

"Isn't this wonderful?" Samantha gushed as she ran her fingers over a rack of dresses. "All the best people are using this shop right now. The designer's dresses are in dreadfully high demand. It was a complete nightmare getting you this appointment." She lowered her voice and continued, "She's fitted three Hollywood actresses, an Indian princess, and European royalty within the past month alone."

"I'm sure you went to a lot of trouble," Rachel said as the sales assistant handed them flutes of champagne. At least there was something decent to drink. "But was it really necessary? We haven't even set a date for the wedding. There's absolutely no hurry to find a dress. Perhaps we could do this another day."

"Harvard darling," her mother said, raising her voice, obviously deciding to include Harvard in the conversation after all. "When are you getting married?"

"Soon as possible," came the deep reply.

Her mother gave her a smug smile.

"That means at least a year or two from now," Rachel said.

"Don't be silly." Samantha pulled out a dress. "It means as soon as we can organize the event. And I think we could easily do that for you within a few months."

"And who's being an idiot now?" Rachel demanded before finishing her champagne. "It takes at least a year to plan a wedding."

"Not if you already have the venue," her mother chimed in with an irritatingly sweet smile and a wicked sparkle in her eye.

Rachel reached over, took her mother's champagne from her hand, and drained that too before handing back the glass. Her mother rolled her eyes and set it on the delicate table beside her. "Was that necessary?"

"Oh, you have no idea," Rachel replied. She was beginning to think there wasn't enough alcohol in London to get her through this shopping trip.

"Of course, you'll be married at Talbot House," Samantha said. "Which means we already have in-house caterers and a wedding planner we can use. Music shouldn't be a problem.

You can always get Jonathan's wife to play her cello, or I'm sure she'd bring her quartet. Although we have enough connections between us to attract someone with more celebrity appeal if that's what you want. And flowers can be sourced locally or from the estate gardens." Her eyebrows went up. "What else is there?"

"Uh, a license? Someone to officiate? Rings? Harvard's family? A reception?" And how about some time to get used to the idea? Only last week, the wedding had been fake, and that had only changed a few days earlier. Surely, she could be afforded a minute to let that sink in.

"We can use the ballroom at the house for the reception." Her mother looked over at Samantha, who held a dress in front of her while posing in the mirrors. "I wouldn't mind having something other than cello music though. Isn't Elton free?"

"He's on tour, Aunt Fran."

"Elton who?" Harvard's voice came through the curtain. "Elton John?"

"Of course, Elton John," Samantha said with a laugh. "Your fiancé's so delightfully...ordinary, isn't he? You are *so* lucky."

"I know." Rachel narrowed her eyes at her cousin. "And he's taken. We talked about this, remember?"

Samantha grinned widely. "What happened to that pinky promise we made as children? Didn't we agree to share everything?"

"That was only because you wanted to get your grubby little hands on my pony, and I was too young to see through you." She'd been ten, and Samantha a far wiser twelve. The pony ended up living at Sam's family home, and Rachel learned the hard way never to make pinky promises with her cousin.

"How about this one?" Samantha held up a dress that had more lace than a curtain in a council flat.

"It looks like something Scarlett O'Hara would wear while running into the firing guns of the Confederate Army."

There was a loud male groan. "Scarlett was on the side of the Confederacy. She would have run into the guns of the Union soldiers. Our kids are gonna grow up ignorant."

Rachel's mother giggled like a teenager. "I do like your fiancé. He'll make a very entertaining addition to the family."

"Speaking of children." Samantha held up an equally awful dress, making Rachel shake her head. "Are you planning to stay on at TayFor once you start a family?"

Rachel's jaw dropped. "We only just got engaged."

"How many times do I have to tell you not to say engaged?" her mother said. "Say betrothed, or promised in marriage, or anything other than engaged. Engaged is what happens to a toilet cubicle when it's occupied."

A chuckle rumbled through the room from Harvard. Great, at least one of them was having fun.

"This one," Samantha said as she held up a mermaid-style dress.

Rachel shook her head. "That's more you than me."

"Do you think?" She studied it, then beamed at them. "I'm trying it on." She disappeared into the changing area.

"Well, that didn't take long," her mother said with a smile.

No, it hadn't. Rachel lowered her voice and frowned at her mother. "Why are you torturing me like this? We only just told you this morning that the *engagement* was real. Did we have to jump into planning today?"

Her mother's hand covered hers. "Yes. We did. Sam had set up the appointment, and we needed some light relief. Face it, darling, you never seem to have enough fun in your life." Her eyes turned sad.

And Rachel hated seeing that look in her mother's eyes. "Fine, I suppose I can try on one dress."

"That's my girl." Her mother patted her hand.

As Rachel made her way across the thick white carpet to the dress rack, Samantha stepped from the changing area. The dress fit like a glove and was perfect on her.

"You look stunning." Her mother was awestruck.

Samantha twirled. "Isn't it glorious?"

"You should buy it." Rachel was completely serious. "I doubt you'll find another dress that needs so few alterations and suits you as well as that one does."

Sam brushed her long blonde hair over her shoulder and gave Rachel a wide-eyed, innocent look that instantly aroused her suspicions. "Do you know what would set it off beautifully? The Talbot locket."

Rachel's hand went to the place on her throat where the locket should have been. The locket Sam had been trying to get her grubby little hands on since they were children. The one Rachel hadn't seen since she'd scratched it from her throat. "You never know, Sam, one of these days, I might cave and give it to you." But then she'd just have to look at it around Sam's neck instead of her own, and the memories it evoked would still be the same. No, it was better off in Benson Security's safe. One day, she'd deal with it, but not today.

"Yay," Sam said. "I always knew you'd come around." She smiled as she posed for the mirrors. "I do look wonderful in this. I might just get it to wear out dancing."

"But it's a wedding dress." Her mother sounded outraged. "You can't wear a wedding dress to a nightclub. The press will have a field day."

Samantha shrugged. "No, they won't. They'll think I'm being fashion-forward or something."

"I'm starving," Harvard called through to them. "How much longer are we going to be? Should I order pizza?"

The three women looked around at all the white dresses and, as one, they shouted, "No."

There was a groan before Harvard spoke again. "Rachel, I need a word."

"Not too long," her mother said. "The designer will be here any moment to go over what you want."

"Oh, goody," Rachel said as she stepped through the curtain, where she found Harvard standing and looking serious. "What's wrong?"

"Elle thinks she's found something." He ran a hand over his smoothly shaven head, and even though her stomach roiled at the thought of what Elle might have found, she still found herself wondering again what he'd look like if he grew his hair out.

"Did she say what?"

He shook his head. "She wants to talk in person."

Rachel's shoulders slumped. "If I run out on this, I won't need to worry about what the blackmailer might do next; Mother and Sam will kill me. You go see what she wants and call if you need me."

His wide hand clasped her neck. "I don't like leaving you alone. I'll call Ryan."

"Oh, please, no. Sam would either seduce him in the dressing room, or he'd get food on the dresses, or I'd beat him to death with my shoe. Or maybe my gun."

His lips quirked as his eyes twinkled with amusement. "Beat him with the gun? You know it shoots bullets, right?"

"It was brought to my attention yesterday that I might have some issues actually hitting a target."

"Rachel," he purred her name, his eyes heating, "we really need to deal with this violent streak of yours."

"But not today. Now go. I'll be fine. Once we're finished here, I'll take a cab back to my place or over to Benson Security if I'm needed. In the meantime, I have Mother and Samantha to protect me." She almost managed to stop from rolling her eyes at the thought of how useful either of them would be in a crisis.

He lowered his mouth to hers and kissed the life out of her, leaving her dizzy and swaying in place while he sauntered out of the boutique.

"Rachel," her mother called, "you'd better not have left."

With a sigh, she returned to the fitting room.

Chapter Thirty-One

"We found a shadow of information in the metadata files of the thumb drive itself," Elle told Harvard once he was in the IT room at Benson Security. "Whoever deleted the metadata attached to the video forgot to write over the space in the trash area to wipe it out entirely."

"Or," Harry said, looking like he hadn't slept in days, "they didn't know enough to clear out the trash storage area too."

With a nod of thanks, Harvard took the coffee Joe offered him. "What've we got?"

"This." Elle hit some keys and the screen on the wall filled with information.

Harvard stilled as he read through the data, then let out a slow breath of a curse. "We sure?"

"As sure as we can be," Elle said tightly.

Harvard turned to Joe. "We need to pick him up and have a chat with him. Do we have a location?"

"Yeah," his childhood friend said, looking every inch the dangerous former army ranger that he was. "Callum and Ryan already lifted him. He's on his way. And he isn't happy about it."

"Like we give a crap," Elle snapped.

Harvard put a hand on her shoulder. "This isn't enough to convict him. We need to be patient. To do this right. Otherwise, he'll get away with it." He turned to Joe. "You and Noah head over to his apartment and see what you can find."

"You're talking breaking and entering; not sure Noah will be up for that. It ain't like we have a warrant giving us permission to toss the house."

"It needs to be done. If Noah won't do it, wait for Ryan. He won't have any moral issues that'll stop him from taking care of business."

Joe nodded. "You calling in Rachel?"

Harvard glanced back at the screen and the one tiny line that had a name in it. "Not until we're sure. The blackmailer's played us all along; let's make sure this information hasn't been planted before we bring in Rachel." Because if a member of her family was behind her attack, it would destroy her.

"Elle, Harry, is there any way to check if this information was planted?" Harvard asked as Joe left the room.

They shared a look where they almost seemed to communicate telepathically.

"There's a couple of things we could try," Harry said at last.

Elle's attention went straight to her keyboard. "But if this is a stretch for us, I don't think your blackmail suspect could do it."

"Let's check anyway," Harvard said as he pulled out his phone to text Rachel.

∿

WHEN THE TEXT FROM HARVARD CAME THROUGH, RACHEL hoped it would get her out of the bridal boutique. Unfortunately, all it said was *Nothing concrete yet. How are you doing?*

She tapped back: *The designer was a bitch, and I should know one when I see one. Sam's bought three dresses. Mother gave up on us and went home. We're winding up with the designer from hell and then going back to my place. Sam has a folder full of wedding ideas that she HAS to show me.*

Sounds like a girls' night. The fool said, having far too much fun at her expense. *Go straight there and set the alarm once you're both in. Don't let anyone inside except a member of our team.*

A chill went through her, making her shiver. *You think the blackmailer is someone I know well enough to let into my apartment?*

Just be extra cautious. I'll be in touch as soon as I know more.

She was grateful he didn't sign off with heart emojis.

"Everything okay?" Sam said as they hailed a taxi.

"Nothing I can't handle."

"That's our Rachel, able to take on the world without blinking an eye." A cab pulled up, and Sam climbed into the back. "Hurry up. I want to show you my ideas before that hunky fiancé of yours gets home. It's bad luck for the groom to see the wedding plans before they happen."

"No, it isn't." Rachel got in beside her. "It's bad luck if he sees the dress. Not the wedding plans."

Sam patted her arm. "I agree that's the case with most people. But for you, it's probably best to play it safe."

Rachel just stared at her as the taxi headed through the streets of London to Hyde Park.

HARVARD STEPPED INTO BENSON SECURITY'S interrogation room and faced the man seated at the table. His suit was rumpled, and his hair stood on end from him running his hands through it. Harvard knew because he'd watched him do it through the one-way mirror while Callum briefed him on what had happened during the trip to pick up their suspect.

"Harvard," he said, looking relieved. "What's going on? Two guys kidnapped me and brought me here. They wouldn't tell me what was happening. But the Scottish one scared the crap out of me. Is this because of my debt? Because I've made arrangements to pay that back. I swear. I'm on top of it. I've stopped gambling. I'm serious about making a go of things at TayFor. Please, call off the dogs."

"No." Harvard took a seat facing Rupert Talbot. "This isn't about your gambling debt. This is about Rachel."

"Rachel?" Rupert turned gray. "Is she okay?"

Harvard opened the folder he'd brought in with him and took out a copy of one of the photos that had been left for Rachel to find. "No. She's not okay."

Rupert leaned forward to look at the photo. He gasped, and what little color remained in his skin drained away entirely. "What the hell?" he muttered. His hand shaking, he reached for the photo. His body swayed. And then he toppled sideways, falling off his chair and onto the floor—out cold.

"What a fabulous idea to sit beside your pool while we did this," Samantha said as she handed Rachel a glass of Merlot before settling into the lounger beside her.

"It was your idea." Rachel sipped her wine, glancing at the skylight above, where the remainder of the sunset turned the clouds pink.

"That's why it's fabulous." Samantha beamed as she drank from her own glass of champagne. "All of my ideas are fabulous."

"No one could ever accuse you of suffering from too much humility," Rachel said, wishing she had more wine, as one glass wouldn't be enough. She loved her cousin dearly, but she was in no mood to watch her gush over wedding ideas. "Where's this folder of yours?" Rachel put her empty glass on the table beside her, feeling slightly light-headed as she did so. They should have eaten before they got into the wine.

"Oh, blast. I must have forgotten it." Sam didn't seem bothered as she watched Rachel over the rim of her champagne flute.

"Honestly," Rachel said, tugging at the throat of her dress. The thermostat for the pool room had to be broken because the temperature seemed to be rising far too fast. "If you made up an excuse just so you could come up here and flirt with my fiancé, then you can leave right now. I don't have the patience to put up with it."

"No." Sam smiled widely, but her eyes were strangely cold. "I know that Harvard belongs to you. He seems to be just as faithful to you as the rest of your family. You're very good at gaining the loyalty of the people around you, aren't you, Rachel?"

"What's that supposed to mean?" Her head spun now, and all she wanted to do was lie down in a darkened room.

"You've always been the darling of the Talbot clan, no matter how absolutely horrid you can be. It grated when I was a child, and I find it grates even more now I'm an adult. Why are you so popular? Do you have any idea? Because I'm at a loss."

Rachel placed a hand on her stomach. Something was wrong. Her brain felt cloudy and the room seemed to zoom in and out of focus. She tried to get up off the seat, but she just became more disoriented, so she sat back down. "You have to call someone," she told her cousin. "I don't feel very well."

Samantha didn't seem to hear her. "You're the one everybody hoped would lead the company one day. The one who inherited a title from your mother, one you don't even bother using, so it's completely wasted on you. *Lady Rachel Ford-Talbot.*" She sneered. "If anyone's a Lady, it's me. But no. The whole world revolves around Rachel. No matter what you do, you're the favored child. You're the one included in the traditions that pass from female to female. And when you're in the room, all anyone can see is Rachel. Even after you were gone for ten years, you walked straight back into the company and had everyone talking about you taking over the helm one day soon. What about the rest of us? We've been there all along. But no, we don't get a look in when you're around."

"Sam, I don't have the energy to deal with your hurt feelings right now. I can honestly say that I don't try to steal your spotlight. I don't even care about it. Now, will you please call the doctor? I think I'm going to be sick."

"And you never share," Samantha continued to rant, growing more irate with each word. "Even that damn locket. It belonged to our great-grandmother, and it passed to you. I'm the only other female in the family that counts. Those bastard children from Theo's many marriages don't have the same stake in this family that I do. They don't have my pedigree. I have just as much claim to our heritage as you. But no. It's all about Rachel!"

"For the love of Prada, if you want the bloody locket, take it." She was about to pass out. She could feel it creeping into the edges of her consciousness. Sam had to call for help. There was something seriously wrong.

"Oh, I don't want it now," Samantha said with a cruel smile. "Because, dear cousin, I know exactly where it's been."

Chapter Thirty-Two

"Want me to get a bucket of water?" Ryan sounded a little overeager as Harvard checked their detainee.

"No, he's coming around. You with us, Rupert?"

There was a groan from the floor. "What?" His glazed eyes cleared somewhat. "Rachel. Dear God. Rachel." He struggled to get up, and Harvard and Ryan helped him back into the chair.

As soon as he was there, he flipped over the photo of Rachel's attack so he couldn't see the image, then rubbed his hands on his thighs. As if trying to remove the contact with the photo. "You think I did that?" Hysteria rose in his voice. "You think I...I...I can't even say it! You think I sexually assaulted my own cousin?"

"Ryan," Harvard said to his teammate, who stood beside the door, "get Rupert a glass of water." Before he emptied his stomach all over the floor.

Ryan slipped out and returned a few seconds later with a bottle of water. He handed it to Rupert, who took a sip before grimacing.

"Someone's been sending Rachel photos of an attack that happened ten years ago," Harvard said, keeping his voice low and calm. "When the photos didn't get the desired result, they sent a video. My teammates hacked the data on the video, and it turns out it was taken with your phone."

"No," Rupert said on a gasp. "No." He vehemently shook his head. "I had nothing to do with this. Nothing. How can you even think that? She's my cousin. I love her. This is...abhorrent."

Harvard sat back in his seat. "Somebody set up her rape. Somebody filmed it. Yours is the only name on the video file."

Rupert slapped the bottle onto the table, making the water splash out. "I'm telling you; I had nothing to do with this. I would never do something like that. Not to Rachel. Not to anyone. I don't know how my name got on the file. If I did, I'd tell you."

The comm unit in Harvard's ear sprang to life. "I think he's telling the truth," Lake said.

Unfortunately, Harvard agreed. He leaned forward. "I need you to tell me everything about the night it happened."

"How am I supposed to know when that was?"

"I'm going to tell you." Harvard put that famed patience of his to good use. "It was the twenty-second of July, exactly ten years ago. Rachel was in London during college vacation and working as an intern at TayFor."

Rupert nodded furiously. "Yes. I remember. It was her last holiday before going into her final year. We spent the summer partying through London's nightclubs. Until—" With a shaky hand, he lifted the water to his mouth and took a sip. He swallowed hard. "Until she suddenly cut everything short and moved back to Glasgow." His eyes welled up, and it was clear he was fighting the urge to cry. "I thought she'd just had a better offer from her friend Harry. She left me a message saying he had a great idea for a business. One that would make them a fortune. And he needed her straight away." A trembling finger pointed at the photo. "But this was why she returned?"

Harvard nodded, feeling sorry for the guy. "Were you out together on that last night? The night before she left?"

Rupert ran a hand through his hair. "I don't know. Back then, I spent most of my time drunk and on the pull. If I managed to pick up a girl, I often left Rachel and Sam to fend for themselves while I took my date home."

"Samantha?" Everything within Harvard stilled.

Rupert nodded. "The three of us tore up London that year."

"Is it possible you were out clubbing the night this happened and that Samantha was there too?"

Rupert looked horrified. "You don't think my sister had anything to do with this?"

"Just answer the question. Is it possible?"

A tear ran down Rupert's face. "What day of the week was the twenty-second of July?"

"A Saturday," Lake's voice said in his ear.

"Saturday," Harvard told Rupert.

"Then, yeah, the three of us were together." The tears were falling hard now. "We went out every single Saturday that summer. It was a joke among the rest of the family, that's why I remember. We didn't miss a weekend."

Adrenaline coursed through Harvard as alarm bells sounded in his mind. "Could your sister have taken your phone and used it?"

Bleak eyes met his. "Yes," Rupert whispered.

Harvard shot from the chair and was out of the door in a few long strides, the sound of Rupert's sobs reverberating through the room behind him. Lake and Callum were waiting on the other side of the door.

"Rachel's alone with Samantha in her apartment," he said, fighting to keep calm. To think clearly.

"Call her," Callum barked.

His phone was already in his hand. He lifted it to his ear and waited as it rang to voice mail. A sense of dread filling him, he changed tactics and sent a text. It felt as though time was suspended as they waited for a reply. Rachel *always* replied. That damn phone of hers barely left her hand.

At last, he looked up at the men he'd grown to respect. The men who cared for Rachel almost as much as he did. "There's no reply."

And then they were running.

"You?" Rachel gasped as the room spun around her. "You took the video? You were there?" She clutched the arm of her chair, silently begging for it not to be true.

Samantha waved a dismissive hand and strode over to the bar in the corner of the room, where she casually poured herself another glass of champagne. "I knew it had to be something dramatic to get you to leave TayFor, just asking you to go wouldn't do it. Nor would some embarrassing photos of you out partying. And I couldn't think of anything else that would do the job." She turned to lean against the bar. "I had hoped to find that you'd been dipping into the company drug stock, but you didn't even dabble. You are such a goody two shoes."

"That smell. Patchouli." Rachel shook her head, trying to clear it. "I thought it was incense, but it was your perfume. I remember now."

"You were very rude about my taste in perfume back then. You said I smelled like a hippie. That was why I doused myself in it for our little party."

Thick, clawing fog filled Rachel's head, making it hard to think. "The men?" She could barely get the words out. Nothing made sense. Nothing.

"Were happy to help—for a price that would set them up for life. You cost them their jobs. And unlike everyone else around you, they weren't keen to forgive your behavior."

"And Terrance?"

"I suspected you might have found out about him." Her cousin sipped her champagne. "It was a tad telling when he didn't turn up for work. I suppose we can thank your security contacts for rooting him out. I have to say, Rachel, they were a very annoying addition to our game."

"This isn't a game."

"It is for me. I got tired of you winning and decided to change the rules. And it worked perfectly for over a decade— until you turned up again. Why couldn't you just stay away? Why did you have to come back and make everyone start comparing us again? Without you around, people could see that I was more than a match for anything you could do. I'm more talented, more attractive, more pleasant to be around. But for some reason, as soon as you enter my orbit, you draw all the attention. Why is that?"

"Maybe because they sense I'm the sane one?"

Samantha's laugh was ice. "I don't know why everyone's so willing to forgive you for being such a bitch."

"*I'm* the bitch? I don't arrange for people to be raped. Or drug them." She stilled. "You've done it again, haven't you? Put something in my drink."

"Of course. How else would I get what I want?"

Rachel looked around as fear made bile surge in her throat.

"Oh, don't worry," Sam said. "I haven't paid any men to play with you this time."

Ringing sounded from Rachel's handbag on the table

beside her. She tried to reach for it, but her limbs wouldn't cooperate. The ringing stopped, and the phone pinged, letting her know a text had come through.

"I expect that's your hunky fiancé." Sam put her glass on the bar. "What does he see in you?"

"Sanity?"

"Typical, even drugged out of your mind, you have to have the last catty word." She strode toward Rachel, put her hands under her arms, and tugged her to her feet. "I am really sorry about this. When you weren't busy trying to show the world that you're better than me, I actually enjoyed your company."

"What are you doing?" Rachel said as Samantha dragged her toward the pool.

"What I should have done the first time," she said. "Making sure you don't annoy me again. Poor Rachel, she got drunk and fell in her pool. Her cousin, Samantha, tried to save her, but it was too late. It's such a tragedy." Her smile was vicious. "But don't worry; I'll console Harvard in his grief."

And then she jumped into the pool, taking Rachel with her.

Chapter Thirty-Three

Cold water rushed over Rachel's head as she sank beneath the surface. The shock of it threw her situation into stark relief. The cousin she'd thought cared about her was trying to kill her. And she might just succeed.

Gathering what little strength she had, she kicked upward. Her only hope was to break away from Samantha and call for help before the drug rendered her helpless.

Again.

As her fingers broke the surface of the water, a hand clasped her ankle and pulled her back down into the deep center of the pool. She forced her eyes open, to see Samantha grinning maniacally as the skirt of her dress billowed in the water around her. It was as if Rachel was looking at a strange underwater fashion shoot. Her cousin's beauty and the surrealness of the situation made it hard to fathom. And with that thought came the dull realization that the drug she'd been given was making it difficult to think clearly.

She had to escape before she couldn't think at all.

A rush of pure adrenaline coursed through her and, with

herculean effort, she punched and fought and kicked until the hold on her ankle loosened. Lungs burning, she swam the short distance to the surface, her clothes weighing her down and her shoes long gone.

Hope surged through her as air hit her face, only for it to be dashed as hands clasped her shoulders and pulled her back under. She'd barely had time to take in a breath before she was trapped underwater again, with Samantha holding her down.

She tried to twist out of her cousin's grasp, but the drug slowed her movements, and it seemed impossible to break free. She was going to die in that pool. In the water she stared at every night. Even if she got out of there alive, she'd never be able to look at the pool again. It was one more thing her cousin had stolen from her.

Which made her furious.

And rage gave her a renewed burst of strength. Desperate, she kicked out, catching her cousin's thigh and sending her toward the bottom of the pool. It wasn't far, but it gave her a few seconds to escape. Rachel didn't hesitate. She clawed her way through the water, scrambling for the side. But as her fingers clutched the tile, harsh hands shoved her face into the hard edge of the pool.

She screamed, blood filling her vision before she was sucked back under. Barely managing to close her mouth before she took in water. Her lungs were aching. Her energy failing. Each movement felt heavier, more lethargic than the one before. Part of her just wanted to give up. To sink into peace. To make it stop.

But the rest of her was desperate to live.

For the man she'd found who made her love him.

For Harvard.

Summoning every last bit of her strength, she wrenched herself from Samantha's hold. Only this time, she didn't immediately rush to get out. Instead, she aimed a kick at her cousin's stomach and almost cheered when she felt the impact. Samantha doubled over, and Rachel surged to the surface, where she grasped the side and pulled herself up.

The water wrapped around her, clinging to her like greedy hands. Determined to keep her submerged. With a cry of desperation, she hauled the top half of her body onto the tiles outside the pool. Gasping for air, she struggled to get her legs to follow. They felt as though they were filled with lead. And her fog-filled mind struggled to communicate with them.

"No," Samantha yelled, grabbing Rachel's ankle. "This time, we end it."

Rachel saved her breath, not bothering to reply; instead, she kicked back with what strength she could muster. It took three attempts but, eventually, her foot connected with Sam's face, sending her back into the water.

With a cry of rage, Rachel hauled the rest of her body out of the pool, then dragged herself across the tiles to the small table where her handbag sat.

"You selfish bitch," Samantha screeched. "Can't you do something for someone else, just once? Stop fighting me. Make this easy on both of us."

Rachel glanced back to see Samantha climb out of the pool. Right beside that smiling gnome Sebastian had given her. The strange sight of her would-be killer and that freakish sculpture almost made Rachel question reality. Maybe she was already drowning, and this whole thing was just a hallucination. The walls moved in and out around her, her limbs barely moved, and her brain was a shattered mirror—reflecting pieces of thoughts rather than letting her think any one thing clearly.

"I should have given you a higher dose," Samantha snapped as she stalked toward her.

Rachel swung back around to the small table and tugged

at the handle of her bag. It toppled to the floor, spilling its contents everywhere.

"Trying to call your fiancé for help," Samantha scoffed, her talons encircling Rachel's ankle again. "It won't make any difference. He won't get here in time."

Rachel ignored her cousin's taunts, focusing what strength she had left on getting what she needed. There. Under the lounger. She just had to reach it.

Her arm stretched, and her fingers skimmed the butt of the gun Callum had given her.

And then she was moving again.

Being dragged on her stomach, back to the water.

"No," Rachel shouted.

Her legs too weak to kick anymore, she was shivering from the cold and the drugs. All she could do was scrabble for anything that might slow her cousin down.

Her hand hit something solid. Cold. Her phone. She grabbed it, twisted, and threw. The phone smacked Samantha on the cheek, and she yelped. It was enough to make her loosen her hold.

Rachel lurched forward, sliding on her belly and reaching for the gun as Samantha screamed with frustration. The gun slipped into her hand, and with one last burst of adrenaline, she fired.

And missed.

For a second, Samantha looked stunned, and then she laughed. "At last, I've found something you can't do." She reached for Rachel's leg.

"No," Rachel shouted before squeezing the trigger over and over. But between her shaking hands and her blurred vision, her aim was completely off.

"I don't know how I'm going to explain the bullet holes," Sam said calmly, as though they were having a polite conversation. "But I'll think of something."

With nothing but hope and desperation, Rachel aimed and took her last shot.

And it hit.

Almost...

The bullet skimmed the side of Samantha's head, leaving a line of red across her temple. Stunned, she staggered back, her hand lifting to the wound. The look of absolute horror on her face when her fingers came away bloody might have been comical under other circumstances. But nothing about this situation was funny.

With pure stubbornness to drive her, Rachel dragged herself across the tile toward her cousin. And while Samantha stood there in bewildered shock, Rachel kicked at her knee.

It was weak. But it was effective.

Samantha's legs buckled, and she staggered backward. With a scream, she hit the gnome, and together they tumbled into the pool.

Rachel didn't wait around for her to surface again. She had to get somewhere safe to wait for Harvard. He would come for her. She knew it.

Half crawling, half dragging herself across the floor, Rachel made it through the open doorway and down the few steps to the hall. There was no way she could stand; her strength was gone, and she was close to losing consciousness. All she could do was pray she managed to stay awake until she made it somewhere that Samantha couldn't get to her.

The stairs down to the bedroom level were harder to negotiate and Rachel bumped and slid her way down them, landing in a heap at the bottom. She moaned with pain but didn't stop moving. There was no time to lose. Crawling, she made her way along the hall to the door that led out of her apartment. The emergency door with the small hallway between it and the outside exit. With trembling fingers, she tapped in the code to open it. It took three attempts but, at last, the door gave way. She toppled through, and the door slammed behind her, locking automatically.

And that's when Rachel crumpled, letting the darkness at the edge of her consciousness claim her. All the while, hoping Harvard would find her.

RACHEL'S APARTMENT WAS EERILY SILENT AS HARVARD slipped inside. He signaled to Lake and Callum, and the three of them spread out to cover the room. They checked the kitchen and dining area, keeping their weapons up in front of them, missing nothing.

There was no sign that Rachel had even been there. Only the fact the concierge had seen her arrive with her cousin and hadn't seen them leave made Harvard believe they were still inside.

"Garage is clear," Ryan said through his earpiece. "Joe's stationed at the front door. So far, no sign of Rachel or her cousin."

"Stay in position," Harvard whispered.

Lake cleared the room, and the men moved down the hall, checking off each room as they went. Soon, the only area left was the pool. As they flattened themselves against the walls on either side of the door, Harvard lifted his fingers and counted them down. On three, they moved.

They were through the door in seconds. Spreading out in standard formation, the men covered all angles and each other's backs. There was no one in the room, but the tiles around the pool were soaked with water.

Lake made a low clicking sound and motioned at something lying on the floor. Cautiously, they crept forward to get a better look. Harvard's heart slammed in his chest—it was Rachel's handbag, its contents scattered over the tiles.

They spread out around the room, checking each area.

"Clear," Callum whispered through their comm as he pointed to the changing room.

"Clear," Lake murmured, indicating the bathroom.

Harvard moved silently, keeping his gun up as he checked behind the bar. Nothing. "Clear," he reported. They had to be downstairs.

He turned toward the other men and started to signal for them to head out and downstairs when he caught sight of something in the pool.

No. Not something.

Someone.

With a roar, he lunged for the water. Only to be held back by Lake.

"It isn't her."

Harvard tried to shove him aside, but Callum appeared beside his partner, and both of them barred his way.

"It isn't her," Callum snapped. "It's Samantha."

Harvard took a deep breath as their words registered. "I'm okay," he gritted out.

After taking a moment to make sure, they stepped aside. Harvard gazed over the edge of the pool, staying calm, as he was trained to do. Her blonde hair drifting around her, a woman lay face down, pinned to the glass bottom. They couldn't make out what kept her from floating, but it was clear she was alone in the pool.

Blonde hair.

Yellow dress.

Samantha.

"Gun," Callum barked from beside one of the loungers, pulling Harvard's attention from the body. "It's the one I gave Rachel." Using the edge of his shirt, he picked it up and sniffed. "It's just been fired."

"Several times." Lake pointed to the holes in the wall and

ceiling.

"I told her to practice," Callum said as he put the gun back where he'd found it. "But she never bloody listens."

Harvard turned from the pool. "Downstairs," he ordered, but the men were already moving.

"Stairs are wet," Harvard said as he led them down to the lower floor. "She came this way."

They moved steadily, sweeping the area with their weapons, barely making a sound. He signaled toward the master bedroom. With Lake and Callum at his back, he assumed breach position and entered the room. They came in behind him seamlessly, spreading out to cover the space and each other. Every room had to be cleared. They didn't know if Samantha had acted alone.

Only once they were sure the room and master bath were clear, did Harvard look up at the pool. Samantha floated above them, her eyes wide and unseeing, her hair spread out around her. She had a gash on her head and a bruise on her cheek. So beautiful, yet so incredibly evil.

Lake grunted and pointed at Samantha's dress. Tangled in the folds of her skirt was the ugly concrete gnome that usually sat beside the pool. It acted as an anchor, keeping her pinned to the bottom.

For a second, they just stared at the gnome and the woman who looked more like an ethereal mermaid than a rapist and would-be killer.

What a waste.

With a shake of his head, Harvard turned to his team. "Move out," he ordered, and they moved, quickly clearing both guest rooms.

There was no sign of Rachel.

"Is there a panic room in this apartment?" Harvard asked Callum.

It was Lake who answered. "No."

There damn well would be one in the house he'd share with Rachel, that was for sure.

Lake crouched and pressed his hand to the hall carpet. "Wet," he said. "What's behind that door?"

"An emergency exit, but I don't have the code to access it."

"Fortunately, we run the security in this building." Lake touched his throat mic. "Joe, emergency override on Rachel's lower floor exit."

"On it," came the reply.

A minute later, a buzz and a click signaled that the door was unlocked. Callum took backup position as Harvard held up his gun. As soon as Lake opened the door, Harvard was through it.

And he almost tripped over the woman he loved.

"Rachel!" Harvard tossed his gun into the corner and fell to his knees beside her. Pressing his fingers to her throat, he felt for a pulse. "She's alive. Callum, we need an ambulance."

"Already calling," Callum said gruffly.

Harvard gently checked her body for breaks and wounds. His main concern was a gash to her forehead, but at least it had stopped bleeding. He only hoped the blow that caused it hadn't given her a concussion. Apart from that, all he could see were bruises and scrapes. Gathering her into his arms, he sat with his back to the wall and waited for the ambulance.

"Drugged?" Lake asked.

"That seems to be Samantha's MO," Harvard said. "So, I'm guessing yeah."

"Ryan," Callum said into his mic, "collect all glasses from the pool room. We'll need to take them to the hospital with us for drug testing."

"You got it."

"She's going to be okay," Callum said.

"Yeah." Harvard brushed her hair out of her face. But it

was no thanks to him. He'd left her vulnerable and missed all the signs that Samantha was a danger to her. He made a silent vow that it would never happen again.

"She's safe now," Lake said as though reading his mind.

"And she's staying that way," Harvard promised.

"Ambulance crew on their way up," Joe said in Harvard's ear. "How's our girl?"

"Some superficial wounds and a gash to her head that's worrying," Lake answered. "But we don't know what drug's in her system."

A couple of minutes later, Ryan appeared at the end of the hall, the ambulance crew close behind him. He held up a clear plastic bag with two empty glasses inside. "Marked where they were for the cops." He looked at Rachel, then turned to the medics with steel in his gaze. "Anything goes wrong with her care, or her condition deteriorates between here and the hospital, I'm holding you responsible." And then he stalked back along the hallway. "Meet you at the hospital," he called over his shoulder.

Lake stepped around the medics as they checked Rachel's vitals before loading her onto the stretcher. He opened the emergency door wide, revealing the service elevator and the stairs facing it. "This way's faster," he said.

As they wheeled her out, Harvard followed. "I'm her fiancé. I go where she goes." His tone dared them to argue.

After taking one look at him, they were smart enough not to.

"We'll deal with the police," Callum said. "And we'll come to the hospital when we're done."

"Her family," Harvard said, his attention on Rachel.

"I'll get Harry to call them," Lake said.

And then the lift doors closed on them, and Harvard thought about nothing but getting Rachel the care that she needed.

Chapter Thirty-Four

For the second time in her life, Rachel found herself in a hospital room with no recollection of how she'd got there. But this time, she wasn't alone.

"Hey." Harvard smiled at her from where he stood beside her bed. "You're awake."

"Why do people say that? I'm the one that's awake; I don't need to be informed about it."

"And you woke up grumpy again." He bent down and pressed a gentle kiss to her lips. "You scared me."

She blinked up at him. "Am I supposed to apologize?"

"No, but promising it will never happen again would be good."

A jolt of agony that wasn't just physical shot through her. "I've pretty much run out of family members out to get me, so I think it's safe to say this won't happen again."

His beautiful face appeared pained. "I'm sorry, Rachel."

And purely from the way he said it, she knew he was not only apologizing for everything she'd been through and the betrayal of her family, but he was also expressing his condolences.

"Did I kill her?" Her mouth was suddenly very dry.

Harvard shook his head. "In the end, it was just a dumb accident. Her dress got tangled in that concrete gnome, and it weighed her down like an anchor."

Rachel tried to swallow, but there was no moisture in her mouth. Of course, Harvard noticed and held a glass of water to her lips. She sipped at it, giving herself time to process what he'd told her. Perhaps she should have felt relief at the news, but all she felt was sad.

"We had lots of good times too," Rachel said once Harvard took the water away. "I...was very fond of her."

He brushed her hair off her face, his touch unerringly gentle. "You loved her, and that's how it should have been. Even after everything that's happened, it's still okay to mourn the woman you cared about."

"I'm...conflicted," she confessed.

"Yeah, we all are. It's normal." He seemed to consider what to say next, and then in the gentlest voice, he asked, "Did she tell you why she did it?"

"She said a lot of things, but mainly, I think she saw me as competition. Samantha liked to be the center of attention, and I took that away from her. Apparently." And then, because he was *her* Michael, she gave him the rest. "I don't know how to behave now. I feel responsible and confused. And betrayed. How did my family take the news?"

He let out a sigh. "Charles blames you for Samantha's death. He refuses to believe she was behind your attack or that she tried to kill you—despite the ton of evidence. Her brother's devastated and locked up in his apartment. Sebastian's keeping an eye on him now he's back home. I like him, by the way. The rest of the family are mainly in shock."

She started to nod, but the movement hurt her head. "What about the press?"

"Julia tapped into her Hollywood connections and helped

us hire a PR company who controlled what story went out. As far as the world is concerned, there was an accident in your pool, and Samantha tragically died."

"Good." She closed her eyes. "How long was I unconscious?"

"A couple of days. Partly from the drug, but mostly from the concussion." He caressed her cheek. "Not sure if the concussion was from Samantha smashing your face into the edge of the pool, or you throwing yourself down the stairs."

Her eyes opened. "How do you know about either?"

"Scene assessment and forensics." He smiled. "That and the huge lump on your head." His smile faded. "Scared the life out of me when I couldn't find you right away."

"I knew you'd figure out where I was," she whispered. "I only had to stay somewhere safe until you did."

"Going by the calls to the cops about gunfire in your apartment, I was about five minutes behind you." He rested his forehead against hers. "It was too long. I'm sorry, Rachel."

"No." She cupped his cheeks and pushed him back so she could look into those dark eyes of his. "You don't take any blame for this. It's all on her. You came for me. You were only minutes away. That's the important part."

"She could have killed you before I got there."

"Seeing as she was trying to drown me, I'm sure you could have just done CPR and brought me back to life."

"This isn't funny."

"I'm not being funny. I'm telling you that I had faith in you. I knew you'd come for me; there was no doubt in my mind." She stroked his cheek with her thumb. "I knew you'd come, because you love me," she whispered. "And I love you."

His eyes sparkled with wicked amusement. "And it only took a near-death experience for you to tell me."

"I'm regretting it already." She pulled him down to kiss those full lips of his.

"Are we interrupting something?" her mother called out, obviously aware she was absolutely interrupting something.

Rachel shifted her head to look around Harvard. "Yes. Come back later."

And, of course, her mother just carried on into the room. "Is that any way to speak to the mother who's been worried sick about you?" She stepped around Harvard to embrace Rachel. "My baby," she said. "I love you so much."

Damn it. Now everybody was getting emotional. Rachel sniffed and swallowed hard as she patted her mother's back in an attempt to reassure her.

"My turn," she heard her father say. And then her mother moved aside to allow her dad to hug her tight instead. "I'm locking you up so that I never have to worry about your safety ever again," he said fiercely. "That means no more working with Benson Security. No more trips to countries where you irritate members of a cartel. No more gun battles on airstrips. No more people out to get you from inside or outside the family. Do you hear me?"

"Yes, Father." She kissed his cheek, and he stepped away, swiping at his eyes with the back of his hand. "Didn't Jonathan tell you that I'm finished with Benson Security, and I'm staying on at TayFor?"

"Yes, but I couldn't believe him until I heard it from the horse's mouth."

"Then consider yourself talking to a horse."

"Good. Good then." He cleared his throat. "I'll go fetch some coffee." With that, he disappeared from the room.

Her mother watched him go as she perched on the side of Rachel's bed. "He's been very upset. We all have. I can't...I can't even begin to get my head around what Samantha did." She blinked back tears, and Rachel reached for her hand.

"It'll take a very long time and a lot of therapy to deal with this," Rachel said.

"Of course, you're right." Her mother forced a smile.

"Where is she?" came a voice from the door. "Where's my granddaughter?"

Rachel let out a sigh as her grandmother steamrolled her way to her bedside. "Must you make such a fuss?"

"No, but I do enjoy doing it." Her gran kissed her cheek. "You look dreadful. Don't they have hairdressers in here?" She glanced around as though one might suddenly manifest. "And the bruises. Next time I'll bring my cosmetics and fix you right up."

Harvard, the suck-up, pushed a chair over for her grandmother to sit in, earning himself a benevolent smile. "Thank you, dear. Now, if you don't mind, would you find me a cup of tea?"

Harvard's lips twitched before he headed for the door. "Be right back," he promised.

"I like him," her grandmother said. "Could you please make an effort to hold the wedding sooner rather than later? You know, before I die?"

"Stop being such a drama queen," Rachel's mum said.

"Oh, don't pretend you aren't thinking it too." Her gran reached out and took Rachel's hand. "I'm rather upset that Samantha's dead," she said. "I should have liked to torture the bloody life out of her myself."

"Mother!" Rachel's own mother snapped. "That isn't appropriate."

"Oh, tosh." She squeezed Rachel's hand. "How are you, really?"

"Tired. Sore. Already fed up with being a captive audience for my overbearing family."

"In other words, you're back to your usual self." Her grandmother sat back in her chair. "Just as I thought. It takes more than a homicidal maniac in a dress to get my granddaughter down. Now, where's my tea?"

Rachel's mother rolled her eyes at her, almost making Rachel laugh.

"Good, you're awake." Elle appeared in the doorway, dressed in what could only be called full Smurfette. She was blue and white from head to toe, and it actually hurt Rachel's head to look at her.

"Did you bring sunglasses with you? Because whatever you're wearing is painful to look at."

"No. I brought cake." Elle placed it on the table at the end of Rachel's bed. "There was more, but I shared a cab with Ryan."

As if hearing his name, he sauntered into the room and grinned at Rachel. "I told Elle it would take more than a near-drowning to kill off the Queen of the Damned."

"Isn't there a limit to how many people can visit at one time?" Rachel demanded. "Is no one policing this?"

"Oo," her grandmother said, her eyes on Ryan. "If I were ten years younger, you'd be just my cup of tea. Speaking of which, could you chase down Harvard and find out where he is with my tea?"

"For a pretty lady like you, absolutely," Ryan said before heading back out.

"I feel nauseous," Rachel said.

"I'll get the doctor." Her mother jumped to her feet.

"Don't bother," Elle said. "It's just Ryan sucking up to her grandmother that's making her sick. After years of working with her, I'm fluent in Rachel-speak."

"She's awake," Isobel shouted as she came into the room, carrying balloons. "We weren't sure if you'd be awake or not."

Callum came in after his wife. "I'm here under duress," he growled.

At last, something they had in common. "So am I," Rachel told him as she peered behind him.

"Don't worry," he said. "We didn't bring the kids."

"Yep." Isobel handed her the balloons before picking up the cake box to peer inside. "We know you're allergic to them. Can I eat this?"

"Be my guest," Rachel said. "Ryan's already been at it anyway."

"Do you have a fork?" Isobel asked as she took the cake to the seat in the corner.

"This is a hospital room. Not a café. No, I don't have a fork." Honestly, this whole experience was agonizing.

"Rachel, stop being rude to your friends," her mother said.

"They aren't my friends," she complained.

"Yes, we are," said everyone except Callum.

"I like your friends," her grandmother said. "They're very entertaining. And the men are rather attractive." She turned to Callum. "Is attractiveness a hiring requirement at Benson Security?"

"No." He frowned at her.

Her grandmother just grinned at him, as though he was being funny.

"One tea," Harvard said as he strode into the room, bringing yet more people with him.

"Good to see you conscious," Lake said with a rare smile.

"You scared the crap out of me," Harry told her as he wrapped his hand around the lump on the bed that was her foot and squeezed. "You even scared Magenta. She actually said she's glad you made it."

"A red-letter day," Rachel said dryly as Sebastian elbowed his way into the room.

"You didn't have to come all the way back from Borneo for this," Rachel told him.

"Don't be a pain in the arse," he said before hugging her too.

"She can't help it." Jonathan took her hand, his eyes turning sad. "I can't believe it was Samantha."

"None of us can," her mother said, hugging Jonathan.

"I can," her grandmother said. "She always was a jealous little bitch."

"Mother!"

"Gran!"

"Mary!" her father added, letting Rachel know he was back too.

"What?" Her gran shrugged. "You were all thinking it."

"For the love of all things Prada, would everybody get out of my room?" Rachel shouted.

"No," everybody shouted back.

Rachel narrowed her eyes at them. "I'm keeping track, and everyone who defies me now will suffer when I'm out of here."

"And you say *I'm* a drama queen," her gran muttered.

Epilogue 1

Harvard crept up the stairs of the apartment building in Thailand's capital city and signaled to his team to wait. They froze in place, blending into the shadows as the person on the other side of the stairwell door passed by.

As soon as he was sure it was clear, he signaled to move forward. In formation, they passed the door and made their way along the corridor to the corner apartment.

Thanks to a local team that owed Harvard a favor, they already knew the exact layout of the apartment and the location of the two men within it. The surveillance equipment installed throughout the living areas kept them up to date on everything that was happening inside.

Which is how they knew that both men were sound asleep in their beds and alone for the first time in two weeks.

Silently, one of his team picked the lock of their front door, and Harvard signaled for them to slide inside. Working as a well-oiled machine, they cleared each room before splitting into two teams and heading to the bedrooms.

Less than a minute later, the men kneeled in the middle of their shared living room, hands tied in front of them and duct tape over their mouths. And, from the smell of things, one of them had already lost control of his bladder.

Harvard removed his mask and crouched in front of them. He reached into his tactical vest and pulled out two Polaroid photos, holding them up in front of their faces.

The other man's bladder gave way.

As he got to his feet, he nodded at his team before pulling out his silenced revolver and shooting each man in the middle of the forehead. Once done, he turned his back on them and signaled for the surveillance equipment to be removed from the apartment. It took mere seconds to get it done. And only a few minutes more to get his team safely from the building.

As they climbed aboard the private plane waiting for them at a small airport outside the city, he sent the video file they'd recorded with their surveillance cameras to the local police.

Rachel wasn't the last woman the men had raped.

In silence, his five-person team buckled in before the plane took off and headed back to London.

"Are you going to tell her?" Megan Raast asked.

The Scottish woman considered herself one of Rachel's best friends. Which, as far as Harvard could tell, meant she spent most of her time trying to wind Rachel up.

"At some point," he said.

Megan's husband, Dimitri, nodded. He'd dealt with the man who'd abused his sister, and out of all of them, could most understand where Harvard was coming from.

"I vote no," Callum said. "There's no telling how Rachel will react."

Ryan barked out a laugh. "We all know how she'd react. She'll have Harvard's balls for not including her."

"True," Megan said with a smile.

Closing his eyes, Harvard settled into his seat and thought about the woman waiting for him back at home. In their new apartment. And their new bed—which didn't have a pool above it.

Epilogue 2

"**Y**ou can't go in there." Megan Raast folded her arms over her pale blue bridesmaid dress and glared at Harvard. "It's bad luck to see the bride before the wedding."

If it had been anyone else, he would have just picked them up and moved them. But if he did that to Megan, she'd most likely shoot him.

"I only want a quick word."

"Tough."

It had been worth a try. "You know those state-of-the-art night goggles you saw the CIA use in Lebanon? I can get you a pair."

The Scot thought about it for all of ten seconds before tossing her blonde hair over her shoulder and stepping aside. "Five minutes. That's all you get."

"I only need two."

Her lips curled. "Then I pity Rachel for marrying you."

With a shake of his head, he entered the guest room in Rachel's parent's house, where his soon-to-be wife was getting ready. Or she should have been. Instead, she stood in front of the TV with the business channel on, glaring at the stock indexes.

"This is completely the wrong climate to take TayFor public," their new CEO said with a frown. "Isn't it bad luck for you to be in here?"

"I think it's bad luck to see you in your wedding dress. I think it's my very *good* luck that you're only in lingerie." He wrapped an arm around her waist from behind and kissed her neck. "I'll tell Megan we're gonna need more than five minutes."

"No, you won't." She leaned back into him as she shut off the TV. "I don't want anything to delay this wedding. The sooner it's over and done with, the better."

"I can't get enough of that romantic side of yours," he said with a grin.

Rachel turned in his hold and draped her arms around his shoulders. "I think this lingerie is proof I can be romantic."

There was no arguing with that. "A corset *and* stockings? Not sure I'll make it through the ceremony knowing this is beneath your dress."

"If you do, there will be a reward in it for you."

"Yeah?" He teased her lips with his, feeling that sensation of coming home that he always felt when kissing Rachel.

There was a thump at the door. "Four minutes," Megan shouted.

Harvard heaved a sigh as he rested his forehead against Rachel's. "I might have to cut my ties with Benson Security altogether, just to see the back of that woman. I never thought I'd say this, but I've met the one person who tries my patience."

"Welcome to my world," Rachel said drolly. "And you'd miss doing the odd assignment for Benson Security. You'd be bored out of your mind if you just worked at TayFor."

She had a point. Although it had been interesting for the

first six months, working to ensure all the gaps in security were plugged and that no one else could help themselves to the company's secrets, the novelty was definitely wearing off.

"I don't want to work with Callum all the time," he said. "I like working with you at TayFor."

"Then it's purely a matter of finding the right balance between your job with me and your job with Callum. Is that what you came in here to talk about?"

"Three minutes," their keeper shouted.

"No." Harvard reached into his pocket. "I came to give you this." He pulled out the jewelry box and handed it to her.

"Shouldn't we swap rings after the vows?" she said.

"Just open it."

With a smile, Rachel lifted the lid and gasped. "I've never seen anything like it."

"Here, let me help you put it on." He took the intricately designed locket from the box as Rachel held her hair up from her neck.

Once it was clasped, she lifted the locket to examine it. "It's beautiful, Michael. Where did you get it?"

"I had a jeweler in Paris make it for you." He pointed at the cut-out designs. "This is an English rose for you. And this is a blue violet, the official flower of the state I was born in. The vines represent the ties that bind us together, while the gladiolus stand for the loyalty, protection, and faithfulness that we give each other. The orchids remind me of your exotic beauty. And the full-petalled roses are for a love that will never end."

Rachel blinked her eyes rapidly. "If you make me cry and ruin my makeup, I will refuse to say I do."

"I'm glad you like it." He brushed a kiss over her lips.

"Two minutes," the pain in the ass shouted.

He cleared his throat. "There are a couple of flowers on there that your mom and gran picked. So, something of your heritage is represented. I can't remember what they are, but they can tell you."

A tear escaped to run down her cheek, and Harvard kissed it away.

"You are everything to me," Rachel whispered.

"I love you too," Harvard said.

"One minute," Megan called.

"I'm going to kill your matron of honor," Harvard grumbled.

"Get in line," Rachel said before tugging his head down for a kiss.

About the Author

Janet Elizabeth Henderson was born in Scotland but now lives in New Zealand. She writes romantic comedies, romantic suspense and futuristic romance. When she isn't writing she can be found on Facebook or Instagram hassling her readers with all sorts of nonsense. In her spare time, she takes care of two children, too many pets to count, and a very long suffering husband. She loves to hear from her readers so don't forget to meet up with her on Facebook, or visit her website for more books.